T0365656

Death of a Green Soldier

MICHAEL WRIGHT

WESTBOW
PRESS
A DIVISION OF THOMAS NELSON

WestBow Press books may be ordered through booksellers or by contacting:

WestBow Press
A Division of Thomas Nelson
1663 Liberty Drive
Bloomington, IN 47403
www.westbowpress.com
1-(866) 928-1240

ISBN: 978-1-4497-9798-0 (sc)
ISBN: 978-1-4497-9799-7 (e)

Printed in the United States of America.

WestBow Press rev. date: 7/17/2013

CHAPTER ONE

Mark Welch stepped off the plane into the dark, cold, bitter winter night. The sharp German wind cut right through his coat and collar. He began searching for the military vehicle that had been sent to pick him up. It was difficult to find in the shadows of the gray buildings in the dark night. The traffic in Frankfurt was always busy around the airport, making the task of finding one truck out of hundreds even more challenging.

Dark clouds churned out snow in a rash of flurries and hid the moon. The charcoal night blended with Mark's confusion from hours of flying. He had flown from one continent to another. Now his journey was on its final leg.

Mark thought about his new world and how he would fit into it, unsure of what to expect. Until now he had lived a simple life in a small town filled with country people who had never wandered out of their own county—and now he had wandered out of his own nation. He was in a strange place with a people who spoke a different language and lived a culture that only resembled life back home. He felt as if he might not have the resources or recourse to control life as he was used to. Deep inside he was absolutely frightened.

Mark was a young man with sandy-blond hair who stood a slim five foot nine inches. When he graduated from high school, he had weighed a mere 135 pounds. Once the army was done with him in basic training, he had added another thirty pounds of muscle. This didn't exactly make him a mountain of a man, but it did give him strength he had never felt before. Mark was secretly hoping this would be an advantage he perhaps would need to survive.

Finally, after walking around in the freezing cold, he found the vehicle. There were two other soldiers with the driver waiting as Mark climbed into his ride. They had been sitting in the vehicle to keep warm. The truck they rode in was different from what Mark was used to. It had two bench seats in the cab. The back, where they had placed all their luggage, was covered with olive-green canvas, the same color as all their uniforms. The other two passengers had the same scared look in their eyes. They were trying to peer out of the steam-clouded windows while the truck sped off down the snow-covered road.

The ride to the new barracks was long, and Mark's mind was full of curiosity and wonder. He thought about what Christmas might be like as the December cold sliced through the canvas doors of the truck. Maybe it would be something more than it had been in the past. There was very little talk. Perhaps the rest of the new recruits were thinking about the same thing.

Looking out the truck window as they drove, Mark noticed how the snow made the landscape brighter than it would normally be. The trees outlined the farmland for what seemed like miles. It was surprising how all the land was used for crops. There were no forests or buildings like back home. Mark noted how nothing was wasted since this country was much older than the one he was from. The snow and winter, however, were just like back home. There were very few houses, only field after field flying by as they drove down the road to their new destiny. Mark wondered where the farmers lived. Perhaps they drove from the nearby towns to their farms.

He continued to think of how his life would no longer be the same. It wasn't like he had never seen adventure or adverse conditions. This time, however, seemed different. He kept wondering how it would be in a country a whole ocean away—a whole continent away. He was a world away from anything he had ever known.

Once they arrived at the barracks, rooms were assigned to each of them. Mark spent the night talking to his new roommate, Jacob Multer. Jacob was a young black Cajun man who had never ventured far from home himself. He was the type of homeboy who loved his mother and family and had a strong sagacity of faith in the Creator.

Though Jacob was not exactly an evangelist, neither was he afraid to talk about what he believed in. His five-foot-ten, two-hundred-pound stature was an advantage that helped Jacob accomplish anything he wanted to. Still, it was his spiritual aptitude that kept him safe and on the right path. It was his faith in God that provided all his successes.

The roommates both seemed to have peculiar sources of energy as the night wore on. Perhaps they were just too tired to sleep. They talked until the wee hours of the morning. Curiosity and anxiety fed their minds and imaginations.

"So have you ever been in another country?" Jacob asked with his Cajun drawl.

"No." Mark smiled at the idea. He had never been in another state before the army.

"So what do you think of it?" Jacob asked. Jacob was trying to get his own mind wrapped around the adventure himself.

"I don't know. It's all a little fast and confusing," Mark confessed.

"I know what you mean," Jacob replied. "One minute we're home relaxing, and the next—well, here we are, wondering what's going to happen." Jacob was searching for the right words to explain the unfamiliar sensation of their new beginning.

"So do you know how it's all gonna work come morning?" Mark asked.

"No, there's no way to tell how the army's going to do things, from what I've seen so far." Jacob laughed. He was remembering what he had gone through in boot camp and AIT. "It's impossible to know how to predict the future in this kind of place. I guess they'll let us know when it's time."

"I guess no matter what they do with us, it's got

to be better than what I had going back home," Mark muttered.

"What do you mean?" Jacob asked.

"Let's just say my life was not like the one you've lived. It's not the kind of life I would wish on anyone. I'm here until I can figure out how I'm going to change it. That could take awhile."

Jacob sat up on his bunk, listening intently. "Well, at least you'll have all you can eat and a place to sleep until you do."

"Yeah, that was the idea. The rest should be easy, but it doesn't feel like it tonight."

They began to talk about their lives at home as the night turned into dawn. Jacob talked about life back in the Louisiana bayou.

"You know, my grandmother would cook up some of the best crabs and cornbread you could ever imagine. I miss her and the meals we used to eat. I miss the warm sun on my back as I walked to town. It's a lot warmer at home than it is here, that's for sure. And no snow. This is the first time I've ever seen snow like this. I could have gone a lifetime not seeing it."

It all sounded very comfortable to Mark. It was kind of like a Hallmark card, he thought. Mark enjoyed listening to someone who loved his family and life. Mark enjoyed seeing the look in Jacob's eyes as he talked about all the things he was seeing for the first time. This was Jacob's first real winter. Mark liked watching how Jacob talked about it. It helped Mark take his mind off his own life.

Mark began to talk about his life at home. "You know,

my mother died when I was a small boy. My dad was very cruel. He would beat us every day for whatever reason he could think of. I don't know how he met my mom, but they were definitely opposite of each other. We had a running joke that he beat us three times a day, whether we needed it or not. Christmas for me was not what it is for other people. It has always been empty, cold, and meaningless, with no purpose. I'm sure it will be the same this year."

Jacob kept his eyes pinned on Mark, listening to every word as if he were telling a horror story. He was on the edge of his seat, listening intently.

"Over the last two years," Mark continued, "I have lived in a backpacking tent while going to school. I joined the cross-country and track teams so I could shower every day. I noticed how the runners would sometimes run in the morning, so I did the same thing. That way I could shower every morning and afternoon. A man can never be too clean." Mark laughed. "My mom had worked as a nurse's aide before she died, so I was able to collect a social security check every month. This money paid for my food and clothes. Not exactly the kind of life anyone would dream of living."

"You mean to tell me the rest of your family didn't do anything to help?" Jacob asked in astonishment. "Where were they?"

"They had their own problems. All of us were trying to do what we could to get away. The court system knew I was on my own as a minor. Instead of placing me in a home or in some other corrective situation, my caseworker found a way to have me emancipated. I was my own guardian as long as I was never arrested and finished school.

"I lived a life that felt like was straight out of a Mark Twain novel. It all seemed romantic, except I had to live it for real. Somehow all the romanticism was lost in the cold nights and empty meals with no one to share the time with." Mark talked like this until they fell asleep. Jacob kept it all hidden in his heart. He made a pact with himself to pray every day for Mark, asking God to see him through.

The next morning started out with a staff sergeant knocking on the door. Jacob dragged himself out of bed and opened the door, still rubbing the cobwebs out of his eyes.

The sergeant filled the doorway as he began giving them their morning instructions. "Privates Welch and Multer, you are to report to third squad of first platoon at 0800 hours. Breakfast is in the mess hall across the way. Report to Sergeant Morris before formation begins." The staff sergeant then turned and left with the same full-of-life attitude that he had had when he came into the room.

Jacob and Mark stood still and nodded as if they understood every word they had just heard. Once the sergeant was gone, Jacob turned to Mark. "What do you suppose he meant by 'across the way'?" he asked, imitating the sergeant's attitude and every motion.

Mark thought about it for a moment and then replied, "I guess the only way we'll know is to ask as we go." Doing as they were told, Jacob and Mark went out after they were dressed and began to make their way to the mess hall.

The building was built out of concrete. It was an old officers quarters from World War II. Yet as Mark and Jacob walked the carved stone floor of the hallway, it all still looked new. Even the walls looked like they had been recently built. It was all original. They liked how the German workmanship had lasted over the years.

They walked out of the barracks to see a building across the parking lot directly in front of the barracks door. Past the building was a large open athletic field. On the far side of the field they could see men assembling at a single-story brick building. On a hunch, they made their way to the gathering and discovered the mess hall and its interesting aroma and atmosphere.

The food wasn't exactly gourmet, but after the journey they had had over the last few days, it was filling and helped them relax and become a little more acclimated to their new surroundings. The coffee helped them feel a little more human as well.

When they returned from breakfast, the sun had risen higher in the sky. The snow glistened in the light, making the day seem just a little surreal. They could feel the cold through their boots as they walked briskly back to their barracks. Their faces were numb from the winter wind ever so slightly whisking inside their collars and down their backs.

They began waiting for the troop formation as they looked for Sergeant Morris. They found him standing near the front door of the barracks. He explained what they needed to do. In a firm but pleasant voice he told them, "The two of you will find your places in the third squad of first platoon. It will assemble right there." He pointed to the place in the corner of the parking lot closest to the barracks door. "You will line up off my left. Any questions?"

Mark and Jacob acknowledged Sergeant Morris, hoping to convince him they had understood everything he said. Then, out of nowhere, another sergeant came around and took Jacob to his platoon. Just like that, the two of them were on their own again.

At exactly eight o'clock well over two hundred men were gathered in front of the barracks. A captain found his way to the front of the group and directed the first sergeant to assemble the company. His words were very plain to hear. His voice a deep baritone, he immediately instructed the platoons. "Company! Form your platoons." This made it easy for Mark and Jacob to find their places in the company. It took less than ten seconds for over two hundred men to form a coordinated group that could be commanded at various levels of rank.

Just like that, formation was established and roll call was made. All the men were accounted for in their respective platoons, and orders for the day were issued. After that the company was dismissed to its areas of work. Mark discovered that first platoon operated the warehouse. Mark, however, was to report to the orientation room in the open bay area on the top floor of the barracks.

Ten new soldiers had joined the company in the last few days. Mark was the only one new to the warehouse crew. The week went by in a blur. Mark never was sure what the reason was for orientation. He did learn some basic rules to follow when in town and how to use JAG if needed. He was also made aware of the language program suggested to them to make life in Germany easier and more meaningful. Mark learned that his barracks had been used by German officers during WWII. It was named after the first Polish soldier to die in September 1939. Gerzuski Barracks was also used as a prisoner-of-war camp for captured Allied soldiers. It was only a twenty-minute walk from the Rhine River, just a short distance from the French border.

After a week of orientation, they were finally given their permanent party room assignments. It was a Friday afternoon, and Mark was told to see Kurt Talagan, who would be his new roommate.

Kurt was an ambiguous kind of individual. He never seemed to have any true purpose in the outfit and yet was relied upon for a variety of necessary objectives. Kurt spent a lot of time visiting places like the PX Center. The PX Center was like a snack bar and shopping center all wrapped into one. When Kurt wasn't in the PX he was walking the streets that meandered throughout the base. This made it seem unlikely that Mark would be sleeping in his new room that night. Where would he find Kurt at that time of day on a Friday? Then, out of the blue, there he was. Kurt seemed slightly agitated at having to help Mark move into his room, perhaps a little from having to share his room after living alone for so long.

The two collected Mark's belongings from his

orientation room on the first floor and moved up to the front corner room on the third floor. After everything was moved in and his locker was set up, the two took a few minutes to rest on their beds and began to talk.

Kurt was a tall man who had been around the block a few times. His six-foot frame and eyes that could cut right through to a man's soul were more than enough to make Mark feel intimidated. His mustache was full and curved at its ends, giving him a kind of distinguished, British look as well. However, there was more to Kurt than just his size and appearance. It was easy to see Kurt carried a history of always coming out on top in any situation. Kurt demonstrated confidence in everything he did and said.

Having rested after Mark was all settled in, Kurt finally stood up, walked to the door, and locked it. After the door was locked he turned the key sideways, leaving it in the lock. Mark later discovered this made it impossible for anyone to unlock the door from the outside. Then Kurt opened the two big bay windows wide and returned to his bed. Quietly he took out what looked like a small piece of dirt and used his lighter to warm it up. Kurt pulled out a sheet of paper from beside his bed and began to crumble the small piece of dirt onto the paper. Once this was finished Kurt pulled out a small pipe and funneled the scraps of dirt into the pipe. It was at this time Kurt took out his lock blade knife, opened it, and laid it beside him on the bed.

Lighting the pipe, Kurt looked over to Mark and asked, "So, do you smoke dope?"

Mark looked at the locked door. He then looked at the

opened windows, reminding himself they were on the third floor. His gaze shifted to the knife lying conspicuously on the bed beside Kurt and then the intimidating eyes looking back at him. All told, it took only a second for Mark to evaluate the nature of the situation he was in. "Yes, I do!" he replied without hesitation, emphasizing each word purposefully and ardently to be as convincing as possible.

In truth Mark had never even heard of hash before now. Each time he took a hit from the pipe he would cough and choke like he was about to die. Keeping his thoughts to himself, Kurt could tell Mark had never even seen hash before, let alone smoked it.

"So what kind of dope did you smoke back home?" Kurt asked in a quiet but intent voice.

"We just smoked pot from wherever. We didn't really pay any attention to what kind," Mark choked out. "It was usually wild weed that grew behind a friend's church."

"So you weren't exactly a big-time toker?" Kurt asked with a smile.

Laughing and coughing, Mark answered, "No, it just wasn't all that important to us. It was just something to do."

"So this is gonna really kick your butt in comparison," observed Kurt.

"Going to?" Mark sat on his cot in a daze from only a few tokes. "It already has."

The rest of the day was a blur as Mark found himself staring at the ceiling, not really thinking about anything. His mind was dizzy as his eyes tried to focus on the simplest things. The two of them sat in the quiet of the evening while the hash intoxicated their minds. It was then that Kurt pulled out his acoustic guitar and began to play with the music that had been resounding from the stereo.

Mark was impressed with how well Kurt's playing blended in with the album, though he did wonder if it was the talent that made it sound so good—it was obvious that Kurt had spent a lot of time practicing—or the intense high. In a sense, time was standing still, yet, at the same time, hours had gone by before Mark finally realized that Friday was now over.

Again, it seemed strange to sleep in a place that was completely unfamiliar to him. The high made it more surreal and attainable. Mark found himself in a familiar state of flex. It was times like this that Mark often felt as if he was part of the wall, like he was on the outside looking in. Things were not real. This time it was no different as he recalled the story Kurt told him about the man who had "accidentally" fallen out of the window of their floor and had to be medevac'd to a hospital, never to be seen again. These memories of unusual conversation should have made sleep more evasive. However, the hash acted as an effective sedative. The day seemed more like a hallucination than reality.

CHAPTER TWO

Saturday morning found Mark waking groggily as he sat up and looked around. He was amazed he was still alive. He got himself dressed and then realized that Kurt was gone. The room was quiet. Mark looked around at the furniture and the accessories Kurt had accumulated over time.

The stereo system was state-of-the-art, and the album collection was amazing. Mark was afraid to touch anything, given the way things had gone the day before. Still, it was fascinating to see all the equipment and how Kurt had carefully laid out the room. Mark had never listened to music like he did the night before.

The high he had from the hash had a pleasant, mellow feeling, making it easy to feel the music flow through him. Everything seemed so alive, as though he were in a magical, euphoric place that was like nothing he had ever felt or seen before. Questions started flowing through his mind again. Who was this Kurt guy, and what did all of this mean? Was the night before real? It had to be, given that Mark was now in a different room looking at a lot of fascinating things—unless, of course, his whole life was a figment of somebody's imagination. Mark smiled at that. Good imagination, he thought.

Once dressed, Mark made his way to the mess hall for breakfast. He walked alone and thought about everything that he had witnessed since his arrival in Germany. He began to feel like he was in a whirlwind and didn't know how to get out, but he wasn't all that sure he wanted to. The day before was not representative of how he wanted to change his life, but it did offer something new. He didn't know how yet, but he knew the change felt fresh.

For the first time in a long time Mark was feeling good about a lot of things. He knew where his next meal was going to come from, where he was going to sleep that night, and how to pay for his clothes. For the first time he knew he would have medical, dental, and vision care, and it was all free. Mark was thinking he was going to like being there, at least for now. He thought about this at great length as he enjoyed a breakfast he didn't have to pay for or cook. All he had to do was show up for formation every morning—and now he had to figure out how to survive Kurt.

While Mark was thinking, he began to formalize how to deal with some of the conflicts to his plan. He had lied to Kurt when he told him he used to get high. He laughed at himself as he took a drink of coffee after the meal. Who would he have gotten high with? Really? He had no money to buy anything other than basic foods. Mark couldn't even buy a candy bar without sacrificing something more important.

That wasn't true now. Now he could buy all the chocolate his heart desired. Now he could buy cigarettes by the carton. In fact, he did. Now he could have a stash of all the things he wanted to stock up on. The only reason for all this was the army. However, now it looked like having Kurt as a roommate could put all this in danger.

How was he going to make it though three years of smoking dope and worrying about skydiving out of his third-story window? "That's it," Mark said to himself with determination. He was simply going to ask Kurt to leave him out of using drugs, or he was going to have to find another room.

Then a sickening thought crept into Mark's mind. There was a reason to the story about the guy who went out the window. It wasn't going to matter where Mark went. Kurt would just find another way to shut him up permanently. Kurt did what he did for self-preservation. He wasn't about to just let Mark go his own way. Mark had no ground to stand on to persuade Kurt that he wasn't a threat that he just wanted to be left alone. No, he wasn't going to go anywhere, and he wasn't going to get away with not using. Mark was stuck, and he knew it.

Mark left his good-feeling breakfast not feeling so good after all. He had joined the army to find a way to get out of one problem only to find himself right in the middle of another one. Why was his life so complicated? Mark moaned to himself. He hadn't asked to live the way he did before now. He hadn't asked for the problems he'd walked right into when he moved into Kurt's room. All he hoped was that he would still be walking when this nightmare was finally over.

Monday morning, after showering and getting dressed in his fatigues, Mark went to breakfast. Once again he enjoyed a good free meal and time to just relax and drink the first cup of coffee of the day. That Sunday had been completely uneventful. There weren't even any drugs or stories about people getting hurt or dying. This somehow seemed like a victory to Mark. Maybe it was a beginning to a way he could enjoy his new life. With that thought of hope Mark even went for a second cup of coffee and smoked a cigarette as his mind created a new fantasy world for him to live in.

On the way back to the barracks, he passed the PX center and took some time to go inside. The cigarettes were much cheaper here than they were back home. Mark had only smoked occasionally, but enough to take notice of what he thought was a good deal. He really wasn't interested in being a big-time smoker, but now that he could afford it, he decided to make an investment that would make him feel even more like this was his home.

His dad had been a chain-smoker, and it had always bothered Mark. This was one of the reasons he never really did a lot of smoking. The other reason was he never had the money. Things were different now. Mark had not seen his dad in years, and now he had money. It wasn't like he was rich, but he was definitely richer than he had ever been in the past. Making a meaningless decision, Mark bought a couple of cartons of Marlboros and took his newfound treasure back to his room.

After formation he went to the warehouse with his new comrades and started the routine of cleaning the place up. It began to occur to Mark that this warehouse was a new project. Maybe even the whole company was newly formed to get this whole operation going. The building was made out of concrete, much the same way the barracks building had been made. It was long, its length following the road in front of it. The front wall was a series of bay doors that could be opened manually like garage doors.

Inside there were wooden shelves that ran in aisles along the length of the building. At one end of the building was a set of stairs that went up to an office area where clerks from first squad operated computers. At the other end was an open bay area for shipping and receiving, and past that was still another open bay that was going to be made into more office space.

Mark's current job was to clean up the aisle ways where piles of goods lay that belonged on the shelves. It all had to be organized, listed, filed, and placed properly on the shelves. This seemed like an overwhelming task to Mark. He stood there all alone looking at the mess for what seemed like forever before he began dealing with one item at a time. He thought it would take the rest of his career in the army to complete his first assignment. What a hopeless, dismal feeling.

During the day two more guys showed up. He had seen them in formation every morning, but he never saw them when it was time for work. Now they stood there, talking to Kurt in a private sort of way, looking over their shoulders to make sure no one heard them. Mark realized they were not there to give him any help. Most of the day Mark ignored them, but he did notice they didn't seem to always be ignoring him.

The weekend had come, and Mark woke up that Saturday to see the same two guys in his room talking to Kurt. Noticing Mark's eyes were open, one of them turned to him and asked, "So you're the new guy, huh?"

"Yeah, I guess I am," Mark replied in a confused, fuzzy frame of mind. He couldn't help thinking they weren't as stupid as they had looked when they didn't help him get any work done all week.

"So where ya from?" the other one asked.

"Michigan," Mark replied, wondering why they were there and what they were all about.

They turned to Kurt and said, "Hey, we're gonna get going." They shook hands as they stood up. "We'll be back later to take care of all that." They gave each other a knowing look but were careful not to give anything away. It was obvious they didn't want Mark to know what they had been talking about. The way they looked at Mark as they spoke made it clear that he was going to have to win their confidence. Mark wasn't sure he wanted to do that. At least not yet.

Once they were gone, Mark looked at Kurt. "So, who were they?"

Kurt replied, "Just some friends that stopped by for a little bit."

"I've seen them around before," Mark said as he thought about the past week.

"Yeah, they're just friends. We've been through a lot together." Mark let it go with that and went on with his day.

A few days later Mark saw the same two again. This time it was just outside the warehouse. Like before, they were talking in a secretive manner. Mark noticed they would look in his direction from time to time as if sizing him up.

The first one Mark had seen was shorter and had dark curly hair. He was always smiling, but somehow it didn't seem like it was out of happiness. There was craziness in his eyes. Mark wasn't sure just what it was, but something told him this guy was going to be trouble if he wasn't careful. Mark figured it was best to stay out of his way.

The other one had the air of someone who had never really found a purpose in life. He seemed to always be about the present, not really thinking about how his actions could lead to problems for others. Mark wasn't sure this guy cared either way. No, this one clearly lived for the moment.

The following morning, Mark, again, woke up to the same visitors. This time they were sitting in a small circle passing around the pipe, which they called a bowl. Noticing that Mark was awake they motioned for him to join them. Mark thought to himself that this was exactly what he didn't want to have happen. Once he had taken his place to participate, they passed the bowl to him. Taking a long, slow toke from the bowl and holding it in, Mark looked around to see them looking back at him. They seemed appreciative of his participation. Mark knew this was going to prolong his life for the moment but wasn't sure how it was going to give him a future down the road. For the moment it seemed like the best plan if he wanted to live to face the problem again later.

The taller, blond one spoke first. "So, did you do a lot of dope at home?"

"Nah," replied Mark. "I just smoked once in a while for something to do. It wasn't like I had a lot of money to spend on whatever I wanted." Mark was trying to sound like he had experience, but really it just made him look like another two-bit loser. But maybe that wasn't a bad thing. Maybe it would still make him look like he fit in.

The blond, Robby, looked at him in a strange way. "I spent as much money on drugs as I could. There's nothing like getting a good high."

Mark thought to himself that he was right. Looking like a two-bit loser would let him fit in, the way this guy was talking. "True, but I didn't have enough money to eat every meal. Where was I gonna get the money for drugs?" Mark said, hoping the high was all that was going to be important to them in a little while.

"Well, maybe that will all change for you now that you get paid for just being here," Robby said, laughing.

The other, shorter one, Chris, sat quietly, listening to the conversation. His brown curly hair and wild-looking eyes made Mark nervous. Mark hoped it wasn't obvious to him just how much he was concerned that he looked dangerous.

They continued smoking hash and listening to music until it was time for formation. After formation they went on to their daily duties at the warehouse until break, which was at ten. Once break was on, they took a quick walk back to the room and lit up another bowl. They enjoyed listening to Eric Clapton while getting on a good buzz.

At lunchtime it occurred to Mark that he had not eaten all day. It seemed that smoking hash had taken away his sense of time and priorities—until they went to lunch, anyway. Mark ate heartily and then went back to the room to smoke still another bowl of hash. The rest of the day went by quickly and mindlessly. At five o'clock, the usual quitting time, Mark went back to the room to find yet another bowl of hash waiting for him.

This time, while smoking with the guys, it occurred to Mark that someone had to be paying for all this. He knew it was only going to be a matter of time before this became an important issue. Looking around at the small group he finally found his voice. "So who has been paying for all this?"

They quietly looked at him and just kind of let the question go.

"Let me rephrase the question," Mark continued, feeling brave with his new plan to fit in. "How much is a block of hash, and where can I get one?" Mark was being persistent, because he knew it was important if he was going to have a place there.

Kurt spoke up with his usual quiet and yet deliberate choice of words. "Give me twenty dollars, and I'll get you a piece."

Mark pulled out a twenty and handed it to Kurt. After the bowl was done, Mark went to the mess hall for supper while the others went their own way. After supper Mark returned to his room and found a block of tin foil lying on his bed just under his dust cover. Picking it up, Mark realized it was the hash he had asked for. Moments later Kurt returned to the room, and Mark quietly showed it to him. "Look what I found just laying around."

Kurt smiled and went about his own business. Mark began to prepare some for the bowl. When it was ready, he asked, "Can you give me the bowl so I can light it up for us?"

Kurt handed the bowl to Mark, and he lit it up. After taking a hit, Mark looked at Kurt and asked sheepishly, "So, do you smoke dope?"

Kurt smiled and reached for the bowl, replying, "Why, yes, I do."

CHAPTER THREE

Days turned into weeks and weeks into months as Mark went through the motions of being a soldier. Christmas had already become a blurred memory. That didn't matter much, as the last few years he had seen Christmas without any meaning. It had been a long time since Mark had been with his family, and this year had not been any different. In fact, this was the first time in his life that he had every day on a schedule and knew what was going to happen from beginning to end.

The days were getting longer as spring was coming into all its glory. Mark could not remember the last time he just sat outside and listened to birds singing. One day in particular, Mark was sitting with his back to a tree just outside the barracks. Guys were milling around, enjoying the warm air and bright sun, just as Mark was. There was some music blasting from one of the windows. The song was "Crimson and Roses" by Tommy James. Mark couldn't ever remember hearing this song before. It was a catchy tune, and Mark enjoyed it a lot.

Sitting against a tree with his legs stretched out and

crossed, Mark was in a stoned state of mind. A robin flew down and rested on the toe of his boot. It seemed to be singing to him. It was such a profound moment that Mark was sure it had some sort of meaning, but he had no idea what it could be. At the same time, the moment was euphoric, as Mark was sure it was meant to give him encouragement that he was somehow in the right place at the right time. Life was beginning to seem good again to Mark—like there really could be hope.

That Friday night, when Mark returned to his room from supper, Kurt had the lights turned off and had lit some candles. There was some incense burning, giving the room a unique odor. The room had been arranged so that their lockers were between the door and Kurt's bunk. On the other side of Kurt's bunk were a nightstand and the wall. There was a desk immediately to the right of the door. Mark's bunk was in that corner so that it would be seen as soon as one walked into the room and looked to the left. It was necessary to walk past Mark's bunk to go around the lockers to Kurt's bunk. Since the door was in the right corner of the hallway wall to the room, it was impossible to see anything going on where Kurt had his bunk. The stereo system was on a set of homemade shelves in the corner opposite the door. There was a window between Mark's bunk and the stereo system and another window between the stereo system and the nightstand by Kurt's bunk.

With this layout it was easy to sit on the floor on the window side of Kurt's bunk and smoke hash while listening to rock 'n' roll like Eric Clapton, Grand Funk, Jethro Tull,

Pink Floyd, and Crosby, Stills, Nash, and Young. This night seemed different with the extra attention given to the appearance of the room. Kurt took out a small package of paper and opened it up. Laying a small mirror on the floor, he took a razor blade and formed two white lines on the mirror with whatever was in the paper package. Kurt then took a ten-dollar bill and rolled it into a type of straw. He then quietly placed the bill to his nose and snorted up one of the lines of white powder on the mirror. Handing the bill to Mark, he said, "Your turn."

This was exactly like the first day Mark smoked hash—but with one small difference. While Kurt was up changing the album on the stereo, Mark bent down to snort up the second line. All of a sudden the line was gone. Mark hadn't a chance to even start snorting it.

Confused, Mark looked around on the floor to see where it all went. Realizing that breathing out before breathing in had caused the white powder to blow away, Mark began to wet his fingers and tried to get it up off the floor and lick it off his fingers.

Kurt returned from changing the album. He looked at Mark and asked, "Do you know any martial arts to protect yourself?"

Mark thought about the few things he was taught in basic training. "No, not really."

"Well, how about if I teach you some simple moves, then?" Kurt asked as he stood up to begin a lesson.

Mark stood up and took a position in front of Kurt, readying himself for his first lesson. After one deft move, Mark was out of breath and on his knees, wondering what had just happened as he looked up at Kurt. "What was that?"

"Well," Kurt replied, "you didn't move away from my elbow."

"Ah, I guess I didn't know I was supposed to or when I was supposed to move," Mark said, trying to regain his breath.

"Well, you do now." Kurt smiled. That was the end of the lesson.

Mark thought about it for a while and realized Kurt must have seen him lose all the white powder on the floor. While they were finishing up the last bowl of hash of the night, Mark asked, "So what was that white powder, anyway?"

"Coke," Kurt replied.

"I've heard of it, but I don't really know what it is," said Mark.

"Oh, it's just something that makes you feel mellow."

"So are we gonna get any more?" Mark asked.

"Not tonight. It's kind of expensive," Kurt responded. With that they put the bowl away and went to sleep for the night.

The next day went on as if nothing had ever happened with the coke. As Kurt was getting ready to leave, Mark's voice broke the morning silence. "So, where you headed today?"

Kurt kept his back turned as he continued to dress himself for the city. "Oh, just going to town. I have some errands to run."

Mark thought about it. He had never been to town

and figured he had been at the barracks long enough. "Sounds like a good idea. I think I will go to town on my own adventure. I need a break from these walls."

Once Kurt had left, Mark put on his civilian clothes and headed for the front gate. Hailing a taxi, he took his first venture into the city of Karlsruhe, which was a stone's throw from the barracks. Mark took the taxi so he could have his own guided tour of the city. This way he would know where different places were, like the train and bus stations.

Mark discovered there was a restaurant right around the corner from the barracks that served really good food. He got out of the cab to walk. Taking this opportunity, he went into the restaurant and looked over the menu. Mark thought the veal and mashed potatoes with gravy looked particularly good.

This seemed like a really good idea. He had always wanted his own private little hideaway like this—a place to go when he wanted to be alone to eat and think. Besides, the meal really looked good with a glass of milk. Maybe he'd come here for an after-dinner thinking time, a stein of beer, and a cigarette. Now this was a feast he would never find at the mess hall. Mark began to have an appreciation for why a lot of the guys would find a place to eat off base. It all seemed very appealing.

After he'd walked around the city awhile, it was beginning to get late, and Mark thought about the bar around the corner to the barracks. He returned there to enjoy the supper he had been savoring all day. It felt good to be alone with his thoughts and relax by himself. That's when it hit him—*to be himself.* That was a thought that provoked deeper ideas about who Mark Welch really was and what he was all about. It was about time he started to get his head together and figure out the plan that had taken him to Germany to begin with.

Everything had been happening so quickly and yet only as each day came and went, only a few moments at a time. Everything was happening mysteriously, it seemed. What was everything? Every day was filled with smoking hash three or four times a day and drifting from morning till night. Mark wasn't even sure what his true job was at the warehouse anymore. What was he doing here? Where was he going in the years to come? Mark had much to think about. He tried to relax, drinking his beer as he smoked cigarette after cigarette alone.

He looked around the dimly lit little restaurant. There was a small crowd of German folks joking and talking at a distant table. The streetlight glow through the windows added to the interesting atmosphere of the room. Mark sat in the corner at his table smoking and drinking and contemplating the last several months. He realized he had come no further since the night he and Jacob had talked when they first arrived. Mark wondered what had become of Jacob.

It was amazing to Mark how a man could so easily slip from being naïve to a heavy drug user in a few short months. Although he was never sure just exactly what would happen if he didn't use, he knew he was afraid to find out after his first initiation. Mark found himself in the middle of large group of users and began participating without even so much as a whimper. No argument. No fight. He just reached out his hand and took the drugs like it was the most natural thing he could do. Wow. And now—now he was in a door less room with no obvious means of escape. He felt like he was boxed in with no one around to save him. He was going to have to save himself.

Finally it was time to go back to his room. The coming day, perhaps, would shed more light to the questions plaguing his mind—questions like who he was and what he was becoming.

That didn't happen. Again, it was a day filled with smoking hash and wandering about the post and nearby Karlsruhe. While he did appreciate the freedom of going where he wanted to go and having the money to buy the little things, he also felt conflicted—enjoying his newfound habits and yet being more lost than ever. He was prisoner of his own devices. He had heard that phrase before. Now he knew what it meant.

Again, weeks were going by with the same routine of smoking hash with everyone supplying when it was his turn. And like the others, Mark not only took his turn at buying but also enjoyed feeling like he was part of something. This quality had been missing in his life before. Maybe that was part of the addiction—being part of something larger than himself.

It was a Saturday morning, and Robby was looking for someone to go to town with. Feeling adventurous, Mark volunteered to go with him. Mark was thinking Robby knew how to speak *Deutsche*. Maybe, with Robby's knowledge and experience, Mark would learn more than he already had about the city.

Once in the cab, Robby spoke up. "Do you speak English?"

The cab driver nodded his head yes. Mark began to believe he had been wrong in his hopes.

Robby continued, "Can you take us to the downtown jewelry store? I need to update my look. This old watch and necklace are going out of style."

Mark noticed that Robby spoke all English. It began to occur to him that Robby was not as sharp as he wanted everyone to think he was. The way Robby spoke to the cab driver and the way he bragged about himself made Mark think this was not going to be as much fun as he had originally thought.

Still, it was good to spend some time with someone other than Kurt. Maybe in time Mark would make more than one friend and learn more about Germany.

Mark's father had been a soldier in the Third Army group under General Bradley. Mark had always had an interest in history, and now he was getting a chance to see what his dad had seen over thirty years before.

There was so much hatred between Mark and his dad, but there was also a sense of importance in knowing who his father really was. Somehow Mark thought it would give him a better understanding of who he himself was. That gave every trip to Karlsruhe even more importance.

The day was uneventful, but Mark learned more about bus and train stations, streetcars, the airport, and taxi drivers. In one taxi the driver sat quietly as he listened to Mark and Robby talk. Once the driver was convinced they were good people, he asked them if they would like to buy any of his watches.

Robby asked about the goods the driver was selling. That was when the driver pulled up his sleeve and opened up his coat. Before their eyes were dozens of high-quality watches the driver was peddling to the highest bidder.

Mark watched as Robby went through the motions of bartering with the driver to get the best deal he could on a good watch. It was a delightful exchange to see. In the end both felt like they had just made the deal of their lives. That was all that mattered.

Another month had gone by when a pleasant surprise took place. One morning in formation Mark noticed two new guys in his squad. It was easy to see they had never been there before. They had the same wide-eyed look about them he had had when he first arrived.

After formation they walked together to the warehouse. Mark was the first one to speak. "I'm Mark. So where are you two from?" he asked, excited at the possibility of having new friends.

"I'm Jeremy, and I'm from Phoenix," replied one of the men. "I'm not sure where he's from," he said, pointing to the other soldier.

"I'm Jason from Boston." His accent was distinctly Bostonian. It almost sounded British.

"What about you?" asked Jeremy.

"Oh, I'm from Michigan. It's hard to say which city, as I moved around a lot the last few years," replied Mark as he thought on his past. "So what will you guys be doing here?"

"No idea," replied Jason. "We haven't been told anything specific yet."

"Well, we'll know in a little bit. Maybe you'll be helping me. God knows I need the help," Mark stated with defiant determination.

As they approached the warehouse, one of the sergeants came up to them and sent them all to where Mark had been working to arrange the shelves. Mark had been able to get a lot of it done, but there was so much more to do that it seemed like forever in the making. Now there were three of them.

Mark had blond hair, Jeremy had red hair, and Jason had dark brown hair. They came to be known by some as the rainbow gang when they weren't called the three musketeers. *A strange thing to be called*, Mark thought, but at the same time it gave him a sense of belonging. This was something that made him feel better than he did just hanging around with Kurt and his buddies.

Belonging was something Mark had longed for, and it had seemed a very long time in the making. Now it seemed he was a part of a lot of things. This was the first one that didn't seem illegal or dangerous to his freedom.

At lunchtime Mark asked them, "What are you guys doing after lunch?"

The two looked at him with an awkward glance.

Deciding to take the chance, Mark asked, "Do you smoke dope?" He wasn't sure why he asked. After all that time he'd thought about getting away from it, here he was making it an issue himself. Mark confused himself at times, and this was one of them.

"I have," replied Jeremy in a slow, quiet voice.

"Well, if you're interested, you can join me, but we can't do it in my room. I'm not sure how my roommate would feel about that," Mark said, wanting to give the impression that his roommate would never approve of drugs. That would keep his roommate safe if things went bad. At the same time, Mark would find out if these two were what they said they were. Mark was really hoping for someone to be close to. He needed someone he could talk to that wasn't going to turn his world upside down any more than it already was.

"That's okay," Jeremy said. "We can go to my room. I don't have a roommate yet."

After lunch they went to Jeremy's room and locked the door the way Mark had been taught. They pulled three chairs into a small circle, and Mark prepared the hash and lit the bowl. They passed it around quietly, each one watching that the other two took a lung full of smoke and held it in. Once confident that no one was a narc, they all relaxed and began to talk of home and their uncertainty of what to expect in their new adventure. It seemed like déjà vu to Mark, only this time he was the one provoking the drug use.

It was unclear to Mark why he was acting this way. In the beginning he was looking for a way to avoid using. Now he purposefully initiated it. Silently he was searching his heart as he continued to promote the hash. The motions were strange, yet comforting. This all seemed wrong and yet strangely right. Mark was definitely in conflict with himself as he went through with what he had already started.

The rest of the day went by like every day always had—with one exception. Every break they would go to Jeremy's room and smoke a bowl. Mark felt like a robot that just did what it was programmed to do, going through the motions even if it meant going against all that he had believed in before he arrived there.

Later that evening, Jeremy asked, "Where can I get hash?"

Mark thought about it for a minute. "Give me a twenty, and I'll get you some." Jeremy did as Mark asked. Taking the twenty dollars from Jeremy, he went back to his room.

Kurt was just getting ready to put an album on as Mark walked in the door. "Hey, Kurt, do you have any hash on you by chance? I know someone who wants to buy some. I took their money and told them I'd be right back."

This seemed to make Kurt happy. Somewhere on the far side of his bunk, Kurt came up with a block of hash and traded it with Mark for the cash. Mark was beginning to get the impression that Kurt just might be a dealer. Too afraid to ask the question, Mark just took the hash and went back to Jeremy, no questions and no problems. It seemed simple and safe.

After returning to Jeremy's room it occurred to Mark that his life had become all about drugs. There was no time for soul-searching as he had planned before. He just wasn't taking the time to know who he was or where he would be going once his time in the military was over. After all, that was the whole reason he had joined the military to begin with. Drugs had never been factored in. Now everything was changing. It was all different from what Mark had planned. What was he going to do about it? It was like he was trapped in a new life with no boundaries and yet faced a locked gate at every turn. Now it was more confusing than ever.

Mark thought how good it would be to have someone to talk to, to have a father to sit with and offer his advice and experiences as they worked out a plan together for Mark's life. How wonderful that would be.

Who knew? Perhaps he would have a sense of this now that he had found two new friends. These two seemed to have the same spirit and attitude that Mark had before. It all seemed too good to be true. Only time would tell. Time was the one thing Mark still seemed to have. However, he knew even that would run out eventually.

Every morning the three would meet in either Jeremy's or Jason's room and smoke a bowl before going to breakfast. They would walk together, talking about what ever came to their minds. Most of the time it was nothing that would change the world. Still, it was changing Mark's world. Breakfast was the same—mindlessly talking about music, cars, girls, what life was like back home, and what their plans were for when they finally went back to the world.

Jason's plan was simple. He had always wanted a disco, a place he could show off to his friends back home and where he could enjoy selling alcohol while drinking from his own stock. He would talk about how the building would look—the type of speakers he would use and the state-of-the-art stereo equipment he would have. One day Toshiba was the best. The next day it would be Pioneer. The speakers never changed: Bose was always revered as the best of the best.

They would sit at break time, lunchtime, suppertime, and nighttime listening to loud rock while smoking a bowl. It wasn't long before other newcomers from all over the company would join them from time to time. It was always the same: joyful conversation while getting high with what always seemed like their best friends, finding peace in their hearts. It was a utopia if there ever was one. Life did seem to be the best it ever had been.

One Friday night late in summer's heat, the three of them were gathered in Jason's room smoking a bowl. They began to talk of the usual things.

"So what are you going to do, Jason, when it's your turn to blow this place?" Jeremy asked. It was always the same question to Jason, because of the way he talked when he answered it.

"I'm going to open a disco where anyone can come in for drinks and great music," he replied with anticipation. "It's going to have all sorts of colored lights that flash with the music and a huge strobe light hanging in the middle. All dance floor in the middle and booths around the walls on all sides. There will be a huge sign above the front door: Draco's Disco. That's what I'm gonna do. What about you?" he asked, putting the question back to Jeremy.

"I haven't decided yet. I know I want a house, but I've got my mom to take care of, and I've always wanted to have a really hot car. I know I want to live in a town, and I don't want to have to worry about mowing the grass, so I'll just stay in Arizona where it's all sand and just use rocks to decorate my lawn," he said with his trademark smile.

"What about you, weasel?" Jason asked, staring at Mark as if to taunt him.

"I don't know yet. That's been one of the reasons I'm here to begin with. You know I enlisted in the army just so I'd have some time to figure it all out," Mark replied.

"What!" exclaimed Jason. "What a fool. You could have done anything you wanted to do once you were out of school, and you choose to come here. You're a fool. That's what you are—a fool."

"How do you figure?" Mark responded defensively. "I had no job, no money, no food, no place to stay, no family, and no future. Here I have food, a place to stay, free medical and dental, a steady paycheck, and time to get my head together. Yeah, I see what you mean. I am a real fool all right," Mark pointed out sarcastically.

"Still, this is the best you could come up with? I would have found something different to do to buy time. Anything has got to be better than this place," Jason countered.

"Oh yeah? Well, what are you doing here? The war's over, and so is the draft. So tell me, how did you end up here if you didn't enlist?" asked Mark.

"Really? I thought you already knew," Jason began. "I was sent here to avoid prison time. I was caught stealing and was given a choice. It was either prison or the military. I chose the army because I didn't want to be stuck on a ship and the air force wouldn't take me. Only the army cooperates with the court systems for this kind of thing."

"Yeah, that's why I'm here," started Jeremy. "I was facing a sentence and given the same choice. It was either two years in the army or five years in prison. In the army you have freedom to move around, get paid, and get thirty days' leave every year. That's why I'm here."

"Wow, you guys only have two years?" Mark asked, surprised. "Well, I guess I could have enlisted for two years. I originally signed up to be a combat engineer, but I was colorblind. Since I was signing up for three years I was given a choice of either MOS or permanent party location. I asked for Fort Lewis in Washington and combat engineer, but since the one fell through I didn't get either."

Jason laughed. "Wow, did you get screwed!"

"Not really," replied Mark. "I still have the time and all the other things I needed to figure out a plan for the rest of my life."

"So how's that working out for you?" asked Jason.

"I admit it's been slow," Mark reflected. "The only thing I have been able to accomplish is to learn how to do drugs and ask myself the same questions over and over in my head. My problem is I don't have anyone back home to talk to about it. No family, no real friends, and no resources."

"You know why you don't have any friends, don't you?"

asked Jason with intent. "You're a weasel. You always find a way to get things from other people without paying anything back. That's what a weasel is, you know. You use people."

"How do you figure that?" asked Mark, surprised.

"Because that's what you do!" exclaimed Jason.

"Okay, let's go with that," countered Mark. "I buy my share of dope. You do your share of smoking it. So what's the problem?"

Jason didn't know how to reply to that. He just stared at Mark and continued smoking the hash. While he took in another toke, Jeremy spoke up. "I hope you're enjoying the free hash, because I don't remember you buying any for a while," he said to Jason.

"Well, actually, he has," Mark said. He was lying, however, and he looked at Jason as he spoke.

Jason looked back with hidden surprise. He didn't know if Mark really believed what he was saying or if he was telling Jeremy this to protect Jason's image and make an extra effort to work out the animosity.

The rest of the night was quiet as they sat back listening to music and smoking more hash. Everything seemed to be back to easy street, but it was all building up inside Jason a little at a time.

Chapter Four

It was a Sunday morning. The sun was bright and the sky was clear. Summer was gone, and fall was in full term as the leaves turned into a rainbow of colors just like they did back home. Mark admired the color and smell as the days grew shorter, and the brisk air carried a unique atmosphere of life about it.

Breakfast was already becoming a memory of mindless talk, free coffee, and cigarettes. The guys had started the day the same as all the others. On the way back from the mess hall they talked about doing something new.

"So, Mark, have you ever done acid before?" Robby asked.

"No, but I've heard of it. Not sure what it really is or does. Why?" Mark inquired.

"Well, I think I know where we can get some. It's not something that you do by yourself. It should be a group experience. Everyone should stay together and do things as a group," replied Robby.

This didn't seem like a big deal to Mark. After all, they almost always smoked hash together. It would seem like a waste not to do acid together too—unless, of course, one of them was going to a concert or something. After only taking a few moments to think about it, Mark decided he was in. The whole group of about ten pitched in their share of money for the acid, and Robby was off to buy it.

After what seemed like an eternity Robby reappeared with the goods. It was what they called purple microdot. It was very small. It had to be handled very carefully, because if it dropped, it would never be found again. It was that small—just a very small dot of purple.

Mark looked at it, wondering if this was for real. He'd spent so much money for such a very tiny piece of nothing.

"Are you sure this is what we were talking about?" Mark asked.

Jeremy spoke up out of his own experiences, which Mark trusted. "Oh yeah. Don't let the size fool you. This stuff will mess with you for at least twelve hours. You don't want to be alone when it kicks in either." This helped Mark feel better about joining the rest of the guys in this new experience.

"Okay," Mark said with a sense of doubt. "If you say so."

With that Mark placed the little tiny dot of acid under his tongue just like everyone else did. It would take at least a half hour to kick in. It was then that Mark realized he had to use the latrine. It was a sit-down job, so he was going to be a little while.

"Hey, guys, I'm going to the latrine. I have to use the stall for a while. I shouldn't be long," Mark explained to his friends as he went down the hall to the latrine to occupy a stall.

"Okay, but give a yell if you start to feel it kick in," Jeremy stated with a little concern.

Once in the stall Mark found the Sunday comics someone had left on the floor. While waiting for nature to take its course, Mark picked up the comics to read. It was then that an unusual experience began to take place.

The comics came to life. Each character actually talked and walked larger than the paper it was printed on. They were so colorful and so full of life. All Mark could do was watch in awe. They moved as if they were alive. The written words were in Mark's ears.

He must have been loud in his appreciation for this bigger-than-life experience, as he could hear talking and laughter just outside the stall door. Peering through the spaces between the stall door and the stall walls, Mark could see his friends standing just outside talking about him. He began to laugh as well, realizing what he was doing with the comics. It was time to remove himself from the stall. Mark had not completely forgotten what his original mission had been. He knew he needed to clean himself up.

As he reached for the toilet paper, it looked like the whole stall had become as large as his barracks room. He reached up what seemed like the whole length of his arm to retrieve the toilet paper. The roll was so large he was not sure if he could handle it. Once the process was finished and his pants were pulled up, Mark opened the stall door, which now seemed like a gate to a zoo pen.

He stepped out of the stall, and life seemed to be more normal—with one exception. Everything stood out like it never had before. Jumping out at Mark with remarkable splendor and wonder were colors Mark had never even known existed. The pastel colors he had always heard about but could never see were now jumping off the walls and floor. The sounds of people talking and laughing had a high-stereo quality about them. Everything seemed to be more alive.

They went back to the room and talked and laughed about all sorts of mindless, unimportant things, as though they were going to change the world with all their knowledge. Philosophy was abundant. While Mark participated in this social gibberish, he kept his thoughts about what was really happening in his mind. It was like he was in a type of Halloween horror house for fun, and yet all was normal deep in his mind. It was like being consciously drunk.

It was too hard to know just how much time had gone by when they decided to go for a walk as a group. Mark went along but had no idea where they were going. Perhaps no one from the group did. They made their way to buy food in Karlsruhe and then went to a bar. There they talked to some of the civilian young people and drank beer. They felt like they were invincible. Nothing could hurt them, and nothing was so big that they could not solve or conquer it. They were superhuman.

Mark had no idea how many bars or places they went to. The last one was much easier to remember, because the acid was beginning to wear off. They were in a bar for special services. Each of them had his own booth. Women came to each one of them and offered their unique attention. All this was for a price, of course. Mark was left out. Between the acid and the beer, Mark was out of money. That was okay. He wasn't sure if this was something he was ready to do anyway. Everyone had his or her own timing. Yet for Mark it was more about a deeper moral value he still didn't know how to express. He thought it strange he could do all the things he was doing but still couldn't find it in himself to participate in what most thought was the most natural thing to do next to breathing.

Mark sat alone waiting for Jason and Jeremy to finish enjoying themselves. They came out of their booths, which were made private simply by pulling a curtain across the aisle end. Both seemed to be very happy and subdued.

The three found their way back home on foot. During their walk back to the barracks Mark wondered what had happened to the rest of them. They had started out as a group of about ten or so, and now it was just the three of them. So much for group activity.

This was an experience Mark was very happy to have had. He wasn't sure he could remember what the experience was, of course. It was all a blur of color, noise, size, and sometimes distorted motion. Not one set of actions seemed to have been connected with the rest—just a series of activities that may have happened over his whole lifetime and yet all took place in a few short hours. This one experience was like a huge revelation of what his whole life had been since his arrival in Germany.

Again, questions flowed through his mind. *What does it all mean? Does it have to mean anything? Is there any meaning to anything in life, anyway?* Mark decided to just let it go and try to sleep. He was beginning to be tired of the nagging questions he brought to himself. The fact was he was getting tired of himself. Not remembering much about the walk back, Mark found himself in his bed. He was feeling like the whole day had just been one giant dream. Maybe it had been.

The next morning proved that the all of yesterday was true. Friend after friend would say something as they passed in the hallway or on the street. It was obvious to Mark that he was now some kind of celebrity. It was apparent to all that this once completely innocent man was now a full-fledged drug user.

At first Mark felt a sense of importance. He felt that he belonged to what he thought was an elite group. However, as the day wore on, Mark began to realize there was no prize in what he had done to himself. He was now living a lifestyle of drugs. There were questions Mark was always asking himself. He had enlisted to change his life for the better. He was supposed to be working on a plan while doing his tour. Now it seems all the challenges he tried to leave behind were gone. They no longer followed him like a stray dog longing for food. Still it was as if things were not right. Perhaps the fog from the drugs was making it all too cloudy to see right.

Mark kept hearing something that was wasn't making any sense. From time to time he would hear his friends say, "Just do your own thing." The only problem was that if a person's own thing was different from what everyone else was doing, then it wasn't so cool. This made the whole idea seem contrary to Mark. It was becoming clear that not everyone was sure of what he or she said and thought. Many people wanted everyone to think they were, but they weren't.

The acid was a great experience to have, but it still left him empty in the end. It had not seemed like it was all it was cracked up to be. There was a sense of relaxation in taking it. It was the kind of trip you didn't have to pack to go on. However, when you came back, things were exactly as you left them. There was no change in your life and no experience so good that your life had a timeless change to it. All it was for Mark was an escape from the things that tortured his mind. However, since Mark always kept his mind with him, it couldn't even be that.

Once on a trip, you could be anywhere you wanted to be or do anything you wanted to do. The only trick was to keep your head about you. Mark was thinking of how he had seen and heard things he didn't see and hear when he wasn't on a trip. Once on the trip, all the colors and sounds were exceptionally heightened, and interestingly, at the same time, his mind was still intact.

Mark had heard stories of people going on trips and not coming back. The question was this: was every trip the same? Sometimes Mark secretly hoped he could be on a never-ending trip. Then he wouldn't have to worry about being responsible for the rest of his life. Deep down it wasn't what he wanted. He just wanted to know how to be true to himself and live to enjoy it.

Fall had fully arrived, and the sounds of football were in the air. Mark enjoyed walking outside for any reason, just to be able to smell the fall air and see all the colors of the trees. There was a sense of freedom that just made him feel good about being alive. This was the first time Mark could remember feeling that freedom and having time to just relax and enjoy a day as he thought it should be enjoyed.

It was a Saturday night when opportunity came knocking. Kurt was about to be released to go home. This was something most of the soldiers were always talking about—being free to do what you wanted to do when you wanted to do it. The whole idea seemed like a dream. Now it was Kurt's turn to fly the friendly skies back to the States and enjoy life any way he saw fit.

Before going, Kurt had been working on an opportunity for Mark. Of course, Mark was not aware of it. Kurt saw Mark after lunch in their room. Looking at Mark with a sparkle in his eyes Kurt asked, "Have you ever thought of making some extra money?"

"What do you mean?" Mark asked with unusual interest.

"Well, you can have your own source of dope to sell and use. What do you think?"

"Yeah, okay." Mark surprised himself with his response. "How would I do that?"

"I know someone who is interested in getting some speed sold, and I told him about you," Kurt replied in calm yet intense voice. "What do you think?"

"Yeah, I can do that." Mark was enthused by the idea.

"I think that would be pretty cool. I'd like to be able to sell and know where my next bowl of hash was coming from. How much do I need to invest?" As the words flowed freely from his mouth, Mark was shocked to hear himself talk like that. He was saying things he never knew he felt. Was that him talking? It felt like it. It sounded like it. He just wasn't convinced it was true.

"Well, we just got paid. Do you have three hundred on you?" Kurt asked.

"Yeah, I do." Mark pulled out the money and handed it over.

"I will be back around suppertime. Remember, you can't tell anyone about this. No one can know where you get this stuff or what you paid for it. From this money you can easily make over a thousand. You tell people what you paid, and they will put pressure on you to lower the price. This will make it difficult for the other sellers and most likely make it tough for you to be able to sell again. Trust me, you don't want that." Kurt was very clear on this idea as he took the money and left to buy the goods.

Suppertime came more quickly than Mark imagined it would. Just as he promised, Kurt showed up in the room, his movements quiet and brisk. Making sure they were alone, Kurt pulled out a large, clear Ziploc bag full of yellow powder.

"So, Mark, are you ready?" Kurt asked.

"I think so," replied Mark, sitting on his bed as he watched this whirlwind of motion come through the door. "What do I do now?" Mark asked.

"Get yourself a mirror or a sheet of glass. Mirrors

work best, because you don't have to explain why you have one. Get a razor blade to line up the speed. Put a small amount in each piece of paper. Make sure all the hits are the same size." Kurt explained it all to him in a training sort of tone. He showed Mark what each hit should look like. The hits were the same size Mark remembered seeing the coke come in the night he blew it all over the floor.

"Use masking tape to keep the hits closed. I would sell each one for ten dollars. There is enough yellow jacket speed here to make at least a hundred hits. If you do it right, you will have a couple of hits left over for yourself to do for free," Kurt continued.

"Ah, okay," Mark replied as he took the bag and sat on his bed, taking in all that Kurt was telling him. This was a big moment for Mark. He was excited, but at the same time he began to think about what could happen if he was caught.

A lot of new questions began to come to his mind. Where would he hide it until it was all sold? How would he go about telling people that he had it and not have any narcs find out? How would he keep the money safe once the sale was made? New opportunities, new problems. Life just seems to keep changing, Mark thought.

After the speed was delivered, Kurt left just as mysteriously as he had appeared. Giving the whole situation more thought, Mark decided not to do this in his own room. He walked down the hallway with the bag hidden in his jacket. He knocked on Jeremy's door. Mark figured that if there was anyone he could trust, it was Jeremy. Jeremy always seemed to be levelheaded and never given to anger or extreme acting out, no matter what the situation was. He just seemed like the logical choice.

"Hey, what's up, dude?" Jeremy asked as Mark walked in like he lived there.

"I've got a proposition for ya," replied Mark.

"Oh yeah? What's that?" asked Jeremy.

"Have you ever sold dope before?" asked Mark.

"Well, yeah, but it's been a while. You have to be careful not be caught is the only catch," reflected Jeremy. "No one cares about you once you get caught. Everyone cares about you until they have what they want. Then the whole world disappears."

"What about you?" Mark asked. "Would you disappear if you knew I had something for sale once it was gone?"

"Well, no!" exclaimed Jeremy. "What do you got?"

"Yellow jacket speed." Mark smiled as he pulled out the bag. "But I need some place I can prepare it and sell it. I don't think my roommate will let me use our room. I'm not sure he's prepared for me to get into drugs this deep this fast. Still interested?"

"Oh yeah," Jeremy stated with his trademark smile.

They began to gather all the things they needed to make this project work. After obtaining a pair of scissors, paper, masking tape, a mirror, and a razor blade, they began the task of putting the packets together for sale.

Once there were at least thirty packets ready, Jeremy went out to find prospective customers. Mark trusted his judgment of people, as Jeremy seemed to always be able to see people for who they really were. After only a matter of minutes people began to knock on the door for a hit.

They had their money in hand and were very willing to keep the whole affair quiet.

It only took another hour for Mark to have the rest of the speed ready for sale. After about two hours, business seemed to be slowing down. However, Mark had already made back his three hundred dollars. Looking at what he had, Mark decided that he could start partying with the rest since he had all his money back.

There was another reason Mark had made this decision. He still did not have a safe place to hide the goods, and now the word was out. The risk seemed to be rising faster and faster. He didn't have a plan to keep the whole thing safe from being caught. The only thing left to do was to get rid of the rest as fast as he could. How? This seemed like a simple question, but he couldn't very well just throw it in the dumpster. That left only one logical answer: speed party.

Mark rounded up all his drug buddies and began to give it out like candy. Everyone participated, but some had concerns. They had to pay for their first hit, and now it was free? How was that fair? Mark let them know it only seemed fair that he made back his money. After all, the second hit was free, and some took a third. That seemed like a fair deal to Mark. It was only a short time before all the arguments seemed to fade away. The rest of the night was a blur of fast thinking and nonstop running around.

Mark found himself extremely happy in this state of intoxication. He really enjoyed being high on speed. He had never experienced this feeling before, and he enjoyed it more than anything he'd ever felt. It was very difficult to explain. There were remarkable joy and excitement over anything and everything. Mark loved the feeling of excitement, the feeling of being on the edge of danger and succeeding in overcoming whatever that danger might be. He felt like a hero without the conditions that make heroes. Christmas and birthdays seemed to have been all wrapped up into one big party. It was all too intoxicating to overlook. Mark loved this and wanted more. He never wanted it to end.

Hours went by like minutes. There was always something to do, no matter how mundane. He cleaned his room, showered twice, emptied the trash in the bathroom, swept the hallway, and visited with friends like it was a going away party for a rock star. To Mark, this was the most awesome experience he had ever had in his whole life. It was great.

The next morning was a whole different story. By six o'clock the high was over. Mark was smart enough to know any good thing could be overdone. With this in mind, he had limited himself to only two hits. Now he had a price to pay. His body had never been in this much pain before. It felt like all his veins and arteries were in revolt against him. No one had ever told him about this side of being high. Hash just made a person sleepy and hungry. Sometimes a person could enjoy a small sense of euphoria. This was much different. The euphoria was very enjoyable for sure. However, the pain that took its place was almost unbearable. All Mark could do was lay in bed and moan.

Jeremy came in the room to check in on him. Seeing Mark in so much pain, Jeremy did the only thing he could think of. He found some aspirin and gave Mark four to help him recover and feel almost normal again. It did seem to help, but it was going to be some time before he felt good enough to feel like a real human being. Jeremy told him to drink all the water he could, but not all at once—just a glass an hour, a little bit at a time. Mark had to be careful not to drown himself by drinking too much water too fast.

By the end of the day Mark was feeling better and decided to go out to his favorite restaurant for his favorite meal. Mark loved the veal they served and wanted a beer to help him sit back and think about the weekend.

Walking at dusk and listening to the birds as he made his way to his favorite hideaway, Mark enjoyed his meal in quiet solitude and sat back once done with a stein of beer. There was nothing like the heavy, full taste of German beer to help a man relax and think about his place in the world.

Mark began to think about how in only nine months he had gone from a small-town country boy to a drug dealer. How had this happened? Just two short years ago he was living in a backpacking tent, looking for his next meal, and now he was enjoying all the benefits of being a soldier.

Yet in spite of all the wonderful things the United States Army was giving him, Mark wanted to risk it all to get high and make money. His ability to make good decisions was falling apart. How smart he was— and yet how stupid he was for risking his freedom and reputation. It all seemed very contrary to what he knew was right and good.

CHAPTER FIVE

It was a Friday night, and Mark was on his way to a Jethro Tull concert. He had bought the ticket at the NCO club, and the concert was in Heidelberg. He was becoming a quick student of using the Euro rail system. He could buy a ticket that could be used over and over for that month and go anywhere with it. Mark had already taken trips to Heidelberg and Mannheim. This particular night Mark was on his way to Heidelberg to hear a band he loved to listen to in his room, to a concert that he hoped would be unforgettable.

It was. The concert was more than just alive. It was amazing how good things looked and sounded with a bowl of hash under his belt. The music spoke to his soul. The band was larger than life. Mark had heard that was how a concert could be, but now he knew. Hearing about it and living it were two different things. The experience was more than unforgettable. It was magnificent. Mark would have this experience seared in his heart and mind forever. It was something that could never be taken away from him.

After the concert Mark was on his way back to the

train station when he came upon a stranger who was selling an acoustic twelve-string guitar. Mark had learned to play some before joining the army. He missed his guitar, but he never talked about it. This seemed like an opportunity he just couldn't let go.

There was only one problem. The guitar was being sold for a measly forty dollars—forty dollars Mark didn't have. Ah! But what he did have, by chance, were two blocks of hash. This value came to forty dollars. Would this stranger be interested? It seemed like everyone Mark rain into smoked hash, so why not ask?

"Would you take hash for the guitar? I don't have the money on me, but I need a guitar. I miss playing," Mark stated in desperation.

"Sure, okay," the man replied.

This answer was like music to Mark's ears. They made the exchange in a manner of seconds, and just like that, Mark was the proud owner of a Framus twelve-string acoustic guitar. The night was more than Mark could take. This was the Christmas he had missed when he first arrived. He'd gotten a true gift out of nowhere for a measly two blocks of hash. Good deal.

Mark held his new prize with passion as he made his way to the train station. Once in the terminal, Mark felt the call of nature. Perhaps it was from all the excitement. Nonetheless, Mark made his way to the restroom still clutching his guitar.

Once in the stall, Mark stood his guitar in its case on one of the front corners. One of the things Mark appreciated about German stalls was how they were made more like closets than stalls. The completely enclosed room made Mark feel safer as he went about his business.

That's when he noticed it. There was a strange hissing noise that echoed inside his stall. He looked all around his toilet trying to figure out what was making this unusual sound. Then it caught his eye. There was a shadow moving around him. Mark looked up and saw a man in a shirt and tie leaning over the top of his stall, licking his lips and whispering something in German.

Shocked and somewhat scared, Mark yelled at the top of his lungs, "Get out of here before I break your face!"

The man jumped back down in the other stall. The sound made Mark think he may have broken a leg or something as he tried to get out of there. The stall door slammed against Mark's as the man ran out of the restroom. His footsteps could be heard echoing on the stone floor as the man flew away.

Mark finished his business in the restroom and found his way back to the terminal area. His mind was bothered by the experience. There were large posts that held up the roof of the station. Mark noticed a man peeking out from behind one staring at him with what seemed to be fear. Mark finally realized this must be the man that had been so disgusting to him in the restroom. Mark quickly made his way to the train that would take him back to the barracks. Continuing to look over his shoulder, Mark made sure he ended his journey alone.

Back at the barracks, Mark took out his guitar and played it some. From that day on, from time to time, when Mark was alone he would play his new guitar and listen to what he could so as to learn new songs or make up his own.

He had to relearn much of what he'd once known, as it had been a long time since he had last played. The guitar had always been a part of his life. Mark could remember when he was very little, his mother had bought him a toy plastic guitar, and it had made him feel like he was king of life. That was the feeling he had now.

Weeks went by as Mark enjoyed playing when he could. He was just beginning to forget about all his problems and had even cut back on smoking hash. Life had some new surprises for Mark

Chris showed up in Mark's room one morning. Hearing some movement in the room, Mark got himself out of bed and saw Chris standing in the middle, looking around like he was lost. "So how did you get in here?" Mark asked, a little unnerved.

"Oh, Kurt let me in on his way out. It seems you take longer to get up than he does," Chris said. "Let me know when you're ready to talk. I've got something you might enjoy."

Mark got himself ready for the day. Once he was showered and dressed he turned his attention to Chris, who had been busying himself in a bag he had brought with him.

"So what's up?" asked Mark as he put the finishing touches on his uniform, preparing for the day.

"I know about the speed Kurt sold you. I was wondering if you were interested in buying other things," replied Chris.

"Depends on what you have," Mark replied, trying not to sound overly excited.

"I've got some coke if you're interested." Chris looked at him with his crazy eyes.

"How about if I just buy a couple of hits to see what I think?" countered Mark.

"Yeah, that would be fine. I'll be around if you decide you want more." With that Chris handed over two hits as Mark handed over the money.

Once Chris was gone, Mark placed the two hits in his pocket and went about his day. From time to time he would put his hand in his pocket and feel the two hits. In doing so, Mark began reflecting on what it all meant. What was he doing, buying and selling drugs like a dealer with no conscience? Yet that couldn't be, as his conscience had been talking to him all morning. Mark began to laugh at himself as he thought about how his thinking would sound to anyone hearing it.

Later that evening Mark took the two hits of coke to Jeremy's room to see if he was interested in having one. Jeremy was sitting with Jason smoking a bowl of hash.

"What are you guys up to?" Mark asked as he entered the room.

"Not a lot. Just listening to some jams and getting stoned." Jeremy grinned as he took another toke. "What about you, man? What are you up to?"

"Well, I just got a couple of hits of coke. Only problem is there are three of us," Mark remarked, puzzling over the dilemma.

"That's not a problem," quipped Jason. "We can always smoke it."

"Are you serious?" Mark asked, surprised. "I've never heard of that before. How does that work?"

"You just pour some of it into the bowl with the hash and smoke it just like you do hash by itself," Jason replied. "It's easy."

They sat down, and the three of them made a circle, like always, to share a bowl. Since one was already going, they just put in a little coke and went about smoking it. Jason and Jeremy seemed to enjoy the new mix. Mark, however, couldn't tell the difference. He didn't feel any more stoned than he did when it was just hash. The important thing was that they enjoyed it. That being the case, Mark knew he could sell the coke to more than just the traditional coke user.

Later that night, after Mark was done smoking the coke with his buddies, he went back to his room. He got ready for bed, hoping Chris was going to show up again soon so he could make a deal. The idea still sounded strange to Mark. Making drug deals—that was something he never thought he would be doing. Now here he was, making a second deal to sell a quantity like he was in the big time. On the one hand, it was a kind of adventure that Mark was becoming addicted to.

On the other hand, it felt like things were starting to get way out of hand. Mark kept asking himself—was the risk worth it? It wasn't like he was going to be making money beyond belief. He could if he did it right, but he just couldn't bring himself to make a profit off his friends.

The whole thing just seemed like he was in another world. A dream world. A nightmare.

The next morning, while Mark was getting ready for the day, Chris showed up again. Mark heard the knock on the door and let him in. "Have a seat, man. I've just got a few more things to do, and then we can get down to business."

"Sounds cool," Chris answered enthusiastically.

Once Mark was ready, he took a seat near Chris and lit up a bowl. They had passed it back and forth a few times when Chris finally broke the silence. "So you ready to take some coke?"

"Yeah, I am," responded Mark. "I just found out you can smoke it with hash. I didn't notice much out of it, but my buddies did."

"Oh yeah," answered Chris. "I do it all the time. It's more of a mellow buzz. Of course it makes the high a little more expensive, but hey, that's good for you and me, right?"

"Well, then, let's do this," Mark replied. He pulled out the money he had been stashing for such an opportunity, and the deal was done. Mark waited a day or two before getting it ready. He kept it hidden in the floorboards near Kurt's bunk. This was a secret hiding place Kurt had just recently told him about.

This time Mark did all the prep work by himself. Once he had all the hits done he went to see Jason and Jeremy in Jeremy's room. "Hey, you guys interested in making some money?"

"Yeah, sure," Jeremy exclaimed. "Whatcha got going?"

"What about you, Jason?" Mark asked, wanting to know if Jason was trustworthy at this level.

"Well, okay, I'm in. What do I gotta do?" Jason slowly responded as if knowing that if he wasn't, a lot of things would change.

"I've got some coke. It's not a lot, but I'll give you half the profit of what you sell. How does that sound?" Mark answered.

"Yeah, I'm in," Jeremy declared.

"Yeah, so am I," Jason said.

Mark gave each one of them ten hits to sell. He kept the rest for himself to. Each went his own way to find buyers. The barracks was full of drug users. They all had their own reasons that varied as much as there were users. It only took an hour to sell all that Mark had purchased.

Once done, they met in Jeremy's room and divided up the money as Mark had promised. This seemed to make Jason and Jeremy happy. Mark also felt a sense of accomplishment. He had a great deal of money in his pocket, and he liked the feeling that he had a group of guys he could count on to buy his goods as needed. Mark went to bed feeling like he was climbing to the top of the world. The only thing left was to continue to convince Chris he could be counted on. The last thought on Mark's mind as he slept was that he was going to hell.

The next night, the three of them decided to go to the bar to celebrate their success. After showering they met in Jason's room. There was a particular bar in Karlsruhe that catered to military personnel. There was always a big band playing there every weekend. The three went to the bar to drink the night away, celebrating their financial success.

Jimmy Jones had been stationed at Karlsruhe for two years by the time Mark arrived. To most, he was just a truck driver who lived with a local woman in town. He enjoyed a great deal of drinking and the culture of the German people. However, there was a secret side to Jimmy that only he knew. Not even the family he lived with could guess his other "vocation."

Jimmy was in the shadows as Mark and his friends went to town. He followed at a distance. He had been suspecting something was amiss for a while now. Jimmy had been watching Kurt until Kurt had also moved into town. The distance between Kurt's new residence and the barracks made it more difficult for Jimmy to do his job. He was very good at his job, but it was impossible for anyone to be in two places at the same time. Jimmy had to make a choice of whom he was going to follow and whom he would have to cut loose for the moment.

Jimmy had known Kurt was a dealer for a long time. The trick was in catching him at it. He had no proof of what was so obvious, and proof was needed for Jimmy to close the case. After two years of trying to prove what he knew about Kurt, Jimmy decided to start tailing Mark. The idea was to make a better connection to Kurt and his other affiliates and shut down larger ring of drugs. It was larger than they had first imagined. To do this he had to make friends and wait until the most opportune time. Newer people were always more vulnerable to manipulation.

Until now Jimmy had only been watching Mark and his friends from a distance. The time was now coming to move closer to the group. To do this he had to find the one person he thought he had the best chance of gaining the needed information from. He knew it wasn't going to be Mark. Kurt would have done his job of indoctrinating Mark to the code of silence.

Jimmy was always a table away in the mess hall, within listening distance when he could. He worked hard to be able to hear the three as they talked and argued. Jimmy was narrowing the field of choices. Soon he would make his move on the most vulnerable one.

Having been convinced that Mark could deliver, Chris made a decision to start using Mark as a regular seller. Chris went to see Kurt at his apartment in Karlsruhe.

Knocking on Kurt's door, Chris could feel his heart beating a little fast with anxiety.

"Hey, come on in," Kurt muttered as he opened the door for Chris. Kurt had been waiting for his arrival for a couple of hours when he finally showed up.

"Thanks, man, I've been kind of tied up with a few things," Chris remarked as he entered the apartment. They sat down at the table to talk as Kurt pulled out a couple of beers. While they drank, they talked about their plans for making as much as they could before Kurt left for the States. His time in Germany was growing very short now.

"So once you're gone who are we going to find to replace you? I mean, I know I'm gonna be the new contact with the Dragoons, but who will fill my shoes?" asked Chris. They seemed stumped over the prospects. *Dragoon* was the term most dealers gave to the local German suppliers. The dealers they were working with used the term to identify who they were. The American connections used it to keep names out of the picture.

Chris continued, "We really can't count on Robby. He is just too much of an airhead. He would either talk too much and get himself and us arrested, or he could get himself killed by the Dragoons. Either way, he is just not a good choice. Who else is there that we know will not get too selfish or stupid?"

"That's a good question," Kurt responded. "The only one I can think of is not the best choice in the world. However, I think if we bring him along a little at a time, he just might prove himself. I know I've sold to him, and he pulled it off. Now you've done the same. It's a good start. We just have to keep it up. Well, actually, you will have to keep it up. I'm leaving in a couple of days, so really you're on your own."

With that, they finished drinking quietly. They both knew whom Kurt was thinking of. From there they made plans on how to prepare their new prospect.

Chapter Six

The sun was starting to descend in the west as men began to congregate back at the barracks. Chris made his way to there with more drugs for Mark to sell. Arriving at the barracks Chris quietly climbed the stairs to Mark's room. He kept thinking about how he was going to convince Mark to move up in the drug dealing business. Knocking on the door, he felt his pocket for the package to give himself confidence for what he had to do.

Mark answered the door. "Hey, come on in," he said, closing the door behind Chris. "Have a seat. I'll be right with you."

Mark got out some hash, and they sat down to a bowl to relax and discuss the reason for the visit. Chris started the conversation. "So how did you like selling the speed and coke?"

Mark thought about the question. "Well, it was kind of intimidating. I know that sounds a little childish, but I was scared. No one wants to go to prison just for trying to enjoy their lives. All I want is to know that today is better than yesterday and tomorrow will be better than today."

"Well, which would you rather have—feeling good or starting to get used to going through every day with no high?" Chris asked with an intent in mind.

"What exactly are you talking about?" Mark asked, his curiosity piqued.

"I know how to set you up with a steady supply of hash and speed. You do like both, right?" Chris said. "What do you think? Are you interested?"

"That depends," Mark cautiously answered. "It depends on what exactly you have in mind and what it's going to cost me. When I sold before, I felt like it was a onetime deal. Now I feel like you are asking me to get into this on a full-time basis. Am I right?"

"How about if we go at it slow, a little at a time? I bring by a package when you can afford it, and you sell the package. If things go well and you like what happens, then we start going a little larger until you think enough is enough. How's that sound?" Chris asked, just as he and Kurt had talked about.

Mark sat and thought about it for a while as they smoked another bowl. When the bowl was near its end, Mark began to stare at it, as if the bowl was symbolic of the plan. It was becoming clear this was a sign of what would happen if there were no more to refill the bowl. All would just burn out into ashes and that would be the end of what was there.

After considering it all carefully, Mark finally agreed to the terms. "Okay, so what do you have for me today?"

"I have the speed if you're interested. Same price. You're still new at it, so I'll explain the rules if you haven't already guessed them. You pay up front. That way if anything goes wrong the suppliers don't lose. They don't like losing their money. They're in it solely for the money. They'll kill anyone who looks like a threat to them or their profit. You will never see them or know who they are, unless you get to the point where they think you're ready. There will be no threat to you because you'll never know who they are and you will always pay up front. Do you understand?" Chris had spelled it out in very simple but intense terms. It was clear this was a serious business, and yet it was just that—a business.

"Yeah, I think I understand," Mark answered quietly. "All I have to do is have the money. That's the thing," Mark said, wanting clarification.

"What's that?" inquired Chris.

"Well, what if I don't have the money when you bring the goods around?" he reasoned. "I mean, I know I don't get the goods, but wouldn't it be better if I asked for it when I was ready rather than you bringing it here when you had it?"

"I see what you mean," replied Chris. "For now that'll be fine. If I were you, I would always have some money stashed once you build up a savings of some kind. That's how it works. Once the goods are available they run a risk of storing it. They have to know there are people out there that can move it. If you let them think you're dependable and then lead them to think otherwise—well, let's just say life won't be the same for you. It gets dangerous. They're willing to go through a waiting time so you can learn for now, but once you get there don't regress."

"Okay, I got it. I'll sell what you have today. Give me more time to think about what you're asking of me. This is a big thing to me. This isn't something you just do for the fun of it. My life isn't much, but it's all I've got. Just give me some time to think it over," Mark requested, knowing that he was at a crossroads.

Mark knew if he continued down this road there may be no return. Still, if he stopped here, then he could be considered a threat, and he didn't want that either. Besides all that, he did like getting high every day. The addiction was in full bloom. There was a lot to consider.

Mark wasn't proud of his current lifestyle, but it was the best he had felt about himself perhaps his whole life. It didn't seem like a good time to see it all end in one stupid decision.

Mark said good-bye to Chris and then went down the hall to smoke some hash with Jeremy. Jeremy invited him into the room with no words exchanged. They sat down, and Mark lit up a bowl while Jeremy put on some tunes. They listened to mellow rock as they passed the bowl back and forth, Jeremy with his same usual grin, like he had some kind of secret.

Finally, after a couple of bowls, Jeremy asked the question burning in his mind. "So what's going on?"

"I'm not sure," Mark answered. "One minute I'm living the dream. The next minute the dream takes a turn that could turn into an even bigger dream or an outright nightmare."

"What are you talking about?" Jeremy asked, knowing there was much more than Mark was sharing.

"I was approached today with the opportunity to be a full-time dealer—I mean, a bigger dealer than I am now," Mark began. "Now I only sell as it comes to me on a hit-and-miss basis, just something that kind of falls out of the sky. Now the supplier wants to know if I am ready to step it up. To be more dependable. To take more risks—risks not only with the authorities but also from the suppliers. I guess once you start this there is no turning back. I'm not sure what to do. I mean, what happens if I say no? It's quite clear what happens if I say yes. I don't know what to do."

Jeremy listened with great interest and concern. He understood all too well the place Mark was in now. This was one of the reasons he was in the army—not only to pay the penalty for his crimes but also to escape those who wanted to hurt him for what he'd made them lose when he was busted. Not a good place to be.

They smoked a couple of more bowls in the quiet with only the sound of music giving them peace of mind. The hash settled their nerves and concerns. They sat relaxing until it finally occurred to Mark he had work to do. He still had the package of speed that had to prepare and sell before he was caught with it. One never knew when a health and welfare inspection would take place. He had never seen one, which meant they were due.

Mark went back to his room and prepared his package for selling. After a few hours it was ready. Since it was the weekend, Mark figured he had time in the morning to sell all he had. After hiding it all in the floorboards, he went to bed, confident he would see things more clearly in the morning.

Morning came, and Mark woke in a maze of mixed emotions. He took his time to get dressed and eat breakfast. After breakfast, Mark sat alone in the mess hall, contemplating how he was going to pull off this next selling spree. He was hoping to eventually no longer need his friends to do the selling for him. Still, the more he thought of it, the more he saw using his friends as a buffer to keep him out of the picture should a narc be watching from a distance. What a dilemma. The last thing he wanted was for his friends to be caught doing his work.

Mark returned to his room to retrieve the goods. He was just getting ready to leave his room when he heard a knock. Mark looked through the peephole and could barely make out the face. He carefully stashed the goods under his jacket in his shirt. Again, the knock was on the door. This time Mark answered, "Who is it?"

"It's me, Jeremy," came a voice from the hallway.

Mark opened the door and let Jeremy in. It was apparent that Mark was agitated, so Jeremy just asked, "What's going on?"

"Nothing," Mark replied. "I was just getting ready to go do something."

"Need any help?" Jeremy offered, knowing what Mark was up to.

"You know, I have always appreciated all that you have done for me," Mark started. "Sooner or later it's going to get a little more complicated. That means there are going to be a lot more risks. I can't keep asking you to do that."

"Well, actually I'm seeing it differently," countered Jeremy. "The way I see it, you're doing us all a favor by having a faster and more reliable supply. I can't keep letting you take all the risks for something I want just as bad as you do. Besides, I know a lot more about all of this than you do. I know the risks. I'm in, and I'm not asking your permission. You're stuck with me."

Mark smiled at the new alliance. He liked knowing he had someone he could not only count on but trust as well. It felt good knowing Jeremy felt that way. He really was a friend. That felt as good as using did. Maybe better.

With that they left the room to go door-to-door peddling their goods. They took their time to talk with each customer so as to build a rapport filled with support and confidence so that if any trouble were ever in the air, someone would speak up. By midafternoon everything was sold.

Back at Mark's room they lit up a bowl to relax after experiencing a time of anxiety and apprehension. After the first bowl was done and the second was lit and going, Mark spoke up. "Hey, once my roommate's gone, how would you like to move in? I don't like the idea of taking the chance on getting someone who I don't know or can't trust. Interested?"

"Yeah, sure, man," Jeremy responded with his usual candor. "I think that would make things a lot easier. Any idea of how to do that?"

"I think I just have to put in a request with the first sergeant. They wouldn't have any reason to deny it. I don't think they know who I am yet," Mark said hoping he was correct.

With that they kept on smoking into the evening. It was getting late when they realized they hadn't had anything to eat yet. Mark decided to take Jeremy to his own little secret place for quiet time.

After they enjoyed a good meal they relaxed, drank beer, and made small talk to end the night. The day had brought about a lot of changes that Mark wasn't ready to take in. Jeremy's company made the whole thing easier to accomplish with less thought and more action.

Sometimes that could be a good thing. Sometimes it could create risks that didn't have to be taken. Mark considered this as they sat quietly drinking beer and enjoying the quietness of the hideaway. However, it did not change the fact that he was now a full-time drug dealer and that getting caught was just a matter of time.

CHAPTER SEVEN

Jimmy went to breakfast in the mess hall, keeping an eye out for Mark or any of his friends. The morning was uneventful as he finished his coffee. After realizing no one was going to show, he went to the PX to see if there was anything of interest happening there.

Once convinced there was nothing to see there, Jimmy went on to the warehouse to catch up on the small talk taking place while they worked. It was always interesting to hear all about how the guys got high using whatever was available at the time. It was from this kind of research that Jimmy knew who was doing what. He needed to do this now more than ever, as time was running out. If he was to ever catch and prosecute Kurt Talagan, he needed to find out what was up with Mark Welch.

At the warehouse, Jimmy saw Mark and watched him as he and Jeremy went to the PX. Jimmy followed and bought more coffee to avoid looking conspicuous. Jimmy sat and drank his coffee, hoping to hear Mark say or do something he could use.

Mark and Jeremy had gone to the PX to eat, having

slept in and missed breakfast. Jimmy watched them sit down at a table as Mark talked to Jeremy. Jimmy got up to sit at a table closer to them. He had an inside advantage, as Mark and Jeremy both thought of him as just another truck driver for the warehouse and a friend who simply liked to drink too much and loved his German family. Moments later Jason came in and joined the other two.

"So what are you two up to this morning?" Jason asked, noticing he had not been invited to go with them to breakfast.

"Oh, nothing," answered Jeremy, trying not to give too much away. "We were just talking about something that happened to him last night," he continued, pointing at Mark.

"Oh, it's not that big of a deal," countered Mark, trying not to involve more people than necessary.

"Well, what is it?" Jason asked, still wanting to be included.

"Let's just call it a business opportunity," Jeremy replied, excited about the possibilities he envisioned.

"Okay, so what is it?" Jason continued, now interested himself.

"Okay," Mark answered, still uncertain how much to say. "I had someone offer me a chance to sell all the time. The only thing is, once I start, there may be no getting out. On the other hand, if I don't want to participate, I could still be facing a very short future. I'm not sure what I've gotten myself into."

"Mark"—Jason laughed menacingly—"you are more of a fool than I ever thought. The only thing you know how to do is make bad decisions. How did you get into this, anyway?"

"I don't know," Mark responded defenselessly. "One minute I'm just a green soldier looking for a way to have a future worth living. The next minute I'm doing drugs and listening to rock 'n' roll like it's some kind of prophet. Now … well, let's just say I'm in a corner with only one way out, and I don't think I can see what it is. Any ideas?"

"Yeah," Jason quipped at the chance to give ill-fated advice. "Take the chance and deal. They say to keep your friends close and your enemies closer. The only way to keep your enemies closer is to be in league with them."

This sounded like good advice to Mark. He sat and thought about it for a while as he drank his coffee. Finally, after a long moment of silence, he replied, "Okay, I'll go ahead and do it. Are you going to be a part of it?"

Laughing, Jason responded, "No way. Are you kidding? I've been building my future by sending money home to invest in a disco, remember? I don't need any of this. It's all you, buddy. It's all you."

"Hey, man, I really appreciate all your support," Mark said mockingly. "There's nothing like keeping your friends close, right?"

Jeremy smirked as he looked at Jason. "So you spend a lot of time living what you believe, huh, Jason?"

"I'll tell you what," Jason said, defending himself. "I'll do what I can, but I don't want to be part of the guys you do business with. I'll help you after you have the goods to sell, okay?"

"Just remember," Mark stated with an intense tone,

"there are only three people who know what's going on now, and you're one of them. If anyone finds out …"

"What?" Jason responded. "What are you going to do? Kill me? I don't think so."

"You're right," Mark finished. "It won't be me. These people have every intention of protecting their interests. They don't think of this as a game. You know now. Even if you walk away from all this at this very moment, you know. If it gets discovered, they'll think you did it because of how you're acting now. You're in it now, man, just as deep as I am."

Now all three sat in silence as they drank more coffee and smoked their cigarettes. While they sat quietly, thinking about what Mark had said, Jimmy sat back, reflecting on everything he heard. This was exactly what he was looking for. Now Jimmy thought he could also have someone he could pull into his confidence to get what he really wanted. He needed someone who was willing to testify to this conversation. Even more, he needed the actual activity to take place. Conspiracy was a big thing and hard to prove. Trying to carry it out was even bigger.

Finally, the three quietly got up and left for the mess hall. Lunchtime had arrived, and they were deep in thought about their lives. Jimmy followed at a safe distance, hoping to discover even more.

They walked casually to the mess hall and ate quietly. Once finished they went to Mark's room. They saw Jimmy coming up the stairs as they entered Mark's room but thought nothing of it, since, as a platoon member, he was considered one of them. He nodded hello as he passed them while they were entering Mark's room. Jimmy made his way to the latrine to sit quietly in a stall, thinking this would throw them off if they became suspicious.

After a short time he left the latrine and went back down the hallway to see if he could hear anything through Mark's door. There was music playing and some voices, but nothing told him anything new. Jimmy left for the PX to plan his next move.

Chris and Kurt talked about the next few days while they packed up all of Kurt's belongings in preparation for his departure back to the States. "I talked to Mark. He seemed interested in our proposal."

"So what did he say?" Kurt asked.

"He's interested, but he's also considering all the dangers he thinks comes with it," Chris replied. "He thinks he has no choice. I'm not sure it's the best way to get him to buy in."

"It's not, but he's already there, so let's go with what we have," Kurt said sinisterly. "I think he'll settle down. In either case he's the only choice we have now that we're out of time."

"Did you talk to the Dragoons? Tell them about Mark?" Chris inquired.

"I didn't give his name, but I did tell them about him," responded Kurt. "They don't have a problem as long as business isn't interrupted and he behaves himself. If things don't go like they think it should, then they'll make changes. I won't be here for that, but you will. Really, when you think about it, this whole thing is up to you, not me. I don't have any investment in it anymore. Just be careful how you bring him around."

Chris thought about it quietly and finally blurted out, "I think he'll do just fine. He doesn't know anything that could hurt me or them, and he isn't the kind of person who would give up information just to save his own skin. I don't know how, but I can see that about him. I think it'll be just fine."

"I think you're right," Kurt said, "so let's finish getting all this packed so you can get on with it and I can go home."

With that they finished packing up all of Kurt's belongings for the movers to take. They would be shipped to his stateside home. In a few days Kurt would be on his way to a new life, and Chris would be left to take over the business. Everyone would win.

The following week was pay week, and everyone was ready for his check. Once Mark was paid he was able to make the deal that Chris had offered. Mark went to his room after getting his paycheck and waited for Chris.

Just before supper Chris arrived with the goods. Mark let him in the room so they could talk.

"So are you ready to do business?" Chris asked as he lit up a bowl.

"Yeah. I've been waiting for you. I have another question," Mark answered with anticipation and anxiety.

"What's your question?" Chris said with a hint of impatience.

"Does it matter if I choose to involve anyone at my

end? I mean, do I have to give up any names, or can I 'share' this end of the business with anyone I choose as long as I'm sure they're reliable and I'm the one taking the risk?" Mark asked with sweating palms.

"Yeah, that's fine," Chris answered with a breath of relief. "How you go about moving the goods is all up to you as long as the job gets done and everyone is dependable."

"Okay. So I don't have to tell you who I have help me, then?" Mark repeated.

"Nope. Just as long as you believe in them. If it goes bad, though, you'll have to give them up or take it all on yourself. Can you do that?" Chris asked.

"Guess I'll have to. I think it's a good move. It gives me a barrier from anyone who would be a narc. He knows more about any of this than I do. I feel like it's a win-win," Mark said with conviction.

"Okay then. Let's do this. I have places to be and people to see," Chris said.

With that they made the exchange and Chris was on his way. From there Mark placed the goods in his hiding spot and went down to see Jeremy.

"Hey," Mark said as he was let in Jeremy's room. "The goods are here. You ready to do some packing and selling?"

"Yeah," Jeremy said as he grabbed his keys and went to the door. They went back to Mark's room and made up the packages. They were just about finished when they heard a knock on the door. Before they could respond they heard Jason.

"Hey, it's me. Let me in."

Jeremy opened the door after Mark put the goods under a blanket to hide them. When the door was closed again, they went back to finishing the job.

"So why didn't you come get me?" asked Jason, a little offended.

"I didn't want to attract more attention than I had to. I figured we could come get you once we were done getting things ready. That way no one would be suspicious about what we were doing," Mark answered, trying to be clever.

"Okay," Jason said. "So is it all done?"

"Yeah, I guess it is," answered Jeremy. "You ready to go look for buyers?"

"Yeah, sure," answered Jason. "How do you want to do this?"

"I was thinking we would go down to your room, and you bring them in a few at a time," Mark said.

"I don't think so," Jason responded with a flare of anger.

"Relax, I was joking." Mark smiled. "Actually, we could do that, only get together in Jeremy's room. He has no roommate, and he won't be there in a few days, anyway."

Jeremy thought about it for a moment and agreed. "Yeah, you know what? That actually sounds like a great idea. By the time they figure out something was going on, we can always say we were looking for help for the move."

They went down to Jeremy's room one at a time with Jeremy going first. Jason and Mark followed. They made sure at least five to ten minutes passed in between them. Once they were all there, Jeremy and Jason would go collect money and then take the goods back to the customers.

It took several hours, but they finally finished the job. After all the money was collected, Mark gave them each a share for taking the risk to help. This time, however, Mark sold it all and didn't keep any to party with. He knew he would need to have a savings for the next time Chris brought him business.

They retired to Mark's room again to smoke a bowl and call it a day. Once the bowl was done, Jason left to go about his own personal business. This left Jeremy and Mark alone. Taking the opportunity, they went to Mark's favorite hideaway for supper.

Chris returned to see Kurt. "Well, he did it. He took the goods. He has the help of a couple of friends. He doesn't know I know who they are, but I do. I know Jeremy will do well for him, but I don't like Jason. He seems too interested in helping himself at anyone else's expense."

"Well, keep an eye on things. Look for anyone Jason may talk to. If it looks like trouble is brewing, do what you have to. Just remember—no chances. The risk has to be worth the reward. Look for the right opportunity. Make sure it sends the right message in the right way to the right people. No sense doing something one-dimensional if you don't have to," Kurt advised. "Make it meaningful or you will be repeating it too often."

Chris took the advice to heart. Inviting himself to

a beer in Kurt's refrigerator, he sat down to reflect and plot out a plan. He didn't know if there was anyone Jason would talk to, but he wanted to have an idea in mind in the event that there was and he had to follow through.

Jimmy was in the bay room on the top floor when Jason came through looking for customers. He watched Jason and followed him at a distance to see what he was up to. Jason saw him but figured he was just going to the latrine. Jimmy positioned himself so he could see how often Jason and Jeremy went in and out of the room and went back and forth to each of the other rooms.

Jimmy knew what was going on, but he also knew if he just went in and caught them, he would either have to use drugs himself or give up his real identity. He was going to have to come up with a way to get one of them to talk. The most likely candidate was Jason. He could tell this from the conversation they'd had in the warehouse. Jimmy wanted to talk to the powers that be, but he also knew that if they were aware of what was going on they would jump the gun and blow the bigger opportunity. He was going to have to pull this off on his own.

There was one other option. Jimmy decided to include his department backup. The Central Intelligence Department was covering a variety of projects and was already understaffed, but if anything went wrong he needed to have someone know what was going on. With this in mind, he decided to go to the PX, where there were some pay phones, and make a call. He would have to be careful, as there wasn't exactly a private booth there. It would too easy for anyone to hear.

For the next few days, the three woke up in the mornings and went to Mark's room for their usual routine of smoking before breakfast. Once they all had their meals, they sat down to eat and talk.

It was then that Jason looked at Mark and asked, "So what now? I mean, are we going to just keep waiting for the next time like we're sitting on pins and needles? I don't like this. I feel like we're on a merry-go-round or something, just waiting for someone to give us another push."

Jeremy looked at Jason with livid eyes. "Look, you act like you've never been here before. It's no different from what you did before. Don't act like this is all new to you."

"What are you talking about?" Jason responded anxiously. "It isn't like it was before. First of all, back home I had places I could go and more people I could count on. People I grew up with. The whole neighborhood was like family. We don't have any of that here. Secondly, Mark here isn't exactly the most experienced guy I've ever worked with. He doesn't have a clue what's really going on. Do you?" He looked directly at Mark.

Mark looked pointedly at Jason as if he was about to fly across the table. "Let me see if I have any idea of what's really going on. If I stop selling, maybe I can go on with my life, but most likely my contact will have to cut his losses. I'm pretty sure that means cutting me. I also have a pretty good idea that if I do keep selling, it's only a matter of time before someone catches on to what we're really doing, and that will be the end of free walking and chilling without waiting for the dreaded health and welfare. That's the good news. There is the outside chance one or more of us could end up in a cemetery. How does that sound? Think maybe I have some idea of what's going on?"

"You don't understand," Jason said, defending himself. "There are all sorts of people that know we sell. They live in every room on every floor of our barracks. I don't know hardly anything about any of them. Do you? I don't think so. I have to be honest—I can't honestly say I have seen all of the guys I've sold to actually use the drugs. So how do we know we haven't already sold to a narc?"

Jeremy looked a little taken aback. "He has a point. We need to do something. We need to have a smoke party. Make sure everyone we sell to is there. Maybe do more than one so that it's easier to know everyone is trustworthy. What do you think?"

Mark thought about it for a moment. "You're both right. I like the idea. We can still use your room. First we have to finish getting permission to move you into my room. Then, while we still have the keys, use your room for the parties. We can do it this weekend."

"What are you talking about?" Jason asked a little defensively. "When did you guys decide to move Jeremy into your room?

"I thought it would be better than getting a roommate

I didn't know or trust. I didn't think you were interested in living that close to me," Mark answered.

"You're right," Jason said with defiance. "You're way too much of a fool for me to be interested in living with you. I'd probably be dead in a month."

Mark nodded, and they all finished smoking and drinking their coffee, completely unaware of who was sitting at the table next to them. It wasn't even a thought. Jimmy was taking notes in his head and would be looking for the parties. And he had more confidence than ever that Jason was the way in.

Chapter Eight

That Friday night they met in Jason's room for a change—mostly for the sake of variety, but partly just in case someone was starting to pay attention to them. It really didn't make any difference, because Jimmy knew what the real deal was. This was, however, completely unknown to them.

Once behind locked doors, Jason pulled out his bowl, and they lit it up and began to plan. Jeremy figured out the first thing to do. "Let's go one group at a time. We can probably put anywhere up to six guys in the room at a time with us. We need to have one of us on the outside, though, as a lookout. We need a plan for cutting things short if it looks like trouble."

"A plan? What kind of plan do you mean?" Mark asked.

"You know, like maybe a type of secret knock or some other way to let the other two in the room know if there's trouble," Jeremy answered.

"Well," Jason said, "if you think about it, my room is next to Jeremy's, so we can use the windows or the door.

If the authorities are outside, they could see the windows, so I could use the door. If they are in the hall, I can use the window."

"How are you going to use the window?" Mark asked now that he could see the plan coming together.

"We can agree to a special knock for the door and then take a string and run it from one window to the other," Jason said as he formulated the plan in his head.

Despite all the time they'd been living there, they had never thought about the windows. Mark began to have a little more respect for Jason but still looked at him like he was not his best friend. Mark didn't like how Jason was always treating him with animosity. He didn't trust Jason, but since Jeremy seemed to be happy with him, Mark went along with the plan. Still, something about him didn't feel right. It was a good plan, but it was Jason's plan.

They all looked out Jason's window and realized how close the windows really were to each other. It would be easy to run a string from one window to the other.

So they did, with an object tied to the end of the string in Jeremy's room. The other end was tied to the radiator in Jason's room. The string was thin enough for the windows to close on it and strong enough not to break. If Jason saw trouble, he could pull the string, and everyone who needed to know would be able to act on it.

Now they needed a plan for hiding the drugs if there was trouble. Mark got to thinking. "We already have the string in place. Why not just tie the drugs to the string and pull the drugs into the room? The only thing left is to have a place to hide them in here. Do you have any loose floorboards that can be pulled up?"

Jason was amazed at Mark's thinking. "You know what? I think I do. Look over here. I think someone used to use this spot for hiding something." They played with the boards until they gave away their secret. Looking at the location of the spot in the room, they realized they could put a piece of furniture over it to complete the plan.

"Did I tell you the first sergeant gave us permission to move you?" Mark asked.

"No, you didn't. That's cool. What about an extra key?" Jeremy asked, seeing it all coming together.

"Yep. Got that too," Mark said as he handed a key to Jeremy. "We have two weeks to get it done, so that leaves everything clear for us to follow through on our plan. We're all set."

That night they moved everything they could into Mark's room. Kurt had already moved his things out, so it was easy to get it done. They left an end table, a stereo, and some chairs in Jeremy's room. Jason moved a couple of his chairs into the room as well. It was around eight or so when they were done.

"So what do you think? Should we go ahead and smoke some hash with some of the guys tonight? That will cut down on how many times we do it tomorrow and Sunday," Jeremy pointed out.

"Yeah, let's do it," Jason said. "Let's figure out who to do first."

"Okay. Why don't we start with the guys who work

in the shipping and receiving area? They live on the same floor, so it would be easy to round them up," Jeremy said. Jeremy went to get his room set up while Mark and Jason went to invite the guys for a small party.

It wasn't long before they had all the guys together and a bowl lit up.

"I'm gonna go. I've got some things to do. You guys have a good time," Jason said, excusing himself to keep an eye out for anyone who might be catching on.

That night went just as they hoped. Everyone they invited enjoyed more than two bowls of hash. They had everyone on the third floor and half the second floor eliminated from their list before they had to call it a night. They were getting too stoned themselves to keep it going.

The next morning they went to breakfast. While they were relaxing over some coffee, they watched to see who came in to decide whom to invite next. Some of the black soldiers would never associate with them. They were from big cities where prejudice was prevalent. They were just as prejudiced as some of the whites. It wasn't going to be easy to pull them in. Mark knew it was going to be up to him to find a way to cross that barrier.

"I noticed those guys will talk to me when they think no one else is watching. I don't know why," Mark said. "Maybe they think I'm more innocent. I don't know. Maybe it makes it more difficult for them to hang onto their prejudice. I don't think they want to hate me. I think they feel like they have to because I'm so white. If they think no one else will know, then maybe they will agree to some free hash," Mark said, trying to convince himself.

"Okay," Jason replied. Better Mark than him, he thought. "You will be in the room by yourself, though."

"Why? I'll just tell them Jeremy's going to be my new roommate and that he won't be a problem if they aren't. I don't think they'll have a problem with me wanting to have my back covered," Mark said.

Mark went to the black soldiers and did all the talking. He knocked on Jared's door first. Mark figured Jared was more of a leader of that group than anyone else.

"Hey," Mark said as Jared opened the door. "How would you like to have some free hash?"

This caught Jared off guard. "Sure. What you have in mind?"

"Jeremy is moving into my room in a few days. In the meantime we're using his room for a type of hash party. I'm 'expanding' my 'dealings' a bit. I was hoping you might be interested in having a convenient source for yourself. If you are, I'll be in Jeremy's room with a bowl to share with you. I just want to be sure everyone I sell to can be trusted. I trust you, or else I wouldn't be here talking right now. I don't know about all your friends. I'd feel better seeing them participate. You know what I mean?" Mark was hoping for Jared's buy in.

"Yeah, I know what you mean," Jared said. "How do I know I can trust you?"

"Well," Mark said, "you can always beat me like you own me if things go bad."

"And you know I will," Jared quickly replied.

"Yeah," Mark said quietly, "I know you will. Jeremy will be there too. If he's gonna be my roommate, then he should get to experience all the trouble I get to have."

"Yeah." Jared hesitated. "Yeah, I guess that'll be okay. Just don't double-cross us."

"Don't worry. I won't. I've got a lot more at stake here," Mark reminded him.

This made it easy for everyone to participate. The impression was given that every party was a complete secret. For all practical purposes, they were all secret.

Everyone they invited got stoned, and Mark, Jason, and Jeremy all began to feel better about the idea of getting caught dealing. They now knew no one in the barracks could be a narc. A narc was not allowed to do drugs.

However, it still left the other possibility. An informant could do as much as he wanted to. An informant would almost have to get stoned to put off any possible thought that they were keeping tabs for CID.

However, the party idea helped with this dilemma as well. After all, what were the odds that an informant would risk all of his friends finding out that he was the one who turned someone in? This was another good reason to be smoking in groups, and it also made it easier to ask one of the guys about others. The plan gave them what they were looking for: confidence.

By the end of the weekend Mark was convinced the whole barracks was trustworthy. However, that still left those who lived off base. On the other hand, it wasn't very often any of them were looking for drugs. Most of the ones who lived off base were married and had no interest in drugs. Neither did most of them have any interest in disrupting anything that went on in the barracks. Their only interests were taking care of their family and staying out of trouble and away from danger. That being the case, all seemed well to Mark.

Jimmy knew there was a plan to root out any possible narcs in the barracks. He somehow had to know what was going on without putting himself at risk. This made it difficult to keep tabs on them. He wanted to keep track of the party sessions, but if he was in the hallway or anywhere near where they would see him, well, then he would be at risk.

Jimmy understood that if they were going to do business, then they would do it where it would be hard to catch Mark and his sources. The trick was to find out what was going on in the room. Once Jimmy knew what Mark had going, he could find a way to bust everything wide open.

He thought about it for a while and wondered what was going on with Jason. Jimmy decided to wait until Monday. When Monday morning came, Jimmy took the chance and went to Jason's room. Jimmy stood by the window at the end of the hallway and waited for Jason to come out. He knew if Jason had any visitors it would be difficult to do his job and not give anything away.

It seemed like forever, but Jason finally emerged from his room and headed for breakfast. Jimmy made his move. "Hey, Jason!" Jimmy shouted just loud enough for Jason to hear. Walking to him, Jimmy continued, "Would you be interested in going to breakfast with me someplace like the PX? I don't feel like eating alone today."

Caught off guard but not thinking anything about it, Jason replied, "Yeah, sure. You buying?"

"I guess I can," Jimmy answered, not really prepared for that.

Jason smirked. "Just joking. Yeah, I'll go. I could use the change."

They went to the PX, where it was easy for Jimmy to talk while eating and drinking coffee. He hoped there would be fewer ears about.

With that part of the plan out of the way, Jimmy had to think of a way to start talking about their possible drug activity. He wasn't so much interested in what they were using or how often as he was in how they were getting it. That would be the real trick—finding a way to steer the conversation to that end.

Once they had their food and were seated, Jimmy posed the anticipated question. "So you guys seem to always have a hash party going on. I miss having a good toke every morning."

"You used to smoke?" Jason replied with surprise.

"Oh, yeah, when I was in the barracks. I don't get around like I used to now that I'm hooked up with my fiancée. I wasn't the biggest user around, but I enjoyed it from time to time," Jimmy responded, feeling good about the approach.

"Yeah, we do too. I never used to smoke like I do here, but I do like it," Jason said. "So why did you move out of the barracks?"

"I like the lifestyle of living in a home and going to work every day. I've got a woman and family now. It's not like it used to be. A lot of things have changed. It used to be you could just go to the room next door and know you would have something to smoke. Everyone had everyone covered. I don't think it's like that anymore. How do you get your supply so easily nowadays?" Jimmy flinched inside himself when the question fell out of his mouth so bluntly. He was afraid it would give the whole thing away.

"That I can't tell you," Jason wisely answered. He was becoming suspicious of this whole setup now. Everything was beginning to feel out of place with that question.

"Yeah, I understand. I don't know why I even asked. I know better. I guess I miss being part of it all," Jimmy said, hoping this comeback would be enough.

"I know what you mean," Jason replied. "I like being a part of things too. It makes life here feel more like home."

"Yeah. Sometimes I miss that. Then I think about what I do have and realize I have more than most people here do," Jimmy followed up. He was hoping this was not a setback. He kept kicking himself in his mind, making it more difficult to keep his plan moving.

"Hey, man, I gotta go. I have people waiting for me," Jason said, hoping not to tip Jimmy that he was on to his game.

"Okay. I'll see ya around. Thanks for joining me. I hate eating alone all the time," Jimmy said.

With that, Jason went on his way. He headed back to the barracks to wait for the best opportunity to check in with Mark and Jeremy. He was confident he might be on to something and was nervous about it all.

Jimmy went on his way as well. He was feeling like he may have just lost the whole case. He just didn't know how to read Jason, and now he was sure he had mishandled everything he had been so confident he could do an hour earlier.

Mark and Jeremy ate their breakfast quietly, too stoned from the days before to be sure of what was real and what was still part of the hallucinations. Taking their time, they ate, drank coffee, and smoked cigarettes as they waited for their minds to finally get a grip on reality.

It finally occurred to them that Jason hadn't joined them. "Do you think we should have woke him up?" asked Mark.

"I don't know. I wasn't thinking much until now," Jeremy answered. "Maybe."

They finally got up and found their way back to the barracks. Mark unlocked their door, and Jeremy was about to make his way down to Jason's room. It was then that Jason came out of his room and walked determinedly to them. He all but pushed his way into their room.

"Hey, what are you doing?" Jeremy asked, almost being knocked backward.

"Sorry, man. Just let me in," Jason whispered.

Mark noticed everything that was happening and blurted out in a forced whisper, "What's going on?"

"I'll tell you what's going on. I think I found a narc!" Jason quickly replied.

"What?" Jeremy couldn't contain himself. "Who?"

"I think Jimmy might be a narc," Jason quickly replied. "He just bought me breakfast and started asking some strange questions about our use and how we get it."

"Are you sure he wasn't just interested in getting some?" Mark said, hoping for the best. "Maybe he was just looking for some hash?"

"Maybe, but what if he wasn't?" Jason countered. "What if he's the guy we gotta be looking out for?" Jason, like the rest of them, was filling up with paranoia.

"There's only one way to find out that I can think of," Mark answered as he thought it all through. "Maybe I can have my supplier check him out. I'm thinking they should know each other for as long as they've both been here." It was then that Mark realized he may have given too much away.

The other two pretended not to notice. "Do that," Jeremy said. "See what you can find out. I don't like any of this. The timing, the questions, who it is … I don't like it."

They all sat down and smoked a bowl to calm their nerves. After some thought they decided Jason should keep his distance for a day or two just to see how things began to shape up. Jeremy was already moved into Mark's room, so they shared all the same risks. It wouldn't be long, Mark figured, before Jeremy would know whom he got his dope from.

A famous quote kept running through Mark's head: "Three can keep a secret if two of them are dead." It was a quote from Benjamin Franklin, but somehow Mark figured it might mean something different for them if all of this came apart. He smoked another bowl to calm him down more.

It was another couple of days before Chris showed up. Jeremy and Mark were getting ready for the warehouse when Chris walked in the door.

He seemed a little surprised to see Mark with a roommate. Mark realized right away what the situation was and asked Chris to walk with him. He was headed for the latrine to finish getting ready for breakfast. While they walked down the hallway, Mark spoke up. "I know what you're thinking, but it was the only way I could ensure I got a new roommate I could trust. I didn't want to have to go through what Kurt went through when I first moved in."

"That was good thinking, but don't you think you should have given me a heads-up?" Chris inquired.

"Sure, if I knew how to get hold of you when I needed to," Mark answered. "Something needed to be done to make sure I could do what I have to. I had to think fast and act. There's more, but not here," Mark replied quietly but with a sense of urgency.

Chris could feel Mark was about to unload a serious problem, so they agreed to meet at the warehouse. From there, Mark went back to his room, and Chris went down the back stairwell.

"So what did Chris have to say?" Jeremy asked, anxious to know what was going down.

"He was a little taken aback, but agreed I did the right thing," Mark replied as he finished getting ready to go.

"What does that mean?" continued Jeremy.

"It means he's okay with you being here." Mark smiled.

"Well, that's all fine and dandy, but what about what Jason told us?" Jeremy insisted. "Did you tell him about that?"

"Oh, that—no, not yet. I told him we needed to talk, but not here. We're gonna meet at the warehouse and go from there. No doubt he needs to know," Mark responded with concern.

They went to breakfast, leaving without Jason as planned. After formation they made their way to the warehouse, acting like nothing was amiss. Jimmy had made his usual appearance, but none of them gave away that anyone knew what was going on. Mark was hoping Jimmy would never be the wiser until they had it all sorted out. Jimmy had the same hope about Mark. The whole thing was one act with each trying to convince the other.

Around ten o'clock, Chris showed up at Mark's desk. He looked like he had just come through a rainstorm. "Is it wet out?" Mark asked.

"Yeah, better wear rain gear," answered Chris.

"What do you mean? We're going out?" Mark questioned with more concern than curiosity now.

"Yeah. We can't talk here. The walls have ears," Chris pointed out.

Mark grabbed what he had. When they first arrived at the warehouse, the weather had seemed fine, but now it had all changed. Once outside they began talking as they walked toward the PX for cigarettes. "So what's going on?" Chris asked.

"Well, as you know, I have two other guys helping me move the goods," Mark started. "One of them was approached by Jimmy a couple of days ago. Jimmy took him to breakfast at the PX and started asking questions about the hash we use and where we get it. It wasn't so much the actual questions as it was how he asked them and how he acted. Jason was spooked. He doesn't get spooked like that very often. It made Jeremy worry as well. To tell you the truth, I really don't know anything about Jimmy, so I wanted to ask you. I figured for as long as both of you have been here, surely you would know something."

"I see," Chris answered quietly. "This does pose an interesting problem. I haven't seen Jimmy around in ages. I was told he was playing house with some German woman. He has kids and everything. I don't know. It seems odd he would stay away for so long and then all of a sudden show up and ask questions like that."

After a few moments of silence, Chris started back up again. "Okay, don't worry about it. I'll have him tailed and see if there's anything going on. You did right to tell me. What are you doing about Jason?" Mark was apprehensive that he had told Chris who it was, but he decided not to say anything, as the real problem was still at hand.

"We all agreed to keep our distance until I talk to you. Don't worry. They don't know who you are yet. I'm sure Jeremy will figure it out before lunch, but he's really cool.

I still don't know about Jason. I'm kind of stuck with him until this all gets figured out," Mark replied.

"Well, how do you know Jason isn't the problem?" Chris asked. "I mean, did anyone see him having breakfast with Jimmy?"

Shaking his head as if to lose a headache, Mark replied, "No, not that I know of. I didn't think of that. Why would Jason do that and make us ask questions? Wouldn't he want us to be relaxed? That would be a big risk to take just to make us worry."

"You can never tell with these guys," Chris answered. "They just don't always do things that would make sense. I suspect they sometimes do things to keep us off balance.

"Okay. Like I said, keep your plan, and I will get back with you as soon as I can," Chris directed as he began to walk away. Then he was gone in the rain. Mark finally made it to the PX and got a pack of cigarettes. He bought some coffee too, but the rain made it impossible to drink as he made his way back to the warehouse.

Jeremy was waiting at Mark's desk when he got back. "So what now?"

"We wait," Mark whispered.

Jason walked over with some vehicle parts that needed to be stocked. The whole idea was to act like he needed help. "So?" he asked quietly.

Again, Mark answered, "We wait. I'll know something shortly. That's all I know." Mark took the parts and looked at them then handed them back to Jason. After that they all split up and went back to their usual routine of warehouse business.

The day went on as normal, with one exception: they didn't meet for their usual lunchtime and break time toke. When suppertime arrived, Mark changed his clothes and decided to go to his hideaway for supper. Jeremy went with him, and they relaxed over some beer and cigarettes after they had eaten their meal.

"So how long do you think we'll have to wait?" Jeremy asked.

"I don't know. It's not like I've ever been in this situation before. I don't think Chris has either," Mark answered. "I don't know." Jeremy nodded for both understanding Mark's point and having full acknowledgement that Chris was the supplier. They finished their beer and started to head back. They were walking along the outside fence to the barracks when all of a sudden Chris was behind them. "Hey, hold up. I talked to the suppliers, and they said to plan on a dry spell until they know more about Jimmy. I think they suspect he's working with CID or some local law enforcement. That's all I can tell you for now. If you want anything, you'll have to look elsewhere." Looking directly into Jeremy's eyes, Chris continued, "Jeremy, you seem to have a good head on your shoulders. Remember ... keep all this quiet."

Mark was taken aback a little by Chris talking to Jeremy like that. However, he kept to the discussion. "Well, won't that put a damper on my ability to move goods once things go back to normal?" Mark asked.

"Yeah, but it's better than taking an unnecessary risk. Look, that's how it is, so just act like there's nothing going on and stay out of sight or trouble," Chris responded. With that, he turned around and walked away into the dusk.

Jeremy, Jason, and Mark began to hang out again. They would go to the NCO club and drink rather than go to their rooms and smoke. It was a change of pace, but it gave Mark a chance to free his mind from the overuse of hash. Out of the blue the questions began to come back like an old pain. Mark had forgotten that part of himself. It was like his old world and new world had just collided.

That Saturday, Mark got up early and went for a walk on an old two-lane road that was never used. Mark had never walked very far down this road, as there was an old Do Not Enter sign on it. He knew it was only meant for cars, but he still didn't want to push his luck.

This day was different. He kept on walking for what seemed to be forever. His mind wondered to the old days back in the States. He thought about how things were when he first arrived in Germany. He was so deep in thought he almost walked right off the road into the river. The bridge was gone. Mark studied the area where the bridge should've been for a few minutes, and finally, it dawned on him: the bridge had never been replaced after it was blown out during World War II. Looking to his right, Mark saw the new bridge for the expressway that now crossed the Rhine.

Mark was amazed at how history was juxtaposed with the modern era. It was fascinating that life in this new world had been made after so much devastation from all-out war.

Reflecting on all of this gave Mark hope. After all, if so much could be recovered after such a brutal war here, then surely he could find a way to live a new life once he left this place when his time in the army was done. The only thing he had to do was live—survive all the possible things that could go wrong.

He was getting tired—not so much physically tired from the walk, but tired from all the mental and emotional drama he was living with. What originally gave him relaxation and a sense of purpose now wore him out. It was all falling apart. This was not the kind of adventure he wanted. These were the kinds of adventures no one ever came back from. It was a very dark, dismal feeling Mark had now.

He walked back to his room to find Jeremy worried about where he was. "Where've you been?" Jeremy blurted out angrily. "You've been gone for quite a while!"

Mark was taken aback by the verbal assault. He wasn't expecting anything like that from Jeremy. "I went for a walk. I had to think about everything that's been happening," he replied defensively.

"Yeah? So where'd you go?" Jeremy continued, his anger still visible.

"I walked to the Rhine. In fact, I almost walked right into it. I didn't realize the bridge was still out from the war!" Marked exclaimed. It was then that Mark noticed Jeremy's usual smile was missing.

Finally, it occurred to Mark that Jeremy's point of view was right. "Hey, look, I'm sorry. I really do appreciate the fact that you care. Thanks," Mark replied, more calmly than before.

"No problem. Just don't do it again. Let me know when you're going somewhere so I can do what I can to help," Jeremy answered, but his anger was still evident.

CHAPTER NINE

That night they went to the Non Commissioned Officers club again. It was just down the street from the barracks. In fact, they had to pass it every day on their way to the warehouse. This made it very convenient. This particular night was more difficult than most for Mark. He couldn't figure out why, but he just couldn't stay at the bar.

He took his leave from the rest of the guys and made his way back to his room. He was almost to the barracks when he ran into one of the guys who worked on the warehouse computers. Struggling to remember his name, Mark was finally able to get it out. "So, um, Daniel, what are you up to this late in the evening?"

"Oh, just went to get something to drink, and then it's off to bed," he replied.

"You got something to drink?" Mark was surprised. "What did you get?"

"Some vodka." Daniel smiled.

"No way!" Mark was even more surprised. "I didn't know you drank alcohol."

"Have to." He smiled again. "How else could I survive being here? You know I'm not much of a drug user."

"So what else do you do for fun?" Mark inquired.

"Well, I like to play chess," Daniel said.

"No kidding. I used to play all the time when I was a kid. Want to play a few games?" Mark asked, hoping he would say yes.

"Sure. Just let me go to my room and put some things away," Daniel replied with a grin. "I'll be back with the game."

With that, they agreed to meet in Mark's room. Daniel grabbed some orange juice from his room and they drank screwdrivers while they played. Daniel could have beaten Mark in his sleep. It was unclear if that was how good Daniel was or if Mark really was that bad.

By the fourth game Mark was toasted from the vodka. He could barely make it to the latrine to relieve himself. After the fourth checkmate, Daniel decided to call it a night and took his game back to his room.

Mark could barely remember going to bed. It took no time at all for Mark to fall asleep. He had the most vivid dream he could remember in years. He dreamt he was leaning out the window and almost fell the three floors to the concrete below.

When morning came, Mark got out of bed and went to the window, remembering his dream. He noticed a lot of vomit was dried on the windowsill and on the wall outside. A little perturbed by the whole thing, he looked at Jeremy and asked, "Who did this?"

Jeremy just stared at him.

"I'm serious!" Mark exclaimed. "I want to know who did that! It's not right to make that kind of mess and just leave it."

Jeremy still just stared at Mark with no words to speak. That's when it slowly dawned on Mark. "You know, I had a dream last night that I almost fell out of this window. What happened?"

Jeremy finally found his voice. "You just got up out of bed, walked to the window, opened it, and vomited. The more you vomited, the more you leaned out the window. I had to grab you before you completely fell. It was close. I was kind of scared."

"Wow, it was all like a dream last night. I think I had one screwdriver too many," Mark said as his mind went back to the dream. "Well, I guess I have a mess to clean up. Know what, though? I'm not touching the puke down there on the steps below. I think I'll leave that for the birds. They have to eat too, right?" Mark joked.

Mark may have been joking, but as he collected the cleaning supplies, he couldn't help thinking just how close he had come to being dead. How was it that Jeremy woke up out of a deep sleep and was able to rescue him from himself?

Mark began to remember an event from a long time ago, when he was very young. While he was cleaning, his mind went back to his childhood. He would go to church with his aunt and learn about God and Jesus. Until now it was all a very distant image in his mind. Now all of a sudden it was becoming real. It also made him very afraid deep inside. He didn't want anyone else to know, but this kind of experience made his think about his death. Mark thought it was true. Near-death experiences did make you think about God and eternity.

He spent the rest of the morning trying to clean off the outside wall without doing a repeat performance of close-call falls. He finally had it done when Jason came to visit. "Hey, guys, I know we agreed not to do any drugs. I was thinking that was because we didn't have any to use. I just found out there's going to be an acid party this afternoon. I was thinking about joining them. What do you think?"

Jeremy smiled and looked at Mark with anticipation. "Cool. I'm in," he said.

"Well, I can't be the only one sitting here straight. Where we meeting?" Mark asked. Deep inside, Mark was hoping this would help him forget his recent adventure and fears.

"Just down the hall. I think it's going to be gray microdot," Jason said.

"Gray? What's the difference between that and what we had last time?" Mark asked.

Jeremy began to educate Mark on the finer points of commercial acid. "Well, purple microdot is strychnine cut with speed, whereas gray microdot is mescaline cut with speed. Mescaline will make you laugh for hours. It's a hallucinogen all by itself."

Mark was curious about what exactly all this was doing to his brain. He wasn't too worried, however, as he didn't really think he was using that much of his brain anyway. He met the rest of them down the hall. He was looking forward to having some fun and taking his mind off all the stress the three of them had been dealing with.

Mark met the rest of them down in Rick's room. Rick was just another guy in the maintenance department. Like the rest of them, he enjoyed a good high and had passed the hash-smoking test they did weeks earlier.

"So who has the acid?" Mark asked, ready to pay his bill.

One of the guys took his money, and moments later he got his tiny little dot of gray. Mark placed the hit under his tongue just like before. It took about a half hour before it began to take effect. It was obvious when it did.

One by one, each of them began to laugh over the silliest things. The way things were placed on an end table or how somebody looked while they were laughing. All that was necessary was to look at something, and it was instantaneously funny. It was like humor was magic.

The group went from the room to the open bay up on the top floor. They moved like they were part of a herd. Mark noticed Jacob was playing pool with a nylon stocking on his head. This was a common practice with the black guys due to the kind of hair they had. Mark had never asked about it, but figured it was one way they kept their hair tamed. Normally the sight was so common he would have thought nothing of it, but this time Jacob looked so funny, Mark laughed uncontrollably.

Jacob was not a user, but he was also not ignorant to what was going on. Having a unique sense of humor of his own, Jacob played it up to make Mark laugh even harder. "What's so funny? "

"I don't know," Mark answered, not wanting to tell Jacob the truth.

"You like the way I play pool or something?" Jacob asked. He took his pool stick and placed it over his shoulders, doing a completely impossible shot.

"Yeah." Mark laughed. "I've never seen pool played like that before. "

Jacob made shapes out of his nylon cap, knowing Mark would think it was the acid. "So what's wrong with the way I play?" Jacob continued to goad Mark. This time he went around the table on all fours. Mark could hardly breathe he was laughing so hard.

The truth was Jacob missed Mark. They never saw each other, and Jacob spent a lot of time praying for Mark and the chance to talk to him without appearing to interfere with his life. Little did he know Mark would have accepted the talk very well. Mark was looking for some sound insight. However, today was not the day for it.

The group was probably in the bay area for over an hour, but it seemed like just a few minutes to Mark. From there they decided to move on.

"Hey, Mark!" One of them shouted. "If you're done playing with Jacob there, we're all going to the theater." There were two blockbuster movies playing there, *Jaws* and *The Green Berets*.

"Hey, I'll catch ya later, Jacob," Mark told him as he went his way with the group. When they got to the theater, it was already dark outside. It seemed to take forever to walk the short distance to their seats as the previews began to wind down. The first movie, *Jaws*, was larger than life. The color scheme was full of primary colors and pastels. Mark watched in awe, totally unaware that he kept blacking out for most of the movie. He could only remember bits and pieces, and then it was over. There was a long intermission before the next movie, *The Green Berets*, would begin.

Mark had to use the latrine, so he got out of his seat. Without thinking about where he was sitting, he made his way to the back of the auditorium. He searched for the doors to the bathrooms.

Once in the bathroom he went about his business. The colors continued to stand out, and each sound and object had its own life about it. What usually took only a minute or two seemed to be a whole lifetime as Mark flushed the urinal and washed his hands.

After his hands were dry, Mark turned and opened the door to leave the bathroom. He walked a very long way before he realized … he was not where he thought he would be. What should have been the exit from the bathroom to the theater was in fact a very long hallway lined with bare incandescent lights about every twenty feet. On the opposite wall were hung mops and brooms.

Mark was extremely confused. Where was he? He had never been in this place before. He spun around so many times trying to figure things out that he had no idea which direction he had come from. He stopped and thought about it for a little while, and it occurred to him that he had a fifty-fifty chance of getting it right by just choosing a direction to go back. He thought he remembered the lights being on his right as he walked in. Using that memory he kept them on his left to find the door he had used to get there.

He guessed right and found a door at the one end of the long hallway. Mark opened the door and found himself back in the bathroom. That's when he realized he had simply opened the wrong door to exit. This time he opened the other door, but looked out for a minute to make sure it was where he wanted to go.

He was not sure how long he had been off on his unexpected adventure, but he was once again in the lobby where the snacks were sold. There he saw one of his platoon sergeants dressed in a tuxedo. Mark was convinced it was the acid that made it look like that. He could not help laughing at his own imagination of seeing his sergeant like that. Sergeant Olsen saw Mark laughing and asked him, "Hey, soldier, what's so funny?"

"I'm sorry, serge, but you look like you are dressed for a wedding or something," Mark replied. At the same time he was suddenly in a panic as he realized what he had just said.

"Well, that's because I am," Sergeant Olsen answered. "Is there anything wrong with that?"

Suddenly feeling more sober, Mark answered, "No, serge, I was just joking." Mark walked as fast as he could into the theater to retake his seat, feeling almost as lost as he had been in the closet in the bathroom. It seemed like forever before he finally found his companions and sat down.

Mark was unsure how much of the movie he had

missed, but it didn't seem important, as he really wasn't following any of it anyway. He kept finding himself lost in the huge screen full of color and jungle. For the rest of the film, Mark thought he was in the jungle—with the exception of the rare moments when he looked at his seat and the others and realized he was in an auditorium. It was confusing yet wonderful to be in two different worlds at the same time.

After the movie all the guys went to the lobby and made plans to go to the bar from there. Mark didn't think he could handle many more of his strange adventures. He was happy to discover a couple of the other guys were going back to the barracks. He didn't want to walk alone. He wasn't sure if he would end up where he wanted to go. This way he would have a guide.

Mark thought it was going to be morning by the time they arrived at the barracks, but it was only eleven o'clock. He found his way back to his room and decided to get ready for bed. The day had been much more than he thought it would be.

Mark was almost ready when he had a sudden sensation. This larger-than-life feeling made him extremely afraid. It was like a dark shadow was hovering over him. He couldn't see or hear it, but he was completely sure there was something or someone else in the room with him.

Immediately Mark turned on the lights to see who was there, but there was nothing to be seen. He was not able to explain it, but he was sure there was something there. He even knew exactly where this thing was. That was even more frightening. Mark knew beyond doubt this presence was hovering above him in one corner of the room. It was dark in nature and was trying to talk to Mark.

Completely filled with terror, Mark tore open his door and ran down to the latrine. He didn't know what that would do for him. He just knew that, whatever that thing was, it was completely capable of following him down the hallway.

Mark stood in the far corner of the latrine staring at the doorway, waiting to see if it came in. He didn't see anything, but all of a sudden it became clear that this presence was hovering above him in the latrine. Whatever it was, it wanted him. It wanted his soul.

With a start, Mark ran, again, down the hallway. This time he went into one of another guy's room. Donnie was sitting on his bunk listening to some music as he smoked a bowl. "Hey! What's up, man?" he asked, surprised to have a visitor, especially since he'd thought his door was locked.

"Oh, nothing. I just got bored being alone in my room," Mark lied. He sat down in a chair across from Donnie and kept looking at the door to see if the presence would find its way in. Donnie noticed Mark was agitated and completely out of breath.

"Would you like some to calm you down?" Donnie asked, trying not to be nosy.

"Yeah, thanks, man." Mark took the bowl and pulled in a deep lungful, hoping for some immediate relief.

An hour went by as Mark helped Donnie finish up

a bowl. It was then that Mark was finally convinced it would be all right to go back to his room.

"Hey, man, thanks for the help," Mark said.

"No problem. Whatever's going on, good luck," Donnie said.

"Good night, Donnie," Mark replied before walking slowly back to his room. He was greatly relieved to find Jeremy in the room when he opened the door.

Mark sat down and started to blurt out the whole story. "You won't believe what just happened to me."

"You're right," Jeremy replied, realizing how agitated Mark was.

"I think I just had a demon try to talk to me," Mark said. "It was like this dark shadow was hovering over me and trying to talk to me. It sobered me right up quick. At first I thought it might be the acid. I don't think so now. It followed me down to the latrine. I know it was real, man. I know it! Do you think it was the acid?"

"I don't know, to be honest," Jeremy said with some of his own fear. "I've heard of this kind of thing before. I don't normally talk about it, but I have to tell you, I do believe in Satan. I mean, I don't worship him or anything, but I know he is real."

"I wish you hadn't said that." Mark winced. "I mean, I know he's real too. I know God is real. What I don't want to know is that Satan was my visitor. Why would he be here?"

"I was told once that drugs can open the door to let the Devil into your life," Jeremy replied. "I don't know if it's true, but what if it is?"

"You are not helping me right now. You need to know that." Mark was beginning to really freak out.

"Sorry. I'm sure I'm wrong. It's gotta be the acid," Jeremy said, trying to convince them both. "I mean, really? The Devil wants to be here, in an army barracks? I don't think so. I'm sure he has better things to do than go around torturing people who are already being tortured. I mean, what would be the point of redoing something already being done?"

They both finished getting ready for bed. After the light was turned out, Mark began to remember what he had been thinking about that morning when he was cleaning up his vomit.

First he was having memories of God when he was a young boy. Now he was having near-satanic experiences. He couldn't help but wonder what was going on. What if he was losing his mind? What if the drugs were destroying his ability to separate fantasy from reality? He lay awake most of the night contemplating how his life was going. That was the furthest Mark had ever felt from being who he wanted to be. It was a very lonely and empty feeling.

CHAPTER TEN

Sunday night was more of the usual for Jimmy. He was out for a walk in the neighborhood, trying to think what his next move would be. Jimmy had wanted to meet with CID to talk about what he thought he knew. The problem was exactly that—what he *thought* he knew. Jimmy had to have more concrete proof, at least something that gave strong suspicion that Mark was a dealer. Jimmy couldn't go on his own gut feeling. If I had only been more patient with Jason, he thought.

Maybe all was not lost yet. It wasn't like Jason had alienated him. Perhaps he could find another chance to talk with him and get Jason to loosen up more. How could he earn Jason's trust? That was key.

Jimmy was so deep in thought he didn't notice the car pull up behind him—a dark gray sedan with three men inside. It pulled up quietly so as to take Jimmy by surprise. Two of the men were out and had Jimmy before he knew what was happening. He didn't even have enough time to yell for help or fight. In one deft move Jimmy was in the car, and off they drove into the darkness.

The sun began to rise bright in the east as men began to wander down to the latrine. Mark woke up just like the rest of the men. It was the beginning of a week after a hard weekend of the usual drinking and drugs. For Mark, however, it had been even more so. The memory of dark forces now haunted him. He wanted to just lay there and dream it all away, but Jeremy moving around reminded him that life was going to go on and he had to be part of it.

Getting out of bed, Mark walked to the window overlooking the front steps of the barracks. He looked at the sky to see what kind of day it was going to be. Taking a stretch, he yawned and then looked below to see what activity was about. That's when he saw it. Mark had to look several times after blinking his eyes in case he wasn't seeing right. Still unsure of what he was looking at, Mark called for Jeremy to come look.

"What is that?" Mark asked in horror, knowing the answer before he asked the question.

Jeremy made his way to the window and looked down. "It's a body," he whispered, still unsure what he was looking at as well.

"Who is it? Do you recognize him?" Mark asked, still shocked and horrified. "What do you think happened? Suicide? What is going on?"

Mark knew Jeremy had no more idea than he did, but with the lack of anyone else to ask, he spoke out of shock.

"I'm gonna go down and see what happened. You stay here and get ready for the day. Don't keep looking out. It could make it look like you did something. Just get ready and wait for me to find out what I can." Jeremy sputtered out the words as he quickly got himself dressed and shot out the door.

When Jeremy was able to get to the open barrack doors, there were several people there he did not recognize. The military police were arriving and began to make a type of barricade to keep people away.

Jeremy was finally able to get a look at who was laying in a heap of hopelessness at the base of the steps to the barracks. It was Jimmy. He lay on his belly, but his face was looking at the building. Jimmy's head looked like it had fallen from a high point, and his body was broken and still. It was difficult to tell through his clothes, but Jeremy was sure Jimmy's spirit was no longer with them. There was no doubt. Jimmy was dead. Jeremy felt his stomach start to churn, and he knew he was getting sick.

Containing his physical discomfort, Jeremy asked the people who were standing there what had happened.

"No, but I'd say he took a nosedive out of the top-floor window," said one of the sergeants who had been on duty for the night. "I didn't hear anything. You'd think I would have at least heard a thump, but I didn't."

Jeremy thought about it and asked himself why. What would be going on in anyone's life to want to take a flight through the top window?

Jeremy had another notion about what had happened, but he didn't know it for a fact. He didn't want Mark to be thinking about it either. Jeremy returned to their room, thinking about what to tell Mark. It wasn't like they had been friends, but it meant something for Jimmy to be laying out there like that.

Mark was pacing the floor, anxious about what was going on below. He knew the military police were there now, and everyone in the hallway had a theory. Jeremy made his way back to the room. "It's Jimmy. It looks like he jumped out of the window upstairs. He's all broken up. He's dead. I've never seen anything like it."

"I've heard stories," Mark sat down and muttered. "Remember when I told you about the first time I did hash? Kurt told me he had thrown someone out the window. He let me think they lived. I don't think he jumped on his own. Does Jason know?"

"I'm sure he knows there's a dead body. I haven't talked to him yet. I'm gonna go get him now. We need to talk," Jeremy stated like he was in charge.

From there, Jeremy went to get Jason. A few minutes later the three of them were sitting in Mark's room. This time there was no bowl. There was way too much going on to take the chance.

Jeremy started the conversation. "It was Jimmy, just like I said earlier. Everyone is saying he jumped out of the window above us. I don't think he jumped. Thinking about all that's happened, how people were contacted—I think he had help."

"So you think I'm responsible for this?" Mark asked in a panic.

"No, but I think the people you work with did it. I think he is lying here as a warning. I don't know who the warning is for. It could be for us, or it could be for whoever was talking to Jimmy. Maybe both," Jeremy continued.

"Oh, great!" Jason exclaimed. "Now they think I'm in with Jimmy?"

"I don't know!" Jeremy exclaimed in his own frustration. "All I know for sure is Jimmy is dead and it's no coincidence that he is lying out there, right in front of us. These people mean business, and now we're in it deep. I can't prove it, but that's what I believe."

They sat and let it all sink in. After what seemed like hours, Mark spoke up out of a spontaneous urge. "I need to talk to Chris." The words were out before Mark had a chance to use caution. Jason looked at him with a small look of consolation. He had suspected Chris was the source but never really wanted to know. Now it was all out of the bag.

"So what are you gonna ask him?" Jason quivered.

"I don't know. I guess just tell him what we saw and see what he says," Mark considered. "I'm sure he already knows if what Jeremy says is true. He'll have to say something. If all of this was meant to be a message, there's no sense not making sure we understand what we are looking at. He will have to know something, and he will want to make sure we know."

They all agreed this made sense. The only problem was Mark still didn't know where Chris was or how to contact him. They would just have to wait for Chris to show up. They were confident that Chris would want to talk as soon as it was convenient. Until then all they could do was watch out the window as the mess was cleaned up and wait for formation to begin.

It was ten o'clock when formation was finally called. They went through the usual routine—with one exception. The captain made an announcement about Jimmy's death. There may be some people asking questions, he said, so the men needed to make sure they cooperated with the law. That wasn't exactly what the plan was for the three, but they gave every appearance that they would behave just like everyone else.

Lunch had ended before Chris finally appeared. Mark was sitting at his desk, pretending to work while trying to understand everything that was happening. Hearing a noise, he looked up. "Hey, there you are," he said, relieved at seeing Chris.

"Yeah, I was waiting for things to calm down a little," Chris answered in a quiet voice. "I heard there was some activity going on at the barracks this morning. What have you been up to, Mark?"

"Me? Oh, no, man. It wasn't me. I woke up to all this. You know what's going on, and I would appreciate it if you told me what happened," Mark blurted out with tension in his voice.

"Okay, sure." Chris smiled. "Let's go for a walk." Once they were a short distance from the warehouse, Chris continued, "You remember how I told you I would talk to the source? Well, we talked, and they said they would check things out. They decided it was necessary to make a statement that no one would misunderstand. They want whoever is—was—working with Jimmy to know they are being watched. How did Jason react to it?"

"He acted just like I did. He doesn't seem to be worried about getting the same thing so much as upset that it happened," Mark answered. "I don't think he was working with Jimmy. I think if he had been he would have kept his mouth shut."

"Well, maybe," Chris quietly said to himself. "Still, I think he needs to be taken more seriously. I think until we know for sure where he stands, you need to be extra careful. It's not easy to do what they did and not get caught. However, if they do you, the last thing you're going to be worried about is if they get away with it. You'll be dead. So don't fool with this. Be careful."

Mark nodded. Watching Chris walk away he thought about Jason and wondered how he was supposed to do everything Chris said. The only thing he could think of was to talk to Jason and do what Jason had advised before: keep his friends close and his enemies closer. It was time to keep Jason close.

Sergeant First Class Billy Olsen was busy overseeing the warehouse operations with Lieutenant Danson. The phone rang. "Sergeant Olsen here," he answered.

"Sergeant, this is the first sergeant. You need to report to the captain as soon as possible. He has some things to discuss with you."

"I'll be there promptly," Sergeant Olsen answered before he hung up the phone.

Once in the captain's office, Olsen sat down,

wondering what this was all about. Looking at the desk for clues, Olsen began with "So, what have I been called here for, sir?"

"Oh, I was looking for some help," the captain muttered as he flipped papers on his desk in search of a document. "What do you know about Private Welch?"

"Not a whole lot. I read his file, but there isn't anything that tells much about him. He enlisted on his own. Has no record, with the exception of being emancipated when he was sixteen. No real family to speak of, and he barely graduated from high school. I think he has potential in the army from what I've seen in his performance," Olsen replied.

"Well, I agree. That's what makes this whole mess so disconcerting. It seems the police think Sergeant Jones was murdered. They can't find any evidence that says he voluntarily jumped, but there's all sorts of evidence of a struggle. How does a man struggle to commit suicide?" the captain said. "There has to be more to this than we can see right now."

"So what are you saying?" Olsen asked with interest. "What does Welch have to do with any of it?"

"I'm saying it's time we did some of our own investigating. We need to pay more attention to what's going on with our own boys. What they talk about. What they do. I don't like this kind of thing going on anywhere, and now it's in my own home. Drugs are one thing, and I don't like that it's running rampant here. Now we have murder. Murder! How could I possibly be happy about this?" The captain's voice illustrated his anger.

"I still don't see what Welch has to do with any of it," Olsen persisted.

"Somehow there seems to be a connection between him, Chris Shultz, Kurt Talagan, and the German drug gang in this area. That's all I know," the captain stated, still frustrated.

"Well, what did you have in mind?" Olsen inquired. "What do you want us to execute, and how? It's not like we do this kind of thing every day."

"How should I know?" the captain muttered. "All I know is it's time to get organized and start fighting back on the drugs and the violence. It was the drugs that led to this. I'm not interested in finding a fall guy. I want to restore morale, a sense of safety, and better mental health for the whole company. The drugs and violence have to go. Get with the others and come up with a plan. I will try to do the same. I need help, and I think you want to be part of the solution. Am I wrong?" He looked sharply in Olsen's eyes.

"No, sir, you are not wrong," Olsen answered. "But why me? Why didn't you call Danson down here? He's the guy in charge, isn't he?" Olsen asked, still lost on what his role was supposed to be.

"Danson doesn't know how to tie his own shoes," the captain said, shaking his head at the idea.

"I will get it started. I just hope we know what we're doing. It could get a lot worse. I would hate for anyone else to end up like Jones did."

With that, he left the office and went for his own walk around the post. Sergeant Olsen was convinced things were going to get a lot worse before they started to get better. He continued his walk, forgetting all about his daily assignments. This was much more important. He was now on a mission to save his charges. He knew it was going to get messy.

Jason worked alone at the warehouse and thought about his part in all of this. He couldn't help thinking that if he had kept his mouth shut Jimmy would still be alive. He knew he hadn't actually pushed Jimmy out the window, but it was still somehow his fault Jimmy was dead. It was a cold, dark, sickening feeling to know his actions had initiated a string of events that led to Jimmy's death. He knew it wasn't over. Jason looked for a corner in the aisles of the warehouse to sit and hide in—a dark, lonely corner that would shield him from the rest of the world. Jason sat, frustrated, knowing no such corner existed. He cried out of his feelings of helpless condemnation, for he felt Jimmy's blood was on his hands.

Chris knocked on the door of the apartment and waited for the door to open. A tall, dark-haired young man let him in and asked him if he wanted a drink. Quickly Chris answered, "Oh yeah. Make it a strong one."

"So did you talk to your boy Mark?" the other man asked, sitting in a shadow in the corner of the room.

"Yeah, and how do you know his name?" Chris answered.

"You do know we have a lot of help in our line of work, right?" he answered. "You didn't tell me everything."

"He's scared you might do the same thing to him. I don't blame him," Chris continued. "He's still convinced Jimmy was working alone. What did you find out?"

"We didn't find anything that told us any different yet either. It is, however, easy to overlook things. I like the message, but I don't like having to do it. Don't overdo the pressure, but make sure the message isn't forgotten," the man said intently. "I don't want to have to do this again. Not with anyone. It's too ugly."

With the day at its end, Mark met Jeremy in their room. They were quiet for a while before Mark finally broke the silence. "I don't know how much more of this I can take. This was not my plan for my life. How do I get out?"

"You wait. Right now everyone else is just like you. Their nerves are raw, and their sense of self-preservation is sharp. Wait. Just wait," Jeremy advised.

"What do we do about Jason?" Mark was still anxious. "I don't think he's guilty of anything except being with us. I know he didn't work with Jimmy. It just doesn't make any sense for him to do that."

"Did you hear me?" Jeremy said. "I said wait. Keep Jason with us and wait. If he's innocent, it'll continue to show. If he is guilty, he'll give it away. Just wait."

"How do you know so much about this stuff?" Mark asked, distracted by Jeremy's apparent expertise.

"I've been there before. It's one of my reasons for being here. It wouldn't surprise me to discover that they're following me. Investigate me. If I were you, I would be more concerned about me than Jason. I am," Jeremy said as he sat in thought. "I think I need to lay low. Maybe I should find another room."

"No, don't do that," Mark said. "It'll only give them more reason to suspect we have something to hide. Do like you said. Follow your own advice and just wait."

They both got themselves ready for supper and went to the mess hall without speaking. The rest of the evening passed quietly. Jason came down, and they visited together, drinking some whiskey and Coke while listening to music.

"So what's the plan?" Jason asked.

"Jeremy thinks we need to just wait it out," Mark answered.

"Sometimes things get better just from time," Jeremy added. "If we're all doing what we say we are, then we have nothing to worry about." With that, they drank one drink after another in no particular hurry.

It was around eleven thirty when Mark woke up. Still feeling intoxication he looked around the room. He woke up Jason up, who was passed out in a chair. Mark was amazed he hadn't fallen off. Jason got up and lay down on Jeremy's bed. Jeremy was passed out on a rug on the floor with his usual smile.

That was enough for Mark. He took off his clothes and went to sleep in his own bed, leaving the stereo on. Morning would bring a whole new light to everything—and, hopefully, the answers they all wanted.

CHAPTER ELEVEN

The three of them woke up the next morning, a little confused about where they were and why they were sleeping like that. Jeremy got himself up off the floor and looked at Jason lying in his bed. He had a perplexed look on his face. Jeremy began to shake Jason. "Hey, man. Get out of my bed. What are you doing, anyway?"

Jason looked up with his own confused face. "I have no idea. Where am I, anyway?"

"You're in my bed. Do you mind?" Jeremy looked at him, irritated.

"Oh, sorry, man. How'd I end up here?" Jason asked.

"That was kind of me," Mark looked at them in his own daze. "I woke you up because you were passed out on the chair. I thought you were going to your own room. Instead you just stood up and went over there and lay down. I was in my own drunken stupor, so I just let it go."

Jeremy was finally able to relax the anger that had been mounting. He started remembering how the night had ended. He had been tired from all that had happened that day and from the alcohol. The rug had looked like a comfortable place to just rest for a while. He hadn't realized it would be for the rest of the night. It wouldn't be right to blame Jason for the same bad decision.

They let it go and got ready for the day with their headaches and upset stomachs. The day went on normally, as did the rest of the week. It seemed to them that no news was good news. Each day took them that much further from the murder. On the one hand, the police hadn't discovered anything, but on the other hand, nothing was happening to them either.

That included no new flow of hash or speed to be sold. That left only one thing to do. They went to the PX and bought some more whiskey and Coke. On their way back to the barracks they ran into Donnie. Donnie was always a quiet follower. He was polite and caring and always gave the impression that he was a stand-up kind of guy.

"Hey, you guys interested in some mad dogs?" he asked with gleam in his eyes.

"Where'd you get those?" Jason asked.

"Some guy I know in the engineering unit." Donnie smiled. "I've got about ten racks if you want some."

This sounded inviting to all of them. "Mad dogs" was the nickname for Mandrix, a prescription sleeping pill sold in any German drug store. Sometimes there were people who had a way to liberate some illegally. This was one of those times.

They each took two racks. It was very dangerous to use these with alcohol, and they all knew it. A person had to be very careful not to use more than one or two at a time, especially if he had been drinking a lot.

They each took two and started drinking their whiskey. In time Jeremy and Jason disappeared. Mark was too wasted to understand what they had said or where they were going. Since he was on his own, he decided to wander down to Donnie's room.

Donnie was getting ready to go somewhere. It was unclear to Mark where it was, but Mark invited himself to go with Donnie. He didn't seem to mind, so off they went. First they went to the NCO club and had some drinks. Mark had some difficulty walking, but he made his way to keep Donnie company.

After drinking there, they walked around the post. It was getting late, and they were both getting hungry. In the state of mind Mark was in, he decided they needed to go where he thought there would be food. "Hey, Donnie, let's go to the mess hall and see if we can get in. There has to be food there."

"Yeah, okay," Donnie agreed in his own drunkenness.

Once at the mess hall they looked at the doors and the windows. Mark had some experience at breaking and entering, but all of this escaped him. The only thing he could think of was his hunger.

They sat down on the steps of the building, trying to decide what they were going to do. Mark suddenly had an idea. There was an old mess hall just outside their barracks that was being used as type of church. However, Mark was convinced it would still have food inside. "Let's go to the Bible study place by our barracks. I bet they have food."

"Maybe. Or maybe we should just go to bed," Donnie answered.

"Come on, man. I'm hungry."

They made their way back toward their barracks and went straight to the building. Feeling more adventurous, Mark decided to check out the roof to see if there was a way in through the ceiling.

He climbed a ladder on the side of the building until he was at the top. He looked around but found no way to enter. The chimney was extremely wide, and Mark saw another ladder going down the middle of it. Mark reached for it from the edge of the chimney. He hung on to the corner of the chimney, trying to reach the ladder. He realized he would have to let go of the chimney and jump to grab the ladder.

Mark would never have had the courage to do such a stunt sober, but he wasn't sober. Letting go of the chimney, he was able to reach the ladder and climb down. Donnie was watching this, completely terrified Mark would fall. The last thing he wanted to see another dead body lying on the concrete. Once Mark was down, Donnie told him, "Are you nuts? You need to just relax! Sit here, and I will check out the door around the corner."

"Okay, but don't take too long," Mark answered. "I am really hungry."

"You just sit here and wait. Don't do anything until I get back," Donnie said, full of fear and stress.

Once Donnie was out of sight Mark began to notice a window well with the window open. Thinking this was just a small hole dug out around the window, he couldn't resist. Standing on shaky legs, Mark walked to the window well and stepped inside it.

There was no bottom. Mark fell for what seemed like forever. He looked up as he was going down, and it felt like the whole earth was swallowing him up. He became horrified that the earth had opened up a gateway to hell for him. Suddenly, he landed with a violent jerk. A loud noise that sounded like empty tin cans being thrown all over the place caught his attention. Mark fell back onto a concrete wall but didn't fall. A light shot through the darkness and blinded Mark's eyes.

Mark blinked a couple of times and could finally see Donnie with a very alarmed look on his face. The light was coming from a doorway in the hole Mark had jumped into. There were pop and beer cans all over the floor of the room.

Donnie ran over to him. "Just how stupid are you, man?" he yelled out of anger and fear.

"I don't know. Why?" asked Mark, sobering very quickly from the fall. "What did I do?"

"You idiot! You jumped into a door well!" Donnie exclaimed. "How have you lived as long as you have?"

"I don't know," Mark answered with his own amazement. "I really don't know. Can you help me get out of here?"

Mark was getting more and more sober as Donnie helped him walk. He looked up at the top of the hole, wondering how he survived the fall. Donnie helped him up the steps he had found when he left Mark sitting.

They went straight to their rooms. Mark got himself

ready for bed. He turned out the light using the switch by the door. He walked across the floor to his bed. He was trying to fall asleep when he began to feel a sharp pain in his ankles.

Mark got up and stumbled back to the light switch. Once the light was on he sat down on his bed and looked at his ankles. Immediately he fell back on his bed. His ankles were all black and blue and swollen to the size of the fat end of a softball. Now the pain was increasing beyond what he could bear.

The only thing Mark could think of was to go down to the Commanders of the Quarter and ask for medical help. He got himself dressed again and stumbled to the door and then to the stairs. He couldn't walk anymore, so he sat down and slid himself down the three flights of steps to the first floor. "Hey, can you guys help me?" Mark shouted out to the two sergeants watching the front door.

They immediately got up and ran to help him. "What happened?" one of them asked.

"I fell into a hole, but I thought I would be all right," Mark answered. "I was wrong."

They called the medical center, and one of them walked Mark across the parking lot to them. Mark was left there alone with the medics and waited for help in a lot of pain. Finally, one of the medics came to him. "So what happened?" he asked as he lifted one of Mark's legs.

"I was high on Mandrix and had been drinking—" Mark started, but was abruptly interrupted.

"*No!* No, you weren't," the medic answered. "You were walking along in the dark. Then what happened?"

Mark looked at them with surprise but continued, "I was hungry, and I saw what looked like a window well, but it was a door well. I jumped in and landed on a lot of cans. Now it hurts like I broke them both."

"Well, let's look at them and see what we have," the medic responded calmly before examining his ankles. "No, they're not broken, but they are very badly sprained. You will have to stay off them for a while."

"How am I going to do that? Don't I have to walk to get to places like the mess hall and work?" Mark asked, confused.

"We have crutches, but don't use them unless you have to," the medic said. "Do you have a ride back to your barracks?"

"I'm right across the parking lot from here," Mark answered.

"Well, we can help you get back, but you will have to miss work for a while," the medic told him. "Here is your medical excuse. Remember, there were no drugs involved. Do you understand?" he asked Mark as he wrote out the excuse for him to keep.

"Yeah, I understand," Mark answered.

The staff helped Mark back to his room. Jeremy and Jason were there, trying to see what was going on. "What happened to you?" they asked together.

"I jumped into that door well you see right outside that window," Mark answered, pointing to the window by Jeremy's bed.

"What for?" Jeremy asked, half laughing and half in shock.

"Because I'm stupid," Mark replied, trying to lie down and take off his pants.

"Wow. Don't you know when enough excitement for one year is enough?" Jeremy asked him with a serious look of dumbfoundedness.

"You are way out of control, buddy. Way out there," Jason uttered in disbelief. "You do live a blessed life, though."

"Oh yeah? Well, I don't feel blessed," Mark said in pain.

Jason laughed. "Well, that's the whole point. You jumped into a ten-foot hole and only have two sprained ankles. Man, you should be dead. Don't you get it? Dead. Wow."

"You may have a point," Mark said as he thought about it. "Still, I'd rather be blessed in a more traditional way. You know … with no pain."

Jason went back to his room, and the other two finished getting ready for bed. Mark lay in the darkness thinking about everything that had happened to him from the time he arrived in Frankfurt until now. Everything kept mounting to a greater and greater extreme. Jason was right. He was out of control. Things were going to have to change now—and change fast. If they didn't, he wasn't going to live to tell about them.

The next morning Jason came in to see if Jeremy needed any help getting Mark ready for breakfast. "This is way too funny, buddy," Jason said, trying to help Mark stand up.

"Yeah, I'm laughing so hard I hurt," Mark replied sarcastically.

They laughed as they continued to help Mark, still in disbelief. Mark slowly put on his pants and reached for his crutches. He sat for a few minutes, trying to decide how he would use them. Both ankles felt the same amount of pain. How was he going to do this?

After thinking about it, Mark stood on the crutches with both feet on the floor. Once up he turned sideways to the bed. Mark was thinking he could use the crutches to lift both feet at the same time. He was wrong again. Once he was off his feet he fell flat on his back on the floor. On the way down he felt something brush his right ear.

Mark lay on the floor, feeling his ear to see if he'd hurt it. It was then he noticed the bunk post. His ear had just brushed it. Mark thought about it and figured that if he had been a few inches closer to the bed on his way down, the post would have struck him at the base of his skull where it met his neck. It would have killed him. Shivers ran down his spine as he stared at the bunk post.

"What's wrong?" Jeremy asked. Mark's face was even paler than normal.

"Do you realize what just happened?" Mark whispered. "I should be dead yet a second time. My head just missed that bunk post when I fell. I felt it brush my ear. You're right, Jason. I am living a blessed life. I should have died last night and again now. Why am I still alive?"

Wanting Mark to relax, they brushed it off like he was just being dramatic. With one at each shoulder, they helped Mark make his way to the mess hall. They sat him down and got his meal and drinks.

Mark was very appreciative, and they enjoyed the meal, feeling like they have just defied death. Mark finished his meal and sat back quietly drinking coffee and smoking a cigarette. Unsure how the next week would work out, he took the pills the medics had given him and waited patiently for the other two to do what they had to before they made their way back to the barracks.

The rest of the day Mark spent sitting in his room, listening to music, and drinking whiskey. Drinking to help ease the pain, he started remembering back to when he was a child.

He could remember going to church with his younger brother when they lived with their aunt. Mark remembered memorizing Scriptures for prizes. He was amazed how long ago that time seemed, but in reality it really wasn't that many years ago. Mark thought to himself that perhaps it wasn't the number of years that made it such a distant memory, but the number of events. Mark's life had been anything but mundane. Every year of his life saw dramatic changes that were just too hard for his mind to keep up with.

Now, however, Mark had nothing else to do but remember. He couldn't perform his duties at the warehouse. He wasn't even able to stand in formation. It was all he could do to make it down to the showers. Mark had decided he would shower once every one else was at work so he could take his time. He had to move way too slow to keep up with the activity of the normal workday.

It was the middle of the week when Mark was approached by the first sergeant for a drug test. An orderly came to his room. "Mark, the first sergeant is directing me to inform you to take a drug test."

"I see. Do you know why?" Mark asked, feeling like he was being picked out.

"No, I think it's just your turn. I'll be back with the bottle," the orderly said as he left Mark's room.

The orderly came back to his room and helped Mark to the latrine to do the urine test. Mark felt like he had this all under control. After all, it had been a long time since he had had anything to smoke or snort. With confidence, Mark filled the bottle and handed it to the orderly from the urinal. Once the paperwork had been completed, the orderly helped Mark back to his room.

Mark sat alone listening to music as he pondered why it was now he had to take the test. The only thing he could think of was what he had told the medics when he jumped into the hole. Then another thought came to mind. Maybe it was the fact that Mark did jump into the hole. It was, after all, a very stupid idea. In the end it really didn't matter why he had to take the test. What mattered was that he was still alive and had all the time in the world to think.

His mind, again, began to drift back to the days of Scripture memorization. Mark slowly began to remember one verse and then another. At first, they had no real meaning, but as time went on, they slowly began to make connections with one another. Mark could remember something about the Roman road to salvation. He kept thinking the same words over and over. The Roman road. What was it? He had never been out of Michigan until arriving here, so it couldn't be Rome. What did it mean? Now Mark wished he had paid more attention to the actual lessons and less to whatever seemed more important at the time.

Mark now wondered what had been more important back then. He lay down on his bunk, trying to remember his childhood. At first all he could remember was the violence. His dad and his older brother had been very violent. Their only answer to every problem was to hurt someone. Over the years it had gotten very old.

The only break in it was the one year he and his younger brother had been sent to live with their aunt. That one year was the only memory Mark had of reading the Bible or ever hearing anyone talk about God instead of using God's name for cursing.

Mark laughed to himself as he remembered the first time he had sworn. They had all been called to the dinner table. Mark had just seated himself when his mother asked if he had washed his hands. He had not, so he had to go the bathroom to wash them. It was frustrating to him as a small boy that he muttered under his breath.

The whole dining room became quiet. The silence was deafening to Mark, so he turned around to see what was going on. They were all staring at him as he stood in the bathroom doorway. After a long silence, his mother told him she never wanted to hear those words come out of his mouth again.

Mark had thought about it and could only think she must have meant the z word, Jesus. (Mark was too young to know how to spell at the time—all he knew was that the middle sound was a z.) Mom must mean the z word. It was a word his dad used all the time. However, Mom definitely made him feel like that was a word not to be spoken, at least not like that. At his current age, Mark understood it better. To that day he could not force himself to use that word. It was one of the few things his mom had been able to imprint in his brain before she died.

Mark began to wonder what his younger brother was doing. Mark got up from his bunk and made his way to the one desk they had in the room. He sat down and began to write a letter. It felt strange to be writing anything, let alone a letter. It took a long time, but time was the one thing Mark had now.

It was suppertime before he finally had the letter done. Mark was amazed they had envelopes. He put the letter in an envelope and wrote his aunt's address on the front. That was the last place he knew of his brother living at. He hoped his brother was still there, but if not, he knew his aunt would get him the letter.

Mark had written how he missed his bother and hoped he was doing better than Mark was. Maybe his brother still remembered the ways their aunt wanted them to learn and actually know how to pray. Mark began to realize the only way he was ever going to make it out of this nightmare was if God helped him. He decided he needed someone who would pray for him.

The next morning, having kept the letter a secret from his friends, Mark made his way to the front desk, where he found an orderly. Mark handed over the letter and asked if they could mail it. Mark paid the postage so they could get it properly stamped. He saw them lay the letter in the outgoing mailbox and turned to make his way back to his room.

Now that the letter was out of the way, Mark's mind kept thinking about Jimmy, the demon, and the fall. He didn't know how, but somehow they were connected. He considered something he had heard of that year with his aunt. Was spiritual warfare this real? It had always sounded like something imaginative that only happened inside someone who had simple life struggles. Did this warfare get violent like this? Was it really a life-and-death struggle? Mark started drinking even more. He used pain for the excuse, but really it was fear. He couldn't prove it, but he knew there was something larger at work.

The rest of the week Mark spent hanging around in his room drinking whiskey and listening to music. He spent a lot of time getting drunk, continuing to tell himself it was to help stave off the pain. The pills were good, but the pain was almost unbearable at first. However, as time went on, it did get better, and by the end of the week, Mark found he was able to go down the hallway and back on his own with little trouble. He noticed one ankle was healing faster than the other. This helped a lot as Mark began to regain his mobility. He was down to one crutch by that Monday.

Mark missed being able to do things for himself and couldn't wait until he was able to work again—work, the one thing Mark didn't think he would miss. He missed work, because without it, he had no real activity going on in his life. The only visitors he had were Jeremy and Jason. Jeremy had to visit him. They were roommates. Jason didn't have to, but he did.

Mark and Jason seemed to now have a stronger bond than they did before. They were both directly connected to Jimmy's tragic death. That was something that was still not going away, but it was getting easier to sleep at night. The drinking made it a lot easier. The trick was to not drink so much that it made him vomit. That was how Mark survived the week after he once again cheated death and fate.

To some it seemed he was a kind of hero. Mark didn't see it that way. The way he saw it, he was some kind of lucky idiot. He had no business living life this carelessly. It had to stop. That was the trick. How could he make it stop?

The following Monday Mark was called into the captain's office. He had to make sure he was properly dressed. This was a serious request. Mark was sure they had somehow discovered evidence that connected him to Jimmy's death. He ran it over and over in his mind. Every time it made no sense. How could they make a connection to something he hadn't done?

Mark waited in a chair outside the office feeling like he was on pin and needles. Finally, he was ushered in by the first sergeant. Mark stood at attention in front of the captain's desk.

"Soldier, do you know why you are here?" the captain asked.

"No, sir. I was not told," Mark answered with a crack in his voice.

"Your drug and alcohol test came back positive," the captain responded. "Can you explain that?"

"No, sir," Mark was surprised. He felt there was no way it could have been positive. Mark did not realize the Mandrix he had taken were one of the things that would be discovered.

"Well, we have to do something about this. We cannot have any of our men using drugs," the captain said. "I am referring you to the CEDAC program. You are to report this morning to be set up with a counselor and get started on a program. Any questions?"

"No, sir," Mark barked out as trained.

"That is all," the captain said as he busied himself with the paperwork on his desk.

Mark turned and left the office, angry that his test was positive. There was no doubt to Mark the whole thing had been a setup. He would have thought differently had he realized it really was his own fault. It would be years before Mark was finally able to see this.

Doing as he was told, Mark made his way to the CEDAC building. Everyone knew where this building was. Mark had been told it was only a matter of time before everyone was a member of this elite group. He had never believed he would be there.

Once again, Mark found himself wrong. It seemed to Mark that he was spending a lot of time being wrong. It was time he started doing something right. Maybe this would be a new beginning. Maybe this was the answer to the prayer Mark had barely had the courage to pray. He didn't dare utter the words even close to audibly. Mark was afraid the dark force he had encountered a few months earlier would hear him ask for help. He didn't know if he could survive that kind of attention. The one thing Mark wanted to do more than anything else was survive his own stupidity and make it back home.

Mark entered the lobby of the center and looked around for direction. There was a sliding window on one wall with a room behind it. On a hunch, Mark went to the window. "Excuse me, I was told to come here for a counseling program."

The lady behind the window answered, "Okay, have a seat and someone will be out shortly to talk to you."

Mark had been waiting for a short time when a man came out. It seemed odd, as he was not wearing olive green, the color of their fatigues. "Sir, if you will follow me, we will ask you some questions and get you started."

Mark followed him down a short hallway to a room with a desk and some chairs. "Okay," the man continued. "Here is a short questionnaire for you to fill out. After you are done, open this door, and someone will come and walk you through what to do from there. Any questions?"

"No, I don't think so," Mark lied. He had dozens of questions but wasn't sure any of them should be asked.

He filled out the form and opened the door to see what was next.

Before long, a woman came in to talk to him. First she took the time to read the form he had filled out. There were a lot of questions about his health history, drug use, and mental state. Mark studied her while she was reading to study him. He noticed that, unlike the first person he talked to, she was wearing fatigues. She was a specialist fourth class and carried herself as if she was somewhat intelligent. This made Mark wonder why she was there.

Finally, she finished reading and introduced herself. "I am Marylyn Myers. I have been assigned to your case. Our main objective will be to do whatever we need to do to restore you to the place you need to be as a soldier and a person. What kind of questions do you have for me? It's okay. You can ask anything you want. Nothing here will be reported to your superiors. Everything that is said and done here is completely confidential."

Mark had a lot of doubts about that. The one thing he had learned about the army was that nothing about a soldier's life was confidential. "Really? How can that be? I mean, how will they know I was successful? Won't you have to write some kind of report to prove I did all I was supposed to do?"

"Well, first of all, that was quite a few questions just now." She smiled. "I think that I will treat them all as one. I think what you really want to know is that everything really is confidential. We are licensed counselors. By law everything has to be kept private unless you request otherwise. Even then it is sometimes impossible for us to share anything that is said or done here, especially if it involves other clients. Does that help?"

"I guess we will find out," Mark replied, still a nonbeliever. "So what do we do first?"

"First we get acquainted. I learn a little about you, and you learn a little about me," Marylyn answered. "What do you want to know about me?"

"Okay." Mark thought a minute. He wanted to ask personal questions to prove she was not as honest as she wanted him to believe. "How old are you? Are you married?"

She let a small giggle out and smiled. "No, I am not married, and I am twenty-six. You probably didn't think a woman would let her age be known, did you?"

Mark was honest. "No, I didn't. I also didn't think you would share anything about your personal life. I figured that would be a hindrance to what we have to do here."

"Well, you're wrong," she answered politely "If you don't see me as a real person, someone who has some life experiences, then you won't believe in anything we are trying to do here. Ask some more," she said, tempting Mark.

"Okay, why are you here? Why do you want to help a bunch of guys that most think are losers?" Mark asked more honestly.

"First of all, none of you are losers," Marylyn responded with conviction. "People get lost in life. Sometimes it's just a matter of making a wrong turn. Sometimes it's from trauma in childhood or just one major event. There are all sorts of reasons people get lost. Guess what? You're just a man who got lost and really just wants to find your way back to where you think you belong."

Mark sat for a little while, thinking about what she had said. He was also surprised that she was giving him the time to think. Finally he looked at Marylyn and asked, "So what? Is there some kind of a map? A compass?"

Again, Marylyn smiled. "You could say that. All we have to do is help you find it. You see," she continued, "it's inside you. You have both the map and the compass. My job is to help you find it. I don't have any of the answers. You have them all. This isn't a job or an assignment. It's an adventure to discover who Mark Welch really is and why he is hiding behind all of what we are looking at now."

The session went on like this for an hour. Once the session was over, Mark made an appointment with her for a few days later. Leaving the building, Mark wondered if this was going to be the one thing that would help him finally find all of his answers like she said. Wouldn't that be a miracle, he thought. He could find what he had been wanting for so many years. And all he had had to do was use an ungodly amount of drugs and almost kill himself and see other people killed to do it. It somehow didn't seem like it was worth the price.

CHAPTER TWELVE

It was a nice, sunny Saturday morning. Mark was finally able to walk without crutches, and he, Jeremy, and Jason were looking for some time away from it all. Once all three were together in Mark and Jeremy's room, they began discussing what to do for the day.

Jason spoke up first. "I was thinking we could do some shopping in a downtown market. There are all sorts of things to buy—novelties of everything imaginable."

Mark had no idea what that meant. "I like the idea of being out. Sounds good."

"I agree," Jeremy responded with a little perk in his voice.

They got ready to go to the market area. The walk was long but worth the effort. It wasn't long before they lost sight of each other. Each of them looked things over to find that one thing that would feel like the find of a lifetime.

None of them found anything that stood out. The only thing that made the trip worth it was getting out and walking in the sunlight with people who had nothing to do with the army or the drugs that had enveloped them for so long.

They met for a bite to eat as planned. "So where do you guys wanna go to now?" Jeremy asked, determined to keep going.

"I'd like to go to Heidelberg," Mark heard his voice say. It surprised him, because he wasn't sure what made him think of it.

"Yeah, that sounds good," Jason agreed.

"Okay then. After we eat, let's say we go?" Jeremy said.

Once they were done they went to the train station and found seats on an open car. There were no doors on this train and no glass in the windows. It was a train used by the everyday blue-collar workers to get to their jobs. The seats were arranged so that each pair of benches would face each other. That way people could talk as they traveled.

There were some short stops along the way where a canteen could be found for food and drink. The guys thought it would be cool to get off at one to eat get something to eat just so they could say they did it. The train waited for twenty minutes at each stop, just long enough for people to get a bratwurst and a beer and eat as they rode. Being free and out in the open made the food and the beer taste even better than they probably would have otherwise.

None of them were sure how long the trip lasted, but every minute was worth it. The guys were having the time of their lives.

"Have either of you ever been here before?" Mark asked in wonder.

"I haven't, but I've heard they do a simulated burning of the Heidelberg Castle. It was bombed during World War II," Jeremy answered.

"Wow that sounds cool. Can we see it?" Mark asked excitedly.

"I don't think so. I think they do it every Saturday night. So unless we stay that late we'll miss it," Jeremy answered.

Mark looked disappointed. Jason seemed to be a little disappointed himself. They started walking around until they found another marketplace and separated to find the treasure that was waiting for them.

Mark was off in his own little world as he looked at furniture and objects to see if anything would capture his imagination. Turning a corner in the market area, he saw it.

Mark had never even heard of tapestries before. Now he was looking at some of the coolest artwork he had ever seen on a large carpet. He wondered why anyone would put such good artwork on the floor to walk on.

"Wow, these are awesome," Mark heard himself say out loud.

"Thank you," came a voice. It was a woman who was sitting off to one side. Mark figured she was the saleslady.

"Why would someone want to walk on this kind of artwork?" Mark asked in wonder.

"Oh, it's not for the floor," she said. "You hang it on a wall. It's like a huge picture."

"Really?" Mark asked in disbelief. "You hang a carpet on the wall? I've never heard of that before."

"It's not a carpet. It's a tapestry, a work of art to be enjoyed at one's leisure," she informed Mark.

Mark looked through all the tapestries she had. One caught his eye like nothing he had ever imagined. It was a picture of Jesus Christ with His hands out as if He was asking a question. His heart was visible and ringed with barbed wire. A knife had been stuck through His heart, and blood was leaking down in large drops. There was a crown of thorns on His head. His eyes were focused on the viewer so that no one could escape His sight.

Looking at Jesus' hands, Mark noticed there were holes in them. These were from the nails that had kept Christ on the cross. Mark remembered how Christ was crucified—nailed to a cross with a crown of thorns on His head.

Mark couldn't take his eyes off the tapestry. Everything about it said it belonged to him. After looking at it for a very long time Mark decided this was the treasure he had been looking for. This was why he was there that day. He made the purchase and held it close as he looked for his friends, who were still shopping.

Jeremy and Jason had both also found some things that they wanted for their rooms. Jason had found a small table that was easy to put together. Jeremy had found a unique pipe he figured they could use for hash. It was a carving of a bearded man's head. They decided to have something more to eat and then head back to the barracks.

After they were back in their rooms, Mark looked for a place on the wall to hang his new treasure. He decided on the wall in the corner near the stereo. He went about hanging it when he realized he didn't have anything to use to actually put it on the wall. The saleslady had not mentioned it, and he had not thought of it. Mark decided to roll it up and place it under his bunk until he had the problem solved. That's where it stayed for the time being.

Chris had other connections for his drug dealings. The sources had stayed the same. They were still the Dragoons. However, he needed to have other avenues to move what he picked up. One of his "clients" was a young German man who lived in one of the apartments near him.

Claude was half-French and half-German and had lived in Karlsruhe for many years. He had learned to make his living off others by convincing them he was completely trustworthy. Then, when it was most convenient, he would take what he could and then move on. He was a conman. One of the best.

Claude found Chris to be a very challenging mark. He knew Chris had a lot of money on him from time to time to do business with the Dragoons and his other clients. The trick for Claude was to know the right time when Chris had a great deal on him and then find a way to take it without Chris knowing.

The problem was that Chris didn't trust anyone with

a cup of coffee, let alone any of his money. After months of working with Chris to earn his trust, it finally dawned on Claude that he would have to change his approach.

Claude was also a dealer. He would get his supplies from Chris just like all the other clients. Claude began to develop a new plan to get as large of a deal from Chris as he could, but on credit. He would have to get the drugs with a promise he would pay him once the goods were sold.

This seemed unlikely, knowing how little Chris trusted people, but that had a better chance of working than getting his hands on money. With that plan in the rough, Claude began to work his magic from years of practice. He understood this would take a long time, but the amount he was after was worth the wait.

Claude had to develop a client base of his own to be able to move the goods once he had them from Chris. Claude had considered simply defrauding his clients by taking their money and running. However, he figured it would be easier to hide from one man than it would be to hide from twenty or thirty. Claude didn't know if Europe was large enough to hide from that many people. It would have to be Chris to keep it simple and cleaner. Besides, the way Claude had it figured, he was smarter than Chris and thus had a better chance of getting away with it.

Mark kept his next appointment with his counselor, Marylyn. They talked about how he started using marijuana when he was in high school. Mark talked about using hash in the barracks, being careful not to mention names. Marylyn seemed very interested in Mark's stories, and she found him funny sometimes.

The more they met the more Mark began to see Marylyn as a woman rather than as his counselor. He thought about what would happen if he told her this. The way Mark had it figured was that if she knew, then they would have to give him a different counselor, and he would never see her again.

This posed three problems for Mark. First of all, he would hate to never see her again. He didn't know the advantage in that since he was starting to like her. Second, he would have to start all over in the counseling process. That would mean he would be tied up in the program much longer, and it could interfere with his finishing his tour in the army. Mark didn't want that at all. Third, Mark didn't know what kind of counselor he would get to replace Marylyn. The way Mark saw it, he was very lucky to get her. Mark was relaxed with her and she was easy to talk to. Mark liked that she was very easy on the eyes. All things considered, he decided to keep his thoughts about her to himself.

For one of the sessions Mark brought a camera to see if she would let him take a couple of pictures of her. When he came to her office, she was sitting at her desk getting ready for him. "So how are things going for you today?" Mark asked as he walked in.

"I'm doing very well, thank you." Marylyn smiled. "Go ahead and make yourself at home."

Mark sat down, stealing looks at her, trying to figure out how to ask about the camera. "So what are we going to talk about today?" he asked, still working things out in his mind.

"Well, where did we leave off the last time you were here?" Marylyn asked, using her training to keep the responsibility on Mark.

He smiled. "Honestly, I don't remember. Did you take any notes?"

"Well, let me see." She began looking around her desk to find the notes. After finding them, Marylyn began scanning to see what the last thing was they talked about.

Mark took out the camera and posed the question. "I was wondering if it would be okay if I took a picture or two of you?" He was beginning to feel embarrassed now that the question was out.

She seemed very pleased with the idea. "Yeah, okay." She smiled with hint of shyness. It began to be apparent to Mark that maybe she liked him a little too. She sat a simple pose in the corner of the room. Then she let him take another picture of her standing in the corner with her hands behind her back.

All of a sudden, Mark began to feel a little awkward. This was all unusual for him. He had never been close to a woman like this. He had no idea what to do next. Smiling, he put the camera away. "Thanks. I'm not sure what I'm going to do with these." Mark was attempting to hide his true intentions of having pictures to look at when they were apart.

"That's okay." Marylyn smiled shyly. "You only live once, right?" With that out of the way, Marylyn looked for a way to move on to something more comfortable. "I think I found what we talked about last time."

"Let me guess," Mark started. "We talked about me getting high." They both gave a short laugh. That was why he was there to begin with.

"So tell me more about what it is like to get high," Marylyn said to get things going.

"Wow, how can I explain this?" Mark began to think. "It's kind of like your mind is far away from what was real before. You feel like all the pain and worry are gone. All there is is what's around you—the walls, the air, the music if you're playing any. Music gives it all more meaning. It makes the experience richer, if you know what I mean."

Marylyn began to share. "You know, I have never used drugs myself, and I have often wondered what the attraction was to them."

Mark tried to describe more what a high was like. "Using hash is easy once you get past all the coughing and choking—kind of like when someone first starts to smoke. Still," Mark continued, "I don't feel like I'm doing the experience justice by simply using words. To really know, a person would have to actually smoke it. It is different for everyone. No two people have the exact same experience."

After many sessions, Mark felt like he had her trust. She certainly had his trust. In his heart, Mark felt like it was time to start convincing Marylyn to try using herself. It felt to Mark like their roles were beginning to change.

Marylyn began completing her notes on the session.

She smiled, thinking about the picture taking, and decided not to include any of that. Then she began to think as she sat at her desk. She wondered if there had been a shift in control in their sessions. In the beginning, this client, Mark, was exactly that—a client. Now she wasn't so sure. It was like things were changing. Marylyn was beginning to feel like she was losing her role as the guide. She was losing control of the process.

Mark, too, began to realize everything in therapy was changing. It wasn't something he had planned, but it did seem to have its advantages. What if his reputation changed? How would his drug buddies act? Would he be known as the guy that smoked hash with his counselor? He laughed at the idea in his head. Then he began to think that wasn't so funny. If he really cared for this woman, then he wouldn't do anything to ruin her reputation. This was becoming very serious.

It began to occur to Mark that she would lose her job and any respect she had earned from her friends and family. He decided if he did this he would have to keep it a secret for the rest of his life. Mark had learned to like and respect Marylyn. He wanted to be free of his current situation, but he also wanted to have friends apart from his world of drugs. His mind was definitely conflicted.

Mark realized his heart was also conflicted. He wanted to love her but knew it was impossible for it to work. He wanted to be rid of her but found it difficult to not think about her. He wanted to be rid of the drugs but loved using them. He wanted to go home with a plan.

That was the biggest problem of all. What home? He still had no home.

Mark always had been a man with no place to call his own. How wonderful it must be, he thought, to have grown up in one place with a family that loved you and to have had the same friends for the last twenty years and life-changing experiences with other people whom you still talked to and called friends.

There were many times Mark had heard people tell him how lucky he was to have the freedom he had. To Mark, however, it didn't feel so lucky. He felt lonely and empty inside. The counseling sessions had helped him realize this more than ever. The drugs helped him fill that emptiness with meaning. The only problem was that the meaning was false. The drugs were doing extensive damage to his body, and now he was becoming aware of this. In the end, Mark realized, Marylyn was helping him to see that he would be left even emptier than he was now. It was hard for him to imagine being even emptier. He had to do something and do it soon. Time was running out.

The next day's formation seemed like any other. At the end of the formation, mail call was done. Mark never stuck around for that. Who was he going to get a letter from? He certainly never wrote anyone. On this day, however, Mark had a strange desire to stick around and just listen to each name being called out. He wanted to watch the reactions of those who did get mail.

Finding a place on the steps to sit, Mark watched. The whole thing reminded him of a Christmas party. He wasn't sure why he thought of it like that. Still, watching each man wait with a small amount of anticipation, he thought he was right. It was like Christmas.

Mark sat there deep in his own thoughts when he thought he heard his own name. He laughed to himself at the idea. He needed to wake up out of his own daydream and pay more attention. He heard his name again. That can't be right, he thought, but he finally found his voice and answered, "Here!"

Mark walked to the mailman and reached out his hand. There it was: a letter addressed to him. Mark looked at the envelope and saw his brother's name on it. He had forgotten about writing him. Mark certainly never expected his brother to write back. It was only a dream. His reality wasn't supposed hold promise.

He held the letter in his hands as he walked to the warehouse. He didn't dare open it. He was afraid of what it might say. He was afraid of what it might not say. Mark was afraid of finding out his brother still cared about him, and yet he was afraid of finding out that he didn't. The anxiety was eating his stomach. All he could do was just stare at the envelope.

It was lunchtime, and he went with Jeremy to the mess hall. Walking in silence, thinking about the letter, Mark finally posed the question to Jeremy. "So do you think I should open this or just keep it as a souvenir?"

"What? Are you nuts? Open it! You have to know what he has to say," Jeremy advised. "What are you going to do with a souvenir letter? It's a letter from your brother."

The idea did seem silly once it was out in the open.

Things always seemed different once he heard the idea out loud. Sometimes Mark's mind had its own way of interpreting things. The rest of the world always put a different light on a subject once it was out in the open.

Mark ate lunch with the letter still in his pocket, unopened. After lunch Mark had to go to his session with Marylyn. He decided to hear what she had to say. It wasn't that he didn't trust Jeremy. Actually, Mark trusted Jeremy more than anyone. No, the reason was that it would add to the imaginary romance going on in his heart.

Mark knew it was imaginary, but it was the closest thing to a real relationship he had ever had. High school had not held experiences like that for Mark. He was too busy just trying to survive day to day in terms of staying clothed and fed. How was he ever going to be able to call a girl up or invite her over? Where would he call her from? Where would he invite her to? Mark had no home and therefore no phone. It could never happen.

"So what do you think, Marylyn? Open it or just let it go, knowing my brother actually wrote to me?" Mark posed the question as the session began.

"What would happen if you opened and read it?" she countered.

"I would find out what he really thought about me. I will know if he cares or if he doesn't care," Mark answered.

"Do you think knowing may give you some answers?" Marylyn probed.

"Yeah." Marked laughed quietly. "Do I really want to know the answers?"

"Do you? You are the only one that can decide that, Mark. This is one decision that is yours alone. While you make that decision, ask yourself this. If the roles were the other way around—your brother in your shoes and you in his—would you want him to read what you had to say?" Marylyn's voice sounded distant as she spoke.

Mark thought about what she said and tears began to run down his cheeks. The whole idea of someone who knew him caring about him was hard to hold on to. Mark didn't understand why. "Why is this so scary for me? I mean, it's only a letter."

Marylyn's answer stabbed the darkness, splitting a large hole for light to shine through. "Because it is sometimes hard to accept that we are capable of being loved. Sometimes we think we are so terrible and so low that we don't deserve love. The truth is that we do deserve to be loved. Maybe it's time to look the lie right in the eyes and prove it is a lie."

Mark could feel the hot tears on his cheeks. He was embarrassed of them, yet he could do nothing except hold the letter in his trembling hands and begin to open it. It took longer than it should have because of his shaking, but he finally got it opened. He tried to retain the envelope's condition so that he could place the letter back in it like a treasure if it said what he hoped it said.

Mark read the letter over and over to make sure he understood it correctly.

"So do you want to share what he wrote?" Marylyn asked, trying to get a feel for what Mark was going through.

"The letter isn't full of life-shattering news," Mark answered. Truth was, it didn't even speak to his heart like a wisdom-filled scripture. "It's what it doesn't say that means the most to me. Nowhere in the letter does it say to not write again. It's quite the opposite. Once all the home news was given about who was doing what, the letter says he is looking forward to hearing from me again. He was happy to hear I am doing okay."

Mark placed the letter back in the envelope and just sat in his chair staring at it. It was a few minutes before Mark realized it was getting wet spots from his tears dripping on it.

"Well, that's good, then," Marylyn said. "So what now?"

Mark excused himself. "I need to go for a walk."

The only thing that kept going through his mind was how none of this could be right. Why was he crying so much over a stupid letter? What kind of a man was he, anyway? Sitting in that room with Marylyn watching him cry over a stupid letter from his brother was embarrassing. The question kept coming back. Why was he crying over the letter? He remembered what Marylyn said, but could that really be true?

The evidence was staring Mark right in the face. What she said had pricked his heart as much as the letter did. Her words had to be true. Mark found a place to sit alone and just stare off into space thinking about it all. How was he loveable? What had he done to deserve anyone's love, let alone his brother's love? He cried. It felt good to let it out. His eyes were hot, but his heart felt a release he never knew was possible.

He had abandoned his brother to live his life alone. His brother was okay. He was living with their aunt. Still, Mark had left him without a word. One day he simply went to school and never went back home. That was four long years ago. His brother still cared.

Mark pulled the envelope out of his pocket and looked at it. He left the letter in the envelope. He just wanted to make sure it wasn't all a dream. Mark talked to himself to reassure himself the letter was real. The new warmth in his heart was real. Everything was going to start changing. Mark could sense this, but he didn't know how it would change. He didn't know what it all meant.

Back in Jeremy and Mark's room in the barracks, Jeremy and Jason were talking as they drank whiskey. They hadn't had an opportunity to smoke hash in what seemed like a long time. They continued to drink as they listened to music. Suddenly there was a knock on the door. Old habits die hard, so Jeremy and Jason looked around to see if there was anything to hide before they opened it. There was nothing, so Jeremy opened the door to find Donnie facing him with a smile.

"Can I come in?" Donnie asked as he looked to see who else was there.

"Sure." Jeremy stepped aside to let him in.

"How would you guys like to have some hash?" Donnie smiled even wider. While he asked, he reached into his pocket to retrieve a couple of blocks.

"Are you kidding?" Jeremy asked in disbelief.

"No, I'm serious," Donnie said as he handed the two blocks to Jeremy.

Jeremy opened his hand and stared at the hash with a blank look on his face. The moment must have been longer than Jeremy realized, as Donnie started to laugh at his reaction. "Yes, it's real." Donnie smiled.

"Wow, how much?" Jeremy asked, reaching for his wallet.

"For you guys? Since you took care of me when I was down, it's free this time. I owe you guys. I just wanted to say thanks. Thanks." He grinned and turned to leave. He didn't want them to have the chance to say no.

Mark entered the room as Donnie was about to leave. It was clear to Mark that something was going on, but he couldn't quite get a grip on it. "What are you guys up to? Or should I be asking?"

"You won't believe it," Jeremy answered. "We just got some free hash."

"No way." Mark smiled. "How?"

"Ask Donnie," Jason answered. "He's Santa Claus today."

"Oh yeah?" Mark smiled in disbelief. "And where did you get this? No, wait. I don't need to know. Thank you, Donnie."

With that Donnie left with a good feeling in his heart. The three also felt good about the first gift given to them in a long time. Mark locked the door, pulled out the dusty bowl, and loaded it up. The three began to smoke like the old days. They joked a little about it and then just sat quietly, enjoying a unique moment. It was then that Mark remembered his tapestry and asked if they knew anywhere to get hooks to hang it.

"Did you try the PX?" Jason quipped.

The answer was very obvious, so all Mark could do was smile and take another toke from the bowl. No, he had never thought about the PX. Sometimes he really did think he was stupid—in a good way, of course.

CHAPTER THIRTEEN

It was another Friday night, and Mark was in the mood for a veal dinner. He hadn't been to his favorite haunt in a while and decided to rectify that. This time he wanted to be alone. He was still doing a lot of thinking about his brother, his counseling, and the tapestry.

On his way to the restaurant, he was suddenly walking beside Chris. "Hey!" Mark said with a start.

"Hey yourself," Chris answered. "What have you been up to lately?"

"They tested me positive for drugs," Mark answered. "I'm getting counseling in CEDAC, and we haven't had any drugs in forever. How have you been?"

"I just got back from the States," Chris answered. "My apartment is just a couple of blocks over from the barracks." Chris handed Mark the address and left with "Come see me when you can. I've got something for ya."

Mark went inside to eat and then relaxed with a stein of beer to think over the last couple of weeks. He began to think about the crossroads he was at. He had to make a decision. He either had to keep doing and dealing drugs and run the risk of being arrested, or he had to leave it all behind. To do that, he would also have to leave all his friends behind. How was he going to do that? He sat back with a cigarette, contemplating it all in a daydream.

A week went by with Mark attending a couple of bland counseling sessions and smoking dope every day like he used to. Friday was finally there again, and Mark realized he hadn't seen Chris all week. He had said he was back from the States. Surely his leave was over, yet not once did Mark see him in formation or at the warehouse. Mark wondered what Chris was up to. He hoped he wasn't going AWOL. If Mark went to see him while he was AWOL, it could mean a lot of trouble for both of them.

After supper Mark decided to go see Chris in the dark to make it harder for anyone to follow him. Arriving at the apartment, Chris answered the door with no qualms or concerns. "So where have you been? I thought you would have been in formation and at work. Are you going AWOL?" Mark asked quickly.

Chris laughed. "You don't know, do you? I'm not in the army anymore. I was discharged two weeks ago. I moved back here because I have such a good thing going. So here I am." Chris smiled like he had just won the lottery.

"Wow," Mark thought out loud. "You're here as a civilian. Do you understand the risk you are taking? You're no longer going to be tried as a soldier if you get caught. They will try you regardless of who you are and put you away for life. Are you out of your mind?"

"I'm not going to get caught. I know what I'm doing." Chris sounded very sure of himself.

"How are you going to explain your income with no job? Self-employed? What's your business to show that?" Mark couldn't believe the words coming out of his mouth. He wondered where he had learned all that.

"I'm a businessman. I've got a line of goods I keep in boxes here to show if anyone comes looking around. I did my homework, don't worry," Chris answered with a smile. "Now let's get down to business. Like I said, I'm a businessman."

Chris pulled out some hash blocks and counted out ten of them. "Here, I want you to sell this. Do you think you can do it?"

"Yeah, sure. But I don't have the money right now," Mark confessed.

"Don't worry about it. Just makes sure I get the profit that's coming to me, just like you used to. Remember, this is a business. Right now I trust you," Chris said with a sharp stare in his eyes. This sounded strange to Mark, as Chris never trusted anyone. It felt good.

"Don't worry. I will," Mark answered, a shiver going down his back. With that, Mark took the hash and put it all in his jeans pocket. On the walk back to the barracks Mark got to thinking about it and decided he needed to walk more.

Things were beginning to make themselves clear to Mark. He was addicted—not just to the drugs, but also to the adventure, the edge of danger. All of this was a much larger problem than he had realized. This new revelation took time to settle down in Mark's mind as he walked the dark streets of Karlsruhe. It was late by the time he decided to go to his room.

Once in the room, Mark laid down on his bunk. He was too tired to get undressed and go to bed properly. He fell asleep, his thoughts becoming dreams. Mark dreamed he was selling hash to an undercover cop and was arrested. Then, all of a sudden, the dream took a turn, and he was back in his small-town "home" in Michigan, walking the streets at night like he used to. Memories began to flow through his mind as he slept.

All of a sudden there was a strange siren sound and a lot of yelling in the hallway. Mark could hear voices shouting out "Get up! This is a health and welfare inspection! Get up and open your doors and file down stairs and go outside and wait."

Mark began to panic. He suddenly remembered having ten blocks of hash in his pocket. Quickly he took them out and slid them under the dust cover on his pillow. From there Mark went down stairs as told and waited. It was a very lonely and fearful time of waiting. Mark's hands were sweating, and his heart was racing. He had no doubt they would find the stash. What was he going to do in prison? What was he going to tell Chris?

It seemed like hours, but before very long someone came out and asked, "Specialist Welch? Where is Specialist Welch?"

"Here," Mark felt his voice shout out.

"Come with me," the man said. Mark didn't notice what his rank was, but at the moment it didn't matter.

He followed the man up to his room. Inside, Mark saw his lieutenant and sergeant first class standing beside his bunk. Mark stood in the doorway, frozen as he took in the scene.

"Soldier, would you please come over here?" the lieutenant said.

Mark walked to his bunk to see what they were looking at. His bed looked just like it had when he'd left. There was nothing touched. Mark was confused why they sent for him.

It was then his Lieutenant reached under his dust cover and pulled out the hash blocks. He took one and unwrapped it. Looking at it as if he had never seen anything like it before, the lieutenant called for the sergeant to look at it.

"What do you think this is, sergeant?" the lieutenant asked.

"Sir, it looks like hash. It looks like dope," the sergeant replied in a calm but confident voice.

"Soldier, do you know how this got here?" the lieutenant asked.

"No, sir. I was out all night. I came back to my room this morning when the health and welfare inspection was called. You can see my bunk is still made. I haven't slept all night, sir." Mark was amazed at how quickly he'd come up with his lie.

"Well, since this is your bunk, you will have to take a ride with the military police and have them take your statement. Good luck, soldier," the lieutenant said.

They took Mark to a vehicle, and he rode to town,

where there was an office and a processing facility. Mark's mind never stopped with all the terrible scenarios that he could imagine. He was sure he would be placed in a cell until some kind of hearing was held. Then he would be court-martialed and sent to prison for selling drugs. He had no doubt his life of relative freedom was now over.

They arrived at the military holding facility. Mark was taken inside, where they put his name on a waiting list to talk to an officer. "Soldier, you need to come over here to be fingerprinted," a corporal told Mark as they finished writing down his name.

Mark walked to him and allowed them to take his hands and get his fingerprints. Mark looked around and asked the simple question. "So how long will I be here?"

"Not long. It's not like you were caught killing anyone. Once we are done with your fingerprints, we will take a short statement from you, and then you will be free to go," a young officer spoke.

Once they finished his fingerprints and his short statement explaining why there were drugs on his bunk, Mark was released. He couldn't believe his luck. However, there was going to be a hearing to determine his innocence or guilt. Mark had thirty days to come up with a good defense and try to avoid prison.

Mark went to talk to a lawyer in the Judicial Adjudicate Guidance office. He signed in at the front counter and talked to the clerk. "Is there a lawyer I can talk to? "

"I can check," the man said. "Just hold on a few minutes. Have a seat in the waiting area."

Mark took a seat and waited for someone to come

out to speak with him. It seemed like forever, but in a few short minutes the clerk was back. "There are none available at this time. Maybe you can come back next week?"

"Okay," Mark replied. "I'll try to be here next week."

Mark left the building disappointed. The only option left to him was to figure this out on his own. This was going to be a very difficult task, but it wasn't like Mark had any choice. Mark felt like he was in a terrible nightmare— even worse than when he found Jimmy's body lying under his window. It was a very dark feeling.

For the next three weeks Mark practiced saying the hash was not his. In truth, he was correct. Chris had given the hash to him to sell and expected to receive the profits from the sales. That being the case, the hash was not Mark's property. It was a clever concept but true in philosophical content. Standing on this principle, Mark held in his heart that it was not his. He had hoped that his belief of that truth would be enough to convince the judge of his innocence.

Chris had been busy trying to establish a solid drug business. He was hoping to be able to retire young on some distant island where he could sip alcohol all day on a beach and sleep with whomever he wanted to at night. Chris had a dream and was working toward that goal. In fact, Chris was working so hard to build a dream that he wasn't keeping an eye on the present.

Claude could see that Chris was in a generous mood. Seeing how much Chris was willing to risk to jumpstart his business made Claude begin to believe his plan would work. He went to see Chris to approach him with his devious plan to help him get a good start.

"If you give me one hundred blocks of hash, I will find my own distributors and sell it all for you in a short amount of time."

"I don't know," Chris replied, trying to think it through. "That's a lot of hash to give out without any collateral. Don't you have anything for me to hold onto until you start to bring in a profit?"

"I might," Claude lied, hoping that Chris could see his effort to please Chris.

"Look," Chris countered. "What if your distributors aren't honest with you? It will only take one to put you in the hole, and then I lose too. That's a really big risk. Why should either of us take that kind of risk?"

"Okay," Claude said. "How about only fifty blocks, and I will take good care that I pick only people that I know will pay up front? Once I have the money from those fifty I should have enough of my own profit to buy more from you. The more you can give me to sell, the more you are moving."

Chris knew what Claude was saying, and it sounded good. What sounded like a risk was giving the hash out without a deposit. That just didn't sound like good business. However, Chris had known Claude for a long time now, and he knew they both wanted a successful business and had similar goals. What Chris didn't know was how dishonest Claude was. Claude had been, once again, successful at hiding his true nature.

"Okay." Chris gave in. "I'll trust you with fifty. You need to return here in one week with my profit so that I have proof to my suppliers that you are serious, and we can both start to build our dreams."

Claude left Chris's apartment with fifty blocks of hash. He knew he could sell them in a day or two and then be on his way with the cash. With that plan in mind, Claude went to find his buyers to liquidate his stash.

Two weeks had gone by, and Mark was notified that his hearing had been moved up. They told Mark the judge advocate was going on vacation and wanted to clear his caseload. Immediately, Mark was filled with more anxiety. It was like a paradox. How would he ever convince the judge he was innocent if he was this anxious? On the other hand, how would he be able to lessen his anxiety if he couldn't convince the judge? It was a vicious cycle.

The day arrived for Mark to go see the provost marshal. He was given a ride in the company jeep provided by the captain. When Mark arrived at the holding facility, his hands were all sweaty again, and his mind was running rampant as all sorts of wild fears raced inside his head.

Mark kept trying to relax using breathing techniques his counselor had been teaching him. To his surprise, they actually seemed to help. Mark sat patiently in the waiting room with a guard while the judge was hearing other cases. Feeling nervous, Mark began to talk to the guard, "So what is the judge like?"

"Oh, he hates drug dealers. He has no patience for them," he answered.

"Well, what if I'm innocent?" Mark asked, feeling his anxiety grow.

"Why? What happened to you? Why are you here?" the guard asked.

"I was out all night visiting friends. When I returned in the morning, a health and welfare inspection was called. They found hash under the dust cover on my bunk. Anyone could have put it there. I was just as surprised to see it as they were," Mark convincingly said.

"Well, I guess you could ask for a polygraph test," the guard said as he thought about it. "That would convince the judge if you really are innocent."

Mark agreed that was a good idea and decided to talk about that to the judge once he was inside. Moments later, his name was called, and Mark nervously walked into the judge's chambers to have his case heard.

The judge was an older man with a determined look in his eyes. He spoke with a low-pitched voice, a deep meaning evident in every syllable. "Young man, it says here you have been found in the possession of hashish. How do you plead?" The judge looked straight at Mark with piercing dark eyes as if to say, "I dare you."

"I am innocent, Your Honor," Mark heard himself say. "The hashish was not actually found on me. It was found on my bunk in an open area. I was not even present when they found it."

"I see," the judge said, listening intently. "Perhaps you'd better tell me what happened."

"Well, Your Honor," Mark started, "I had been out all night, as I said in my statement. I had just returned to my room when the inspection was called and we were ordered to go wait outside. I think it is in the report. I had not even slept in my bunk. It was still made. This is the first time I have ever been in this situation, so I am extremely nervous. I don't know if it would be good for me to take a lie detector test, but I'm telling the truth."

The judge sat back, thought for a few moments, and then replied, "I will tell you what, young man. I would rather let a hundred guilty men go than convict one innocent man. You seem like an honest young man, and you do not have any priors. I believe you. Therefore, I will dismiss your case. I will record that you are not guilty of the charges. However"—the judge leaned forward into Mark's face—"I want you to listen to me good. Stay away from those potheads!"

Mark couldn't believe his ears. He was actually found not guilty. With all the proper military courtesy he could muster, Mark replied, "Thank you, sir."

"That is all. You are dismissed," the judge said, looking at his desk for the next case.

Mark all but ran out of the chambers with a huge smile on his face. He was found not guilty. Mark had no desire to contain his sense of relief. A party was in order. He was not guilty. Mark rode back to the barracks in the jeep, but his mind was soaring high above them, as he felt free of every sin he had ever committed. It was an incredible feeling.

The end of the week had come, and Chris was expecting Claude to return with his money. The weekend came and went with still no Claude. Chris was becoming concerned. His first thought was that maybe something had happened to Claude. Maybe Claude had been caught, or perhaps he was just sick.

Chris waited for yet another week, and still Claude didn't show. Taking matters into his own hands, Chris went around to other people he knew would know Claude. No one had heard anything, good or bad. This was serious. Someone should have heard something by now.

It was late at night when Chris had gone to visit Claude. After waiting awhile, Chris became confident that Claude was alone. Looking around on the street and in the hallway, Chris was sure no one was around. He pulled out his gun and knocked on the door. After knocking on the door, Chris made sure the gun was out of sight so Claude would not be able to see through the peephole that he was armed.

Claude was unaware that Chris knew where he lived. It was a big surprise for Claude to see Chris knocking on his door. Claude had lost track of time and did not realize Chris would be looking for him so soon. Claude opened the door to let Chris in. Chris pushed the door open and stuck the gun in Claude's face. "So you thought you could cheat me out of my money?"

Shaking in fear, Claude answered, "No, man. I have your money. I just don't have it here. Honest. I was going to come see you in the morning. I just didn't have time to do it today."

"Oh yeah? So where is it?" Chris asked, hoping Claude was being honest.

Realizing he would lose it all if he gave up the money that quick, Claude tried to buy time. "It's not here. I can go get it in the morning. I never keep my drug money where I live. That way if they try to bust me they don't have all the evidence."

"That's okay, Claude," Chris said as he pushed him into a chair. "I have the solution." Chris took out the rope he brought and tied Claude's hands. Then he helped Claude stand and walked him to the door. "Listen. If you talk to anyone or shout or try to run, I will kill you. Do you understand?"

Claude nodded his head yes. Chris found one of Claude's jackets and put it over Claude's shoulders to make it look like Claude and Chris were just out for a walk. It was a long walk to Chris's apartment, but in the dark, Chris was able to pull it off much easier than he had imagined.

It was late when they finally arrived. Chris had cleaned out a closet to keep Claude in hiding until Claude told him where to find the money. There was just enough room for Claude to sit with his knees bent. Chris didn't want him to be comfortable, because he wanted Claude to tell him where his money was. Chris was losing control of his thinking.

For three days Chris kept Claude in the closet. During the day Chris would leave the apartment to run errands and do other business. On the third day, while Chris was out, the landlady came around for a routine check of the apartment.

She began the inspection of the place by first checking

the kitchen sink to make sure the water ran and drained properly. From there she went into the bathroom. First she flushed the toilet. While the water ran for the toilet, she ran the shower and the bathroom sink. All the plumbing seemed to be in order.

Next she opened the coat closet to inspect the doors and the hanger bar. To her horror she found a tied-up man who smelled as if he had not been allowed to use a bathroom in a while. She covered her face with her hands as her eyes gave away her shock. Not thinking, she shut the closet door and the apartment door and ran back to her office.

On the fourth morning, there was a knock on the apartment door. When Chris opened the door, several German police officers rushed in and beat Chris with rubber clubs and then handcuffed him.

Once he was subdued, they began the search for Claude and found him just as the landlady had said. The officers took care of Claude. Chris was arrested for kidnapping and possession of illegal drugs.

While Mark was feeling a sense of relief, he found ways to celebrate his freedom every day. Sometimes it was the little things, like enjoying a cup of coffee as he walked from the PX to wherever he wanted to walk. Other times he would meet with Jeremy and Jason and smoke a bowl as they chuckled about how the judge had talked to Mark.

The days grew in number as Mark found it more and more difficult to get in touch with Chris. He wanted to find a way to make it up to Chris for losing the hash when he was busted. It was strange to Mark that Chris never showed up for the hash Mark had lost.

The longer time went on, the more Mark began to forget about Chris. Finally, Mark became convinced that Chris must have moved or something. Back in the barracks, Mark continued with Jeremy and Jason to smoke hash to celebrate life. In doing so, Mark forgot about his change of heart from the letter his brother had sent. Once again he was becoming lost in the daily routine of a drug addict's life.

Before his next scheduled session with Marylyn, Mark was getting excited to tell her about his recent adventures with the legal system. He was all excited to tell her how he had "won" his freedom. It was impossible for Mark to contain himself. "Did you know I had to go to court for possession?"

"Oh yeah, I was informed by your commander," Marylyn said. "So how did it go?"

"Well, I'm here, right?" Mark answered with a big smile. "I told them the truth, and they actually believed me. I never thought they would believe me."

"Why wouldn't they?" Marylyn asked from a therapeutic perspective.

"Because when it comes to drugs, if you're the one caught, then you must be the one guilty. The fact is in most cases they're right. They could have been right in this case. Think about it. I am here to see you by order, right?" Mark countered, still amazed he was believed.

"I see." The therapist in Marylyn came out. "So are

you saying there is a chance you were guilty? Remember, by law I have to keep all things confidential unless there is murder, child abuse, or a possible suicide involved. In this case none of these things exist. Please feel free to speak the truth, or everything we do here is a waste."

"What you are asking feels very dangerous. What if I asked you to take a risk that would make me more willing to take the chance on you?"

This took Marylyn by surprise. She was not sure how to take his question. It was realistic yet provocative. Deep inside, Marylyn was exotic and yet timid in the way she thought. She was confused for the first time in a way she hadn't seen coming. Neither had Mark.

"What did you have in mind?" Marylyn asked hesitantly.

"What if we did something that made me more comfortable believing you?" Mark asked, still confused himself.

"Okay," she said, thinking. "How about dinner at my place tomorrow?" She couldn't believe the words came out of her mouth. Still, she didn't want to take them back. There was something about all this she just had to see through.

Mark, surprised to hear her give such an invitation, couldn't stop himself, "Yeah. That sound good," he responded.

That night Mark could think of nothing but going to Marylyn's house for dinner. He didn't know what to expect, but he had so many feelings going on it was difficult to think straight. It took great mental strength just to brush his teeth before bed—the kind of strength Mark didn't know he had.

With determination and desire, Mark itemized his thoughts down to what he decided was most important. Mark had to focus on a goal that would keep him sane to the end. That would help him be able to see his way home and avoid going to prison or deeper into the drug world.

After lying in bed awake half the night, Mark finally decided on what he had to do. He would take some hash with him to test her. Depending on her reaction, Mark would somehow know what to do to move on. It wasn't perfect. In fact, it was totally unnecessary, but it was a plan that helped him sleep.

The next day the same mundane routine at the warehouse played out. Jeremy and Jason worked together on a project to improve workers' ability to find standard stock items. Mark's main responsibility had been changed to the nonstandard stock items. This left him with little to do but think of the dinner he was going to have with a woman.

In some ways, he thought, she was pretty. Then again, maybe it was because this was the first time in his life it seemed like a woman showed any interest in him—even if it was more clinical than relational. Some attention was somehow better than none. He knew his mind was filled with fantasies. The fantasies, though, felt better than anything that had filled his mind in a very long time, so he just took it in and enjoyed the daydreams.

Finally, when it was quitting time, Mark walked briskly to his room to shower and put on some civilian clothes. It was while he was dressing that it occurred to him that the only clothes he had were T-shirts and jeans. What if she was expecting something more? Mark laughed to himself—if she was, she should have said so. Inside he smiled. This was who he was, so this was who she would see. There was no sense pretending to be something different. After all, wasn't that what she had worked so hard to teach him? To be himself?

He arrived at her home just as they'd agreed. It was a quaint house with a sense of the country about it. Mark was pleasantly surprised to see Marylyn dressed in a denim jacket and jeans herself. He felt much more at ease.

Marylyn smiled as she greeted him at the door. "Come on in and make yourself at home."

Mark smiled and walked in. The place looked simple and clean. It had definitely been decorated by a woman. This made the home very pleasant to be in. "I like your place," Mark said as he sat down.

"Thank you. It's not much, but it's mine," she said as she put the finishing touches on the meal.

Mark realized what she was doing and asked, "Do you need any help?"

"No." She smiled. "But thanks for asking. Would you like some wine?" She had prepared a simple meal of spaghetti with garlic bread. There was a tossed salad to go with it. It was the kind of meal that put Mark at ease, and the wine was the perfect finishing touch. Marylyn had poured Mark a glass even before she had asked.

"Yes, that would be cool," he said as he stood to look around more.

She invited him to the table as she began to place everything on it. It felt good to her to have someone to share a meal with. Mark suspected it had been a while for her as well.

As they ate, they made small talk about the house and Germany. It was after supper that Mark decided to put his test into action. "So why did you become a therapist?"

"I had always wanted to help people. I always passed out at the sight of blood, so being a doctor or nurse was out of the question." Marylyn laughed.

"I know what you mean," Mark said, remembering his childhood. "I remember once my younger brother cut his wrist on some garbage, and I blacked out just from the sight of it. I pass out at the sight of needles too." Mark smiled.

"Oh yeah," continued Marylyn, "I don't do needles either."

"I remember you said something in one of our first session," Mark said, laying out his trap. "You said a therapist had to have experiences so that they could be more of a guide. You said it was important to know where you were leading your client. Do you remember that?"

"Yes, why?" she asked, intrigued by the setup she saw coming.

"Well," Mark continued, "I was wondering—what do you know about the world of drugs? In all our sessions it is always you asking the questions or answering one of mine with a new question. This time I was wondering, since we are not in counseling, what you really knew."

Marylyn thought about it for a moment, trying to

think of the right answer. Finally she had to admit there was no right answer. "I have never done drugs. I never had a reason to. I have thought many times what would I say if I was ever challenged with that. Now here I am, and even with all the time I have had to think about what I would say, what I would do, I have never figured it out."

"Would you like the chance to try it?" Mark exposed his bait.

"What? You mean do drugs?" Marylyn was both intrigued and terrified by the idea. She could lose her job and her reputation if it ever got out that she had done drugs. On the other hand, how could she do a better job of helping clients if she had no experience or idea of what it is like? This was a life dilemma with a moral aspect. What was the right answer?

Mark, feeling brave, pulled out the block of hash. He asked Marylyn for a sheet of paper and took out his lighter. She watched with intense interest as Mark prepared a bowl of hash. Once finished, Mark put the bowl to his lips and asked the question. "Would you like to smoke some dope?"

Marylyn thought about it a little longer. Then on a whim she nodded her head yes and watched Mark light the hash and take a toke of it. Once Mark's lungs were full of the smoke he handed the bowl to Marylyn.

Marylyn was hesitant to take it, but after a short second she reached her hand out and meticulously took the bowl and began to suck on the pipe like she had just seen Mark do. Holding it in, she began to cough and choke. There was a moment when she thought it just might be possible to die from coughing. Taking a second toke, Marylyn handed the bowl back to Mark. They passed it back and forth in silence until it was finished.

"So?" Mark inquired with a smile. "What do you think?"

"It feels heavy on my lungs," Marylyn said, trying to be objective. "I didn't realize just how heavy the smoke would be."

"That might be why so much residue builds up in the stem of the pipe," Mark thought out loud. "Sometimes we take a pipe cleaner and clean out the stem. The cleaner is so thick with this thick liquid paste that we wipe it on cigarettes and get high off that. Most of the time it's a better high than the actual hash."

"I can see how that would be," Marylyn said, breathing heavier than normal.

"So?" Mark again asked. "You didn't answer my question. How is the high?"

"I can see why someone who wanted to escape would rely on something like this to help them. I only agreed to this because I know hash is not physically addictive. It is, however, a hallucinogen. It would be the perfect choice to do an experiment like this to see why so many people turn to drugs like they do. Did you know most people who 'experiment' with drugs are really experimenting with a new way to get away from the old problem? Whatever that old problem may be," Marylyn said, trying so hard to take more of a clinical approach than a personal one to this whole event.

Mark was determined to take her down the road of

being more personal. "That's all fine and good, but are you trying to deal with an old problem?"

Marylyn hesitated. "No," she said. "I'm not."

"So it would be safe to say that even after trying out the drug, you still can't claim to know the way from experience. Do you want to know something?" Mark continued. "I don't think you have to lead the way from experience. I think sometimes you can lead the way just from common sense. Do you believe in God?"

Marylyn thought for a moment as she looked for the new trap in his question. "Yes. Yes, I do. Why?"

"Well," Mark began, "I was thinking how Christ did a lot of leading that way. Yet they say He lived a perfect life. I don't think that was an oversight or just something that was by chance on God's part. I think it was a deliberate plan on God's part for Jesus to be perfect and yet lead the way."

Where that idea came from Mark had no idea. Sometimes things just came out of his mouth from out of nowhere. He had to stop and think about what he had said himself. Mark was hoping it made as much sense as it felt it did.

Marylyn smiled. "Yes, I think you are right."

They sat and finished the wine as they talked more on the subject. Between the bowl of hash and the bottle of wine, Mark was feeling more than a little toasted. He considered the romantic angle of the evening. He wasn't sure just what it was, but somehow it just didn't feel right. Was it because she was his counselor? Was it because he knew there was no future in it? Maybe it was the whole list of reasons not to get involved with her. Whatever it was, Mark decided it was time to leave.

"So will you be okay tonight?" Mark asked, hoping to make this his escape from making a huge mistake.

Looking a little surprised by the question, she answered, "Yes, I think so. Why?"

"I was thinking I should probably go while I can still say my name and see where I'm going," he replied, making what he hoped was the perfect excuse.

Marylyn appeared to be in thought for a moment and then nodded. "I think you might be right. I can hardly think myself right now."

They said their good-byes, and Mark began the long walk home. He hoped to encounter a taxi, but if he didn't, the walk was worth not losing her as a friend. He knew there were those who would call him a fool, but somehow he felt like he would be a fool if he had gone any further. Besides, who says she would have wanted that? It wasn't like she was outright asking for anything more. Perhaps the whole idea of the possibility was in his mind alone. Mark decided that was where it would stay.

When Mark was finally back at the barracks, there was a lot of talking going on in every room. Mark caught bits and pieces here and there, but was unclear whom it was all about. It was apparent that someone had been arrested and was going to prison, maybe for life. Obviously, this worried Mark a lot. Whom were they talking about?

Back in the room, Mark found several of their smoking buddies with Jeremy and Jason. They were all in a big circle, smoking a bowl and talking about the news.

"What are you guys talking about?" Mark asked with increased curiosity.

"Chris," Jason said quickly. "He was arrested for kidnapping a guy. They say this guy was all tied up and kept in his closet. Something about he owed him money or some such thing."

"No way!" Mark exclaimed in shock. "How? Why? When?"

"I guess it was recent, but no one knows for sure," Jeremy said as he stared at the bowl.

"I don't believe it." Mark sat down, stunned. "Why would he be that stupid?" Mark did believe it. He thought about all the times he had seen the craziness in Chris's eyes. The whole thing was more than believable once he thought about it more. Mark realized he would no longer have a connection for drugs. He was torn in two by the idea. On the one hand, it was exactly what he needed. On the other hand, Mark didn't feel ready to give up his life of drug use. Mark felt a surge of anger coming on.

CHAPTER FOURTEEN

Mark wasn't clear himself if it was a matter of anger or a matter of just being lost inside, but he had all sorts of mixed feelings that had to come out. Anger was all that he could recognize. It wasn't logical or even practical. It was just a pure, raw set of emotions that Mark didn't know how to talk about or act out.

During the night Mark made a decision. He lay thinking about the drug test that had come out positive and the counseling he had to go through. He thought about how so many things had come about because of that. Mark decided that if they wanted a positive result, then they were going to get one. He didn't know how yet, but he would give them what they wanted. Maybe then all this would come to an end. It wasn't a rational decision, but it was a decision that gave Mark a new purpose: to put it all to an end.

Friday night was dark and very cool. Mark wore his heavy field jacket as he waited for a taxi. The plan was to go to the bar and do some heavy drinking. Standing in a downpour, he finally saw a taxi coming his way.

The ride seemed quick as Mark did nothing but think about how he was going to get drunk and then come back for some dope smoking. Once in the bar, Mark began to look for a table. He found one where some of the guys looked familiar to him.

"Hey, what are you guys drinking tonight?" Mark asked as he sat in the empty chair at the table.

"Just rum and Coke," one of them answered.

Mark made his order and began drinking to catch up to them. They began talking about a lot of different things. Drugs finally came up. "I know I've seen you guys before. Do any of you ever use speed?" Mark asked, getting even drunker.

"Well, since you brought it up, you did sell me some once," one of them replied. Mark didn't know who it was for sure, as the dim light made it difficult to see the more he drank.

"Yeah." Mark smiled. "I knew I'd seen you around before. So what's going on tonight? Does anyone have anything worth doing?"

"What are you talking about?" another guy asked.

"Okay, let me explain. I'm looking for something more than just a few drinks. I've lost some friends, so I lost all my connections. I'm just asking. It you don't have anything that's cool. I'm not looking for any trouble," Mark explained as he drank the rest of his Rum and Coke.

The guy sitting on his left let out a sigh. "You see that guy over there at that table?" He pointed to a man on his right who was right behind Mark.

Mark turned around to look. "Yeah, I see him."

"He might have some heroin if you do that kind of thing," he said in a low voice.

"Oh, man," Mark said, almost in distress. "I don't use needles. I can't handle needles. They make me pass out."

"It's up to you. You asked, and there's something over there to help. That's all I know." With that the guy on his left got up and went to the restroom.

Mark thought about it as he took a couple of more sips of his rum and Coke. Finally, he began to convince himself that he could always drink it. As long as he took it, he would have to get high. In his drunken state of mind this all made sense.

Finally having drunk in enough courage to go through with it, Mark got up and went to talk to the guy at the table behind him. "Hey, man," Mark started in a drunken slur. "I was told that you might have something that can ease the pain."

"Who told you that?" the man asked, looking at Mark like he was unwanted trouble.

"See that guy at the table behind us?" Mark pointed to him.

"Yeah," the man answered.

"They say they know you and you might have something I can use," Mark said quietly.

"I see," the stranger said hesitantly. He sat glancing between Mark and the table he'd come from. "I'll tell you what," he finally said. "Take this packet and hand me a twenty without making it obvious." He handed Mark a small packet as they shook hands.

Mark handed him a twenty, pointing to the bar as if to ask him to buy them both a drink. The man got up and went to the bar. Mark waited a few minutes then got up and went to the other end of the bar to sit by himself.

Mark still had a Coke can with him and in one deft move emptied all the powder in the packet into his Coke. He had just finished this maneuver when two men dressed in shirts and ties approached him.

They sat on both sides of Mark and began to question him. "So what are you up to this fine evening?"

"Not a lot. Just getting drunk," Mark answered as he began to drink his Coke. "Do I know you guys?"

"Not yet, but maybe you will," answered one of them. "We heard you like using."

"Oh yeah?" Mark was becoming suspicious even in his inebriation. "And where did you hear that?"

They both pulled out their identification. "We are with CID, and we have reason to believe you are involved in things you shouldn't be."

"CID?" Mark questioned. "What exactly does that stand for?"

"Central Intelligence Division," one of them answered.

"So what do you want with me?" Mark asked, a little concerned.

"We saw you buy some dope," the other one answered.

"What?" Mark looked shocked. "What are you talking about?"

"You know what we're talking about. Why not just

admit it, and then we can talk more from there?" They both seemed to be talking together now.

"I'll tell you what," Mark answered. "Why not frisk me? You can look anywhere you want. I don't have any drugs on me. All I've been doing all night is drinking." Mark was telling the truth. It was true he had put the drug in his Coke, but drinking was exactly what he had been doing all night. This made him very convincing.

Frustrated, the one on Mark's left lifted his eyebrows to the other one as if to say they had him. The other one shook his head no and got up to leave. "We will be watching you. We will catch you. We know all about you," he said as he stood.

"Well," Mark hesitated, "I guess you know more about me than I do, because I don't seem to know anything about myself anymore. When you get the chance, fill me in so I can catch up with myself."

Mark couldn't believe he had said that. He figured it had to be the alcohol talking. He was finishing his Coke about that time when he started feeling just a little bit sick. Mark figured it was all the alcohol and the excitement of dealing with two CID agents who were so bold as to confront him face-to-face. Once again, Mark was walking away a free man. He wondered just how much luck and grace he had left.

Mark made his way back to his room and decided to call it a night. He had no idea where Jeremy was off to, but it didn't matter, as Mark just wanted to lay down and sleep. With any luck his upset stomach would go away and he would feel better in the morning.

He had turned off the light and was lying in bed. He could feel his stomach continue to churn more and more. Mark began to think about the heroin he had drunk with the Coke. Was it possible that it was acting like a poison?

Mark began to sweat, and his thoughts ran wild with ideas of dying of some kind of poison. He didn't know what he was going to do. Then all of a sudden it didn't seem to matter. He knew he was about to vomit. There was no time left.

Mark got up and ran for the door. He turned on the light and realized he had no time to make it to the latrine. He ran for the window. Throwing open the bay windows he immediately leaned out and released gut-wrenching vomit.

It seemed like it would never end. Everything Mark had ever eaten seemed to now be on the ground below. The cold air felt good on his face as he finally had a moment to breathe and regain some kind of control. He didn't dare move from the window for fear he would be cleaning up a mess on the floor. He didn't think he was up for that.

Mark was regaining his strength and breath as he leaned out the window, gazing at the ground below in the darkness. Wow, he thought, the heroin must be kicking in. He could swear the ground below where he had been vomiting was moving.

Studying the mess below more carefully, Mark was sure it was moving. It was not just an illusion. It was moving. On a hunch Mark called out, "Hey! Who's down there?"

"I am," a voice from below answered.

"Who are you and what are you doing down there?" Mark answered, filled with curiosity and disbelief.

"It's Darren. I'm vomiting. I think I'm sick" came the answer in a faint but now very recognizable voice.

In sudden horror and yet comical awareness, Mark realized he had been vomiting on top of someone else who was vomiting. What were the odds? Mark decided to slowly close the windows and turn out the light before Darren put it all together. If Darren ever realized what has just happened, he would kill Mark. This secret of all secrets.

Still, it was funny. Yet it was the kind of funny story he would never be able to tell anyone—at least not anyone there. Remembering back, he could hear the words in his head: "Three can keep a secret if two of them are dead." Mark wasn't interested in dying just yet.

The next morning Mark thought he was feeling better. He certainly had a slight case of hunger. Maybe that was a good sign. He must not have been poisoned, or else he wouldn't be feeling better this quick.

Mark went to the mess hall to get breakfast. He wasn't sure what he felt like eating, but he thought he would at least try some toast or maybe some biscuits and coffee. Mark collected his food from the counter and found a table.

Mark had eaten one slice of toast and one biscuit as he drank coffee. Then it hit with a surprise. He started to feel the food come up in his throat. Mark closed his mouth tight as he got up to run to the latrine. Turning the corner to the short hallway where the door to the latrine was, his mouth could hold no more. Vomit sprayed out of his mouth on the line of men waiting their turn to get trays for breakfast. It was one smooth motion as he ran around the corner. Mark wasn't sure just how many, but he could hear the cussing as he ran into a stall to worship the porcelain god. Worship he did. It seemed like forever again as Mark emptied his entire digestive cavity of anything he had in him.

It seemed like hours—and maybe it was—before Mark was finally able to stand and breathe. He had tears in his eyes and sweating everywhere from the workout. For a while he wasn't sure if he was going to live. After resting for a while, Mark was finally convinced no one was left in the mess hall. That made it safe for him to go back to the barracks without anyone waiting to beat him up.

The rest of the day Mark spent on his sickbed. He was way too sick to want to do anything but rest. He had no energy to do anything at all—no drugs or alcohol or even food. He was barely able to go to the shower.

Several days passed with Mark feeling no energy and not being able to eat. He showed up for work, but didn't tell anyone what was going on. Not even Jeremy. Mark knew better than to try to eat in public. He was afraid of performing any more undesirable baptisms. Mark had no desire to make anyone angry with him for doing the unthinkable to him like he had done in the mess hall.

Once a day Mark would try just to drink water. He knew he needed water. At first it wouldn't stay down. Then Mark decided to just sip every once in a while.

Perhaps he could trick his stomach into thinking there was nothing in it. Mark figured if he did this enough then at least he wouldn't get dehydrated.

The weekend had finally arrived, and Mark was feeling a little braver. He decided not to do the mess hall routine. Going to the PX, he bought some food to go. Once back in the room, Mark prepared the waste can and began to eat at the desk with the waste can beside him. He ate only a little at a time. It took over an hour before Mark was finished.

At first it seemed like he was finally able to keep the food down. Then it happened. The vomiting wasn't nearly as violent, but it was complete for what he had eaten. It took only a few short moments. Mark thought this was progress. Lying in his bed, thinking, like he had been every day of that week, Mark made one decision. Never again would he even think about drinking down some heroin. Most definitely the risk was not worth the reward. For all the "trickery" he may have pulled off on the CID officers, he was paying the price.

For the rest of the day Mark continued to sip water, just like he had all week. It seemed to Mark that he was finally getting better, as he was growing restless. He didn't feel like sleeping as he had at the beginning of the week. His body was recovering. Hopefully, it would just be a matter of time before he could eat and be back to his normal routine.

On Sunday morning Mark was feeling the best he had felt in what seemed forever. Having no doubt in his mind, Mark went to the mess hall, feeling like he could eat everything they had.

Mark filled his tray with eggs over easy, bacon, ham, toast, and coffee. Mark took his treasure to a table and dug in to the meal he had wanted for a long time. Once Mark started to eat it was uncontrollable. He all but swallowed his food whole out of incredible hunger. The meal was over in just a few seconds. Once finished Mark sat back to enjoy a cup of coffee.

He had just finished his coffee when, once again, he felt his stomach reject all that he had shoved into it. Knowing what was about to happen, Mark went to the latrine on a full run. It was like déjà vu. Mark once again sprayed the whole mess hall line as he turned the corner to the latrine.

This time it was different. He didn't feel sick like he had all week. Perhaps he was vomiting simply from eating too fast. He spent most of his time in the latrine waiting for his chance to escape. Mark thought about that for a minute. He actually felt like he could run. Peering out of the latrine door to see if anyone was looking, Mark made a mad dash for the exit door and ran all the way back to the barracks. Even though he wasn't able to keep his breakfast down this time, he knew he was finally better.

At lunchtime Mark tried to eat again. This time it was much better. Not only did the food stay down, but it felt also good to be full. Of course, Mark took his time to eat rather than trying to fit it all in his stomach at the same time. That helped a lot. Mark sat back to drink coffee like he used to. He even enjoyed a cigarette as he relaxed.

Jeremy and Jason had gone to town to enjoy their weekend. This left Mark alone with his thoughts. It felt good to have some time alone once in a while.

Just as Mark was relaxing, Jacob joined him with his own coffee. "So how ya feeling?" he asked with that familiar Cajun accent.

"Hey!" Mark exclaimed with a smile. "Haven't seen you in forever."

"I know." Jacob laughed. "It's been great."

Marked laughed at that. "I bet it has. What have you been up to?"

"Just staying out of trouble. Ever try it?" Jacob asked more seriously.

"Try? Oh yeah. Succeed? Not too often," Mark said.

"You know what the problem is, don't you?" Jacob asked, hoping Mark knew.

"Actually, I don't. I know the more I want it, the harder it is to get," Mark said.

Jacob thought about it for a minute. Then he picked up a napkin and unfolded it. "You see this napkin?" Jacob asked as he held it up. "Do you think you can separate the front side of it from the back side?"

Mark looked at it for only a second and laughed. "Of course not. Why?"

"Well," Jacob started, "that's how responsibility is with freedom. You can't separate one from the other and have what you want."

Mark thought about it as he held the napkin in his hands. "Okay, so what are you saying?"

"I'm saying that you want to have freedom but you are not taking the responsibility to make it happen. It's like that with God, you know," Jacob said like he was a wise old man.

"I think I know what you're saying," Mark said as he thought about it. "What about God?"

"God will help you if you make the effort. It has to be an honest effort. You have to really want it. You can't fake it with God. He knows what you're thinking and what your heart is. You, however, must be the one to trust God and act on that trust." Jacob talked with a command of the wisdom that God had granted him.

"Wow, where did you get all that?" Mark asked in amazement.

Jacob smiled at Mark's total unawareness of the Scriptures. "You do understand that God will always be with you, right?"

"Oh yeah? Why would God care about me? What have I done to deserve His help?" Mark asked in complete bewilderment.

"God loves you because you are you. He created you just so He would have you to love. You are God's gift to Himself. At least that's what my grandmother always taught me," Jacob answered. "Do you want your friends to like you because you make them like you or because they want to like you?"

"How could I make them like me? It's not like I have

special powers. Of course because they want to," Mark said, wondering where this was going.

"Well, God is like that too. He could have created you to like Him, but He wants your love because you choose to love Him—just like He chooses to love you. That is why He would help you—just like you would help anyone you loved. It's really not that difficult to understand. Just think about it." Jacob looked at Mark, hoping that Mark understood what he was saying.

They sat and finished their coffee while Mark thought about all that Jacob had been saying. It really did make sense. Still, how would he leave the world of drugs without all his friends wondering what he was doing? Certainly that part of it couldn't be that easy to do. Mark treasured his friendship with Jeremy, and he was addicted to the drugs. Between his friend and the drugs and living drug free, Mark didn't know how it would all turn out.

On the other hand, if Mark didn't leave the world of drugs, he would either end up dead or in prison—or, at the very least, with no family, future, or home when he returned to the States. Nothing else had worked. Maybe it was time to try it. On the way back to the barracks, Mark stopped at the PX and bought some hooks to hang the tapestry. Mark was thinking maybe it would inspire and encourage him to make it work.

That evening Mark had the tapestry hung by the time Jeremy came back. They started up a bowl of hash when Jason came to the room. The three of them sat down to the hash, some music, and some good old-fashioned talk about whatever was on their minds.

Then they started looking at the tapestry. They began to philosophize why Christ would be asking them to let Him in their hearts and what the barbed wire on His heart and the crown of thorns meant. It was a very deep discussion.

"So do you think He still looks like that now that He's risen?" Jason asked intently.

Mark was amazed that Jason even knew that Christ had risen from the dead. "Do you really believe He did rise from the dead?"

"Oh, I don't know," Jason confessed. "They say He did. His body was never found."

Mark's memory began to return to when he was young and had a chance to learn the Scriptures for prizes. "Did you know there was a crowd of people who saw Him go up to heaven? Thomas, one of the disciples, was shown the holes in Jesus' hands and the hole in His side from the spear when He was still on the cross. Yeah, I think He still looks like that, at least some."

Jeremy listened like he was in his favorite class. "So you're saying that Jesus is still alive today? So where is He?"

"In heaven, I guess," answered Mark. "The Bible says He is sitting at the right hand of God and is constantly talking to God about each of us as we pray."

Jeremy laughed. "Well, I guess He won't be talking to God about me. I never pray."

"I know," said Mark in thought. "I don't either. Maybe it's time I start."

They continued to smoke and look at the tapestry as

they listened to music. It somehow looked different with the lights off and only candles burning. Sometimes, Mark thought, it looked like Jesus' face glowed and His eyes never left Mark's. In some ways it was very comforting, yet in other ways it was almost scary that Christ never took His eyes off them.

They must have smoked four bowls of hash before almost passing out from being stoned. In his deepened high, Mark thought maybe this was how the Indians used to go into the spirit world to discover what God had for them to see. Mark was hoping that as long as he was already stoned, maybe he would see what God wanted him to see in a way he had never seen before.

There was a lot to think about as Mark remembered the lunch with Jacob. Now, with the tapestry and the return of some of his memories of the Scriptures he had learned, maybe what God was telling Mark was to get his act together and start trusting God with all the things he had doubted. There really was nothing left to lose. Mark was thinking maybe Jeremy would understand after all.

Later that night, after everyone was asleep, Mark got down on his knees and prayed a short prayer. "God, if you are real, show me by giving me a way out of the army with an honorable discharge." Mark believed that for this to work, he had to trust God to do just that. Mark made a deal: "God, if you deliver me from my own stupidity, then I will serve you for the rest of my life." He didn't know any other way to prove to himself that God was real and truly did love him.

CHAPTER FIFTEEN

After breakfast on Monday, Jeremy came back to the room. "Hey, how ya feeling now, man?"

"Better. I'm not vomiting when I eat. Breakfast actually stayed down again today," Mark happily replied. "Looking forward to lunch." He smiled.

Jeremy smiled back. "That's good. I was hoping I would never have to clean up after you. I was beginning to worry about your health."

Jason came into the room like he was Jeremy's shadow. "Hey, you guys hear the news?"

"What news?" Mark asked, glad for a new subject.

"Well, last Friday they took Guy away for going AWOL from his guard post. Actually, he was just buying cigarettes at the PX—you know, like we always do. Then just last night they arrested Joey while he was walking back to the barracks from the NCO club. I heard they planted drugs on him so they could put him away." Jason was sounding like a radio news broadcaster.

Both sat in silence for a few minutes. Finally Jeremy spoke up. "What's going on?"

"I don't know," Jason answered sullenly. "There's another rumor that the army has to 'clean house' because of how Vietnam went. The Soviets are still trying to find our weaknesses. Maybe they just feel like we're making them look bad. I don't know."

They lit up a bowl and silently listened to music and gazed at the tapestry until it was time for formation. By the end of the day, Mark felt like he needed all the friends he could get. He invited both Jason and Jeremy to the hideaway for supper—his treat. Mark felt it was time to start lining out what he needed to do before the army did it for him.

They ate supper and made small talk. Each one talked about his own thoughts about what to do to survive the "cleansing." No one, it seemed, was going to survive it without giving up either his freedom or his habits. That was how it was looking, at least.

Finally, as they were finishing up their meal, Mark ordered another round of beer. "I was thinking, guys, you know, about what to do. It's no secret that I first joined the army to buy time to figure out what to do to improve my life. Jason, you made it very obvious to me that I was not doing this very well. I need help."

The other two sat in silence, not sure what to say or what Mark was really asking. Jeremy finally broke the silence. "So what do you want from us?"

"I think it's time to quit. I think if I don't stop on my own I will be spending time behind bars just like Guy, Joey, and Chris. I'm just not really up to that. I have no desire to be put in a position where I have to name names.

If I just outright quit, then they have to frame me like everyone thinks they framed Joey. If any of that is true," Mark answered, his hands on his head.

"You really think they're just going to forget you exist? Do you remember how they have you on CEDAC and you went to a court martial?" Jason asked.

"Yeah, I remember. I remember every minute I'm awake. You have a better idea?" Mark asked.

Jason sat, silent. Despite the fact that Mark was not really addressing the heart of the issue, Jason didn't feel he had any alternative solution to offer. "No, I don't. I just think you are not using your energy on the right issue."

"I know it seems that way. Still, I was thinking about what a friend told me recently. I know you're gonna laugh, but what do I have to lose?"

"What's that?" Jeremy asked.

Mark started to chuckle. "Ask God for help to get me out of the mess I put myself in."

Jason and Jeremy looked at each other with skepticism. Then Jeremy had another thought. "I know some people may say that's just nuts, but after all I've seen, I think God has to be with you. You've lived through too much for it to be just plain luck or coincidence."

"I tend to agree," Jason added.

"Question is, how do you do that?" Jeremy asked.

"I don't know. I guess just do exactly what I was told. Pray, trust, and pray again. I think I have to be honest in every situation or I'm not really trusting God," Mark said as he thought it through.

"What do you mean? Be honest about what?" Jason began to worry.

"First, I have to believe they won't ask me questions about who is doing what. Second, when they ask me questions about myself, just tell the truth. See what happens," Mark conjectured.

"Well, that's gonna take a lot of guts," Jeremy said, taking in all Mark was saying."

"I know. Funny thing is I'm no hero. I don't have any guts," Mark replied as he thought about all he had been through.

"Oh yeah? Well, from what I've seen, you could almost be my hero." Jeremy laughed.

"So what do you want from us?" Jason asked.

"Just understanding. I'm not interested in betraying anyone. I promise I won't give any of you up for my own personal goals. I just don't want to lose your friendship or your trust as I try to turn my life around. I think if I stay here any longer I'm not gonna make it."

Both of them looked at each other for a moment and then looked at Mark. "We got your back as long as you have ours," Jason warned.

Jeremy nodded in agreement. Those words were too hard to speak, but he felt them nonetheless.

With that they finished their beer and made the silent walk back to the barracks. It was time for Mark to start fresh. He prayed quietly as they walked that he really did have the support of his friends.

That Monday morning Mark decided to put all that he had been learning and thinking about to the test. Mark wondered whether God was real. It seemed like He was real. When he thought about the night, he was positive a demon was in the room, Mark was sure He was real—if demons were real, then God had to be. How could there be one without the other?

Monday after formation, still a third friend was taken in on charges that he had run his room key down the side of a sergeant's car, causing extensive damage. At lunchtime half the guys from the hallway were meeting in Mark's room to talk about it.

"I heard that Guy was getting a dishonorable discharge for abandoning his post," Jason said. "I guess one of the guys working with the first sergeant had heard this from the captain."

All the guys in the room started talking at once, upset over the news. "I heard that Joey was going to prison at Fort Leonard Wood in Missouri. I heard he would get something like ten years for possession," Jeremy said.

Mark listened to all that was being said. Suddenly he had a thought. "What about John? What's going to happen to him?"

One of the other guys spoke up. "I heard they beat him up pretty bad in one of the back rooms. Now they're gonna charge him with destruction of property. I'm sure they will give him a bad conduct discharge or something."

Mark had to think very seriously about his new commitment to telling the truth. He had finally decided how to show his trust—to admit his guilt when asked and just believe that if God really was God, then He would deliver him from evil.

Then again, with this news Mark was beginning to think maybe this was a bad time to put it all on the line. But maybe it was the best time. If the army really was cleaning house, then it would only be a matter of time before Mark was arrested. He would need a larger power than himself. The way Mark saw it, only God could get him through all this. With any luck it would be a while before Mark really had to put it to the test. For now it was more of an agreement in his mind.

That afternoon Mark was called to take another urine test. This was a follow-up test for the CEDAC counseling process. They wanted to see if Mark had quit using drugs and was making progress. Mark was confident that this time he would be caught.

He knew it was coming, so he had stopped to see one of the girls in the warehouse office. Mark knew she was pregnant. The army was going to give her a medical discharge for pregnancy. He wanted some of her urine so when they tested his they would find him pregnant.

Mark had heard they did not test by sex or name. They simply used the social security number for reference. They tested for a variety of things, including drugs, alcohol, and pregnancy. It seemed to Mark that if they saw just how poor their system worked, they would have to revamp how they did the tests. It would buy him time.

Diane was sitting at her desk when Mark finally had the courage to ask her.

"Diane, how ya doing?"

"Not bad. How's your day going?" she said.

Mark smiled, trying to get the words out just right. "Well, funny you should ask."

"Uh-oh, what's going on now?" she asked, now looking up at him with real attention.

"Well … I was wondering … you know how you're pregnant?" Mark began.

"Yeah, I do know. Why?" she asked, suspicious.

"Hmm. How do I ask this?" Mark smiled. "I was wondering. Since they do their drug testing by social security number and not by name or sex—well … can I have some of your urine?" It was finally out.

"What? *No!*" Diane was very emphatic. "What do you think I am?"

"Well, actually, I think you're pregnant and was thinking about the look on the captain's face when he says he has to let me go for being pregnant." Mark laughed.

"Well, I think you're sick and you need to leave," Diane replied with a very disgusted look on her face.

Mark was disappointed to discover her unwillingness to challenge the system. He was just going to have to let them see all the drugs he had been using since he started. It would make Marylyn look like a bad counselor, but that was going to have to be how it was.

Mark met the medic at the warehouse door, ready to go have his test done. They went to the clinic, and Mark filled the bottle with his own urine. This would be the first test, Mark thought. Now he would see if prayer really did work. It would only be a day or two before Mark was told the results.

The rest of the day was filled with his thoughts. Mark

kept talking to himself about what prison was like. He thought about the story of Joseph being in prison after being falsely accused of raping a woman. God delivered Joseph from prison, but it took ten years for it to happen. Ten years was a long time to be in prison.

Mark thought about Chris. He had heard that Chris was in prison for life for kidnapping that man. The rumor was that Chris was going insane. Mark wondered how anyone would know. It wasn't like any of them had been there to visit. Mark's mind kept wandering like that all day, skipping from one thought to another. It was very hard to concentrate on his fate or his work.

The next day was no better. Mark found himself daydreaming at his desk. He couldn't help wondering what he was going to do or how. The only thing he did know was that he had to follow his plan. He just had to trust God.

All of a sudden there was a lot of commotion. Mark heard a lot of yelling but couldn't figure out what was being said. Jerking himself out of his daydream, he looked behind him. There were flames climbing up the shelves along the outside wall behind his desk. They kept the inner tubes for truck and jeep wheels along that wall. Boxes full of rubber were now on fire. The wooden shelves were also burning. All Mark could do was stand there and stare. Jeremy came and stood beside him. "Is that a fire?"

"Yeah," Mark said in a soft, bewildered voice. "I think it is."

"Hey! Wake up! What are you doing? Soldier, grab

that fire extinguisher and put that fire out!" Sergeant First Class Billy Jones yelled, his anger and frustration intense.

Mark and Jeremy, all of a sudden, acted like they had just woken up to nightmare. Jeremy grabbed the fire extinguisher, while Mark began to look for another. In a few minutes there were several soldiers working to put the fire out. They opened up the big bay doors and got the boxes separated on the ground outside so that the fire would not spread and would burn itself out.

The fire took all morning to put out. The whole building was filled with smoke, so there was no more warehouse work for the rest of the day. They all went to lunch, talking about everything that had been happening. The main topic was how the fire started. Who started it? Why?

"I think it was spontaneous combustion," Mark heard one guy say. Thinking about that, Mark had remembered a barn burning down when he was young. He had heard that spontaneous combustion occurred when heat was covered up by a burnable substance like straw or paper or cloth. The boxes were not set up like that. How could it have been spontaneous?

"No," Mark heard himself say. "It had to be lit by someone. That's the only way it could've happened."

Jeremy thought about it. "But who?"

Jason spoke up. "I saw someone behind the shelves not too long before the fire. Maybe he did it?"

"Who did you see?" Mark asked.

"I couldn't tell. They were dark, and it was kind of

dark behind the shelves. They were wearing green, I think." Jason laughed. "Besides, it wasn't like I thought it was important at the time."

They all laughed at that. All everyone wore was olive green. All lunchtime they talked about it with great interest. It was both exciting and scary. "How do they know it was a soldier? Maybe it was a terrorist." Then they laughed at that. Why would a terrorist want to burn down a parts warehouse that had little to do with the security of the US Army in Germany? It had to have been a soldier.

After lunch Mark was in his room smoking a cigarette and drinking a beer. He had just put on an album when he heard a knock at the door. Mark opened the door to see Harold standing there. "Come on in," Mark said. Harold was one of the black soldiers who worked in another section of the warehouse.

Once in and seated, Harold asked the most common question that day: "Did you hear who started that fire?"

"No, why do you ask?" Mark wondered why Harold, who was black and hated whites, was in his room asking the question like he was Mark's best friend.

"I started it," Harold confessed.

Mark stared at him in disbelief, surprised Harold was trusting him with this kind of news. "Why are you telling me?"

"I don't know. You don't talk, and you always seem fair with everyone. I also know you were there when I started the fire. I wanted everyone to think you did it. Now I don't want that. I'm scared, but I also want out of the army with an honorable discharge. What do you think they will do if they find out I did it?" Harold asked, staring at the floor from his chair.

"I don't know what they'll do. Why did you want them to think I did it?" Mark asked, confused.

"Well"—Harold looked up at him—"I certainly didn't want them to think I did it."

"Why did you start it?" Mark asked.

"I figured if the warehouse burned down, then they wouldn't have anything for us to do and would have to send us home," Harold said with his head in his hands.

Mark laughed. "All they would do is make us rebuild the warehouse, clean up the mess, and find other things for us to do. We belong to the army. They aren't gonna just send us home like they did in school. Everyone has to serve their time."

Harold thought about that and shook his head. "What am I going to do?"

Mark looked at him as he took a drink of beer. "Hey, you want a beer?"

"Yeah, thanks, man." Harold smiled. "That sounds good." Harold took the beer and drank it as he thought. "One thing's for sure—I can't go around telling people."

"Why did you tell me?" Mark asked.

"Like I said, you were the only one there when I started it," Harold said.

Marked laughed. "So now if they do figure it out that you did it, does that mean you're going to think I told?"

"Nah, I know better," Harold said with conviction. "I know where you've been and what you've been through. I know you won't talk. You have too much to lose to want to risk everyone thinking you're a snitch. That would be a mess."

"That's for sure," Mark said quietly. "So now what?"

"I guess just wait to see if they find out," Harold said, looking like he was doing better.

They both drank another beer and listened to music. Mark thought about how different it was to be drinking with Harold, given how much Harold hated him just for being white. It was truly an odd thing to experience, yet at the same time it felt good to cross that line in such a pleasant way—just two men sharing a beer and listening to music.

Days went by before Mark heard about his urine test. There was no news about who had started the warehouse fire. Rumors flew that one of the guys who were just arrested for drug use was responsible. From time to time, Mark would see Harold walking, and they would look at each other with that knowing look. It was obvious that Harold felt better about not getting caught. At the same time it continued to feel good to Mark that a barrier had definitely been crossed. He hoped that somehow this all made a difference for Harold as well.

On Friday afternoon Mark was working in the stockyard. He was working on the inventory when a sergeant came to talk to him. "Welch, the captain wants to see you."

Mark knew it was about the urine test. He had been waiting for the results to come back. He locked the gate to the stockyard and walked to the barracks where the captain's office was.

Mark checked in with the orderly, sat on one of the chairs lining the wall, and waited for the captain to call him in. The day had been uneventful until this moment. It had actually been nice to be outside. Now being called in to do the follow-up, Mark couldn't help wonder what CEDAC had recommended. There was no doubt in his mind that there was going to be a lot of concern on the captain's part over the positive results.

"Soldier, go on in," the first sergeant directed with his bass voice. Mark got up out of his chair and walked into the office, feeling like his life may be at its end. Once in the office he stood at attention, waiting for the next command from the captain.

"At ease, soldier," the captain stated. He kept looking at the papers on his desk. "Do you know why you are here?"

Mark thought for a moment, not knowing whether he wanted to answer at all. He wasn't sure if he wanted to give away anything he might know. It was worse than playing poker, Mark thought.

"Well, you are here because the results have come back on your drug test. As I am sure you must know by now, it came back negative. Good job on cleaning up your act."

Mark was in disbelief. He had been sure that with everything he had done it would be positive. He stared at the wall in complete shock and finally heard his voice say, "Excuse me, sir, did you say 'negative'?"

"That's right, soldier. I did say 'negative.' Again, that was a good job. You need to continue to keep yourself clean. I am sure it is not an easy thing to do here in these times. I want you to continue to follow through on the CEDAC program. I will meet with you again about your progress in a few weeks. That is all, soldier," the captain said, finishing the meeting.

Mark left the office deep in thought. He was supposed to report back to the warehouse and thought he was on his way there. When he finally came to his senses, Mark found himself sitting at a table drinking coffee at the PX. He was completely unaware of how he had gotten there. He didn't even know if he had paid for the coffee he was holding in his hand. One thing he was certain of was that a lot could happen in a week. Around here, a lot could happen in a day.

It was five o'clock, and Mark decided he needed to at least go back to the barracks and talk to Jeremy and find out if he had been missed at the warehouse. He didn't want to get into any more trouble than he was thinking he was already in. There was a lot to think about.

Jeremy walked in the room right behind Mark. "Hey, there you are. So what happened? What did they say?"

"More than I imagined," Mark replied. "The drug test came back negative, and they want me to keep up the good work. They want me to finish the CEDAC program."

"No kidding," Jeremy said, letting it all sink in. "What else did they say? Did they say anything about the rest of us?"

"No, just that the test came back negative. How? How could it be negative after all the drugs I've done in the last couple of weeks?" Mark asked, still not believing what he had heard. It was like it was some kind of a trap. But that didn't make any sense either.

"I don't know. Nothing makes any sense anymore in this place. I think you need to take it as God answering one of your prayers. Right? You know what's been happening around here lately. It sounds like it's your get-out-of-jail-free card," Jeremy said as he thought about what he was hearing.

"I think you're right. But why me? What did I do that was so special that I should be treated differently?" Mark asked, feeling like he had just been pardoned from a life sentence for no reason.

"Does it matter? I mean, really, the only thing that's important is that you have a second chance. Ask Guy or Joey or any of the other guys that are gone if they would take this chance if they had it," Jeremy answered, determined to make sense of it all himself. "The only thing that matters is whether you get your life back and do something with it once you have it. Right?"

"Yeah, you have a point. I have been wanting a way out of this nightmare. We all have been dreaming of leaving this place the right way." Mark talked like he was in a dream.

Out of habit more than anything else, and feeling like there was no good answer to find in the natural world, they lit up a bowl to take it all in. While they smoked and listened to music, Mark looked at the tapestry and asked God under his breath to help him see the right way to go. Mark was asking for wisdom as he smoked hash and sought God's will. He wondered how many ministers could do that and get away with it. Then he realized no one said he would get away with it, so he ought to stop being so smug about it. That's when it hit him. Mark began to realize he was in sin. He had heard that word a lot. What was sin?

Mark decided to go to his favorite haunt. The last time he was there the three of them had made a pact to do the right thing. He didn't know if he would ever see it again. Once he agreed to trust God, how much time did he have before it was a done deal? Would he go home a new man? Wow, Mark thought. In the years to come, who would ever believe what he was about to go through now?

Mark ordered his usual veal with mashed potatoes and beef gravy. He liked to have either corn or peas and tossed salad. It made Mark feel like he was at home—or at least what he thought a home would feel like. Mark liked to drink milk and then have coffee with pie after the meal. Once he was done with the meal, he would order a dark German beer and sit back in his chair and smoke as he thought about his life. Where had he been? Where was he now? Where was he going? It was all like a big dream to him. Mark wished this was all about someone else and not him.

Mark was uncertain how long he had been there. It was a comfort knowing it was a Friday night and he had all the time in the world to get back to the barracks. Yet, at the same time, that was just it. Mark suddenly realized time had a value it never had before. All his life Mark had

had time. That was all he had. No matter what was going on, he'd had time.

Then, once he graduated from high school, he had no time. So Mark enlisted in the army to buy time. Three years would normally be enough time for anyone. Mark thought about it. Now all of a sudden there was no time. He still had eight months to go before his three years was up. Was all that time gone now? Had he spoiled it all? Was he stupid? Was he a hopeless case and a criminal? Was he really all about using drugs?

Then again, where had this opportunity come from? Had God answered his prayer? Mark thought about how he had prayed for help and wanted to believe in God. He remembered the conversation he'd had with his friend Jacob in the mess hall and the napkin representing responsibility and freedom. How did that go? He could separate one from the other and have it keep its consistency. That was really cool how Jacob had used the napkin to show him that. And he was right. Mark thought about it a lot as he sat and drank his beer until it was time to go back to the barracks.

CHAPTER SIXTEEN

Saturday morning should have been filled with rest and relaxation. It was supposed to be a day of catching up with who you were and where you had been. This Saturday began a little different. The three friends had just finished breakfast and walked back to their rooms.

Suddenly, there were voices in the hallway shouting for everyone to get their gear and report for formation.

At first everyone thought it was a health and welfare inspection. They all began to open their doors and file outside. "Soldiers! What are you doing?" came a shout from one of the sergeants. "This is not a drill. This is a yellow alert. Pack your gear and get ready for formation in one hour!"

"What?" one of the other guys asked the group in the hallway. "What is he talking about?"

Jason spoke in his usual obnoxious way. "Hey, don't you get it? We are on alert for going to war. They said it's not a drill. They always start out as drills. Yellow means we will probably stand down. In other words, go back to normal. Just pack your duffel bag like they said and get ready to go."

All the men went to their rooms and began packing their web gear: helmets, shaving kits, wool socks, fatigues, and canteens—everything a soldier would need in a battlefield. Most of the guys kept what needed to be packed ready to go so they would be all set when this happened. Others who weren't so intuitive did not, so they enlisted the help of those who were already set. Within the hour everyone was ready and outside.

The afternoon sky looked very blue as the sun shone through the wispy clouds that floated by. The wind felt good on Mark's face as he held his helmet in his hands. The formation had not been called yet, so most were talking among themselves. Mark sat by himself off to one side, thinking about what might be happening.

He had never considered the possibility of going to war. It was supposed to be peacetime. His plan for the army had been just to take everything in and hopefully figure out what to do with his life during the three years he had signed up for. He had not signed up for this. Every time he had a plan something would happen to spoil it all. Now it was happening again. The only bright spot in all this was that it wasn't his fault this time.

Mark thought about what war was like. He had read books and seen movies. He remembered a class he'd had in high school about warfare. It was gruesome. War was something to pretend to like, but when it became a reality, it was downright scary. Mark knew he just would not be able to go to war. He needed a new plan.

Mark thought about the Rhine, which he was familiar with from the few short walks he had taken. If he planned things right, he could jump in the river and catch a ride with one of the cargo boats. Maybe he could work on a boat and go to Sweden or Norway and hitch a ride on a boat back to Canada or something. Michigan was a border state, so he could find a way to get back home from time to time.

Being a deserter was a serious thing. Mark knew this. But so was war. The idea of having someone shooting at you or being blown up was not Mark's idea of fun. He knew he couldn't do this. This was nuts in his mind. His cousin had been in Vietnam, and Mark had no desire to go back to the jungle after they had already left. His mind was made up. He was not going to the party he'd been invited to.

"All right! Listen up! Form your units and fall in!" the first sergeant yelled out. "Captain, the company is ready," Mark could hear him say as the captain took his place at the front of the company.

"Men, we have been put on a yellow alert. That means there is a possibility of going into some kind of military engagement. There is also the greater possibility of being ordered to stand down. In that case, we will all put our gear back on the shelves and go back to our normal routine. This particular alert is for some action going on in Greece. For the moment that is all I can tell you. To be truthful, that is all I know. I will now order all of you to relax and visit with one another, but stay in the meeting area. I am waiting on word, so I want everyone here when it is time. Lieutenants, keep track of your men. Allow bathroom breaks. Men, smoke 'em if you have 'em. That is all."

With that, the men all went back to what they were doing: talking, thinking, and rechecking all their gear. Mark went back to his spot to think some more.

"Hey, what are you doing over here all by yourself?" Jeremy asked.

"Oh, just thinking. Are you ready to go to war?" Mark asked with a distant look in his eyes.

"No." Jeremy laughed. "Why? Do you really think we're going?"

"Think about it," Mark said with reserve. "Is there anything about our lives here that has gone like it should?"

"Good point, but I still don't think we're going to war," Jeremy said with confidence.

"I hope you're right." Mark let out a heavy sigh. "I don't think I could do it."

"Well, with any luck—and you have to admit you have been lucky—we won't have to find out." Jeremy smiled.

They sat quietly smoking cigarettes and thinking about the idea of going to war. Finally, Mark broke the silence again. "Funny how war seemed so inviting when I was watching it on TV and reading about it in the classroom. Now that I could be face-to-face with it, it's not so cool anymore."

"Man, you gotta let it go," Jeremy said quietly.

"How? I mean, here we are, waiting for it to happen or go away for the moment—you know, like a volcano that acts like it's going to erupt. First few times it subsides, but eventually it does blow. This will too. I can feel it," Mark said, a distant, scared look in his eyes.

Jeremy could only nod his head as if he agreed, but inside he began to think maybe, just maybe, Mark was beginning to lose it. Maybe it was paranoia. Jeremy hoped he was wrong but decided to stick close to Mark in case he had to pull him back to reality. He wasn't sure just how easy that would be.

After an hour the captain asked the first sergeant to recall formation. "Men! Fall in!"

The company reformed as the men took their places in their respective platoons. Mark found his spot, but his mind was still planning out the map he was going to follow once he had the chance to go. Maybe it would be when they were issued their weapons. Maybe it would be when they were loading up the vehicles to move out. It would be easy for everyone to think he was in a different truck.

"Men," the captain began, "we have been ordered to stand down. I am happy to say the situation has been temporarily resolved. Pray that it stays that way and there is no need to go to war. No one wants that if it can be avoided. Thank you, gentlemen. You are dismissed."

Everyone began filing back into the barracks. Mark headed back to his room just like everyone else. Once his gear was put back in place, he sat down on his bunk and began to think about what his mind had just gone through. Was he a coward?

The horror of that question made him feel cold inside.

He began to shiver as if he were in subzero weather. Jeremy was just finishing putting away his own stuff when he noticed. "Hey, man, what's wrong?" Jeremy asked as he walked to Mark's bunk and sat down.

"Nothing," Mark answered very unconvincingly.

"Ah, I always wondered what nothing looked like," Jeremy replied, completely sure there was something very wrong. "Did you use something that's making you sick again?"

"No, man!" Mark answered, irritated with himself.

"Okay, but I know there is something wrong." With that, Jeremy got up and went about his own business.

After a short silence, Mark began, "Ever wonder if you're a coward? I think I might be a coward."

Jeremy smiled, glad they were finally getting to the heart of the matter. "Why do you say that?"

"Because all I could think about the whole time was running. It was just a drill, and all I could think of to do was run." Mark stared at the floor, paralyzed by his own fears.

"And you think no one else out there was thinking the same thing?" Jeremy said, wanting to share his own feelings without sounding patronizing.

"I don't know what anyone else was thinking. I'm not sure I care. What I do care about is what I was thinking and feeling. I always thought I was made of more than that. Do you think I would have run if I had the chance?" Mark let his thoughts run rampant.

"Truthfully? No. I was busy thinking the same thing. I had a plan to hitch a ride to Karlsruhe and use my Euro pass to get to England. From there I was going to fly back to the States and find my way back home. But then, I thought, I only have a few months left, so they probably wouldn't make me stay long anyway," Jeremy said.

"Mine was a little more wild. I was going to get to the Rhine, jump in, and catch a boat to Norway or Sweden and then catch another boat to Canada. Michigan borders Canada. I figured they would be looking for me since I was a deserter." Mark laughed.

"You're right. That is crazy. I don't think you would make it in the Rhine. That's kind of a fast-current river. Certainly deep. I don't see you doing all that," Jeremy said.

"Well, the point is, I had a plan to run. I think that makes me a coward."

"Well then," Jeremy said, sitting down beside him in thought. "That makes us both cowards, because I had a plan too. Know what? I think it's time for a bowl. We need to chill out and not be so hard on ourselves. No one can say what is right or wrong when it comes to war. The notion of killing someone or being killed is not normal thinking."

Mark nodded. "You're right. It's time for a bowl." With that, Mark dug out his bowl, and Jeremy prepared his own stash of hash. While waiting for Jeremy to finish, Mark put on some music, and they both sat on Jeremy's bunk and shared the hash for some time of relaxing and thinking.

The next morning Mark went to his session with Marylyn. Once both were seated Mark spoke up. "Do you think using drugs can make a person a coward?"

Surprised by the question, Marylyn began, "So what brings this up?"

"We had an alert yesterday. All I could think of was to run. It was just an alert, and all I wanted to do was go home. Is that normal?" Mark asked.

"Yes. I can't think of anyone who is normal that would want to go to war," Marylyn quickly replied. "The whole idea of death, whether it be yours or the person you are afraid you would have to kill, is revolting to anyone who has a conscience."

"Really? Are you sure? Or are you just saying that to make me feel good?" Mark was looking for the truth, hoping she was right.

"I'm sure. To tell you the truth, I'm happy that's how you feel." She smiled as she leaned forward with her hands held together on her lap. Her eyes met Mark's, giving him a warm sensation he wished he'd had the day before when he felt so cold.

"I think you're right." He smiled. "I don't know if I would've run. All I know is the idea was very tempting."

"It was just another form of escape. Listen, I know we have not talked a lot about this idea. You have to understand. It is very normal for a person to want to escape any kind of situation that hurts or causes excessive discomfort. It's not wanting to escape that is wrong; it's how you escape. The reason drugs are wrong is the real harm it does to your body and the way you think. The idea of wanting out of the situation you are in is not only normal but also healthy." Marylyn was now sounding like the therapist she had always wanted to be for Mark.

"You know, we have never really talked about your childhood, why you were living on your own like you were while you were in high school. We've never really talked about your family. Maybe it's time we did that," Marylyn suggested, maintaining eye contact.

Mark thought about what she was saying. He looked deep into her eyes, trying not to be distracted by his infatuation with her. It was not to be distracted by her long, shiny hair as it hung down past her shoulders when she leaned forward. It seemed so natural to Mark to steal glances of her feminine figure. This was something he didn't see in the course of a normal day. He almost felt like he was a prisoner in some kind of jail—or like he was somehow violating her. Yet he couldn't stop.

Forcing himself to think about what she wanted, Mark finally answered, "It's just that it's hard to trust someone—anyone—with all my 'dirty' secrets. Maybe I'm not the one who created my past, but I'm the one my past is about. Trust seems to be a very hard thing for me."

"That's understandable. I guess what you have to weigh is whether the risk is worth the reward for where it will take you. Of course, maybe that's what you're really afraid of. Maybe you're afraid of what you will discover about yourself. I think what you will discover is that you are a good person with the same kind of challenges everyone else has to face every day. I think you will find out that good people make bad mistakes. Making a mistake does not make you a bad person. It just makes you human," Marylyn said.

The words pierced Mark's heart and soul. He was hearing things he had never heard before. Could it really be true that he was a good person? A good person who has made some bad mistakes just because he was human? These questions had been haunting him long before he had ever even considered using drugs. What Mark was beginning to understand now was that it was his past that made it so easy to make the turn. That was a lot to take in.

Noticing the time, Marylyn said, "Well, at least think about it. Our time is done for the day. I do have other clients—none as important as you, of course," she said jokingly.

Mark smiled as he began to bring himself back to the real world. "Yeah, I know what you mean. I am pretty important." They both laughed, and Mark got up to leave the room. He stopped in the doorway. Turning, he said, "I think you're right. I know you think you are"—he smiled again—"but I think it might be time to do that." Mark left feeling good that in her eyes he was normal.

Back in the room Mark found Jeremy and Jason smoking a bowl. They were seated in front of the tapestry talking when Mark came in. "What are you guys talking about?"

"Oh, just the same as before. Wondering what Christ wanted us to know. Wondering if everything was true about Him why He doesn't make Himself known now." Jeremy looked at Jason as he spoke.

Mark chuckled, in part at himself and in part at his friends. "Really? You don't know why?" he asked.

"Know what?" Jason looked at Mark with a hint of disdain.

Mark smiled at him anyway. "He makes Himself known to us every day." He wasn't sure where this was all coming from, but Mark kept on talking, hoping it would all make sense. "You see Him in each other's eyes every time you trust each other. You see Him in the way things work out every time you tell the truth or trust Him to help you out of the trouble you've put yourself in. I see Him every time He saves my life or protects me from myself. He is real. He is here right now. He always tries to intervene for us when we trust Him to do so. At least that's what I believe now that I have been trusting Him to help me. Every day He opens my eyes more and more to my own value and weaknesses."

Jeremy and Jason sat and listened without speaking. After a moment they nodded as if in agreement and started to share the bowl with Mark. Then, almost as an afterthought, Jason asked, "So you really believe that? "

"Yeah, I do. Why?" Mark asked, knowing Jason was going to say something that would cause tension. That was just the way Jason was sometimes.

"Well, I was just thinking, if you really believe all that, why is it you don't always act it?" Jason's words went straight to the heart.

"I think about that too," Mark started, knowing he had to be honest, at least with himself. "Thing is, it's easy to say it and easy to believe it when it's not put to the test. Then, when the test comes, I forget everything I believe. Not just that, but everything. It's like I panic or something. I admit I'm frustrated with it all. I'm thinking this faith thing isn't like magic. It takes real work and a lot of courage. I'm trying, now more than ever. That's all I can say."

The rest of the night was quiet and serene. They spent the time listening to music, smoking hash, and talking about philosophy as if they would change the world with their infinite knowledge.

A few days later it began to occur to Mark that he had not heard anything of Robby. They were headed to breakfast when Mark decided to ask, "Jeremy, have you heard anything about Robby? I haven't seen him for a while now. Haven't heard anything about him either."

"Not really. The last I'd heard he was missing," Jeremy said as they walked stride for stride toward the mess hall.

"Oh yeah, I'd forgotten about that. No one has heard anything yet that you know of?" Mark asked.

"No, why?" Jeremy said.

"Just curious. I just realized it's been a while is all." Mark let it go as they entered the building for a hot meal.

It was midmorning at the warehouse, and Mark was busy going over the inventory of the yard stock. Jeremy walked up to him. "I think I know what's going on with Robby," he said quietly. "I heard he went AWOL for sure."

"I had heard that before, but you would think there would be more news by now. I wonder if he's okay," Mark said as he contemplated the possible fates a man could meet going AWOL in a foreign country.

"It's hard to say. Robby wasn't exactly the most predictable person I ever met," Jeremy replied, looking at the ground as if he spied some kind of trinket.

"You don't suppose he was mixed up in any of that stuff that Chris was doing, do you?" Mark asked after giving the whole thing more thought.

"They were friends. Didn't you say you met them both at the same time?"

"Yeah, but I always thought it was odd that those two would hang out together. I just can't see Chris trusting someone like Robby. His mouth was never shut." Mark smiled.

"That's for sure," Jeremy agreed. "Still, they do say opposites attract." They both laughed at that.

After work Mark decided to go for another walk to the river. It had been a while, and he liked how the sun would shine on the water in the early evening. The walk felt good as the wind swept through Mark's hair. He liked walking almost as much as he'd liked to run when he was in high school.

He finally reached the water at the end of the road. Mark decided to sit down, letting his legs dangle off the edge of the road as he watched the current run. He smiled inside at the thought of being able to sit at the end of a road and literally see the river flow where the road used to be. His mind began to wander back to what he imagined it had been like during the war when the bridge was blown up.

Mark thought about whether the German army had intentionally blown the bridge up to slow down the advancing Allied army. Maybe the Allies had blown the bridge up to slow down the German retreat, or, perhaps, to keep the Germans from attempting a counterattack.

He was very deep in his thoughts when he saw it. At first it was like a flash of light off the water's surface. Intrigued, Mark studied the spot on the water's surface more intensely. It was on his side of the river off to his right, closer to the expressway that now crossed the river. It looked just like a head bobbing up and down with the waves as the current flowed past. Suddenly, Mark felt a cold shiver run down his spine. Was it really a body? How could it be? It was a steep decline down the bank to where it was lain. Mark was more afraid of what it was than the actual climb down. Even so, the climb down would cause him to fall headlong into the river. Mark thought about how funny it was that a few days ago that prospect had been very inviting. Now, though, it was something to dread.

He wasn't completely sure what it was, and he really didn't want to know. Still, he considered how much it looked like Robby. That would be too much of a coincidence. Mark thought about how easy it would be to dump a body here. No one ever went here, and it was too far from the bridge to be visible to people flying across in their cars and trucks. It could take forever for anyone to discover a body that way.

If it was Robby, why was he lying dead in a river? Could he have committed suicide? Was he done away with just like Jimmy? Mark was beginning to feel more and more like this whole place was more dangerous than it was worth. While he was not sure what he had seen was even a body, the whole idea was revolting, and he needed to find a way out. It was definitely time to go.

Mark walked quickly all the way back to the barracks, praying for God to get him out of Germany. He was hoping to never hear anything about a body being found in the river. He made a decision to never return to that spot again. What used to be a place of refuge had now had been violated, even if it was only in his mind. Mark confirmed in his own heart that it was time for him to go home. Ready or not, he just had to go.

For the next few days Mark went through the motions of working at the warehouse. He kept trying to find things to do so that his mind didn't bring back any unwanted memories. He had even decided not to ever talk about it with any of his friends—not even Jeremy. He did the only thing he could think of to get help. Whenever he was alone, he would actually kneel down and pray that what he'd seen in the river hadn't been what it looked like. He prayed the door would be opened for him to go home early—with an honorable discharge, of course.

Friday morning was going just like the two days before it. Mark was staying busy with his work pretending everything was normal. One of the sergeants approached him. "Hey, Welch, are you busy?"

"Yeah, what do you need?" Mark answered as he kept his eyes on his clipboard.

"I need you to go to the first sergeant's office and see the orderly," he replied in a casual voice.

"Nice," Mark replied. "Am I in trouble again?"

"Nah," the sergeant answered. "Just more routine garbage. Just go and do whatever they ask."

Mark finished up his immediate task and walked to the first sergeant's office. There he saw one of the orderlies behind a desk. "I was told to report here, but wasn't told why," Mark said after he got the orderly's attention.

"What's your name?" he asked, looking at a list on a clipboard.

"Mark Welch," he replied.

"Let's see … ah, here you are. We need a urine test. Just routine," the orderly said. The orderly grabbed a bottle and the paperwork and walked with Mark down to the latrine. Mark found a urinal and filled the bottle as the orderly watched to make sure everything was done properly to keep the test legitimate.

Once done, Mark went back to work at the warehouse, not even thinking about the hash he had been smoking. It was just no longer a worry for Mark after making his decision to trust God to take care of him. After seeing the image down at the river, nothing seemed to matter anymore now.

The weekend went by with the usual smoking dope and eating meals. No one had any money to go to town. It was in between paydays. Mark barely had enough to go to his favorite hideaway for his quiet meals. He scraped up enough to give a decent tip and went to see if he could figure out how he was going to go home. No plan ever emerged.

The following Monday the same sergeant came to

see Mark at the warehouse. "I guess you are becoming popular at the first sergeant's office, Welch."

"Why do you say that?" Mark asked, intrigued with the statement.

"They want you there again, this time right away. Put down whatever you're doing and report now," the sergeant said. "I am to escort you there to be sure you arrive in a timely fashion," he said in a mocking voice.

Mark put down his clipboard and walked quietly with the sergeant, wondering what it was all about. It seemed too fast for the urine test. He took a seat in the waiting area and stared at the wall, thinking about everything and anything until the silence was broken. "Specialist Welch," the first sergeant called out. "Report to the captain's office."

Mark walked into the captain's office and stood at attention until he heard the order for at ease. "Do you know why you are here today?" the captain asked, this time looking straight into Mark's eyes.

"No, sir," Mark answered, becoming more relaxed with the whole idea of being in the office.

"Well, son, it appears you have regressed in your progress with the drug program. Mind telling me what's going on?" the captain asked.

"Going on, sir? I'm not sure what you mean," Mark answered, not knowing what to say.

"I was afraid you would take that stand. You have a good record with the exception of the positive drug tests. The problem is, the drug tests are not definitive proof that you are using drugs. They only point very strongly to that conclusion. That is why I have the authorization to make this offer to you. It is a one-time offer, and you must make a decision in a timely fashion. We have a new program that offers an honorable discharge, but you will be barred from reenlistment. It is called a Chapter Sixteen. If, down the road, you want to reenlist, you will have to have a letter of recommendation from a minister, a psychologist, and a medical doctor stating that you are fit for service. Do you understand everything I have stated so far?" the captain questioned, his eyes now directed straight into Mark's, burning into his mind.

"Yes, sir, I think I do," Mark answered quietly as he considered everything he was hearing.

"Good," the captain continued. "I am offering you a Chapter Sixteen honorable discharge so that you may get on with your life under other conditions. Perhaps this will give you a chance to get and keep your life cleaned up and have a chance to make a life for yourself. What do you think, young man? Would you like to take this offer?"

"Can I have time to think on it? Maybe talk to my family?" Mark countered. He knew he had no family to really confer with, but he didn't want to make his decision until after he had time to take it all in. It was a lot for Mark to process.

"Yes," the captain answered. "But remember, you only have just so much time. I am not sure exactly how much time there is, but I do know it is short. I will try to find out what the time requirement is. You take a week or two to make up your mind. We will talk again soon. Dismissed."

Mark left the office, amazed that the answer to his prayer to go home had so quickly been provided. Then he remembered the conversation he'd had with Jason just a short time ago and knew he was right. God was with him in everything. God was with him all the time. If only he had felt God's presence down at the river. The memory was still haunting him.

Chapter Seventeen

Mark returned to the warehouse with his mind full of thoughts of going home. How wonderful it would feel to finally get out of the whirlwind he had been in for so long! It was hard to tell just how long Mark had been fantasizing when it hit him. Home to where? They usually asked for an address to ship all your belongings. What address would he give them? Where was it he thought he was going? *Nice*, Mark thought. He was going from one dilemma to another.

He thought it was a good thing he'd asked for time to think about it. There was still a lot to get figured out. Right in the middle of his thinking, Mark heard a voice. "So what did they want?" It was Jeremy.

"They want to send me home, Jeremy," Mark said. "My problem is—home to where?"

Jeremy stood beside him as they thought about it in silence. "Well," Jeremy said, "why not where your brother is? At least you have an address. Where is he living, anyway?"

"Hmm, with my aunt," Mark said. "I'm not sure

I'm welcome there. That's the last place I ran from. Of course, it was a long time ago. Things change in time, I've heard. I don't know. I guess I could call him and see what he says."

"Why did you leave there?" Jeremy asked out of curiosity.

"You know, it's been so long I really don't remember. When you're that young, it seems like everything is so critical. Things that seemed so important and then just don't seem so important anymore. In fact, they seem so meaningless I don't remember what they were," Mark said, sounding like an old man conversing with his grandchildren.

They went back to work to finish out the day. Once back in the room, Jeremy broke out the bowl while Mark sat at the desk to think. By the time the bowl was ready, Mark had made up his mind, "Do you remember the other day when I went for my walk? The one I take to the river?" Mark began.

"Yeah, why?" Jeremy asked as he prepared to light the bowl.

"Well, I can't swear to it, but I think I know what happened to Robby. Thing is, I don't really know it. But wow, I can't believe how much it looked like a body. Not just anybody, but Robby," Mark confessed.

"Are you serious?" Jeremy just about dropped the bowl.

"I wish I wasn't, but yeah," Mark went on. "I was sitting on the pavement enjoying the sunset when a gleam of light to my right caught my attention. It was between me and the expressway just on the water edge, too steep to climb down. To be honest, I didn't want to climb down. If it was Robby, then it was too late to help him. If it wasn't, then there was no point in taking the risk. Either way I didn't need or want to know."

"I don't know what to think." Jeremy stared at the floor. It was difficult to let it all settle in his mind. "You thought you saw a body?"

"Yeah, I think I did, and I never want to see anything like it again," Mark said, staring at the floor as well. "Do you remember when Jason asked why I don't act like I believe?"

"Yeah," Jeremy said quietly. "I remember."

"I prayed to God to get me out of Germany with an honorable discharge. The captain just offered me an honorable discharge. The only catch is, I will be barred from reenlisting if I ever want to return to the army. I would need a letter of recommendation from a psychiatrist, a minister, and a medical doctor."

"Well, you know that could never happen." Jeremy smiled. "There isn't a psychiatrist on earth that would think you were sane if you wanted to reenlist."

They both started to laugh. Jeremy got up and put on an album to go with the hash and what was looking like good news. "So you're going home. The final quest to being in this place. Going home." Jeremy smiled even bigger and took another toke off the bowl.

"Yep, it looks like I'm going home—if I can ever figure out where home is, anyway," Mark said, staring at the floor again as he took his turn at the bowl.

Mark thought about the whole problem of not having a forwarding address. It would be okay if it was just a case of mail. The problem was that this time he was the mail. He could send some of his things to his sister's house, but he knew there wasn't any room there for him. Anyway, what good would it do to send his things to one place if he was going to another? The real problem had to be solved.

There was only one thing left to do. He had to call his aunt. It wasn't like he hated her. Nor was the problem that she had no love for him. The problem was her husband. His uncle had no love for anyone. Sometimes, Mark thought, he didn't even love himself.

His aunt was his mother's sister and had no children of her own. They had made an agreement that if his mother had ever died she would take care of the kids. When he was twelve, they tried it, but his dad hadn't been all that keen on it. His uncle was miserable with everyone for the whole year. So he and his brother had to go back—back to the life of mistreatment and abuse. That made Mark angry and started everything that made it so difficult to talk to his aunt now. He felt betrayed. Even though Mark understood the whole thing with his uncle, he couldn't get the idea that he was betrayed out of his mind or his heart.

Maybe it was time Mark learned to give all that over to God as well. It was an idea that Mark had thought about before, but now it had come to a head. Perhaps he just had to put aside his own selfish ideas and give it all to God. That was not an easy thing for Mark. Still, he knew it was time. It was time to make a phone call and turn a new page.

A Scripture suddenly came to his mind. He didn't know where it could be found, but he knew the words. He thought it might be Psalms 119:105: "Trust in the Lord with all your heart and lean not on your own understanding. In all your ways acknowledge Him and He will direct your path." It was time to trust and acknowledge God.

The next morning after formation, Mark decided to talk to his sergeant. "Hey, serge, is it okay if I go to the office to make a call home today?"

"What do you need to make a phone call for?" the serge asked, knowing Mark had no real home to speak of.

"I just need to call home. I need to talk about the possibility of going to see my aunt," Mark replied. Then thinking about it, Mark asked, "Can I talk to you in private?"

"Yeah, sure, what's on your mind?" the sergeant answered as they moved to a more quiet area to talk.

"Do you know about the offer the captain made to me?" Mark asked.

"Why don't you tell me?" serge encouraged him.

"He said I can have an honorable discharge if I take a Chapter Sixteen," Mark said quietly, looking around to make sure no one was paying them any attention.

"So what do you want to do?" the sergeant asked.

"I don't know. For one thing, I don't even know if I have a home to go to. That's why I want to call my aunt. I kind of need to sort things out," Mark replied. "I need help to see my way through this."

"I understand," the sergeant said, looking in his eyes. "It's about a six-hour difference to eastern standard time. So figure out what time it will be there when you call, and just let me know when you head over."

"Thanks, I need the help." Mark was grateful for the permission. He figured it out that when it was three o'clock in the afternoon, or 1500 hours, it would be nine o'clock in the morning at his aunt's house. Not knowing what else to do, Mark found a corner in the warehouse and prayed to God for the right words to say and hoped his aunt would be home.

The whole day his stomach was all tied up in knots at the thought of calling. On the one hand, he was excited that he would be leaving the army. On the other hand, nothing had changed between the time he'd enlisted and now. So what was the advantage of leaving? Then the list began to grow in his mind. The advantages to leaving were getting away from the drugs, having a chance to live longer, and maybe, if he lived with his aunt, being more exposed to who God really is. And maybe, just maybe, he would finally figure out what he needed to do with the rest of his life. The ever-elusive answer.

It was finally three o'clock. Mark let the sergeant know he was going to the office to make the call. The walk seemed a lot longer than normal as Mark kept trying to think of what he would say. How could he ask to go there to live after all these years? He hadn't even written her. What if she said no? In that moment, Mark realized that what he was really afraid of was if she said yes.

He was finally at the counter of the office. Seeing the orderly, he spoke, "Hey, is the phone available for me to call home?"

"Um, hold on. Let me check," he answered as he got up to check with the first sergeant. A few short moments later, he came back. "Yeah, go ahead."

Mark went around the end of the counter and picked up the phone. He knew there wouldn't be a lot of privacy, but it would have to do. His hands began to shake as he tried to dial the number. The first two tries were all messed up. He kept getting the numbers wrong or not spinning the rotating wheel far enough. Finally, the third time was the charm. The phone was ringing.

A familiar voice came over the line. "Hello? Who is this?"

"Hello, Auntie. It's me, Mark. How are you?" Mark could hear his voice, but it seemed like it was somebody else.

"Mark? How are you? It's been so long. I've been praying that I would hear from you," she said very excitedly.

"Oh yeah?" Mark continued. "Well, I'm fine. I'm doing good. In fact, I'm doing so well they are going to let me out early." He lied, not knowing what else to say to explain him coming home so soon.

"Why would they do that?" she asked, concerned.

"You know how they pulled out all the troops from Vietnam? Well, they need to have a place to put a lot of them. Some of us who volunteered were offered an early honorable discharge to help make room for the ones coming back who are making the army their career." Mark hoped this would make sense.

"Oh, wow. That sounds wonderful. I'm happy for you." Her voiced sounded like she meant it.

"Well, here's the thing, Auntie. I haven't had time to get ready to have a place to go."

She cut him off. "Don't worry about that. You always have a place here until you can get back on your feet. You just come home and take some time to reacquaint yourself with home."

This all sounded too good to be true. It took him a minute to get his mind wrapped around it all. "Thanks, Auntie, I appreciate that. Listen, this is the phone in my captain's office, so I can't stay and talk. I will write you the details as I find them out."

"That sounds good. You do that. Take care of yourself. I will be looking for your letter," she said with energy and love in her voice.

"Okay. Bye, Auntie," Mark said as he prepared to go.

"Bye-bye," she replied, and Mark hung up the phone before any more could be said or heard. It was all too easy to be believable. He'd really thought it would all be much harder. He was sure he would be held accountable for some strange accusation, but he didn't know what it would be. He was excited and confused at the same time. There was only one thing left to do: party.

Mark went to his room, hoping to see Jeremy. On his way up the stairs he began thinking about how his aunt had acted. There was no consideration at all about his uncle. That seemed strange to Mark. There was no way his uncle would allow him to even stay the night, let alone as long as he needed. Something was up, and Mark didn't know what it was.

Just as he'd hoped, Jeremy was in the room. "I called my aunt," Mark said. "She actually said I could stay as long as I wanted."

"That's cool," Jeremy replied, hoping it was all good.

"Yeah, that's the problem," Mark said as he found a seat and thought about it.

"What do you mean?" Jeremy inquired, looking confused.

"Well, it's just that my uncle hates everyone. After my brother and I stayed with them for a year when I was a kid, he said we could never stay there again. So why would it be okay now?"

Jeremy just listened quietly as Mark started to stare at the floor, thinking it all over. After a little bit Mark finally broke the silence. "I think it's time to celebrate. You think we can get ahold of anything good? I mean, it's not like they're going to give me another physical or anything. They already tested me positive. Might as well prove them right. Right?"

Jeremy laughed. "I'll see what I can find. I'm sure somebody has something we can get." With that Jeremy left the room on a quest to celebrate a buddy going home, although it was still unclear how long it could all take.

While Jeremy was gone, Mark began to think about that. Maybe he was jumping the gun looking for a home so soon. Then again, it was still important to know he had a place to go. It looked like everything was coming together.

Jeremy came back with a smile on his face. "Guess what I got?"

Mark couldn't help smiling. "What do you have?"

"I've got a lead on some acid. Purple microdot. That should put some color in your world," Jeremy said, sounding like he'd just found gold.

Mark didn't really care for acid anymore, but he didn't mind it either. For one thing, it was cheaper and lasted a lot longer than any other high. Another reason was best expressed by the old saying "A little dot will do ya." It was kind of corny, but it was true. Easy to do, cheap, long lasting—what was not to like? "So when do we get it?"

"Friday. That way we have all evening to enjoy it." Jeremy had it all planned out.

"I was thinking of calling home again on Saturday," Mark said, thinking how strange the words sounded to his ears. It was funny how things worked out. One minute he was just another homeless bum, and the next he had a bedroom in a middle-class home in rural Michigan. It still blew his mind.

"It'll work out. You can sleep till afternoon. By that time it will be morning there and you can call after we celebrate your new ticket and home." Jeremy had it all figured out.

They got ready for supper and went on with their day. Mark spent the rest of the evening letting it all sink in. He had a home. Even if he only stayed there a little while, it would be long enough for him to get a grip on his life the way he had planned on doing in the army but failed. Maybe with the help of his brother and aunt he could do what he couldn't do by himself. He had a home.

Friday was there fast. The rest of the week had gone by with thoughts flying through his head. It seemed like minutes after formation that Mark was going back to the room to get ready for the party. Jeremy was close behind him as they changed into civilian rags.

"I'm gonna go get the acid. Be back in a few minutes," Jeremy said as he hurried out the door.

Mark looked up from doing his shoes. "Okay, I guess I'll be here."

Just as Mark was done redressing, several of the guys came in the room. Everyone was talking at once. Mark just looked up with a blank look on his face, wondering what was going on. He looked to Jeremy to answer his question. Finally seeing his familiar smile, he asked, "Jeremy, what's going on?"

"Just getting the party started." Jeremy smiled. "Here's your hit."

Mark took the hit in his hand and looked around to see if anyone else was taking any yet. "So what's the plan while we trip through the rainbow?" Mark asked.

"Thought we'd start with the movie. They're showing *Jack and the Beanstalk*," Jeremy answered, getting his jacket.

Mark noticed the others already had jackets on. "So has everyone else already took their hits?"

"Yep. How about you? Are you going to be playing catch-up?" Jeremy asked as he headed for the door.

"I feel like that's what I've been doing since we got to the room." Mark chuckled as he put the hit under his tongue. He grabbed his jacket and ran to catch up with the others after locking the door. They were off to the movies.

They walked and joked all the way to the theater. They paid for their tickets, found their way into the auditorium, and sat as a group. They were all excited to see the animated movie in color as no one else would see. They were all anticipating how the acid would accentuate the colors. While they talked among themselves, the lights dimmed and the previews rolled on the screen.

Mark thought back to the last time he watched a movie there. He made a mental note that if he had to use the latrine he needed to make sure he used the correct door to rejoin his friends. It finally began to happen. The acid was kicking in. Mark decided he was going to enjoy his last trip in Germany. On the one hand, he was starting a new life with God, but on the other hand, he was still stuck in his old world.

While unconnected thoughts wandered through his mind, outlandish colors began to unfurl before his eyes as the screen took all his attention. It was as if nothing else existed but the movie living so vigorously in front of him. It was very enticing. Mark was part of the world he was watching.

The plot of the movie was living its way through Mark's being when all of a sudden he saw the Devil. The Devil was a red creature with two cow-type horns coming out of his head. He had a long, red tail with a type of arrowhead at the end. He carried a pitchfork just like all the cartoons Mark had seen of the Devil. It was ridiculous, and yet it was very real.

The image didn't seem to have anything to do with the movie, but Mark figured it was because of the acid. He thought that the Devil was really some other character that his mind just made look like a devil. That made sense to him as his cognitive wits were still about him.

Then Mark realized the Devil seemed to be talking directly to him. He hadn't been paying any attention to his words because he was so involved in the colors and motions. However, the Devil demanded his attention. It sounded like he was yelling at him. "Hey! I'm talking to you! Pay attention!"

"Are you talking to me?" Mark asked in a quiet tone, hoping no one else heard him talk to his "imaginary" friend.

"Of course I'm talking to you. Who else would I be shouting at? You don't think anyone else in this auditorium can hear me, do you?" He seemed to look directly at Mark. It was starting to feel scary. Mark was sure that none of this was right.

"Why are you talking to me? What do you want from me?" Mark asked, getting more and more concerned about his animated visitor.

"What do you think I want? What I've always wanted. What else is there besides souls?" The creature appeared to be getting closer and closer. It was no longer on the screen, but on the tops of the seats in front of Mark.

"Why is my soul so important?" Mark asked, clutching his heart with his hands.

"It's no more important than any of the others, but for now it's the most available one. Does it matter to you? You didn't seem to have any use for it at any other time in your life. It's not like you'll miss it," the creature said, trying to sound persuasive.

"I know that's how it seems, but that's not how it really is. So forget it. I'm not interested in giving up anything to you, least all my soul. This whole thing is nuts. None of this can be true. Be gone!" To Mark's surprise, it was gone. Now it was like the whole conversation had been in his head. Mark was relieved to think that it was all just part of the trip. Yet there was a lingering doubt.

Mark decided to leave the movie and go back to his room and looked for others to join him and. All of a sudden being on acid wasn't something he ever wanted to do again. He left the movie theater and noticed everything around him seemed normal. The colors were just as they should've been. The sounds were just like any other day. The people around him were just as they should've been. The only difference was they were still feeling the effects of the acid, but Mark felt like it had run its course for him. That was all right with Mark.

Donnie, Jason, and Darrin were the ones who went with Mark to his room. Darrin was the most experienced with acid and decided to talk to Mark first. "So you all right now? Are you still tripping and freaking?"

"Actually, I'm not doing either now. Should the acid already be done in me?" Mark asked, hoping it was possible.

"It's hard to say. Depends on how good the hits were. It's always possible to get a bad hit." Darrin smiled, trying to give Mark hope.

"Well, that would explain why I wasn't feeling it the whole walk back, but why was I having a conversation with the Devil?" Mark asked, still looking for a reasonable explanation.

"Man that happens all the time. I wouldn't worry about that. I'd worry if it kept on going on once the high was over. Then you're in real trouble." Darrin laughed, trying to make a joke out of it all to put everyone at ease.

Mark sat for a little bit. Darrin was convinced he was all right, so he left the room to go about his own business. Mark continued to relax on his bunk. He was getting tired of demonic visions, dead bodies, falls into holes, and drug addiction. It was all past getting old for him.

Then he saw a demon again. It was floating in the far corner of the room, diagonally across from the door. The creature had several horns coming out of its head. The head itself looked like a cross between a dinosaur and a reptile. It had wings made out of reptile flesh. It was thick with large, disproportionate muscles. Its teeth were large, and saliva mixed with blood dripped off them. Its eyes were bloodshot, wide-open, and fixed on Mark. The demon's smile was sinister. It didn't speak, but from time to time, it laughed at Mark as if it knew a dark secret that would destroy him. There was a darkness surrounding it as if a cloud of death was always with it. It kept floating above him, its wings twitching back and forth and its eyes always fixed on Mark. It had large, clawed hands that would reach out from time to time as if trying to grab Mark and snatch him away.

"It's here again!" Mark shouted and pointed at the corner. Jason and Donnie looked but didn't see anything. Mark cowered as he scrambled for the door.

"What are you talking about?" Jason asked, almost frightened himself. "There's nothing there."

"You don't see it?" Mark shouted with uncontrollable fear. He had crunched himself into the corner by the door. It was now impossible for him to open the door. His own body was in the way. Mark was becoming frozen with fear. "It's there! It's right there!" Mark pointed at it as he sat in a ball as far away as he could without leaving the room.

"I think it's just the acid playing tricks on your mind," Donnie said, trying to get Mark to calm down.

"Oh yeah? Well I don't! I am as sober as the neighbors are! I'm telling you, it's in this room!" Mark was in the worst panic of his life.

"What do you want me to do?" Donnie asked, hoping that something would bring Mark out of it.

"Tell me you see it! Tell me I'm not crazy!" Mark was certain it was real. "I'm telling you, it's real! I think he's here for my soul. It's a spirit, so you can't see it. I've heard drugs can open the door to such things. Go away! God, please make it leave me alone!" Mark shouted at the figure in the corner.

It was gone. Just as suddenly as it appeared, it was just gone. The room felt at peace. It was safe again. Mark blinked his eyes several times and started looking at the corner with suspicion. "It's gone," he said quietly. "It just ... disappeared."

"Are you sure?" Jason said, becoming convinced the whole thing had been real.

"No, all I know is I can't see it. Look around. See if it just went to a different spot," Mark pleaded.

"What? We could never see it to begin with! How are we going to know if it just moved?" Donnie asked in a panic.

"Okay, okay," Mark conceded. "I'll look. I gotta tell you, I don't feel like it's here. I can't sense it. I think it's gone."

"What did it look like?" Jason asked.

Mark knew his answer was going to send Jason on one of his high-riding responses, but what else could he say? "It looked half reptile and half dinosaur with horns and wings. Its muscles were way out of proportion. But I think it can look anyway he wants to. I think it was just playing with me. In the theater it said it wanted my soul."

"What?" Jason said, before heading in the opposite direction Mark thought he would. "It was in the theater? I didn't know that when we left. What else did it tell you?"

"I asked it what it wanted with me," Mark began, "and it said it wanted my soul. I asked why me? Why not someone else? Why was I so special? It said I wasn't special; I was just more available. So I told it I wasn't available and told it to leave. It left."

"But then it showed up here," Jason added. "Are you sure it wasn't just something from the acid?"

"I think that's what it wants everyone to think. I think that's why it only shows up when I use acid and not hash. It's smart. It wants me divided from all your help. That's what I think, anyway," Mark answered, still shaking from the whole experience.

"Well, I'm outta here," Donnie said, fear in his voice. "I don't need any demons haunting me just because I'm available."

Jeremy walked in the room. "What's going on now?"

Mark looked at him, fear still etched on his face, "The demon's back. Only this time I couldn't feel it. I could see and hear it, but not feel it. When I said, 'God, make it go away,' it was gone."

"What is it with you and demons?" Jeremy tried to joke, but it sounded more like an accusation.

"I don't know," Mark said with all the courage he could muster. "I don't know."

"Well, is it still here?" Jeremy asked, looking around as if he was looking for a mouse.

"I don't think so," Mark quietly answered. "Like I said, when I was panicking, I asked God to make it go away, and it left."

"Okay," Jeremy began, trying to sound like a hero. "How about if we just do an all-nighter? Everyone sleeps in one room."

"Yeah, okay," Mark thought out loud. "That sounds good to me."

"Yeah, me too," Jason said, looking around for anything that didn't look right.

They got their things together and went down to

Jason's room. They took mattresses, blankets, pillows, and some clothes and laid themselves down on the floor with a small desk light on. Jason put on some music at a low volume, and they just kept quiet for a little while.

Once the beds were set up, Mark was still very agitated. He was shaking, and sweat was running down his face. His eyes were wide-open and full of fear. Jason looked at Jeremy and started looking for some Mandrix to help him settle down and sleep. Mark finally fell asleep after taking three. Jeremy lay down for a moment and then lifted his head and looked at Jason, who was lying in his own bed. "So what do you think? Do you think it was real or the acid?"

"Honestly?" Jason paused. "I don't know. You know how much I enjoy harassing him. He makes it so easy. This time, though, he was just way too convincing that he could see something Donnie and I couldn't. We could tell he wasn't hallucinating. I mean, when we left the theater he was perfectly fine. He talked normal, walked normal, and did everything normal. I'm convinced the acid was done for him. I'm no expert by any means, but to tell the truth, I think it was real. At least to him. I've heard of demons doing things like this, but I always thought they were just stories. Now? It's not like him to freak out like that."

"Wow," Jeremy said quietly. "That's all I need. A demon in my room. Any ideas of what to do now?"

"Not really." Jason lay thinking. "I think it's over for now. I guess just get some sleep. Maybe the morning will help us think it out better."

Jeremy nodded and lay back down. Lying on his side, he gazed at Mark, now sleeping peacefully, and wondered. Maybe it wanted him because he wanted out of the world of drugs. Maybe it wanted him because he had been looking to God for some of his answers. After all, it was Mark who brought the tapestry into the room.

Jeremy began drifting off to sleep, thinking that there seemed to be a lot of maybes floating around in his head. Then he was asleep.

CHAPTER EIGHTEEN

The new morning broke bright and early as the three of them began to wake up, confused at first about their surroundings. Mark looked at Jeremy, who was just sitting up. The room smelled of alcohol, smoke, and sweat. Slowly, Mark began to remember the demon he had faced the night before. Searching for a cigarette, he looked at Jeremy and asked, "Did you see it? I mean, last night—did you see the creature?"

"No, man. I guess you're the only one that saw it." Jeremy shook his head.

"I think it was the same one I felt the time before. I didn't have the same sense from it, but I felt the same fear. This time it was even more real. It wanted me, Jeremy. It wanted me just because I was available—whatever that means." Mark was still living the nightmare.

"How do you know he wanted you?" Jeremy asked, intrigued.

"He told me. He talked to me. It was a deep, grinding kind of voice. It scared me so much all I could do was crouch and shiver." Mark was back in the room in his mind. He began to shake again.

"I thought you said it didn't talk to you?" Jeremy asked.

"In the room it didn't, but at the movie it did. He looked different at the movie, but the voice I heard matched what I saw in the room. Jeremy, I'm scared. Who's to say it won't come for me at any time? I mean, where is it written that it will only show up at night?" Mark began to panic again.

"You said it left. What made it leave, then?" Jeremy was still confused about it all.

"Yeah, it left. I couldn't take it anymore, so I said, 'God, make it go away,' and it was gone. Just like that, it was gone," Mark began, remembering more.

"So are you saying God made it go away?" Jeremy asked.

"Yeah, maybe so. I guess He did. That's when it was gone," Mark said.

"So you're saying God is real?" Jason asked, not knowing himself whether he was being obnoxious.

"If that demon was real, then why isn't it possible for God to be real? I mean, who or what made the demons? They had to come from somewhere," Mark reasoned.

"Where do demons come from?" Jeremy asked, his curiosity piqued.

"The Bible says that God made all creatures in heaven and on earth," Mark said, beginning to remember his Sunday school days. "It says that Lucifer was the most beautiful creature God had ever created. He was so beautiful that he became full of pride and revolted against God. The reason he was created was to worship. Music was one of his gifts, but when he turned against God, he was cast out of heaven, and one-third of the angels went with him. I think that's what demons are—the angels that went with Lucifer, who is now Satan."

"How did you learn all that?" Jason asked, beginning to think this was all a bit much.

"I used to like to read a lot," Mark said.

Jason sat back and thought about what Mark was saying. He began to think that if it was all true, then there had to be a God. If there was a God, then there was a way to keep the demon away. There was hope.

The three of them sat quietly, smoking cigarettes and trying to get their minds together. Finally Jeremy spoke up. "Well, is anyone hungry?"

"Yeah." Mark smiled.

"I could eat," Jason said as his eyes lit up. "Let's go."

That afternoon Mark went to the PX to see if he could use the pay phones to call home. It was still a strange concept, but he was hoping to get used to it. Once there, Mark asked the lady behind the counter, "Is it possible to call the States on these pay phones?"

"That depends," the lady said.

"Depends on what?" Mark asked.

"Depends on if you have enough coin," the lady answered smugly.

Mark searched his pockets for coins. Realizing he didn't have enough, he searched his wallet for bills to cash in. He found ten dollars' worth and exchanged it for quarters. Mark dialed the number on the pay phone and inserted some of the coins. He could hear the ringing of the phone. "Hello?" came a voice. It was his brother.

"Hello there," Mark answered. "How are you?"

"Good. I'm doing real good. I hear you're headed home."

"Yes," Mark replied. "I don't know when for sure, but I know it is going to happen."

"Cool. I've got a room all set up for you," his brother said excitedly.

"Hey, I was wondering …" Mark hesitated, not sure if he should ask. "What about our uncle? Won't he be upset about my being there?"

"No, I guess you didn't hear," his brother said. "They got divorced. It was ugly."

"What do you mean?"

"He suspected her of being unfaithful. He even attacked her car with an axe. He threw her down the stairs and beat her up pretty good because of it," he said.

"What?" Mark asked in disbelief. "Was she?"

"No, of course not. He just went nuts. Then he divorced her. Kind of strange, really," the voice on the phone explained.

Mark was quiet for a minute. "Wow, I don't know what to say."

"Well, at any rate, you have a room now. Call when you know when you're coming so we can pick you up at the airport," his brother offered.

"I will. I have to go now. Take care and tell Auntie I'll call again when I know more." Mark hung up the phone and stood staring at the floor. Finally he thought to buy a cup of coffee and found a seat to think. It was unbelievable that his uncle had treated his aunt this way. He was full of mixed emotions. On the one hand, he had a home, but on the other hand, his aunt went through a lot of horrible grief before this was possible. Life was full of strange events that put everyone through a lot of pain. It was easy to think he was the only one that had hard times. It was a revelation to realize other people had difficult lives as well. Yet they didn't have to escape using drugs or other means to handle the rough times. How did they do it? Mark wanted to be able to live life the same way. His way of dealing with life was going to kill him.

Monday finally arrived. Mark had thought about it long enough. He had a home to go to. He knew if he stayed he would either end up in prison or dead. At the very least he would be a complete addict, and that alone was more than he would be able to handle.

After formation, Mark made his way to the captain's office. He had decided he would take the offer to go home. His time waiting his turn in the office area seemed very short as Mark's mind drifted back to Michigan. It was the first time since he could remember that he was excited about going somewhere. Suddenly, his mind was redirected. "Specialist, the captain will see you now," the first sergeant said.

Mark entered the office and stood at attention. "Soldier, I understand you want to accept the honorable discharge we talked about earlier," the captain said as he looked up from his desk.

"Yes, sir. I have recently discovered I have a home to go to, and I feel my time here has run its course. If the offer still stands, I would like to do as you suggested. I would like to get on with my life, perhaps have the opportunity to go in a new direction I have not been able to go in before," Mark said.

The captain realized Mark was still at attention. "At ease, soldier. Yes, the offer still stands, but I want to reiterate that I do not know how long it will take to go through. If you are sure this is what you want, then sign this paper."

The captain slid the papers to the edge of the desk to make them easy for Mark to sign. Handing him a pen, the captain continued, "This paper simply states that you agree to the terms I have already mentioned to you. You will need three letters to ever be able to reenlist in the military, one from a psychiatrist, one from a minister, and one from a medical doctor, all stating you are properly fit to perform the duties of a soldier. However, please read the paper before signing to make sure I didn't miss anything."

Mark lifted the paper and read it. It said exactly what the captain said was written on it. Mark signed the paper. The captain took the paper and looked at it to make sure Mark had signed it properly. "Thank you, specialist. If there are no further questions, you are dismissed."

Mark demonstrated the proper about-face and left the captain's office feeling very out of place. Suddenly he was no longer sure if he was doing the right thing or not. On the one hand, if he didn't leave soon, he was not sure if he ever would. On the other hand, it was like quitting before it was over. He was confused and had no idea where to turn for the right answers. He had never quit something before.

The rest of the day went on as normal. The only exception was the doubt in his mind and heart. What seemed so right all weekend suddenly seemed all wrong. Why would it feel so wrong now? It puzzled Mark to no end. It just seemed to go through his mind over and over.

Monday night Mark tried to sleep, but dreams of everything going wrong kept waking him up. Many times he woke up in a cold sweat. Finding it difficult to breathe, he sat up, trying to figure out what the dream had been. He couldn't remember—he just knew everything was always going wrong. He was always wrong.

Tuesday morning, just like every other workday, Mark went to the warehouse with a headache that was growing increasingly worse. He figured it was from the lack of sleep and the nagging feeling he had been wrong to sign the paper. As the morning wore on, Mark finally went to the lieutenant's secretary, Rose, for an aspirin. "Hey, Rose, you got any pain killers? My head is killing me," he asked, holding his head.

She looked in her desk. "Here you go. Keep the bottle. It's almost gone, anyway," Rose said as she handed it to him.

"Soldier!" a voice came from behind Mark. "Let's go see the captain, shall we?" the lieutenant suggested strongly to Mark. They walked together to see the captain.

Mark was not told why they were going. Once in the office area, the lieutenant said, "Soldier, have a seat. Do not move until you are told to. Do you understand?"

"Yes, sir, but do you mind telling me what this is all about?" Mark asked.

"You will be told what you need to know when it is time," the lieutenant said as he went into the captain's office.

Moments later, the first sergeant approached Mark. "Soldier, I was told you have drugs in your possession. We need to search you and your room. Please stand up and empty your pockets onto the counter." Mark did as he was told. Then the first sergeant told Mark, "Lift your arms straight up in the air." He then frisked Mark thoroughly until he was satisfied Mark had nothing on him. It only took a few minutes. Nothing was found.

"Soldier, come with us. We will go check out your room," the first sergeant said as Mark stood up and followed him up the stairs to his room.

Mark unlocked the door. There were two other soldiers with the first sergeant and the lieutenant. The lieutenant began to immediately go through Mark's locker. He threw everything in the locker onto Mark's bunk and the floor. It was like the lieutenant was in a frenzy to find something.

Mark noticed how hard the lieutenant was trying to find drugs. On impulse, Mark said, "The painkillers I asked for were only aspirin. The term *painkiller* is very common for aspirin. That's all you'll find, because that's all there is."

Finally, after everything in Mark's locker was on the floor, the lieutenant turned to his bunk and tore it apart as well. Nothing was found. The lieutenant looked at Mark. "I will find it. You will make a mistake, and I will catch you."

"Catch me at what, sir? Catch me at having a headache? You already have, sir. See, it is right in front of you. Here is the bottle of aspirin right here," Mark said, holding the aspirin bottle that Rose had given him.

The lieutenant turned in anger and marched forcefully out of Mark's room. The others looked at Mark for a moment. "So are you guys going to put everything back?" Mark asked in frustration.

"No, that's your job," the first sergeant answered as he turned and walked out of the room.

Mark spent the rest of the afternoon putting his things back together. He was just about done when Jeremy walked in. "What happened?" he asked, looking a little perturbed.

"The lieutenant decided I had drugs on me. When he couldn't find any on me, he decided I had drugs in my locker or in my bunk. He left here very angry," Mark answered, still amazed at what he had just gone through.

Now he was feeling better about his decision. He knew there were some who wanted him arrested and put away. It would only be a matter of time before he was in prison. It was now a race to see if he could get home first.

"You do know I have hash in my locker, right?" Jeremy asked, getting angrier.

"What? Why? Why would you keep hash in your locker after all I have been through? You know the hiding place in the floor. Why not use it?" Mark was astonished.

"I don't know. I just didn't," Jeremy said as he sat on his bunk.

"And you think it's my fault that they were in here?" Mark asked, still confused as to why Jeremy had taken such a risk and now blamed him.

"Yeah, I know it's not right, but I'm scared. I think they won't stop at this," Jeremy said, looking at Mark with a blank stare.

"You remember the other guys? Guy, Joey, and John? Remember, they're cleaning house. Now that they have a reason, they'll be after me. Don't let your guard down. Let them think it's only me they want," Mark said, trying to think rationally.

"We're roommates. They'll be after both of us," Jeremy said, regaining his patience.

"Don't worry. I got your back," Mark said, relaxing more as he remembered his prayer to God to protect him from himself and get him an honorable discharge.

They went on with the evening. After dinner, they were getting settled down for bed when they heard a knock at the door. "Who's there?" Jeremy asked as both of them looked around to see if there was anything to hide.

"Jason" came the answer. Jeremy opened the door, and Jason walked in. "You guys okay?"

"Yeah, why?" Mark answered as he sat on his bed.

"I heard you had some help reorganizing your locker." Jason smiled as he sat at the desk. "I can see they didn't find anything. Good job." He kept smiling.

Mark nodded, and Jeremy looked at Jason like he was being some kind of an idiot. "So what's up with you?"

"Not much. Just wondered if you guys want to smoke a bowl. I brought some to share," Jason pulled out his bowl and a small block of hash.

"I don't know if that's safe," Mark said hesitantly.

"I checked around. Everything's clear for now. Besides, if they try to catch us I'll just eat the hash that's left, and if we get caught in the process I'll take the fall," Jason said, being serious.

"Okay, but I won't let you go down alone," Jeremy said.

Jason lit up the bowl, and they started passing it around, trying to relax and get their minds wrapped around what was going on. "So, if I got this right, you signed a piece of paper that says you agree to a Chapter Sixteen honorable discharge. The lieutenant doesn't want to let it go because he's some kind of fanatic who wants you in prison. That's just great," Jason said sarcastically.

"Sorry. I had no idea something like this was going to bring that kind of attention," Mark said as he put it all together in his mind now that Jason had made it easy to see. Mark began to believe he had blown it. How was God ever going to get him out of this? Still, what if He could?

Mark made his decision. He didn't know if it was

rational, but then nothing going on in his life has been, with the exception of his brother and his aunt. He decided he would make the agreement with God again. If God really was real and got him out of this mess, then he would serve God for the rest of his life. Now all he had to do was find the right place and time to pray it. Somehow that made him feel better.

The next morning Mark found a place in the warehouse to have a little private time. "Dear God, I don't know for sure if you are real or not, but if you are, I was wondering … If You can get me out of the army with an honorable discharge, I will serve you for the rest of my life." Mark knew that he had done this once before, but back then he wasn't all that sure he was doing it because he meant it. This time was different. He was definitely serious. In his heart Mark knew he meant every word he prayed.

He began to think about his prayer. It made sense that the only way to make it work was to be honest. Otherwise, how would he know if it was God or not? If he had drugs on him, he had to be honest and admit it. If he didn't have drugs, it would even be easier to be honest, as they wouldn't find any.

After lunch one of the guys from the engineering platoon saw him. "Hey, Mark?"

"Yeah?" Mark answered.

"Got a minute?" the engineer asked, looking around to make sure no one was paying any attention to him.

"Sure, what's up?" Mark asked, getting curious.

Talking quieter, the engineer looked Mark in the eye.

"I've got some acid I'm trying to get rid of. I know they're trying to get rid of you, but are you interested?"

After taking a moment to think about it, Mark finally decided to buy. "Yeah, okay. How much?"

"Actually, I just want to get rid of it. Thing is I hate just dumping it. It seems like a waste. You can have it for free. You probably need it more than I do, anyway," the engineer said, reaching into his pocket.

Still trying to put all his heart into it and keep it making sense, Mark decided to take the acid. "Thanks, man. You're taking a chance even talking to me, you know."

"That's what life is, right? Taking chances," he said. He walked away before anyone could catch on to what they were doing.

Mark pocketed the acid. Thinking about his plan he decided that if he was approached and asked, he would just tell the truth. With confidence, Mark walked to the warehouse and went about his work.

Mark made his way to the barracks after work hours. All of a sudden, he heard a voice from behind. "Specialist Welch, please stop walking." It was one of the sergeants with the lieutenant. "We have reason to believe you have drugs on you. Is there anything you have to say?"

"Yes, I do," Mark heard himself say. "I have drugs on me." He felt a bit of disbelief that he'd said it.

"Really? You think this is some kind of game? This isn't a game!" The lieutenant was becoming furious. "This is serious business!" Then he walked away.

"Sir?" The sergeant ran after the lieutenant. "Don't you want me to search him?"

"No! He's just messing with us. He wants me to look like a fool again. He doesn't have anything on him. I will get him!" the lieutenant said as he kept walking, the sergeant trailing him and shaking his head.

Mark stood in shock. It had actually worked. He'd told the truth, and they'd just walked away. Not knowing anything else to do, Mark just started walking to the barracks and went about his business. His mind was full of amazement. God just might really be real.

He began to look around once he got back to his room. Thinking about it, he knew he could always put the acid in the floor, but it could prove hard to find later. Then he looked at the locker. He reasoned that if he used a piece of scotch tape he could always put it on the back of his locker. Then he could find it when he needed it.

Mark decided to go to supper. On his way he realized he was running low on cigarettes, so he stopped at the PX to buy a pack. Looking around, he saw Jacob. All of a sudden a lot of questions came to his mind. He decided to see if Jacob had time to talk.

"Hey, what are you up to?"

Jacob turned to see who was talking to him. "Hey, buddy. Not much. Just thought I'd do something different for supper. How about you?"

"You wouldn't believe it," Mark said as he sat down with Jacob.

"Oh yeah? Fill me in, man." Jacob wanted to hear it all.

"I was offered an honorable discharge but barred from reenlistment," Mark began. "The problem was that, if you remember, I didn't have a home to go to. On a whim I called my aunt to talk to my brother. She offered for me to live with her until I have someplace to go."

"Wow, man. That is just too cool." Jacob smiled as he listened.

"Yeah, but there's more," Mark continued. "Now the lieutenant thinks I'm some kind of drug dealer or addict. He wants to get me kicked out or put in prison. He does not want me to get an honorable."

"So what are you gonna do?" Jacob asked, concerned.

"Well, I was thinking," Mark began. "I thought about God. I remembered a lot of things you've told me and some things from my past. So I prayed to God that if He is real to get me out of this whole mess I put myself in and let me have an honorable discharge. If He does this, I will serve Him for the rest of my life."

"Okay," Jacob said.

"I figured if it was going to work, then I would always have to be honest, or I would never know if it was God or if I did it on my own. Well, the lieutenant came up on me a few hours ago while I had acid on me. He asked me if I had drugs on me, and I told the truth. He got mad and walked away, cursing me. He said he was going to get me no matter what. Thing is, he had me, and it was like God made him leave me alone."

"No kidding?" Jacob asked, amazed at what he was hearing. "You think God made Himself known to you like that?"

"I don't know," Mark confessed. "I was kind of hoping

you could tell me. That's what I was thinking about when I saw you in here. What do you think?"

"I think it was God. I think God wants you to know He is real and He cares what happens to you," Jacob answered, still amazed that Mark was giving God a chance.

Mark sat looking at the table, smiling at the idea that he might actually be on the verge of turning his life around. It was an amazing feeling and yet still scary. Still, Mark thought, it was a different kind of scary. Like he was living an adventure that was finally worth living—not just risking his life for no reason, but taking a chance on God. He was scared, but his heart was filled with hope and happiness he couldn't remember ever feeling before. He felt good—even better than he felt when he first arrived in Germany and thought he was about to have a new beginning.

Jacob got up and stretched. "Hey, man, I'm really excited for you! I'll keep praying that God sees you through it all. Trust Him. I gotta get going, but remember to pray. That's the big key—praying and believing what you're praying for."

"I will, man. Thanks. I needed the encouragement," Mark said as he stood up to leave as well.

Jacob left while Mark went to buy the cigarettes he'd originally come for. After buying them, he left to go to the mess hall. Looking at his watch, he realized it was too late to get supper there. He decided to go to his hideaway. It was a good time to do this anyway. He was feeling really good about his decisions and God's help.

Suddenly, Harold was walking behind him. "Hey, man, hold up."

"What's up?" Mark asked, surprised to see Harold like this. They never took time to talk, especially in public.

"We need to talk, man," Harold said, looking around. "I need to get something out. You remember when I told you I started that fire?"

"Yeah, I remember. I never told anyone, if that's what you're worried about," Mark replied.

"I know," Harold began. "That's why we need to talk. I know who started the fire, but it wasn't me. I can't say who it was. The reason I told you that was because the guy who started it was worried that you knew he did it. He wanted to be sure he wasn't going to get caught."

"I get it. So now what?" Mark didn't really get it. He just didn't know what to say.

"Well, now I can see you can be trusted. So I figure I need to tell you what I was told."

"Okay," Mark said hesitantly. "Go on."

"Well," Harold said slowly, "I have a friend in the orderly office area. He overheard Lieutenant Danson say he was going to get you no matter what. But he didn't want to do it by planting anything on you. He's sure you will do it for him. He will hound you until you're busted. I just thought you should know. Watch your back, man."

"Why you telling me this?" Mark asked, appreciating the heads-up. "You don't even like me."

"Let's just say I owe you one. Don't tell anyone, but maybe you're growing on me. If you ever repeat it, I'll swear you're lying." Harold smiled but looked serious.

"Don't worry. I won't," Mark assured him with a smile.

Harold turned and left. Mark watched him walk away, thinking about everything he had told him. What he'd suspected was true, then. All of this was about more than just Mark learning if God was real and getting his life back. It was about a literal survival.

Mark went to his hideaway with a lot to think about. It seemed like he had, once again, come full circle. This time it had to be for good. He had to trust and believe in something that was real and true. He had heard that God was real and true.

Remembering what Jacob said, Mark bowed his head quietly in the corner where he always sat to eat and think. Mark prayed, "God, if you are real … I know Jacob thinks you're real. My aunt thinks you're real. There must be a reason they all think that. If you are real, please deliver me from Lieutenant Danson and get me home with an honorable discharge. I promise I will serve you for the rest of my life. I don't know what else to ask or say. Just please help me."

Back in his room, Mark got ready for bed. Once he was lying down for the night, he began to think about everything again and again. Once again he prayed the same prayer. He figured it wouldn't hurt to keep reminding God about who he was and what he needed. After all, it wasn't like he had spent a lot of time with God in the past.

Suddenly, Mark had a new thought. He should have asked Jacob about being demon-possessed. He had forgotten about the demon until just now. Here in the dark, he suddenly remembered how that ugly thing had wanted him.

"Dear God," Mark began to pray again, "don't let that thing get me. Keep him away from me. Don't let it near me. Please, God, protect me." With that, Mark flipped the covers up over his head and tried to sleep. Finally, sleep he did.

CHAPTER NINETEEN

The next day Mark got up to face the challenge all over again. He thought about removing the acid hit from behind the locker and flushing it down the toilet. But if he did, how would he ever know if God was going to deliver him the way he'd been praying for?

Mark thought about it, but somehow it still seemed to make sense to let God deliver him instead of delivering himself. It was a risk, but he was already risking his life with the drugs and the dealers. Somehow it seemed to make more sense to take a risk on God.

Mark went to breakfast with Jeremy. They sat quietly as Mark kept thinking. It seemed like that was all he could do anymore. Finally, Jeremy spoke. "So have you given any thought to what you will do once you're home?"

Mark chuckled. "No. I've been so busy thinking about just making it there. It seems too good to be true that I'll ever see it. With Danson after me, who knows how far I'll get? I had a 'friend' tell me Danson was out to get me, so now I know it's not just in my head. It's all too much for me to dream of right now."

They finished breakfast and went to formation. Right after it was all over, Lieutenant Danson approached him. "Soldier, you need to move to a room on the first floor. You will be moved to the quartermaster squad and work with them until you are either released or sent elsewhere. Do you have any questions?"

"Yes, sir," Mark said out of confusion. "What room am I moving into?"

"Go to the first sergeant. He will have your room assignment. That is all." Then the lieutenant turned and walked away.

Mark thought for a moment about what he had just heard. Then he started to go to the office. He suddenly remembered something the lieutenant said—"until you are either released or sent elsewhere." He figured that meant sent to prison. *Nice,* Mark thought.

The orderly was typing away when Mark walked in. "I'm supposed to see the first sergeant about my new room assignment. Is he available?"

"I'll check. Just have a seat," the orderly said.

Moments later, as Mark was looking at the floor he heard the First Sergeant speak. "Soldier?"

"Yes, first sergeant. The lieutenant told me to see you about a new room assignment," he said as he stood up.

"You will be moving to room 110. The orderly will get you a key. Start moving this morning. Once you're done report, to the quartermaster for your new assignment." Then the first sergeant went to the captain's office.

Mark retrieved his key and went to find his new room. Opening the door, he found the room completely empty.

There was not one piece of furniture in it. Mark began to realize there was a lot more going on here than just getting reassigned. He was being manipulated.

He went up to his soon-to-be former room. Sitting on his bed, he began to think about what was going on. His stomach began to hurt, and he just held his head in his hands. What was he going to do? There was a small, quiet voice deep inside him. "Mark, be still. I am here. I will be with you always." Mark looked around, but no one was there. He wasn't frightened but strangely felt encouraged.

Taking a deep breath, Mark got up and whispered, "Thank you, Lord." He decided the locker should be moved first. He began to empty it out to make it easier to handle. Since it was lighter, he knew he could move it down the stairs by himself.

It took some doing, but by lunchtime Mark had moved his locker, bunk, and nightstand down to his new room. Then Lieutenant Danson walked in, "Soldier, this is all the furniture you will be allowed to have. Pack up all your civilian clothes and personal belongings. Get them ready to be shipped. Stack them in one of the corners of this room. An orderly will have the movers come get it and ship it all home for you. You will not be needing them again until you are either released or sent elsewhere."

Mark did not speak but only listened. Once the lieutenant was gone, he decided that before he even did that, he would go to lunch. The whole morning had been busy, making him hungry.

While things were going on that Mark was not to

know, he did know a secret that no one else would be able to outfox. The way Mark saw it, Lieutenant Danson was not going to be as successful as he thought, no matter what his intentions were. Mark knew he was going to make it home—not just make it, but actually be able to start the new life he had originally planned on as well. God was going to do it for him this time.

As he made his way to the chow line, Mark began to realize that that was the problem. He had always tried to do it all on his own, even back when he was living in the woods. He'd always thought he was alone. Now he was coming to realize he wasn't alone after all. There was hope where no one could see it—no one except Jacob, anyway. Now he could see it too.

Mark was about to have a seat in the mess hall when he heard someone call his name.

Looking in the direction of the voice, Mark could see Jacob. "Yeah, okay," Mark said as he headed toward his table. Jacob moved a chair for him. "Thanks," Mark said as he sat down. "So how've you been?"

"Not bad," Jacob said as he took a drink of water. "I've been praying for you."

"Somehow I know that," Mark said as he chose the silverware he would use. "I was kind of hoping to run into you. I've been wondering about something else."

"What's that?" Jacob asked after swallowing another bite.

Mark took a moment to decide how to ask the question. "I think I might be demon-possessed. I was wondering what you knew about that kind of stuff."

Jacob smiled as he took another drink. "Well, first of all, you're not possessed."

"How do you know?" Mark interrupted.

"Because you don't squirm around like there's something inside you," Jacob said as he continued. "Trust me, you're not possessed. Secondly, I know a lot about demon oppression. It could be that. Tell me what makes you think you're possessed."

Mark hesitated. "Well … there have been two different times in the last few months or so that I have been in the presence of a demon. The first time I didn't see it, but I know it was there. The second time I actually saw it. It was ugly. It had several horns on its head, wings, no feathers, skin like a reptile, big, ugly-looking arms and face—I almost filled my pants. I don't know why I didn't. Why would it want me?"

Jacob smiled. "You are definitely not possessed. You are being oppressed."

"That's bad, isn't it?" Mark asked, interrupting again.

"It's not good, but it's not as bad as you would think," Jacob said as he thought about it. "There's some kind of sin in your life that it is causing. It knows you like this particular sin. If you confess that sin and ask God to take it away and ask God to protect you from the demon, it will go. That's all I can think of for the moment."

Mark sat without eating. He just looked at his food for a few minutes. Then he asked, "Can you help me with this? Do you know how it's done?"

"Yeah, I can help you. There's a trick, if you know what I mean," Jacob answered.

"What's that?" Mark asked.

"You have to be serious. You can't trick God. He knows what you're thinking and what you're feeling. Do not try this and not be serious," Jacob advised.

"Trust me, I have no intentions of playing with this demon," Mark assured him.

"Okay, then. When do you want to do it?" Jacob asked.

"I'm in the middle of moving to a room on the first floor. Room 110. I've got the whole day. Whenever you feel like you've got the time, you know where to find me. Just one thing," Mark added.

"What's that?" Jacob asked, thinking of what he would need to do this.

"It's not that I'm ashamed of God, because I'm not. I'm just not sure I want the whole base to know what we're doing," Mark said as he began to eat again.

Jacob nodded. "Yeah, I agree. Mum's the word."

They finished eating in silence as they thought about what they were going to do. After eating, Jacob went back to work, and Mark headed back to his room to finish moving his clothes. He took his time moving everything. It felt like the end of an era. He had a strange empty feeling as he looked at the room he had been living in for the past year. It held a lot of memories. Now he would be leaving one of his best friends. He felt hollow and lost.

After walking back to his new room, he sat on his bunk and began thinking about the new life waiting for him. Mark wondered if this was how it would feel once he faced the demon and completely dedicated his life to God. Would there be the same empty feeling of leaving the old behind as he began to live the new? It was scary, and yet there was a sense of new adventure. The big difference, he knew, was that there would be no life-threatening dangers as a result. Instead he would be getting rid of the threat.

It was about five o'clock when there was a knock on the door. Mark figured it was Jacob, so he got up to open the door. He was correct. "Come on in," he said.

Jacob looked around for a chair, but there was none there. Standing near the door, he said, "I like your new place. Love what you've done with it."

"Thanks," Mark said, knowing he was being sarcastic. "I'm glad you like it. So what do we do to start this 'project'?"

"Well, it's really not that rough," Jacob began. "All we really have to do is write down the sins you think this demon is urging you to do. Confess these sins to God. Ask Him for forgiveness, and then ask God to banish the demon." Jacob paused. "The best way for all of this to work is to accept Christ as your personal Savior. Jesus says He is the way, the truth, and the life. No one can come to the Father except through Him. You have to believe that."

"Sounds easy enough." Mark sat and thought. "Actually sounds too easy. Are you sure that's all there is to it?"

"Well ... there could be one small problem," Jacob said.

"Okay?" Mark inquired. "And that is what?"

"It is possible the demon will want to hang on to you," Jacob said. "We have to be prepared for that."

"What? How are we going to be prepared for that?" Mark asked, beginning to rethink the whole thing.

"We pray it won't happen. If it does, we keep praying until Christ banishes it," Jacob said with confidence. "There is one more thing to consider now that I remember it."

"Now what?" Mark was losing count of what to do.

"The Bible says that if you banish a demon and do not fill that empty space, it will come back with company, and it will be worse than it was before," Jacob replied calmly.

"What?" Mark exclaimed. "How can it be any worse? How do I fill the empty space?"

Jacob smiled. "Simple. You ask Christ to live in your heart. Ask Him to be your personal Savior and live in your heart."

"And you will be with me the whole way?" Mark asked.

"The whole way, buddy," Jacob said, looking him in the eye.

"Okay then, let's get to praying. Do we kneel or what?" Mark wanted to get started before he became too afraid to face the demon.

"Yeah, let's kneel here by the bed," Jacob said. "But before we do that, let's make up the list to work with."

Mark sat on the bed and pulled out a pen and paper. He wrote down the sins he could think of that the demon might be oppressing him with: using drugs, swearing, smoking cigarettes, drinking alcohol, and not trusting

God. That was all Mark could think of at the moment. His mind was racing with the things the demon could do to him. "Okay, I think I'm done." He handed the list to Jacob.

"Okay then. Let's kneel," Jacob said as he kneeled at the side of the bed. Mark joined him and folded his hands as he closed his eyes.

"Dear God," Jacob began to pray. "You know everything Mark is going through. You know about the demon, and you know about his sins. He has written them down to confess to you. We know you already know his sins, but we also know he needs to confess them." Looking at Mark, Jacob said, "Okay, Mark, read this list of sins and confess them to God."

Mark took the list. "God, You and everyone else knows how I have been using drugs. I know they are harmful to me, but I've been doing them anyway. Please forgive me for using drugs. I also ask that you forgive me for swearing, smoking cigarettes, and drinking alcohol. I know these are not what you want me to be doing. I ask that you forgive me also for not trusting you sooner. Forgive me all my sins, and help me to know how to serve you." Mark then looked at Jacob, not knowing what to do next.

"Lord, Mark wants to ask you to live in his heart and in his life," Jacob said, looking at Mark.

"Yes, Lord," Mark continued. "Please come into my heart and my life and take away this demon and help me to do what is right to trust you to get me out of this mess I have made for myself."

"Amen," Jacob said.

"Amen," Mark said, looking at Jacob. He'd expected more to happen. "So that's it?"

"Yeah, I think so," Jacob said, standing up.

"No sign of the demon. So what do I do now?" Mark asked, confused.

"Live like you think you should. God will tell you what to do. Listen to your heart. He will direct you as you need. He will always be with you. Just trust Him," Jacob answered. "You'll be okay." Jacob got up and went to the door. Then turned to face Mark again. "I know you will be okay. Just do what the army asks of you and you will make it home. God has things planned for you. Just trust Him." Jacob opened the door and was gone.

Mark sat on the bed and began to wait to see what would happen. Nothing did. He thought about how he felt. There was no difference. He was afraid he would feel empty, but he didn't. He felt just fine. In fact, the more he thought about it, the more he felt good. He felt full, not empty. It felt good.

He finished boxing up all his personal belongings. He had just finished the last box when he realized he hadn't eaten yet. Mark was just getting ready to go to his hideaway when there was another knock on the door. He opened the door to see Jeremy.

"Hey, buddy, did you forget about me?" Jeremy asked as he walked in."

"No, man, just got so busy I even forgot to eat. You hungry?" Mark asked.

"I ate, but I was hoping to see you in the mess hall.

So they moved you, I see," Jeremy said, looking around. "So now what?"

"I don't know. The lieutenant keeps saying it's until I go home or they send me somewhere else. I know he has it in for me," Mark said as he thought about the day. "Well, I don't know about you, but I'm hungry. Want to go the hideaway?"

"Yeah, I can go with you. If nothing else we can drink a few beers," Jeremy said. Mark made sure he had his wallet and key. They left the room and went on their way to get supper and drink beer together. For all Mark knew, it could be for the last time.

The next morning Mark got up to begin the day. He went to formation but found his place in a different squad. It felt very unnatural, but he did it anyway. After formation Mark was headed to the quartermaster room when the lieutenant approached him. "Soldier, go wait in your room. The movers will be there shortly. You can make sure everything is packed right and labeled for the move back to your home. You do have a home, right?"

Knowing he was being baited, Mark answered, "Yeah, I do. How about you? Do you have a home that accepts you?"

The lieutenant seemed to be extra irritated at the question. He narrowed his eyes at Mark and moved a little closer like he was about to do something. Mark spoke again. "It doesn't feel all that good to be talked to like that, does it?"

The lieutenant stopped and then just walked away. Immediately after the words were out of his mouth, Mark knew he shouldn't have said it. Still, he thought it was good to stand his ground and not be pushed around like he was someone's property. Then he went to his room just as he'd been ordered.

About a half hour later the movers arrived. Mark asked them questions about how to label the boxes and how to tape the boxes up correctly. Once he was happy with everything, the movers took the boxes and went on their way.

Mark felt like he was finally seeing his last days in Germany. He went to the basement where the quartermaster room was and reported for duty just as he had been directed from the beginning.

Teddy was another newcomer to the quartermaster room. He had been sent there to wait his turn at getting out. Unlike Mark, he was sure they would be sending him to prison. Seeing Mark walk through the door, he went to talk to him. "So are you all settled in?"

"I don't know," Mark said, looking Teddy over. "Who are you, anyway?"

"Sorry," he began. "I'm Teddy. I've been placed here until they figure out a way to send me to prison."

Mark looked at him, surprised. "What makes you think they want to send you to prison?"

"Because that's what the lieutenant keeps telling me," he said, looking down at the floor. "He seems pretty convincing."

"Yeah, he talks like that to me too. Know what?" Mark said.

"What?" Teddy wanted to know.

"That's all he can do. Talk. He has no control over what happens to you. Only you do. Believe that?" Mark asked him.

"I don't know. He seems to be in control of a lot," Teddy said.

"Trust me. He can't do anything if you don't give him a reason. That's the way it works. That's why he's so angry with me. I don't give him anything to work with. He has to let me go. It's killing him inside. That's where it needs to stay. Let him be the miserable one. I'm ready to go home." Mark talked like he knew what it was all about. In some ways he did. He was beginning to feel like he had changed a lot since his first days there. Maybe he had.

"Well," said Teddy, "I guess I can try to not give him a reason. The thing is, I love to use drugs. I don't think he should have the right to interfere. We should have the right to enjoy life any way we think is good."

Mark thought about what Teddy said. "I don't know, man. You do know drugs are very harmful, right? Besides, if you're high all the time, how can you perform as a soldier the way we are being paid to? You see the problem?"

Teddy nodded but was still clearly of his own opinion. Mark looked for the sergeant in charge for the day. Then he got on with the duties he was assigned. The rest of the day was spent learning how to perform new duties and where things were kept.

CHAPTER TWENTY

The next day Mark had to keep his appointment with Marylyn. There was a lot to talk about, as his days in Germany were coming to an end. He entered her office a little early, eager to get the session over with. Mark wanted to start getting on with his life. It was time to put everything behind him.

"Mark, it's good to see you again," Marylyn said with deep appreciation. She had learned to enjoy his company.

Sensing her sincerity, he replied, "It's good to see you too. I was wondering if this was my last session."

Marylyn looked through her paperwork. "I don't see anything here to indicate that. Do you want it to be your last?"

Mark sat down as they were talking and bent his head down, holding his hands as if in prayer. After a few moments, he asked, "What would happen if we did end it today? What kind of things would happen? I mean, would I be somehow punished?"

Marylyn looked at him with a blank stare. "I don't

know what you mean. First of all, the only thing your commander would know is what I told him. Do you remember what I told you? It's illegal to report anything without your permission. That means that once I determine you have done all you need to do, then it's over. You're done. I can determine this simply by you telling me you're done. Is that what you're telling me? Because if it is, then we are done. There are no consequences save one."

Mark picked up on the last statement. "What's the consequence?"

"If you really are not done, you will continue to use drugs, and they will catch you again. If that happens, they may not give you CEDAC as a course of action. They may just simply terminate your enlistment—possibly send you to prison, depending on how they caught you." Marylyn was filled with concern as she spelled out the possibilities.

"So what you're saying is that as long as I quit, I'm good?" Mark asked with hope in his heart.

"That's one way to look at it," she said, wondering what was really going on in his mind.

"Here's the thing. I was offered an honorable discharge, but I would be barred from reenlistment. I agreed to the terms. I don't know when it will be fulfilled. I know it will be soon, because my lieutenant has had me moved to the first floor, and they shipped all my belongings home." Mark wasn't sure how much she already knew, but it felt good to be able to tell her about it.

"So you found a home?" Marylyn said, looking pleasantly surprised. "Where? How?"

"I called my brother," Mark began, "and my aunt answered the phone. She said I was welcome to come back there until I could get on my feet. Do you believe in God?"

Marylyn sat looking at her hands as she held them between her knees. Then, looking in his eyes, she said, "Yes. I don't know that much about Him, but I believe He is real. I believe He exists. Why?"

"I've been praying lately," Mark kept going. "I mean, a lot. Thing is … He's been answering all my prayers. I mean, in a way that it has to be Him. My lieutenant—he hates me. He really, really wants me busted. There have been times when he could have busted me. He asked me if I had drugs on me. I did, so I told him I did. He just got angry that I was playing games and left me alone. When I didn't have drugs, he would search me. He could have planted drugs on me like they did to other guys, but he didn't. He just got mad and left me alone. It's been wild but good—exciting, actually. It gives me hope that I will get out of here without going to prison. Another thing I believe is that if I stay, they will get me and send me to prison—or, worse, I will die of an overdose or something. I have to get out of here if I'm ever going to get away from drugs." Looking at Marylyn, he asked, "What do we do now?"

"What's the advantage of this being your last session?" Marylyn asked, hoping to see his point.

"I don't know that there is one. Maybe I should keep going. I'm only asking to try to figure out what I need to do to make this work," Mark answered, looking in her eyes.

They stared at each other for a moment, but then both suddenly felt uncomfortable, afraid their true feelings would become obvious to each other. Marylyn looked at her watch, trying to pretend to be professional, and then looked back at Mark. "You're right. It is difficult to know what the next best move is. Maybe that's the answer in itself?"

"What do you mean?" Mark asked, intrigued with her thoughts.

"Well, if we don't know what to do next, then let's keep the sessions going. Only now let's work out how we want them to end in your best interest. If you think the best way for you to get out of the drug world is by leaving, then let's work toward that goal. By the way, I think you're right. That usually is the best way. It's just that here it isn't usually an option. But know what? Today it is."

They sat facing each other and began to smile. Then tears began to moisten Marylyn's eyes, and she quickly turned away, pretending to otherwise busy herself. She was hoping Mark didn't notice, but he did. He was happy she did that, because his eyes were beginning to moisten as well. It was becoming obvious to each of them how the other one felt.

Mark, feeling awkward at this new awakening, stood up to leave. He didn't know what else to do. He had never had the opportunity to be this close to a woman before—not one who just might feel the same way about him. In spite all of the things they had been through, it was still a new feeling. It was also a good feeling, but since he couldn't think of what to do next, he simply got up to leave.

"Are we done here?" Marylyn asked, not sure where her question was coming from. She felt as if she wasn't just asking about the session.

Mark felt like she meant more as well. "I'm not sure. I've never been here before. To be honest, I don't know what to do. I've been alone for so long. Come think of it … all my life." Then, smiling, he said, "I'll be back next week?"

Marylyn smiled as she began to understand everything better. "Okay then. Next week. Maybe we can make up a plan now that we know what needs to happen." She was talking both about how to get Mark home and whether there would ever be a them. It was all a little more than she had planned for—more than she was expecting. Until now she hadn't realized what she felt any more than Mark had. It was almost like everything around them was starting over again.

The day ended just as the session did—in a dreamlike world. Teddy seemed busy with his own thoughts. Mark knew he was supposed to be learning a new job, but his mind just wasn't in it either. The sergeant running the operation knew it was a short-term assignment. His job wasn't so much to train Mark as it was to babysit him. That was how the workday ended, and then they were all free to go to their rooms.

Mark was just about to open his door when Jeremy met him in the hallway. "Hey, you ready for dinner?"

"Yeah." Mark put his key back in his pocket. "It's been

a strange day." They began to walk as Mark went on about his new discovery. "I think I might be getting in deeper than I realized."

"Oh yeah?" Jeremy listened with his smile. "How so?"

"You know how I've talked about my counselor," Mark started. "Well, I'd swear she's feeling the same things I am. Only now I'm leaving. It makes everything more clouded. More difficult."

Jeremy smiled even wider. "Oh, I see. So what's gonna happen?"

"I don't know. I've never been here before. I feel like I'm thirteen going on five. I don't know what to say around her anymore. I don't know how to act. It's getting weird, but I like it," Mark confessed. "Any ideas?"

"Here's the thing," Jeremy began. "There is no right or wrong thing to do. Just follow your heart. Make sure that whatever you do, you follow your heart. In the end it will tell you what is best. I don't know how it works. I just know it does."

"Does it always work for you?" Mark asked, trying to believe.

"So far," Jeremy said, looking at him more intently. "It's not like I'm a love doctor or anything, but so far it's worked for me."

"What if my heart says to let it go so I can get on with my life?" Mark asked, hoping it would be wrong.

"Then that's what you have to do. Thing is, I can't decide that for you. Only you can know for sure what's best for you. If she loves you, then she will respect that and make it easy for you." Jeremy was hoping he was giving good advice. It wasn't easy.

They went on to the mess hall and ate dinner quietly. Mark was just finishing up when it began to occur to him. Everything was also going to end for him and Jeremy. He began to realize Jeremy had always been there for him, even tonight. He'd been there for Mark a lot more than Mark ever was for him. "So why have you always been there for me?"

"What do you mean?" Jeremy asked, not sure where Mark was going with his question.

"You have always been a good friend to me. A lot more than I ever was to you. Why? I know I didn't deserve that kind of friendship. Sometimes I think Jason was right. I am a weasel. I do a lot more taking than I do giving," Mark said, thinking about all they had been through.

"Maybe that's how it seems to you, but that's just it. You've never thought more highly of yourself than others. I've always liked that about you. Don't worry—we won't do the gay thing. I like you is all," Jeremy answered, beginning to feel a little awkward.

Mark felt the change in the air. "It's been like this all day, first with Marylin, then with Teddy just for different reasons—and now with you." He smiled, looking at Jeremy as he drank his coffee.

They both smiled as they gazed at the table. Then they lit up another cigarette and smoked as they drank their last cup. They sat looking around, taking in what they knew might be their last time together. That was the problem now. It was hard to know if this was the time to say good-bye. They didn't know anyone who had ever been through this before.

The next morning Mark took his new place in formation. He didn't hear anything that was said, as his mind was still on Marylyn. He kept drifting away into what might have been if he had lived his life differently.

All of a sudden, everyone was leaving, and he was still standing in his spot. Mark looked around, feeling a little embarrassed, and turned to go to the quartermaster room. "Soldier, where are you headed?" came a voice.

Mark turned around, startled. "What?"

"Didn't you hear? The captain needs to see you," his new squad leader said.

Mark turned in another direction and headed to the main office. Once there, he spoke to the orderly on duty. "I'm here to see the captain as ordered."

"Okay, just have a seat." The orderly got up to see if the captain was ready to see him.

Mark sat looking at his watch, wondering if he was going to be sent to another base or sent home. His mind wandered. It seemed to Mark like his mind had done nothing but wander the last week or so. Then he was brought back to reality. "The captain will see you now," the orderly said as he sat back down at his desk.

Mark entered the office with more familiarity than he had ever hoped to have. He stood at attention, but this time he paid more attention to his surroundings than he had before. He noticed more certificates on the wall and personal pictures of the captain's family. It seemed odd to think of the captain as a normal person.

"At ease, soldier," the captain began. "I have the results of the Chapter Sixteen back. Everything has been approved. Your orders are here. You will ship out in a few days. I understand you have shipped all your belongings home. If things go properly, you will beat your things home. Do you have any questions?"

"Actually, I do, sir," Mark began. He wasn't sure what he was going to say, "I was wondering first of all ... why the lieutenant keeps saying things like 'once I'm released or sent elsewhere'?"

"I don't know why he says that," the captain replied. "I'll look into it. Anything else?"

"Yes, sir," Mark continued. "When will I get my copy of the orders so I know what to do and when?"

"You will be leaving this office with them, son," the captain said, frank in his answer.

"Thank you, sir."

The captain handed him his orders. "That is all, son. You are dismissed."

Mark did his about-face and left the office with his orders in his hand. Once he was in the hallway he looked at the orders. He tried to read every detail that would tell him things like flight time and where he was headed.

He was going to Fort Dixie in New Jersey, where he would be processed to be released from service. It looked as if he would be there for a week. The orders had dates and times. Looking for a place to sit, Mark finally found the stairs. He kept reading every detail. The orders said he was to be released with an honorable discharge, and in two weeks he knew he would be back in Michigan—out of what had first been a dream and had then turned into a nightmare. Now it was turning into hope. Mark wondered if the hope would stay or turn into despair again.

Mark did the only thing he could think of. He prayed. He bowed his head right where he sat and said a silent prayer: "Thank You, God, for the orders that gave me an honorable discharge and will be sending me home. I pray that it doesn't end there. Help me to quit the drugs and have a future, the one I couldn't do on my own by joining in the first place. Amen."

Instead of going to his work assignment, Mark decided to go to the PX. It wasn't that he wanted to be AWOL from his job. He just wanted a little more time to think. For a few minutes he walked in the rain without noticing. He was soaked before it finally occurred to him just how hard the rain was.

He was already almost to the PX, so there was no point in turning back. Inside, Mark bought another pack of cigarettes. He was putting them in his pocket when he realized he still had a full pack. That was okay, he thought. He just took one out and lit it up and then headed to buy a cup of coffee.

After he paid for the coffee, he sat at a table to think of what to do next. Looking at his watch, he realized he could call home to let them know the news. He didn't know when he would be in Michigan, but he did know the final date of his time in the military.

Mark went to the pay phones and searched his pockets for change. He dug up enough to make a quick call to his aunt. "Hello?" The voice on the other end sounded like he had just woke her up.

"Hi, Auntie, I'm sorry for waking you. It's just that I have my orders now. I will be home in two weeks. They're sending me to New Jersey first for processing. Once I'm done there I will be coming home." Mark was hoping he wasn't pushing things by calling like this.

"Oh, well, that's wonderful," his auntie said. "Do you know when you will be in Michigan?"

"No," Mark said, breathing a little easier. "I probably won't know until I'm in New Jersey. I just wanted to let you know as I know. I will call you again from New Jersey." He laughed a little as he said it.

"Okay. You be careful. I will be waiting for your call," she said in what sounded like a yawn.

"Okay, Auntie," Mark said. "I will let you go now. Bye."

"Bye," the voice on the other end said. Then Mark hung up feeling like he was almost ready to go.

Suddenly everything seemed surreal. He was walking in a dream as he went to buy still another cup of coffee. He didn't even realize it until it was in his hand and paid for. Looking around, he sat at a table and tried to regain his bearings. It was like he was no longer there but in a dream. He prayed a quiet prayer that this dream would not turn into a nightmare. It seemed like a familiar prayer.

Mark wasn't sure how long he had been sitting there. He suddenly noticed people were headed for the mess hall. Looking at the clock on the wall, Mark became aware that it was suppertime and he hadn't been to work all day. He wondered if he would be in trouble as he got up to go to dinner.

After dinner Mark went up to Jeremy's room to see if he was in. He knocked on the door. "Who is it?"

"It's me, Mark," he said, checking to see if the door was unlocked. It wasn't.

"Hold on," Jeremy answered. Moments later, the door opened. "How's it going?" Mark asked as he walked in. The room looked different. Then he noticed some of Jason's things in the room. Looking around, he saw Jason sitting in a chair on the other side of the lockers. "Hey, man, like your new home?"

"Yeah, but I'd like it more if I was home," Jason said, looking like he was stoned.

With a smile, Mark asked, "Have any more?"

Jason pulled the bowl out of hiding and handed it to Mark. "Have some. We were just getting ready to get something to eat."

Jeremy had the door locked by then and reached out his hand for his turn with the bowl. "Did you want to go with us?"

"I guess I could, but I already ate. I was getting ready for my big move," Mark said, trying to hold the smoke in while he talked. "I got my orders."

The other two stopped what they were doing and stared at Mark and then at each other. Jeremy spoke first. "Oh yeah? Do you have them with you?"

"Yeah," Mark said as he pulled them out. "Here, but don't damage them. I need them to report to my next station." Mark smiled as he watched Jeremy read the paper and then hand it to Jason. Jason looked at it for a moment and gave it back to Mark, still looking at him in disbelief.

"You know what this means," Jeremy said with a smile. "It means we need to have a celebration party."

"Okay, but we need to be careful," Mark pointed out. "Remember, there is one lieutenant that wants to burn me. He will be all too happy to burn everyone else he can in the process."

"That's true," Jason said, sobering up on the idea.

"However, I may have done something to slow him down," Mark said with hope.

"What's that?" Jeremy asked with a little more light in his eyes.

"Well, when I was getting my orders from the captain, I asked him what the lieutenant meant when he keeps saying 'or if I am sent to someplace else.' The captain said he would look into it."

"Wow," Jeremy started, "I hope that didn't make matters worse. Either the lieutenant was acting on his own or he was following orders."

"I know, but I get the feeling he was acting on his own, just trying to be a blockhead," Mark said as he sat at the desk by the door.

After dinner they went back to Jeremy's room and smoked a couple of bowls. It had been a little while since Mark last smoked hash, and he knew somehow this may very well be the last time. He sat in a stoned state of mind, wondering if it wasn't the last how many more times there would be before he could honestly say it was.

The next few days went by in a blur. When he was on duty, his mind was focused on the flight back to the States. When he was off duty, he wondered what it was going to be like to be a civilian. What would he do for money since he would no longer be employed? Simple—he would just have to find a job like everyone else. It would be his turn to take his place as a real adult.

Sometimes it was scary, but sometimes it was exciting. Then his mind would float back to what he needed to do to get ready for his flight. He just couldn't get his mind where it needed to be. He hoped it wouldn't be the thing the lieutenant needed to finally trip him up and kill his hopes for freedom.

Friday morning Mark knew he had to go see Marylyn one last time. It was an unscheduled session, but he would not be there for the one they'd hoped to have. Getting permission from the quartermaster sergeant, Mark went to the CEDAC building. This time he knew it would be the last.

It seemed like forever before Marylyn was finally available. When she finally came into the lobby, she looked a little taken aback at seeing him. She knew it could only mean one thing. "Come on in, Mark," she said in a soft voice.

Mark got up and followed her into her office. He sat down, trying to think of what to say. He wanted this moment to last forever, and yet he wanted it over with so the pain would go away—the pain he didn't feel until he was finally ready to talk.

"So does this mean what I think it means?" Marylyn

asked, trying to look professional. Her hands started to tremble as she pretended to look through his file.

"I don't know what to say, Marylyn," Mark began. "I just know I had to come see you. My orders have arrived. I will be going back to Michigan in a few days. I'm not sure what to do now."

Marylyn knew what he meant but tried to act like he was talking about the therapy. "Well, you will just have to find a way to stay away from drugs by not looking for them once you're home."

"Yeah," Mark said, looking at the floor. Then he looked into her eyes, and the words just seemed to flow out of their own volition. "I don't know what to do about you." He was suddenly embarrassed, so he covered it up with "But you probably know. You probably see this a lot. Is it from the fact that you have been guiding me to the way out?"

Marylyn, taking the lead, said, "Well, this happens a lot with clients and therapists. There is a bonding that takes place, but it's always different for each case. I think this is just from the way we had to work together."

"You think so?" Mark said, wondering if she was being honest or if it really was more.

"Yeah, I think so," she said, composing herself into something she didn't like being.

Mark began to think that maybe he had imagined the whole thing. "Okay ... well then ..." He stood up. "Is there anything I need to sign or do to make this our final session?"

"No," Marylyn replied, still looking at the file in her hands.

Mark nodded and got up to head for the door. "Well … thank you for all you did for me. I hope things continue to go well for you as you help others. You really did a lot for me." Then he walked to the door.

"Wait," Marylyn said in an almost desperate voice. "I just wanted to say I really enjoyed working with you too. You taught me some things I can use to be a better therapist. I hope you find all that you are looking for when you get home."

Mark hesitated and then asked in an almost squeaky voice, "Do you mind if I have your address just in case I get the chance to get in touch to let you know how I am?" The sound made him feel a little embarrassed, but he was glad he asked.

"Sure!" Marylyn exclaimed before she had a chance to control her excitement. She wrote it down and handed it to him. Mark tried to take it, but she held onto it for a moment, as if to say, "Don't go."

Mark smiled. "You take care." Then, out of impulse, he moved closer to her and hugged her. She hugged him back. Mark then turned and walked out. He never turned around to look. He was afraid he would do something that would make him ruin everything he thought it was.

CHAPTER TWENTY-ONE

Mark spent that night drinking at the NCO club. He kept thinking about Marylyn. He thought it might be better than being lost on what to do once he got home. Besides, she was a much more pleasant thought to dwell on than himself. He kept seeing her face as he drank the night away.

"So are you drinking alone?" a voice came from behind. Mark turned around to see Teddy grabbing a chair to sit with him.

"Hey, man." Mark smiled. "What's going on with you? I never see you in here."

"I know." Teddy laughed as he sat down. "I never drink unless I've got nothing else going on. But I'm glad to see you. I was wondering if we could talk for a moment."

"Well, let me check my schedule. I may have a few minutes," Mark joked, taking another drink of his beer. "What's on your mind?"

Teddy got straight to the point. "What do you know about hepatitis?"

"Not a lot. I know one guy who got it from not

properly washing his dishes. I've heard you can get it from dirty needles, but I don't do needles." Then Mark had a sudden start. "Wait! Don't tell me you've been using dirty needles." Mark was getting a little anxious, hoping that this wasn't why Teddy was asking.

"Actually, I did. We only had one between the three of us. We tried to clean it each time with rubbing alcohol, but I guess it didn't work," Teddy said quietly, looking around to make sure no one was listening.

"Yeah, well, it's hard to clean the inside of the needle, you know. You can't just wash the outside of it and expect it to be good again. That's why hospitals never use the same needle twice, even on the same person." Mark was trying to sound even-toned and not get Teddy excited, but it was hard to keep his emotions hidden. "What were you using?"

"Heroin," Teddy said, still trying to keep it quiet. "My urine is getting dark, and my eyes are turning yellow. So is my skin. I don't know what to do. Any ideas?"

"Go to a hospital. A doctor. Get to the medics. Whatever you have to do before you have it so bad it kills you, man," Mark said, getting worried. "You can't just wait for it to go away. You also need to know it's contagious—using the same glass, silverware, or, if it's bad enough, the same air you breathe. Don't mess with it, man."

"What makes you so sure of what you're telling me?" Teddy asked to make sure of the facts.

"It's not like I'm an expert, but I did learn some things in counseling, which is where I learned what I just told you. My counselor is real good at teaching about the diseases you can get from drugs." Mark spoke like he was still in class as he explained the lessons he had learned from Marylyn. "So tell me that you'll see a doctor or something first thing tomorrow. Okay?"

"Yeah, I will," Teddy said as he finished his first drink. Then, after he put the glass down, he walked away. Mark wasn't convinced he would do as he said.

Mark had bought himself another beer when Jeremy suddenly joined him. "Mind if I join you?" he asked as he sat down next to Mark.

"Please do." Mark smiled, enjoying how people kept finding him.

"So are you enjoying your last days of freedom?" Jeremy joked as he ordered a drink.

"Yes, I am," Mark said as he lit up a cigarette. "How about you? How's your night going?"

"I'm doing okay. I was just looking for something different. Thought a drink or two would be a good way to get the night going. Doesn't seem to be a lot of guys around. What are you doing here?" Jeremy asked as he downed his first drink like a sailor.

"I don't have a lot of choices anymore. I know I'm being watched a lot closer than I used to be. You know about my new best friend," Mark said sarcastically. "With the lieutenant hounding me, I need to 'be a better man.'" Mark laughed.

"So you're really going home." Jeremy smiled as he downed his second drink. "I won't be too far behind you. I'm down to my last days here myself."

"Here's to us, then." Mark lifted his drink to Jeremy. "It's too bad I have to leave like this. I wish I could go the way everyone else does. It feels like it's an empty victory."

"I wouldn't say it was an empty victory. Do you remember what you told me about why you came here?" Jeremy asked.

"Yeah, it was to have time to get things figured out so I could have a future. Why?" Mark asked, knowing Jeremy was making a point.

"Well, did you gain time to think?" Jeremy asked.

"I gained some time, but I can't really say I got anything thought out," Mark said, thinking it over.

"Really? I think you did. You got ahold of something you didn't have when you first got here," Jeremy said, trying to encourage him.

"What? What did I get ahold of? I think you've been drinking too much already." Mark smiled as he took another drink himself.

"No, man, listen," Jeremy started again. "You keep talking to me about how God has been helping you, right?"

Mark nodded as he began to listen more intently. "Go on."

"Well, if everything you say is true, then He is real. You didn't have that before. I'd say you got a very powerful aid helping you. If God is real, then I don't think He's confined to just this place. That means He will be with you all the way, right?" Jeremy was beginning to make sense.

Mark thought about his reasoning for a little bit as he nursed his beer. Finally he nodded. "You know what? I think you're right. If that's the case, then I just might make it all the way to old age."

They both smiled and finished their drinks. Mark looked at his watch and decided to head back to the barracks. They walked the short road to the building, stumbling from time to time. Mark had a sudden question. "Tell me again why you're such a good friend. I know for sure I don't deserve it."

"You do," Jeremy answered him. "I'm the one that doesn't deserve it."

They finally got to Jeremy's room. Mark looked around, trying to remember how it had been before he moved out. It had only been a couple of days, but it seemed like a lifetime ago already. Strange, Mark thought, how fast things could change. In what seemed like only a blink of an eye his whole world had been turned upside down and inside out. It wasn't all bad, but it was just as confusing as the day he arrived.

Jason walked in, looking like he had been doing some drinking himself. After he took a seat on his bunk he looked at Mark and started in. "So you think you got all your answers yet?"

Mark looked at Jason, trying to figure out where he was going with his question. It seemed to Mark that he was looking for trouble. "So what's your point?"

"Really? You don't know what I'm talking about?" Jason looked at Mark with disdain.

"Is there something I did to make you so angry that

you want to start an argument for no reason?" Mark looked at him, trying to think his way through it.

"You're a weasel. You always think you can use people and take what they offer without giving anything back. Then you start talking about God like He's the Easter bunny. Guess what? He doesn't exist. It's all in your head. All in your head." It was clear that Jason had a strong stand against believing in God.

"That doesn't make any sense. You start out talking about one thing and then turn it around and talk about another. You don't hate me because you think I'm a weasel. You hate God. But thing is, if God doesn't exist, then how can you hate someone or something that isn't real? If you're going to be angry, start talking sense." Mark was starting to get a little angry himself. He didn't like being pushed into a corner for no reason.

"Okay then, tell me why you think He is real." Jason had been waiting a long time to do this. He had even put off his feelings when they were high and talking about the tapestry. Now was his chance to make it all look like stupidity.

"Before I explain it to you, let me ask you one thing. Do you believe in the wind?" Mark began to lay out his proof.

"The wind? Yeah I believe there's wind. But you can prove the wind," Jason said, defending his thoughts.

"How? Can you actually see it, or do you just see the results of it? You can't actually see air or the wind, but you know it's here. You can feel it, hear it, and, at times, smell it. But no one has ever seen it. Right?" Mark thought he had a sound frame of thought.

"So what's that got to do with this?" Jason countered.

"I have felt God's presence, and I have heard His voice inside me. I still remember the day He told me my mom was dead. I remember it like it was yesterday. I have seen the results of His presence in the prayers He has answered for me—like when He protected me from the lieutenant busting me for drugs. I was honest, and yet I wasn't searched. They figured I was lying and left me alone. Since when does the lieutenant just leave you alone?" Mark knew he was on a roll and wanted to keep going before he lost momentum. "I know people have been praying for me, and that is why I didn't die when I jumped into that hole. I should have hit my head on my bedpost, but I didn't. That would have killed me. I should have gone to prison for dealing, but I was released and found innocent. We all in this room know I was guilty. I had one of the hardest judges on drugs, and he let me go. Me. I have nothing special to offer, but he let me go. Can you explain that?"

Jason stared at Mark like he wanted to just get up and beat him but couldn't. Jeremy had been sitting at the desk watching the confrontation the whole time. Finally he interrupted with a thought of his own. "So where is this all going anyway, Jason?"

"What do you mean? You know God isn't real," Jason protested.

"Well, you heard Mark's explanation. What do you have to argue it? Make it something that makes sense, because we both know everything Mark has said is true—everything except what he said about his mother. We weren't there to see that. But we saw everything else. Right?" Jeremy was getting tired of Jason always complaining about how Mark was always so lucky. "Explain his luck."

"Okay, so I don't have anything to disprove it. But you know it's all a fairy tale." Jason was starting to break down.

"Why do you think that?" Mark began to realize this had more to do with Jason and something that had happened. "What happened to you?"

"If He's real and if He's so great, then where was He for my brother?" Jason started to tear up.

"Well, I could say the same for my mother, you know," Mark said, trying to put it all in perspective. "I know she was a Christian."

"My brother had his whole life ahead of him. There was no reason for him to drown. He was a good kid. Why would God just take him away?" Jason was becoming more agitated.

"Who says God is the one that took him? You know there are demons out there. You have to know, because you know there is a God. Ever think God was with him when he was going? Maybe God made it painless and took away his fear. Maybe God walked with him through the whole thing while the devils were doing their dirty work. Is that possible?" Mark didn't know, but he figured that was how it had been for his mother when she died.

"You know what? I'm not going to do this. You know

how I feel, and I know how you feel. So let's just leave it at that." Jason was getting tired. He knew he didn't have any more to stand on than he thought Mark did.

Jeremy decided it was time to mellow the whole thing out. He had been preparing a bowl for this moment. Seeing both of them slowing down, he took out his lighter and lit it up. "Here you go, man." He handed it to Jason. "Let's do something a little more relaxing."

Jason took it without saying a word. He just stared off into space as he took a long toke. Then, after holding it awhile, he took another one and then handed it to Mark. "You up to doing one more bowl with us? Or are you too holy?"

Mark smiled at him. "Let me have it, man." Mark took the bowl from Jason, took a turn, and handed it to Jeremy. They began to mellow out as Jeremy put on some music to make the night more pleasing.

They smoked until the bowl was gone. Mark looked at Jason. It was obvious to Mark that Jason was hurting inside for a brother he would never see again. Mark sometimes felt the same way about his mother. It didn't hurt as much now as it had when he was younger, but the pain was still there from time to time. It was hard to know a person he once loved would never be seen, heard, felt, or touched again. He finally got up and took a step toward Jason and put his hand on Jason's shoulder. "I know, man. I think about my mom every day. It's been ten years, but I still miss her. Sorry." Mark left for his own bed.

Sunday was the kind of day that looked like it would come and go with no meaning. Mark felt like it was almost a waste. He was beginning to feel like every day should have a meaning of all its own. He was becoming more and more appreciative of all he had.

Mark thought about it as he was getting up for the day. He made his bunk and then got to thinking. This could be the last chance he'd have to have breakfast with Jeremy. Who knew what Monday was going to bring? Once he was dressed he went back up to Jeremy and Jason's room.

They were just getting up themselves. Mark sat at the desk as he waited for them to finish dressing. He thought about the night before, but he didn't know if he should say anything or not. Then Jason spoke. "So did you sleep okay?"

"Yeah, I was out before I hit the bed. I needed that. Thanks for the smoke last night," Mark said as he smiled at Jason.

"Me too. I think I was drunk. I don't get drunk that often. I've never talked about my brother before," Jason said as he went about getting ready.

"I know I've never heard about it before. I'm sorry to hear about him." Mark didn't know what else to say.

"It's all right. It happened a while ago. I'll get over it. Right?" Jason tried to make it look like it would be easy to do.

"Yeah, I guess we all do over time," Mark answered as he waited quietly.

They went to breakfast and ate quietly. They were still recovering from a hard, drunk night and looking forward to resting one more day before getting back to the normal workweek. Jeremy lit up a cigarette as he sat back in his chair. "So do you think you will eat this good at home?"

"I don't know. I think any food in freedom will taste good. Right, Jason?" Mark was hoping to have some kind of resolution in their friendship.

"Yeah, I think you might be right." Jason finished up his last bite before he was ready to light up a cigarette.

Mark finished at about the same time and lit one up as well. They all sat back and relaxed as they enjoyed what they thought might be their last time together. Jason looked at Mark and thought out loud for all of them. "You know … it's always hard to tell what Monday will bring."

Thinking about it, the other two simultaneously said, "You got that right." All three of them smiled at each other, thinking they were finally able to be close for once. Mark took it all in as he smoked and drank coffee. He felt like he would never have friends like these two again.

On the one hand, he was looking forward to his new adventure with whatever he thought God might have waiting for him. Still, on the other hand, he wondered how even God would be able to give him friends like the ones he had with him at that moment. It was hard to really know what God had in store for someone who didn't know a thing about what it meant to follow Him.

They went back to Jeremy's room and put on some music and smoked some hash. Mark got to wondering whether there wasn't something they could do to make the day pass by faster and more enjoyable. "So what do you guys want to do this afternoon? There's got to be something we can do that would be fun."

They had just finished the bowl and Jeremy was hiding it in the floor when a knock came at the door. Jason looked at Jeremy to make sure to give him enough time to put the floorboards back in place. "Who is it?"

"Open up. It's Lieutenant Danson," said a voice from the hallway.

All three looked at each other wondering what it was all about. The lieutenant never came around the barracks on the weekend. Jeremy went to the door and opened up. "Attention!" he shouted as they all complied and prepared a salute.

"At ease, men," the lieutenant said as he walked in. "I smell something unusual. Do you young men have any hash in here?"

"No, sir," Jason answered before anyone else could think. "Why would you think that, sir?"

"Like I said, soldier. I can smell it," the lieutenant replied as he walked around the room. He took his time to look under the beds and through the shelves the stereo sat on. Finally, as a last gesture, he opened up the lockers that were unlocked and lifted items to see what may be underneath them. "I want you all to know I will be personally watching all of you from now on. I know there are things going on that need to stop. I will catch you." Looking at Mark, he repeated himself very emphatically, "I will catch you."

Then, just as suddenly as he arrived, the lieutenant left the room. "You gentlemen have a good afternoon."

"What was that?" Jeremy asked, glancing at Mark with a look of irritation in his eyes.

"Sorry, man," Mark said with a slight smile. "He likes me."

"Well, he can just like you somewhere else, don't you think?" Jason opened up with his own flare of humor.

"I'll see what I can do to keep him at bay. I know he said he wants all of us, but I think he really only wants me. I think I made him angry," Mark said, trying to be more serious.

The three looked at each other, trying to get a grip on what to do about this new problem. "Being popular isn't all it's cracked up to be, I think," Jeremy finally said.

"I think I'd better go and put some space between us. Perhaps from now on the less we see of each other the better for you two." Mark thought this out of concern for his friends. "I'm sorry if I just made your lives more difficult for the rest of your time here."

Jeremy started laughing. "You didn't, man. If there's one thing I'm starting to learn, it's that life is an adventure and we just cannot take responsibility for what other people do. We can only be responsible for how we react to them."

Mark nodded in agreement and then left the room. He wasn't sure where he was going to go, but he knew it had to be away from his friends. It was his turn to make the sacrifice for the rest.

Mark decided with the sun starting to go down he would walk the base one last time. It felt good to feel with warmth after the recent cold days. He just walked around the perimeter of the post to think and reflect one last time on how his life had been the whole time he had been there.

He was lost in thought as he inspected every stone and crack on the street. It seemed important to Mark to try to remember everything he was seeing. He tried to recall all the memories he had made the whole time he was there. He knew he would never be in this place again. Taking his time, Mark finally came back to his own barracks as the sun was setting and the shadows were getting longer and darker.

Looking at his watch, Mark realized it was suppertime. It felt good to have another reason to walk at least a little farther. So supper it was. He sat alone looking around at the mess hall. It all looked different now that he was seeing it through eyes that were not going to see it very many more times.

Mark was drinking a cup of coffee as he began to think. He counted the number of times he thought he would be eating there. At three times a day, he figured maybe it would be nine more times. He knew time would fly by faster now that it was down to single digits.

It felt good to have the time to enjoy another cup of coffee. He sat back after eating and lit up a cigarette. As he began to smoke he thought he should have packed extra cartons of cigarettes to ship home. It would have saved him money once he was back in the States.

Then again, he knew his aunt would never allow him to smoke in the house. Maybe it was time to also stop smoking as long as he was going to have to stop using drugs. The plan to stop seemed simple enough. If he wasn't around it, then he would have to quit. How would he get a hold of any? Cigarettes would be tougher to quit. All he'd have to do would be to go to the store and buy them.

While he was thinking, he realized everyone was leaving the mess hall. It was dark outside. Looking at his watch, Mark realized the mess hall would be closing soon. It was time to go back to his room for one of the last nights he would be there. It was going to be a lonely night. It was time to cut all ties to his friends. That was the only way to protect them from being busted.

The evening was going slow. Mark took his time to get ready for bed. There was no furniture except for his bed and a nightstand. Mark stood by his door and looked at the room. It felt so empty and so cold. Yet at the same time he thought about how in a few more days he would be back in Michigan. It was exciting as well. The feeling was confusing as he kept being taken back and forth by the empty room and the hope of things yet to come. The idea made him smile.

Suddenly there was a knock at the door. Mark was pulled out of his train of thought as he heard a lot of voices in the hallway. Immediately he thought his night was about to be ruined by another visit from his favorite fan: the lieutenant.

He opened the door, expecting to be humiliated one more time that day. "Surprise!" The voices of at least a dozen of his friends flooded his ears as they came into the room, everyone talking at once.

"What's going on?" Mark asked, definitely surprised and concerned.

"It's a going-away party," Jeremy said as he handed Mark a bottle of wine. "Since no one knows for sure when you're leaving the barracks, we thought we should send you on your way while we still had the chance. You don't mind, do you?" Jeremy's smile made it impossible for Mark to resist.

Smiling at the idea, Mark answered, "No. How could I mind?"

Talking with several people at once, Mark noticed the room was as crowded as any room had ever been since he had been there. There were some guys he didn't even think he knew.

Then he smelled a familiar odor. "Hey! You guys aren't doing up a bowl, are you?"

"Yeah, why?" came an answer from one of the guys. "Don't tell us you don't want any." There was a lot of laughing. Mark wasn't sure if it had to do with the question or just all the conversations going on at the same time.

Another knock came on the door. Everyone became quiet on his own as if by signal. They all looked at Mark, who was petrified by what he was seeing and now hearing.

"Who is it?" Mark asked, knowing in his heart it was the lieutenant.

"Lieutenant Danson" came the reply.

Mark looked around the room and spied the big pile of the hash on his bed. While everyone else was looking for a place to hide it, Mark knew there was only one thing left to do. In one motion he picked up the sheet of paper and funneled the hash into his mouth. It was like eating dirt. His teeth were filled with grit and the taste was like dust. He then grabbed the bottle of wine to rinse out his mouth and started guzzling it down, swallowing hash and all.

Mark made his way quickly to the door from the bed, pushing his way through all the guys still looking for a hiding place. "Come on in, sir," Mark said as he opened the door. "It was hard to get to the door with everyone here."

"What's going on here?" Danson asked as he immediately began to search the room for the drugs he knew were there.

"They're just giving me a going away party, sir," Mark answered as he followed the lieutenant around the room. Everyone made way for both of them as the inspection went on. Lieutenant Danson looked everywhere he could think of. He opened the windows and looked to see what might have been thrown outside. He looked under the mattress and inside the nightstand and went all through the locker.

Finally, after exhausting all his ideas and looking very disappointed, he turned to Mark. "I know there are drugs in here. I can smell it." His face was very angered as he tried to make Mark feel insignificant.

Looking into Lieutenant Danson's eyes, Mark replied, "Well, sir, if you can find what isn't here, then by all means confiscate it all and take me in. The only thing in this room now besides all of you is this wine. Would you like some?"

This made Lieutenant Danson even angrier. "I will catch you. You will make a mistake, and that will be the end of it." With his threat made, the lieutenant left the room. Mark watched him walk down the hallway to be sure he was out of earshot for the announcement he knew he had to make.

"Wow" came a lot of voices in unison. "Where did you hide it?"

"I have some bad news. I'm sorry, but I didn't know what else to do," Mark said as he knew he now had everyone's attention. "I ate it all."

It was like killing a boy's puppy. There was complete silence. "No, really," he said, putting forth a faint effort at reasoning. One of the guys was sure it was all a joke and the party was only beginning.

"Yes, really," Mark answered, disappointed himself. "I'm sorry, but we all would have gone to prison, something I am not willing to do. Do any of you have more in your room or something?"

That was too much to hope for. The answer was obvious by the complete silence that now filled the room. The door opened, and one by one they all filed into the hallway with their heads hung low, the disappointment all over their faces.

Mark stood by the door, trying to show his appreciation for their good intentions. "Thanks, man, for trying and caring," he said to each one as they all went back to their own rooms. In a moment, as fast as the room had filled up, Mark was once again all alone with his thoughts.

He looked around to make sure nothing was left that could incriminate him if found. There was nothing, only the brief memory of what could have been. Mark got into bed. He had expected the hash to make him feel high. He was sure from all he had heard that he would feel much different than he did as he prepared to sleep. The only thing he could think of was it was bad hash. He hoped he wouldn't have another week of vomiting like the last time. With that thought, he went to sleep.

CHAPTER TWENTY-TWO

On Monday morning, Mark woke up to a knock on the door, as he didn't even have an alarm clock left. CQ had to wake him up on their way back to their rooms at the end of their shifts.

Mark yelled out, "Okay, I'm up," and heard them walk away on the stone floor in the hallway. He opened his eyes but still felt like he was in a dream. It must have been the heavy sleep he'd had. He threw back his blankets and floated as he sat up on the edge of his bed. This was the strangest feeling he had ever had, he thought.

Mark stood up to walk to the light switch, but it was also like floating. He looked at his feet to make sure they were on the floor. Concentrating, he could feel the cold floor, but it was more like a dream than a reality. "What's going on?" Mark asked himself as he purposely slid his feet to get to his locker. He was beginning to wonder if he had taken something in the night to drug him.

It was difficult, but Mark made himself try to remember all he could to figure out what was making him feel this way. "Ah, the party." Mark smiled to himself.

The hash. It must take time for it to get into his blood stream if digested. Now that he knew what was going on, he decided it was the most pleasant feeling he had ever had in his whole life.

Mark found his towel and toiletries. It took some time in his state of mind, but he took his things and floated down to the showers. It was like discovering the world all over again as Mark searched for a place to put his things and hang his towel. From there he went into the showers.

There were four showerheads in a room that was about an eight by eight square foot. Mark turned on all four showers to get the full effect of the steam. This was often done when a person was alone in the showers. This way anyone new coming in wouldn't have to warm them up. There was also the extra benefit of the warmth of the steam.

There was a new advantage for Mark that morning. Although Mark was colorblind, he could now see colors he never knew existed. There was a rainbow that was hypnotizing him into euphoria.

Mark was not sure how long he had been in the showers when he heard a voice. "You ever going to be done in there?"

Mark started laughing. "Yeah, I think so." He noticed his skin was beginning to get that wrinkled look from prolonged exposure to water. In fact, his whole body was turning pink from the warmth. It was by far the best shower he had ever had. Mark began to wonder if heaven was like this.

It took a long time, but Mark was finally dressed. He made his way back to his room to get his coat and go to breakfast. The walk down the hallway was like walking in a tunnel. The lights were like silver and gold globes giving off life to each living thing that passed through the wonderful rays of light. It was all Mark could do to not outright laugh as he enjoyed his newfound joy.

Finally, as he reached the end of the hallway, he opened the doors to the great outdoors. The bright sunlight caused him to squint as he walked into the wonderful world. The fresh air was exhilarating as he breathed it in.

The walk to the mess hall was filled with a splendor of color. All the greens, yellows, and blues from the grass, light, and sky glowed in their own way as they bounced off each other in a radiance all their own. The paint on the buildings, signs, and posts tried to speak to him with their own colorful story of existence as he walked by them. Mark was filled with awe as he discovered a whole new scheme of life and its own collage of wonderful colors.

Miraculously, he reached the mess hall. Mark began to notice the colors were not the only new thing to his senses. The sounds coming from the building were amazingly different as well. There was a kind of echo as each voice was bouncing off the walls of a cave. The vibrating sounds each had its own unique resonance. It was life in full stereo, filled with reverberation and vibrant beauty.

Mark continued to float as he made his way to the chow line. It was as if his new world had arrived and he was an observer. He was on the outside looking in and enjoying the wonders of being the critic of a masterpiece of creation.

Mark reached the counter and took in yet another new sense. The aroma was in its own realm of splendor. It was as if each odor was its own entity. Every smell had its own distinct boundary of pleasantness. His mouth watered with anticipation of what may soon fill it. His stomach began its own orchestra of sound as it rumbled in anticipation.

Mark enjoyed the meal. It consisted of eggs, bacon, sausage, toast, grape jelly, coffee, and a cinnamon roll for dessert. Mark had to concentrate as he made his way to an empty table. It would have been easy to spill his plunder on the floor. He found it difficult to do the most common of tasks without being distracted by his new world.

Gazing at his feast, Mark sat down and reached for his silverware, only to discover he had forgotten it. Once again he floated to the front of the line to retrieve the needed tools for the job at hand.

Mark made his way back to the table and began to devour his meal. He had imagined it would be more like everything else had been from the time he woke up until he put the first forkful of delight in his mouth. To his surprise, once he began to converge on his plate, he vacuumed it all into his throat like a dog devouring long-awaited meat. It was gone before he had a chance to know how it tasted. Mark had not realized the strength of his hunger until that very moment. The meal was gone in seconds.

This could only mean one thing in his mind. It was

time to get another plateful and see if it was possible to enjoy the flavor. In moments he had a new meal. This time the flavor matched the aroma. Taking his time, Mark was able to appreciate breakfast just as he had his shower and walk.

After the meal he was enjoying a cup of coffee and cigarette when he suddenly realized he was going to be late for formation if he did not get moving. The dream, he thought, was about to be over. He was mistaken.

Rushing back to the barracks, Mark found most of the men milling around the gathering area where formation would take place. Still in a dream state, Mark found his place and waited for the orders to be given to fall in. Everything seemed to be happening like it was a fairy tale. The story was unfolding just as if he were reading it—with one exception. Mark was in the pages he was living. All he had to do was wait for his cue, and he would know it was time to do whatever the story was calling for.

One of the guys was going to drive to Frankfurt on a drop-off run. He needed a man to ride shotgun. Most of the guys knew what was going on for Mark even though he was not aware of it. "I want to take Welch with me to help once I get there," Henry said as he was given the assignment.

"Very well," Mark heard the sergeant say. Then Mark realized Lieutenant Danson wasn't present. This was a pleasant surprise all on its own. He wondered where he might be but hoped the lieutenant would not appear until long after Mark was on the road. To his delight, they were in the truck and leaving the post long before the lieutenant arrived.

The ride was very exhilarating. Mark enjoyed the wind as it blew through his hair. All the colors he'd been enjoying from the time he woke up were still alive and vibrating in his eyes as they flew by his window. The rainbow was moving at sixty miles an hour as he tried to breathe in every shaft of light that reflected the color scheme moving quickly through his mind.

Mark thought about his trip. He compared it to all the acid trips he had been on. He had heard how acid was supposed to bring colors to life, but none of the trips he had been a part of were even close to the one he was on that morning. This was not work. It was not a job. For the first time since he began to wear olive green it really was an adventure—an adventure he hoped would have no end.

The truck began to slow down, and Mark realized they were already in Frankfurt. On the one hand, he was excited, knowing he would be back to this wonderful city again very soon to fly home. On the other hand, it was disappointing, as being there at that time meant the trip was already half over. Mark wanted it to go on forever.

Henry finally spoke, breaking the silence that Mark hadn't even noticed until then. "Hey, are you hungry?"

"What?" Mark answered, taken out of his dream world. "Oh, wow, man. Are we there already?"

Henry laughed as he looked at Mark's eyes. "I wish I was on the same trip you're on. Yes, we are in Frankfurt. Are you hungry?"

"Yeah, man." Mark smiled. "Where are we going to eat?"

"The mess hall packed a lunch for us in the back. I'm not about to take you in public. I may never see you again." Henry laughed. He then left the truck cab and went to the back to retrieve their lunches. Mark waited patiently, not even sure if he could move anymore.

Henry handed him a lunch. Mark didn't know what it was, but then it really didn't matter, as it was gone before Mark had a chance to know what it tasted like. Henry was watching in pure amazement. "Wow, man, did you chew any of that?"

"I think so," Mark answered with a lost look in his eyes. "Why?"

"It didn't look like it." Henry giggled as he took only his third bite from his own lunch. "You still hungry?"

"I don't know." Mark thought about it. "I don't think so. To be honest, I'm not sure. Is that a problem?"

"Not if it isn't to you," Henry said, chewing his food much more carefully than Mark had.

The rest of lunchtime went by without any more discussion. Mark was once again lost in his world of free-spirited observation. There were people walking around who had no idea Mark and Henry were even there. Everyone was going about his or her own business. Mark was watching them when he realized they were not in a military facility. "Hey, where are we, anyway?"

"Frankfurt. Why?" Henry asked.

"I know what city we're in, but where in Frankfurt? I

thought we were going to a military facility." Mark tried to get his question out so Henry could understand.

"Oh, yeah, well, we are almost to the airport. You know, where you will be in a day or two. I have to go to the holding warehouse to pick up the things we came to get. I stopped because once we pick it up and sign the papers we only have so much time to get back. So I thought we would eat first. That way, by the time we get back, it will be chow time again, and maybe we will be hungry. You know … keep it all balanced." Henry was hoping this all made sense to Mark so he wouldn't have to re-explain.

"Oh, okay. Sounds good," Mark said, not really knowing the point but not really caring, either. He just wanted to know where they were. Satisfied with the answer, Mark went back to his fantasy world and soon realized he was waking up to the road again.

Henry had finished his meal, gotten back in the truck, and made the pickup while Mark was finally sleeping off his fantastic high. All Henry could do was smile, knowing what it must be like in Mark's mind at that time.

Mark was trying to get his bearings. He looked at everything going by the window. It was of no use. There was not one single landmark that Mark recognized. Becoming suspicious that they may be lost, Mark looked at Henry for any sign of confusion. There was none. They were not lost. Only Mark was. That was okay with him as long as they made it to where they were going and he continued to enjoy his day.

True to his word, Henry got them back to their post just in time for dinner. Mark got out of the truck to find several other soldiers taking the load out of the back. There was not one thing Mark had to do that day. His whole responsibility was to avoid trouble and finish the day without incident. Mission accomplished.

Mark walked to the mess hall but found it to be the mundane establishment it had always been rather than the pleasurable surprise it had been earlier that morning. Mark let out a sigh as he realized the high was finally wearing off. To his relief, it was none too soon, as he walked past Lieutenant Danson on his way to chow line.

"Soldier, where were you today?" Lieutenant Danson barked out.

"I went to Frankfurt with Specialist Henry, sir. Why?" Mark answered, hoping not to be in more trouble.

"Who told you to do that?" the lieutenant asked with narrowed eyes.

"The quartermaster sergeant, sir. I was just following orders," Mark replied, beginning to wonder what the deal was.

"Very well. As long as you didn't take it upon yourself." Then the lieutenant was gone. Mark wondered how he would ever go on a trip like that and get away with taking it upon himself to do so. It seemed ridiculous to Mark to even suggest it. He figured the lieutenant just wanted to harass him one more time for the day.

After eating, Mark decided to stop by his room for another pack of cigarettes and then go see Jeremy in his room. Mark walked into his empty room and got a pack from his locker. As he was about to close his locker, he saw his orders folded on the same shelf. He decided to read them to refresh his memory on when he was leaving. He read the words and then took the time to read them again to make sure he was seeing it right. He was to be leaving the following morning. *Wow!* It was really happening. He had just had his last full day in Germany. He was leaving in the morning.

Then he began to worry. Did everyone else who needed to know have his ride and ticket all set? This was all new to him. He remembered using his orders to get on the plane to get there, but how was he getting to the airport?

He had to walk past CQ anyway to use the stairs to the third floor. He stopped to talk to the CQ on duty. "Hey, man, do you know anything about me having a ride to the airport in the morning?"

"Hold on, let me look," the CQ said as he picked up his clipboard full of orders to see to. "Are you Mark Welch?" he asked.

"Yeah. Is that it there?" Mark asked in return.

"Yeah. There'll be a driver in a jeep waiting for you at 0600 hours. You are to have all your things packed in a duffel bag and ready to go then. Any other questions?" the CQ asked.

"No, thanks, man." Mark smiled as he began to go up the stairs to see Jeremy. He knocked on the door to hear the usual "Who is it?"

"It's me, man. Mark," he replied, waiting for the door to open.

"Hey, come on in," Jeremy said as the door opened wide.

"You coming in to eat all our stash too?" Jason asked, smiling, a twinkle in his eyes.

"You got any to eat?" Mark said, smiling even larger. "Man, you won't believe the high I've been on today."

"I'll bet," Jeremy said as he sat down on his bunk.

"Hey," Mark started, "I just came to tell you guys I'm leaving at six in the morning. This really is my last night here."

"Wow, it really is over, then," Jason said as he looked intently at Mark. "You really are leaving before us. How's it feel?"

"Like a dream—a dream that could just as easily turn into a nightmare," Mark began. "I know my orders say to go to Fort Dixie in New Jersey, but sometimes I think it's all a trap. It's some kind of trick the army is playing on me to get me to go to the slaughter without a fight. I don't know—maybe I'm just too paranoid," Mark said, thinking out loud.

"That happens with a good high," Jeremy said as he began to look for the bowl. "How about we have one last parting gift? What do you think?"

"Are you sure?" Mark asked, even more paranoid. "You know what happened last night, right?"

"Yeah, I know," Jeremy said. "That's why we only have out what we'll smoke in one bowl. If he shows up, we dip it in this cup of water on the desk there and put it in the floor. We did a trial run last night just to see if it would work."

"Ah … nothing like doing your homework," Mark said as he took a seat, anticipating one more high. He knew it could very well be his last. In fact, it needed to be.

Jason seized the bowl and lit it up for the first toke. After filling his lungs with smoke, he handed it to Mark. Mark took the bowl and looked at it as if it was his very first time. Then he looked at the other two. "You know," he said, smiling, "this is the room and almost the exact spot where I took my very first hit of hash. This is déjà vu." Mark smiled even more and then took a hit from the bowl.

Once his lungs were full of smoke, he passed it on to Jeremy, who nodded in agreement—this was truly a moment to celebrate. Mark, however, knew it would also be the last time he would ever smoke hash again. God willing, this would become a memory that would be lost forever as time marched on in his life.

They finished the bowl, and Mark sat at the desk for a little while, listening to the music that he didn't have in his own room. Once again he was lost in thought. This seemed to be happening to him a lot in his last days there. He thought it was a natural phenomenon, as he was trying to sear into his brain all that he could to take back with him in honor of all he had been through.

Again, there was a knock at the door. Jeremy had just placed the bowl in the floor. Still feeling the intensity of always being followed by the lieutenant, Mark sat staring at the door.

Jason got up and opened the door to find Henry

looking in. "Hey, man, what's up?" Jason asked as he opened the door wider.

"Nothing. I was just checking in on Mark. I wanted to make sure he was staying out of trouble for the rest of the day. Serge asked me to keep him out of harm's way," Henry said, looking for a seat. "What are you guys up to?"

"Not much," Jason said. He looked at Jeremy to see if he was concerned by the visit. Then Mark spoke up. "I was just missing the music. Thought I'd pay one more visit to my old stomping ground before I take that big bird in the sky back home."

"Are all your things packed?" Henry asked, a little eager.

"Most of it is, but I want to shower in the morning, so I still have all my toiletries and a fresh set of clothes sitting out. Why?" Mark asked.

"I was just wondering if it was too late to pack me in your bag." Henry smiled as he lit up a cigarette. "Wish I was going with you. I miss home."

"Don't we all," Jeremy said as he watched the conversation take place. It all seemed a bit odd to both Jeremy and Jason. They never saw Henry in their area and were a bit suspicious of his intent.

Mark began to sense it better himself as he was coming off one high and beginning another from the bowl they just smoked. "Well, I guess I need to get back to my little hole in the wall and enjoy my last night of sleep in this world." With that, Mark got up and went back down the stairs.

He had reached the first floor when he saw his old platoon sergeant standing just outside the doors, which were blocked open for fresh air. "Hey, serge," Mark said as he approached him. "What are you up to tonight?"

The sergeant looked at him with his pipe in his hand and thought before he spoke. "You know you had as much potential as anyone here. Why are you giving it all up?"

Mark looked at him for a moment, surprised to hear him talk like that. "If I don't, then I'm either going to end up dead from some kind of overdose or busted by the lieutenant. He is determined to find a way to get me out of here by way of prison. He told me so."

"You know I wouldn't let that happen," the sergeant said as he rolled the stem of his pipe around in his mouth. "He can't do what you don't let him do."

"I know you believe that, but I don't. I just know if I'm going to have any kind of life at all I have to get out of here. I made it a place of death for myself," Mark countered.

"You know you won't make it out there. It's a different world than it is here. You don't have the skills to live there and be successful or happy," the sergeant said, trying to be convincing.

"I appreciate your confidence in me," Mark said, beginning to get irritated at the words he was hearing. "I thought you had more faith in me than that. If I can't make it in the real world, then how would I ever make in this one?"

The sergeant then turned his back to Mark and continued to smoke his pipe. Mark realized that his decision was very difficult on the sergeant and searched for the words to try to make it right. "You know I have to do this. I have always had the highest respect for you and what you stand for. This thing, though—I don't know how to explain it, but I have to do it. I know I'll be all right. I know it's the right decision for me. I'm just asking that you trust me, just like I have trusted you ever since you got here. I promise I'll be okay."

After Mark said the only words he knew to say, he turned and went back to his room. On the way he asked the CQ to wake him up at 0400 hours so he would be able to get everything done, eat, and then keep his appointment with the jeep. He looked forward to starting his long journey back to the world he had been in when he started. It really was time for him to go home.

He felt like he was dying. It was like he was leaving one world to go to another. Mark began to wonder as he was getting into bed whether this was what it was really like to die. Thinking like that, he began to see it like it was a death—the death of a green soldier and the birth of a new creation. Not knowing the Bible, he wondered if it was scriptural to think of it like that—the old person dying so a new one could live. He didn't know, but that was how it felt. He was a green soldier who was dying. In the morning he would be reborn. It really was the death of a green soldier.

CHAPTER TWENTY-THREE

A sudden knock on the door woke Mark up. It was now four in the morning, and he was about to begin his day on one continent and end it on another. The whole proposition excited him as he jumped out of bed to get ready to shower.

The showers were not nearly as exciting as they had been the day before. Yet the whole day was filled with a wonder all its own. He was going home. He could hardly stand it. Like the night before, he wondered if going through death was this exciting if you were with God. He hoped so.

He was finally ready for breakfast with an hour to go. Mark got himself up to the mess hall to wait for the doors to open. It seemed like forever as Mark kept looking at his watch. It opened right on time at five thirty. He had hoped it would open early just because the workers were ready, but it didn't.

Mark went in and got his breakfast as fast as he could. In minutes he was done and was on his way back. During the walk to the barracks, he tried to remember what it was

MICHAEL WRIGHT

he had eaten. He was in such a hurry that he couldn't even think about what he was putting on his plate. He pulled out a cigarette to smoke as he arrived.

Once back in the barracks, Mark made sure he had everything packed and his orders in his pocket. He locked his room for the last time and took his key to the CQ. "Here, you need to sign this form showing that you turned in your key," CQ said as they handed him the clipboard.

Mark signed the form and took his duffel bag outside to wait on the steps for the jeep. At exactly six o'clock the jeep arrived. "Hey, are you Mark Welch?" the driver asked.

"Yes," Mark replied as he picked up his bag to throw in the backseat.

"Go ahead and climb in. I have to let the CQ know I picked you up so they know you are on your way. Be right back." The driver got out of the jeep and headed into the building to sign the needed forms.

"Are we finally ready?" Mark asked as the driver returned. "I think I've been here long enough. I'm ready to go home."

They seated themselves to get ready to go. The driver started up the engine, and off they went, first through the gate and then down the road. Mark could hardly believe it was finally happening. He was on his way home.

He decided to talk to the driver just to keep his mind off the thought of flying. "So what's your name?"

"I'm Daryl. I usually drive for the major, but they gave me to you today. I can't help notice that your rank is specialist. How is it I'm your driver for the day?"

"I don't know." Mark smiled. He found it interesting that they gave him the major's driver. "All I know is I got special orders to go home. That works for me."

"Wow, special orders," Daryl said the words slowly, as if they were something special in themselves. "So is this some kind of a secret mission?" he joked.

"No." Mark smiled. "I wasn't a very good boy, but they couldn't prove it, so they decided to offer me an honorable discharge just to get me away from their few, proud, and brave."

Daryl smiled. "Nice. So you pulled one over on them, then."

"Not really. I'm the one who'll pay the price in the end. I didn't accomplish anything special. I put my life at risk, and now it's more in my best interest than it is the army's to get out of here before I end up killing myself or going to prison." Mark thought about his words as he said them. He wondered how he would ever explain it all to his brother. He wondered if he ever would explain it. Perhaps it was far better for some things to remain a secret. He had a lot more to think about than he realized.

They reached the airport faster than Mark had imagined they would. That was good, and yet it felt like it was all going too fast. Mark laughed at himself. A few hours ago, it couldn't go fast enough, and now all of a sudden it was going too fast. He didn't have time to adjust. His mind was spinning like a merry-go-round.

They got out and went into the terminal to find the line for military personnel. Mark took out his orders and got in line with his bag. Daryl stayed back by the doors just in case there were problems and Mark ended up staying.

It only took a few minutes before Mark was on the way to his plane. The walk to the plane was short in distance but seemed long in his mind. He kept trying to take in all the little things to make the trip more meaningful. Somehow Mark had thought it would feel more special than it did.

Mark found his seat on the plane and sat down. His duffel bag had been taken at the door to be placed in a closet near the cockpit for the duration of the flight. All he had to do was sit back and enjoy the ride over the Atlantic Ocean. Mark felt like he had waited forever for this journey. Now that he was on it, the journey seemed surreal, like the whole last week had. None of it was real, and yet it was all too real.

He thought back to when he was thinking about dying as a green soldier. He shook his head and thought he really did feel like he was in the process of crossing over. The only thing missing was the hospital bed and a doctor. Inside he was dying so that he could be reborn as a free man. He wondered how free he would be if he still didn't know what his future held. It still felt scary. He still felt alone.

He began to realize that as he contemplated his life, the plane had already flown into the air. They were on their way. Looking out the window, he thought about how he was as far away from the ground as the plane was. For the moment it felt like no matter how high they were, they were not far enough away.

He started to feel tired and fell asleep. From time to time he woke up, but for the most part he slept almost the whole flight to the United States. He finally woke up and began to think about what to do when he landed. He pulled out his orders and tried to figure out how he would get to Fort Dixie when he landed. There was nothing telling him how to do it.

He knew he would have to find a ride, but he didn't have any money on him for such a task. Thinking about it, he noticed he didn't feel any different than he had back in Germany. He was just as alone as he was when made the first flight to get there so long ago.

The flight landed right on time, and Mark found his way to the main lobby area. He looked around to see if he could find a place to rent a car. Then a man in uniform approached him. "Specialist Welch?"

"Yes," Mark answered, wondering where he had come from.

"I'm here to take you to Fort Dixie. I guess you didn't see me when you got off the plane." The man looked very professional but sounded down-to-earth.

"No, I'm sorry. I didn't even look for you. I wasn't told I would get a ride from here. I'm glad you're here," Mark said with a smile. "Thought I was going to have to walk there."

They walked out to the car, and Mark put his duffel bag in the trunk. It felt strange to ride in a car. It was even stranger to see everything written in English. He was home—well, sort of home. He was back in the States.

The ride was short to the post. He had to walk up

some stairs to the processing area. There were rooms for them at one end of the area. The main part of the large room was filled with tables and computers. There were phones ringing and people talking all over the place. There was a hallway where their rooms were. The place set up just like basic training. No privacy. They were not to leave the processing area until they were done and ready to go home.

The orders said it would take a week. Counting the day he arrived, it only took three days before he was to take a plane to Michigan. It flew by so fast Mark could hardly remember whom he had talked to about what. It was less than seventy-two hours including sleep time before he was ready to go.

"Soldier, you are now a civilian. You will need to call your people to pick you up at the airport where you will be arriving." The man speaking was an officer, but Mark didn't know his name or rank. It was all happening too fast.

"Yes, sir. I'll go call them as soon as I know when I'll be arriving." Mark was hoping to know then.

"Very well, then. Carry on." And the officer was gone. Mark was hoping for the information he needed to make the call. He didn't get it. He would have to wait.

It was suppertime. They were served McDonalds regular hamburgers. It was all very strange. Mark was eating real American food. He was just about to finish the last bite when he heard his name. "Welch?"

"Yes, sir," he answered.

"Your flight will be leaving at 1300 hours. You will

arrive in Michigan at 1800 hours. The delay is due to a layover in Chicago. Make sure to call home for your ride. Once you leave there, you are on your own. Any questions?"

"No, sir, I think I'm all set," Mark answered as he swallowed his last bite. When he was done eating, Mark went looking for the phones. They were all regular phones. No pay phones. He didn't have to pay to call home. No overseas operator—he just had to dial and talk. It felt like years since he'd been able to do that—and in fact, it had been two years since he'd left home.

After dialing the number, Mark waited for a voice. "Hello?" It was his aunt.

"Hello, Auntie, it's me, Mark," he answered. "How are you?"

"I'm doing good. Are you coming home soon?" she asked. Hope was in her voice.

"Yes. Can you be at the airport tomorrow at six in the evening?" Mark was hoping the answer was yes.

"Yes. I can be there. Where are you now?" she asked, wondering if he was okay.

"I'm in New Jersey. I am being processed out of the army. They're done with me today, but my flight doesn't leave until tomorrow." Mark was still trying to think of how to tell people why he was leaving the army early. He was hoping they didn't realize it.

"Will you be getting an honorable discharge?" she asked. Mark was shocked to hear the question.

"Of course. Why do you ask?"

"Just curious. We will be there," she said, but she almost sounded embarrassed that she'd asked.

"Okay, Auntie, I will see you then. I have to go now," Mark said, still wondering what had made her ask the question. Maybe she knew why he was getting out early. It was hard to know what she thought. It felt good to know he had a ride all the way home. It was finally done. Soon all of it would be over.

The next day was there in no time. The blur of processing was finally over. A group was transported to the airport in a van. When they arrived at the airport, the door was opened, and once the men were all out, they were gone. All the discharged soldiers were on their own.

Mark made sure he had his ticket in his hand before they left the processing area. Now he made sure he still had it. Convinced he had all he needed, Mark searched for his airline and found his way to the airplane he was riding to Chicago.

The flight took only an hour, and then he found himself walking around, waiting for his next flight. After a few short hours he was on another flight to Michigan, and after one more, he was landing. When the plane touched down, he felt a terrible feeling in his stomach. The nerves of facing his family for the first time in many years were becoming almost unbearable. He didn't know what to do or think. Suddenly he was not as ready as he thought he was a few short days ago. Suddenly it felt like years since he had last seen his friends in Germany. A lot could happen in three days, Mark thought.

Mark walked off the plane and found his duffel bag. He began to look for familiar faces. They had changed a lot, but he still recognized his brother and aunt. They were smiling as they waved to him over the railing.

Mark found his way to the other side and finally, for the first time in years, hugged his aunt and brother. It was a dream, and yet it was difficult. His mind was in a haze. He didn't know what to say or what to do. Mark had all but forgotten about God—not because he didn't believe, but because his mind was so full of fear and anxiety over what to expect.

They walked to the car, and Mark was placed in the passenger side of the front seat. He felt so tired, but it wasn't from the trip so much as from all the anticipation. He was home, and now he felt like he didn't know who he was. It was like he was waking up from a coma or something. He couldn't think of anything to say. So he kept his thoughts to himself.

The car pulled into the driveway of his aunt's house. It wasn't the same place where she used to live. Mark finally spoke up. "Where are we at?"

"We're home. This is where we live now," his brother said.

"Your uncle and I are divorced now. It wasn't easy and I'm not proud of it, but that's where we are now," his aunt said in a quiet voice.

"What are you doing for money? How are you surviving and paying for this?" Mark asked, all confused about how life was turning out for all of them.

"I work in the factory. I get paid good money. We're

all right. Everything will be just fine." His aunt was confident. "We've been doing this for a couple of years now."

Mark had had no idea how difficult other people in his family had it. All he ever thought about was himself. For the first time maybe in his whole life he began to realize this. It wasn't that he was self-centered or selfish; he was just so busy trying to live his own life he had forgotten other people had similar challenges. It was embarrassing. He felt shame for his lack of caring.

"Auntie, I'm sorry for all the hard times you've been going through. I had no idea. I don't know what to say. I'm just sorry." Mark hung his head as he finished saying the words.

"It's all right. You had your own problems to work out. There wasn't anything you could have done about it." Mark nodded in agreement.

"Where would you like to eat?" she asked as they put his bag in a bedroom. "I was thinking of taking you out for your first night home," she said.

"I don't have any money right now," Mark said as he listened. "I get my next check here. They held it to mail here. Then I'll get a separation check, but I don't know how long before that comes in." Mark was hesitant since he wasn't able to pay his way. It was a habit now.

"That's okay, Mark. I wanted to pay. We want to celebrate you being home," she said, almost disappointed at his reaction.

"I don't care, to be honest. Anywhere is good, as long as it's American," Mark finally said as he smiled. "It just feels good to be back to where I came from. To be home. Well, sort of home."

"Mark, you are home," his aunt said. "You have a room. You stay here until you get all your things from the army and you find a job. I know you're twenty-one now and you need to be on your own, but you can stay until you have all your things in order. There's no rush. Tonight, just relax, and let's go out and enjoy you being home."

They went out to eat, and Mark tried hard to know what to say. It was hard to know how to act. He kept thinking about smoking a bowl and lighting a cigarette. Every time he went to speak, he had to think before he let the words out of his mouth. It was very hard. He knew he didn't deserve their loyalty. It was all very humbling. Why were they so nice to him? He hadn't earned it. It all made him sad and even more embarrassed.

The night was finally over, and Mark found his bed just as his aunt had said he would. Looking around, Mark felt like he was an alien in a foreign land. He was home, but it didn't feel like it. It didn't feel bad, but it didn't feel like he belonged.

The more he thought about it, the more he didn't know what to do. Then he remembered his promise. Once he was ready to get into bed, Mark knelt down on his knees and prayed for the first time since he and Jacob had prayed about the oppression. "Dear God, help me to know what to do and how to do it. I don't feel like I belong here, but I don't have any other place to go. Show me what to do and what to say. Thank you, amen."

When Mark woke up the next morning, he had to

stare at the room for a few minutes to think of where he was. Everything was completely different from what he had ever known. This was the very first time he had ever been in that house, let alone slept in it.

It was a basement bedroom. The walls were done in rough wood, giving it a rustic look. The closet doors were also rough wood, but the handles were of a rod-iron style, fake in appearance. The ceiling was pleasant, not the bare floor joist that one would normally think of seeing in a basement. In fact, the whole basement was completely furnished, with carpet, normal-looking walls, and a fireplace in the corner of the main den area. There was a nicely done laundry room that was also used as a mudroom. A door going outside was on the way to the garage.

There was a second door in the middle of the den room wall that also led outdoors. That one was always kept locked. Mark figured this was because the other door went through the mudroom, thereby keeping the dirt out of the living area.

Mark thought his aunt's house was very pleasant. The last thing he wanted to do was smoke in it. Nor did he want to do anything else that would destroy the work and love she had put into her home. So with that in mind, he dressed himself and found his way outside using the mudroom entrance. He took in the morning air and enjoyed the backyard view as he lit up his first cigarette in almost a day.

He stood looking around the yard as he smoked and began to realize he hadn't missed smoking as much as he'd thought he would. Thinking about it, Mark figured that he had been a chain-smoker while in the army. Yet in less than a day he was down to one or two cigarettes in a day's time. Perhaps it was as simple as mind over matter. If he didn't mind, then maybe it didn't matter.

Once the cigarette was out, Mark found his way upstairs to find the other two awake and working on breakfast. Mark stood watching as the two of them danced around each other. They both seemed to know their own roles in the project at hand. "Is there something I can do to help?" he asked, feeling out of place.

"No, you just have a seat at the table. I have some coffee you can drink as you sit and relax," his aunt said.

His brother, Devon, looked at him off and on as he worked at making toast and getting things out of the refrigerator and then returning them for their aunt. Mark was watching Devon watch him. Finally, he couldn't take it anymore. "What is it you want to know, Devon?"

"Oh, nothing," he said as he went about his fetching chore. "Well, okay, it's just that you seem different from how I remember you. It's almost like it's not you."

Mark smiled. "Ah, okay. I understand. Know what? Sometimes I feel like I'm not me anymore myself. I feel very lost here. I was lost in Germany too."

"Really?" Devon looked surprised. "Why were you lost there?"

"I don't know how to explain it," Mark tried to explain. "It was like every day brought about so much change in my life that it kept changing me. The people around me were never the same for any length of time. It was even like that before I went. When I was in high school, my life kept changing. I don't know who I am anymore. So I'm not surprised you don't know me either."

Their aunt was listening to them as she pretended to pay full attention to the cooking. She had difficulty keeping her eyes from watering. Both of the brothers noticed her eyes, and Devon asked, "What's wrong with your eyes, Auntie?"

"Oh, I got some steam in them from the heat on the stove is all. I'll be all right in a minute," she said, not wanting them to know her heartache. In her mind it was too early to start working on too much change this soon. She felt that way even more now that she heard what Mark had to say. It was breaking her heart to know all that he had gone through, even as a child.

The fact was that even Devon had been through a lot, but he was younger, so he didn't remember most of it. Mark, on the other hand, got more of the brunt of it—to the point where he had lived in a tent all alone in the woods. It was a wonder he even finished school.

The day was drawing to its end as Mark tried to make his new room a temporary home. As the afternoon was closing into evening, their auntie came to his room and asked him if he wanted to go to church with her.

"What day is it?" Mark asked, thinking it was a weekday.

"It Wednesday. We always go to Wednesday evening service around seven. I didn't want to wait until it was time to go before giving you the option." His aunt was trying her best to be accommodating, and Mark could tell.

He thought a minute and remembered his promise to God. "You know what? It just might be nice to do something like that for a change. What time do you leave?"

"We try to get out of here by six. I have things to do before the service starts," Auntie said, smiling at the thought of him going.

"I'll be ready," Mark said as he looked around for some clothes. His boxes had not arrived yet, but he still had his dress greens from the military. He made sure they were clean and got them ready to put on when it was time to do so.

During the ride to the church Mark began to replay the promise he had made. God had been very faithful at getting him out with an honorable discharge. Still, in the back of his mind, Mark wasn't sure if it was right to "make a deal" with God to get what he wanted. Somehow it didn't seem right to promise for the wrong reason. It was like he was bound to a bad deal. It was like he'd agreed to be a friend to someone when he didn't even know if he liked that person. It didn't make sense to keep his promise for all the wrong reasons.

Mark found himself in a church pew. It was the first time he had been in a church in over a decade. It had a familiar look about it, and yet it was completely unfamiliar. He wondered if he should even be there as he thought about all the sins he had been committing. Mark began to think if anyone there, including his family, knew even half of all the things he had been involved in, they would chase him out into the streets and cause him to be hit by a car—or, even worse, a truck.

He wanted to get up and run. The service hadn't even started yet, and he felt this was all wrong. How could he have thought he would ever be able to sit there with a clear conscience? Yet here he was. He wanted to find someone to explain this to, but who? His brother? How could he tell his brother what kind of monster he was? And he certainly couldn't tell his aunt. The very notion could cause her to have a heart attack.

He was stuck in the middle of a traditional church service with a crowd of people who didn't know the first thing about sin. He felt like everyone was wearing white as pure as white could be, and here he was wearing black that was darker than night. He stood out like a large rock on a small, sandy beach. He didn't belong and he knew it.

The pastor, an elderly man in a suit, stood at the pulpit and began to sing a hymn. A woman got up and went to the piano in one corner and started playing the melody that went with the song. Gradually, the whole congregation in one accord began singing along with the pastor.

Mark looked for a songbook and tried to find the song and sing along with them. He didn't want to look even more out of place than he felt. It was no use. He was all thumbs. By the time he found the song it was over. He looked around to see if anyone had noticed, but it didn't seem like they did. His first mistake and it had gone unnoticed. That was good.

He was about to sit down when the pastor started another song. "Oh no," Mark said under his breath. This time he looked at one of the others just in front of him and managed to see the page number. Quickly he found it and began to sing as best he could along with the rest of them. Well before the end of the hymn he felt like he could pass for one of them. The sweat on his back was beginning to feel very heavy. Mark was sure he would be found out. Then what? He was afraid to know the answer.

Finally, everyone sat down, and the pastor began to talk about who God was and how man needed to worship Him. It wasn't that Mark disagreed. It was more like he didn't understand everything the pastor was talking about. His mind was spending too much time feeling self-conscious.

Then it began to make sense. Mark wasn't sure how, but some of the words the pastor was saying found their way into his mind and heart. He heard something about the wages of sin being death. He had seen enough about death for a lifetime. He didn't want any more of death. Then he heard the pastor say something about the gift of God being eternal life through Jesus Christ the Lord. A gift. It could not be earned. One could not buy it. It was a gift—a gift that only God could give.

Mark started trying to listen more intently. He focused on every word when the pastor started talking about the Roman road of salvation. Suddenly Mark smiled to himself. He knew what the pastor meant, but it was still a thought that made Mark start to lose his focus.

Then the pastor said "in Romans ten, nine and ten." That was confusing. Was it in Romans ten or Romans nine and ten? But it didn't matter, because the only thing that did matter was what the versus said. The pastor said, "If you confess with your mouth that Jesus is Lord and believe with your heart that God raised Him from the dead, then you will be saved."

That was it for Mark. Those were the words he needed to hear. That was a reason to give his life to God. That was a reason to serve Him for the rest of his life. Nothing else mattered anymore. Mark did believe that Jesus was Lord. He had seen Christ in action back in his barracks room. It made sense then that if Jesus was in his room a year ago, then He had to have risen from the dead two thousand years ago. How else could He have done it?

Now the pastor was saying something about how Christ had defeated sin—that now Satan had no power as long as Christ was Lord of your life. This left a new question in Mark. How could he make Christ Lord of his life?

It was then that people began to go to the altar. Mark looked around. He was wondering what was going on. Why were all these people going up front and kneeling on that railing? He kept watching, trying to understand, when his aunt asked him, "Mark, would you like to go up front and have the pastor pray for your salvation?"

"What do you mean my salvation?" Mark asked in earnest. "What's my salvation?"

"You know," she said, "pray that you receive Christ as your Lord."

"Oh, that," Mark said as it clicked in his mind. He stood up and walked to the altar and knelt like the rest of them. He looked around for a moment, still unsure about all the little things.

Listening to the others, he began to realize all they were doing was praying out loud. That didn't seem so bad. Other people around them were praying for or with them. That didn't seem so bad either. *Okay,* Mark thought, *I can do this.*

Lord, he began, *I don't really know what I am doing. One thing I do know though is that I want you as my Lord and Savior. I need you in my heart like the pastor was saying about confessing with my mouth and believing in my heart so I can be saved. That's what I want. If you can do that for me, I would really like that.* Mark continued after thinking about it. *Lord, if you could also take away the drugs and the alcohol and the cigarettes, I would like that too. I think I've had enough of all that.*

Someone was beside him now also praying for him. He was afraid to look to see who it was. He began to think it really didn't matter as long as they were asking for all the same things. Then Mark got a little more brave. *And Lord, if you can also help me to know what to do for the rest of my life, it would help. This is one thing that keeps getting me in trouble. I don't know what to do. It's like I'm lost or something. Can you help me with that too?*

There was a sudden rush inside Mark. He didn't know what it was or how to describe it, but it was definitely real. He opened his eyes to see what was going around him, but there was nothing there to see. Mark still felt it inside and all around him. Then he realized he had no fear. It was like a friend. It was like there was something there that he somehow knew would always be with him and always be … a guide? Mark couldn't help it. He started smiling, and tears started running down his cheeks.

He didn't feel sad. Why were his eyes so watery? Yet there he was full of something or someone he had never seen or felt before. It was very real, even though none of it could be seen or explained. Mark had no idea how long he was at the altar, but when he was finally ready to stand up, most of the people were gone, and the service was definitely over.

"I'm sorry," Mark said as he looked at the pastor. "I didn't mean to be here so long. I know you have to get things locked up."

The pastor just smiled. "It's all right, son. I don't have to be anywhere but here. Do you know what just happened to you?"

"I'm not sure," Mark said as he sat down in the nearest pew. "What did happen?"

"The Lord is now in your heart and in your life. He has made you one of His."

Mark looked at the cross in the front of the church as he thought about it. "So what does that mean?"

"It means that no matter where you go or what challenges you face, He will always be with you. He will always tell your heart what to do and how to do it." The pastor seemed like he knew what he was talking about. Still, Mark wasn't so sure he really did. Some of what he said seemed too easy.

Not wanting to argue with the man, Mark said okay and then got up and shook the pastor's hand. As he walked to the doors of the church he began to think about what he had been told. Walking to the car he had a sudden notion that he was not alone. It wasn't a frightening thing. It was a comforting thing. Perhaps the old pastor was right after all.

Then it hit Mark. He had died. That was what he was going through from the time he began his journey home. He was dying to his old world. Now, however, he was reborn. He was now a new creature. Mark didn't know if it was scriptural, but he knew it was true.

The green soldier he had spent so much time being was dead. The new person, wearing white like all the people in the church that night, was in the place of that dead soldier. He really was born again. He had found his place in the world now.

It no longer mattered if he had a plan. God had a plan, and no matter what it was, it would fit him. Mark smiled as he climbed into the car and they headed home. He was really home. And it was good.

It was getting late after the three of them returned home. Everyone was in a very good mood. Devon seemed to be more helpful to their aunt than usual. This made it easy for Auntie to go to bed earlier than normal.

Mark was just finishing a snack Devon had made for all of them. Both Devon and Auntie were busy getting ready to sleep. When Mark was about to put his dishes in the sink, he heard his aunt talking in her bedroom. Thinking she was talking to him, he went to her door to see what she wanted.

"… and Lord," he heard her saying, "You know how

I have been praying that Mark and Devon would come to know you as their Savior for all these years. You know how I have knelt before you every day. My sister who is with you now has always wanted all of her children to know you personally. I am so thankful that tonight you have answered that prayer. I praise You, Lord, for all your wonderful works. I also know, Jesus, that this is not the end, but only the beginning. They will have many troubles, trials, temptations, and failures. I know they will sometimes want to fall away from you. I continue to pray that through all these times you will give them the grace and mercy you have always shown me. I pray that for the rest of their lives they will always know how real you are and how big you are. Help them to know that you are the creator of all things, so there is nothing too big for you to give them or handle in their lives. I know this is true. I pray that Mark and Devon will always know this to be true …"

Mark felt embarrassed for eavesdropping on his aunt. He walked away from her door, feeling so good about how much she had always loved and cared for not only him but his brother too. He decided to follow her example and went down to his own bedroom and knelt beside his bed. He thought about the time he did the same thing with Jacob. Smiling, Mark decided to include Jacob in his prayers, knowing Jacob was already doing the same for him.

The following morning Mark got to thinking about his old school buddies. There were only two of them, but he wondered if they were still in town. Looking around, he found a phone book and looked up their parents' names.

"Auntie, do you mind if I call a couple of my old school friends to see how they're doing? Maybe visit for a couple of hours?" Mark asked, hoping it would be okay.

"No, I don't mind. You go right ahead," she said as she poured a cup of coffee.

Mark found the phone and made a call. Matt was still home. He had graduated the summer before but was waiting to go into the navy. They made arrangements to do some things in town. Mark was excited.

After breakfast, Mark waited for Matt to show up. Finally his car pulled into the driveway. Mark went out and climbed in. "Hey, man, how've you been these last couple of years?"

Matt smiled. "I've been doing all right. I know it's been rough for you, though."

"Now how would you know that?" Mark asked.

"Oh, I know you. You never were one to handle change very well. Remember your eighteenth birthday party?" Matt started laughing.

"I remember you puking your guts out," Mark said, returning the favor.

They were finally in town, and Matt was pulling up to another house.

"Where we at?" Mark asked, feeling lost.

"We're at my brother's house. He just got the place a couple of months ago," Matt said as he started to get out of the car.

They walked in, and Matt introduced them. "Mark, this is my brother, Dave. Dave, this is Mark."

Mark nodded at Dave as they shook hands. "Come on in and make yourself at home, Mark," Dave said.

Matt sat down at the table and pulled out a baggy. Mark started watching to see what was going on. He had the uncanny feeling that it was drugs again. That was something he wasn't up to dealing with just yet. Matt took something that looked like tobacco out and rolled a cigarette.

"So when did you start rolling your own cigarettes?" Mark asked.

Matt started laughing. "Has it been that long since you've seen grass?"

Mark sat down, watching. He remembered his prayer and didn't know what to do or say. Suddenly he felt this powerful force inside him. He stood up, not knowing what he was about to do. He heard his voice speak: "I'm sorry, man, but I can't do this. I don't know how to explain it, but it's just not the right thing for me. I'm sorry."

Mark suddenly realized he was outside walking. He made his way to a restaurant and sat down. Looking around, trying to figure out how he'd gotten there, he saw a waitress approach him. "Sir, can I get you a cup of coffee?"

Mark reached in his pocket and remembered he didn't have any money. "I'm sorry, I must have forgot my wallet. I'm a little embarrassed. Is it all right if I use your phone to call my brother? Maybe he can bring it to me," Mark said.

"Sure, it's right behind that counter," she said, pointing it out.

Mark made the call, and his aunt came and picked him up. While he waited for his ride, Mark began to think about what had happened at Dave's house. It wasn't the marijuana that bothered him so much. It was the powerful force he had felt. At first he was thinking he was being judged. But then, the more he thought on it, he began to realize—it wasn't the feeling of being judged. It was the feeling of conviction. He was convinced that participating in such activity was no longer acceptable.

That was eye-opening for him. When he had prayed with Jacob, he had continued in his old behaviors. Now he could no longer do that. Not because of some rule or law. It was simple. He just could no longer do it. The new creation was no longer able to abide by the old lifestyle. Mark smiled at the idea. It wasn't going to be a punishment to live a new life. It was going to be a celebration of new things. That was too awesome to overlook. On the ride home he felt as good as ever. He'd done it. He'd walked away from his old world of sin. He really was a new creature. To be sure, it wasn't him but Christ who was now living in him.